Firefly Hollow

—A NOVEL—

T.L. HADDIX

For Shirley Crandall.
You are missed.

CHAPTER ONE

NOVEMBER 1959

THE LONG, TENSION-FILLED DRIVE BACK to Perry County was one of the most sorrowfully painful rides of Sarah Jane Browning's life. When her mother had called her at the college in Berea the night before to let her know to come home, Sarah was forced to face the harsh reality she'd been dodging for several months.

Her father was dying.

The middle child of three, Sarah had always been close to Ira Browning. To both her parents, really, but her father was her hero. She couldn't bear the thought of losing him, but she had no choice to let go.

Since she wouldn't be returning to school, she packed up all her belongings and loaded them into her old car, then set out to make the drive back to the holler she'd grown up in, a little place outside of Hazard, Kentucky, called Firefly Hollow. A few years old, the car was small but reliable, a real luxury she'd not been expecting.

Remembering the day Ira had given her the keys brought tears to her eyes.

"You'll need a good car to get you back and forth from school. This one has some miles on it, but it still has many more before it's a junker. By the time she rolls her last mile, you'll be able to buy yourself a new one."

Her parents weren't wealthy, so their generosity had stunned Sarah, touching her deeply.

Now, making her way around winding curves, up and down hills, in the car her father had lovingly picked out for her, hoping that she would be in time to say goodbye, she wanted to scream at the top of her lungs. Her grief and guilt were so heavy she felt like an old woman.

When, many miles later, the homestead finally appeared around a bend in the road, tears sprang up, nearly choking her. The white, clapboard two-story farmhouse was a welcome sight with its wide front porch and black shutters. She parked beside the house and sat there for a moment, watching smoke curl out of the chimney. It drifted down low, following the road that wound deeper into the holler, fading into the winter gloom.

The wind gusted around the car, its icy fingers creeping in to curl around Sarah's ankles and legs. Swallowing hard, she grabbed her purse and opened the door.

Her mother came out on the porch as Sarah was ascending the steps. Eliza looked older—worn and tired. For a drawn-out moment, they stared at each other, and then they embraced.

"Oh, Mama. Is he…?"

Eliza pulled back. "He's resting. It'll be time to wake him up soon for his pain medicine. Come on inside." She pulled her sweater tighter around her shoulders as she opened the screen door. "We'll freeze near to death if we stand out here much longer."

Sarah followed her mother into the living room, where her niece, Moira, was playing with her dolls on the floor. Sarah's older sister Kathy was on the couch, watching. She didn't speak, just nodded coolly in Sarah's direction.

"Kathy. Hi, Moira." Sarah kept her voice low, not wanting to wake her father, whose hospital bed was in the dining room.

"Hi, Aunt Tharah," Moira lisped. "I lotht my two front teeth, thee?" The little girl stuck her tongue out through the gap where the teeth had been.

Sarah smiled. "I see that."

Eliza took Sarah's purse and coat. Catching her hand, she urged Sarah toward the dining room. "You need to prepare yourself before he wakes up. It'll be easier for you both that way."

From the couch came a quiet snort. "The rest of us have been preparing for this for months, Mama. Sure must be nice not to have had to worry about cleaning up messes and keeping vigil over a sickbed. But I guess I ain't thinking straight. School's more important than family, I hear."

"Kathleen, that's enough," Eliza said. "I warned you about taking an attitude."

With a seething glare in Sarah's direction, Kathy stood. Sarah saw that her sister was pregnant again, several months gone. "I need some air. Moira, stay right here."

"Yeth, Mommy," Moira said, seemingly oblivious to the undercurrents in the room.

Kathy grabbed a coat from the rack and stalked out the door. Sarah winced, prepared for the slam, but at the last minute, her sister closed it gently instead.

Cheeks hot, Sarah turned to her mother. "I'm sorry, Mama. She's right. I should have come home before now."

"One of the few things that has given your father comfort these last few months is knowing that you were in school. Don't you *dare* apologize. You've not been here, but you've been helping him in a way the rest of us couldn't." With one last squeeze of Sarah's hand, Eliza nudged her toward the dining room. "Go on now. I'll be in the kitchen, getting things ready for lunch."

With a deep breath, Sarah pulled back the curtain that had been hung to give her father some privacy and stepped into the dining room.

Though it had only been a couple of months since she had seen him, the cancer had been busy. Gone was the powerful man who had loved to dance across the yard with Eliza and wrestle with his children, laughing as the three of them combined couldn't bring him down, not even when they were teenagers.

The patient man who'd endured Sarah's learning how to drive, the man who'd held her when she was scared and dried her tears when she cried, was no more. Cancer had reduced her father to a sunken hull of a human being. His skin was nearly translucent, the veins showing through the backs of his hands and eyelids, with dark bags under his sunken eyes. If he weighed a hundred pounds, she'd have been surprised.

"Oh, Daddy." Easing down onto the chair beside the bed, she studied him, trying to reconcile her memories with the reality in front of her. The task was impossible, she finally decided. There were two versions of Ira Browning—the one from before the cancer and the one from after. Try as she might, she couldn't understand how a just and loving God would let such a terrible thing happen to a man as good as her father.

Her mother joined her in the vigil after an hour, and her father woke up soon afterward. He had a few lucid hours, a gift for which Sarah would be forever grateful, and then later that night, Ira Browning closed his eyes for the last time.

The day of the funeral dawned bright, with sunlight sparkling off the light snow that had fallen the day after Ira had died. He was laid to rest in the family cemetery not far up the holler from the homestead, alongside his father and mother, near two of his siblings who had died before reaching adulthood. The family went back home for the wake, and once again, the house was full of people.

"You keep a close eye on your mother," Sarah's aunt Nancy cautioned as they washed dishes. "She's held it together this long, but she's liable to break down tonight, now that all the hoopla is done with."

"I know. I just don't know what to do. How do I help her?"

Nancy laid down the dishtowel. "You be there for her. When I lost my Sam, I didn't want to hear people tell me they understood or that they knew what I was going through when they good and well didn't. I wanted them to let me grieve, let me talk about it, or leave me the hell alone, and it changed from hour to hour. I don't know how your mother's going to react, but just be there for her. No offense to Kathy, but she's as useless in an emergency as teats on a boar hog, given how much she dotes on Randall."

Sarah frowned. "You know she was helpful to Mama the whole time Daddy was sick."

Nancy sighed. "I know. And to give the poor girl credit where it's due, she didn't do a half-bad job. But for what comes next? Eliza needs *you*. Not Kathy."

"How did you handle it? After everyone had gone, how did you get through the days?"

Nancy's first husband had been killed in a mine collapse. Though she'd remarried a few years back and moved to Georgia, Sarah knew her aunt was still haunted by that loss.

She looked out the window and across the valley. "I had no choice. I picked myself up and put one foot in front of the other. And then I met Roy, and he saved me."

When the dishes were finished, Sarah went out onto the front porch, where some of the men had gathered. Her younger brother Jack stood off to one side, not saying much but just watching. Sarah walked over to him and leaned against the porch railing.

Eyes closed, she let the rhythm and cadence of the voices wash over her.

Even though she'd only gone as far as Berea for college, speech was more cultured, more proper, there. She hadn't realized how much she missed hearing the familiar drawls and twangs until just now.

Jack nudged her shoulder. "Don't go to sleep on your feet."

She opened her eyes and shot him a look. "I'm not. I'm just… taking it all in, I suppose. Have you had time to talk to Gilly?"

Gillian Eversole was Sarah's best friend, and she was Jack's sweetheart. Sarah fully expected and hoped to have Gilly as a sister-in-law someday.

Her brother's cheeks grew pink, and he looked down at his feet. "Not yet. I don't know what to say to her."

"'Hello' and 'I've missed you' would probably be a good place to start. She said you've not been writing to her like you used to."

Jack straightened away from the railing. "I'm going for a walk. Come with me?"

"Let me get my coat."

They headed up the road, going up into the head of the holler. The afternoon was quiet and peaceful, and the sun had stayed out long enough to make the temperature almost bearable.

"What's on your mind?" she asked as they came to the swinging bridge that went across the creek to the houses on the far side.

He played with a winter-dead vine that clung to one of the support ropes of the bridge. "I want to ask her to marry me."

Sarah was relieved and pleased. She gave a genuine, delighted smile for the first time in days. "Oh, Jack—"

He held up his hand. "No, it's not that simple. I want to ask her, but I'm not sure it's the right thing to do, not for me and not for Gilly." He looked down at the water moving across the rocks in the creek. "I won't be out of the Army for another year, maybe two. And if we end up going to war like they're saying we might, I can't ask her to wait for me. It isn't fair."

"Is it that you don't want to ask her to wait or that you don't want to wait for her?"

Jack raised tormented eyes to hers. "I'd wait until forever for her."

Tears flooded Sarah's eyes, and he handed her a handkerchief.

"Thanks," she mumbled. When she'd regained her composure, she cleared her throat and tried to figure out what to say. "What if Gilly was the one asking you to wait? Wouldn't you want to know how she felt?"

He closed his eyes and leaned against the support post. "Yeah, I would."

"Well, I think you have your answer. And just in time, too. Here she comes."

Jack turned to look over his shoulder, back down the road toward the house. Sure enough, Gilly was headed their direction, a pensive, uncertain frown on her face.

"I'm going to head back into the house," Sarah said as Gilly reached them. She gave Gilly a brief hug and touched Jack's shoulder. "You two need to talk."

As she walked, she let her mind drift back toward the two people she'd just left. "I hope they can work things out. The alternative would be intolerably sad, and I think this family has had as much of that as we can handle."

Later that night, even though she was exhausted and had gotten ready for bed early, Sarah found she couldn't sleep. At ten thirty, she went downstairs to the kitchen. To her surprise, her mother was seated at the table. In her nightgown and robe, hair down around her shoulders, Eliza looked incredibly vulnerable.

"Hey, Mama." She gave Eliza a soft squeeze, then went to the sink with the teakettle.

"You can't sleep either, I take it?" Her mother had her hands wrapped around a mug of coffee, but she wasn't drinking it.

"No, I can't even shut my eyes." She pulled out the chair next to her mother's and sat. She held her silence, waiting for her mother to speak.

"I can't bring myself to go into our bedroom for more than five minutes," Eliza confessed in a low voice. "Even though he hadn't slept in there for the last couple of months, he was still *here*. I could walk out to the dining room and touch him, see him. If I go back in that room, I'll have to face that he's gone."

Sarah reached out and covered her mother's hand with her own. Eliza clasped her fingers and held on.

"Did you talk to Nancy about it? About going back in there after…"

"I did." Eliza sighed. "And she told me to not let myself have even one night to think about it because if I did, I would never go back in there. Damn it."

"Do you think she's right?"

"Yes. The thing is, I don't know if I want to go back in there, Sarah. Not without your father." Eliza pulled away and sat back. "I've thought about offering the room to your sister and Randall. It's bigger. They could use the space."

Kathy and Randall had moved in when Ira had been diagnosed with cancer and it became apparent Eliza needed help. Sarah privately thought they'd been so eager to help because Randall had seen a free ride on his horizon, but she kept that thought to herself. She was glad, however, that they were planning to move out next week when their rental house would be ready.

"You know I can't begin to guess what you're going through," she told Eliza, "but I'm going to tell you what I think you'd tell me."

Her mother raised an eyebrow. "And what do you think that would be, young lady?"

Sarah gathered her thoughts, choosing her words carefully before she spoke. "Do what feels right to *you* and don't rush into anything. You don't answer to any of us, and you shouldn't have to feel like you do. Daddy wouldn't want that. He'd want you to do whatever you need to do to get through this and hang anybody who feels differently."

Her mother didn't respond for a long time, and Sarah was starting to worry that she'd said too much when Eliza finally asked, "How did you get to be so smart, Sarah Jane?"

"I believe it comes from my mother."

Eliza let out a long breath and closed her eyes. "I've not had a good night's sleep in several months. I'm so tired I can't think straight. Other than sleep, right now, I don't know what I want."

"Would it help if I stayed with you tonight?"

"Sleep in the bed with me, you mean?" Eliza asked.

"Yes. Only for tonight, to get you past the first hurdle. I'd be there in case you got scared or needed to talk."

Eliza rubbed her eyes. "If you wouldn't mind, I think that would... I think I could go in there if you were with me. Thank you."

Sarah took Eliza's mug to the sink, then came back and held out a hand. "Then let's see if we can't get you settled in so you can get some sleep."

"Dr. Spencer gave me something to help me. I don't want to rely on it. Do you think I should take it?" Eliza asked as they went into the bedroom.

"Why don't you try to sleep without it, and then if you need it in a little while, you can take it?"

Sarah tucked her mother in and smoothed Eliza's hair back, much like her mother had done for her when she was a child.

Eliza smiled. "One of these days, you're going to be a wonderful mother."

"I hope so, Mama." Sarah went around and got under the covers on the other side of the bed, turning the lamp off as she lay down. To her relief, her mother seemed to go to sleep almost as soon as the light was out.

Sarah, however, stayed awake for a while longer, her mind dancing unhappily back over the last few days. As she drifted off, an odd sound woke her. Thinking at first that it was a train whistle, she raised her head up off the pillow to hear it better. When she did, she realized that the long, mournful wail wasn't a train whistle at all but the distant howl of a wolf.

"I must be dreaming," she murmured, then closed her eyes and slept.

CHAPTER TWO

THE NEXT SEVERAL WEEKS WERE long and stressful for everyone in the Browning household. When he'd learned he wouldn't survive, Sarah's father had done as much as he could so that her mother wouldn't have to worry about finances after he was gone. But there was still paperwork to complete, banks to visit, and a myriad of other small things needing doing that had slipped by the wayside while Ira was ill.

After a little while, Jack went back to Fort Knox. Kathy and Randall moved out, and life slowly returned to a so-called normal, but the progress went in fits and starts. Every time Sarah thought they were making headway against the grief, at least learning to cope with it a little more, something would knock that impression back down.

After two weeks of trying to sleep in their old bedroom, Eliza had given up. "I can't bear the memories," she confessed during one of the late-night conversations she and Sarah had fallen into having.

"Then don't fight them." With minimal fuss, Sarah helped her mother pack up the bedroom and move into Jack's old room.

By the time January rolled around, Sarah was trying to figure out what to do with the rest of her life. It was a topic that often came up in conversation with her mother.

"What do you want to do?" Eliza asked. "If you want to go back to school, we'll make it happen. Your father set aside some money, and—"

"No. That money is yours, Mama. Besides, I don't know that going back to school is the right thing for me. I don't know what is. Tomorrow, I'm going to go into town and talk to Mr. Napier at the Board of Education. They might still consider hiring me, even though I don't have a teaching degree. A couple of my professors at Berea wrote reference letters for me, and they thought he might be convinced to take me on as a teacher despite my not having graduated, given the circumstances."

Chin propped on her hand, Eliza studied her daughter. "You've gotten so mature the last couple of years, I hardly know what to think. I was so busy with your daddy these past few months I've not had any time at all to spend talking to you. Whatever happened to that boy you were going with at school? You've not mentioned him at all since you've been home."

Sarah shrugged. "You've had more important things on your mind. And as for that boy, he... Joey is a nice young man, but he isn't for me. He, um, he kissed me, Mama. And I didn't feel a thing." She felt her face flush, but she needed to talk about it. "I really thought he might be the one, but then he kissed me, and all I could think was that I'd waited that long to be kissed and it was like being licked on the mouth by a dog."

She'd caught Eliza mid-sip, and coffee splattered everywhere as her mother erupted into coughing laughter. When she could speak again, Eliza was still chuckling. "Oh, Sarah. Never say you told the poor boy that."

Grimacing, Sarah blew out a breath. "No, but I think he figured it out. There wasn't any way to tell him we were done without hurting him. I felt so vain, breaking up with him because of the way he kissed. But I remembered how you and Daddy acted around each other and..."

"You want that kind of love? Is that what you were going to say?"

Sarah nodded. "Yes. I'm sorry."

"Don't apologize, either for mentioning your daddy or for wanting something like what we had. It's my fervent prayer that all my children will know such a joyous marriage." She stood and stretched.

"After you speak to Mr. Napier, if he has nothing for you, swing by the library. I know they were looking for someone there a few weeks ago. If they haven't found anyone, it might be a good fit for you until you can find a teaching job." She placed a soft kiss on Sarah's forehead and gave her a brief hug. "I'm going to bed. Will you be coming up soon?"

Sarah stood, moving to look out the window over the sink. "I don't know. I'm actually thinking about taking a walk."

Eliza frowned. "This late? It's nearly nine o'clock."

"Yes, but the moon's full, and it's almost as bright as day out there. Plus, since that warm air came in today, it's almost pleasant. I won't need more than a heavy coat to stay warm. I've not had a chance to really go walking since I got home, and I'm feeling a little caged in, to tell the truth."

Her mother narrowed her eyes. "Well, come upstairs with me first if you insist on going out tonight. I want you to take a pistol with you. If we really have been hearing a wolf, you don't need to be out there unprotected."

Several times since the night of the funeral, they'd heard distant howls.

Once Eliza had outfitted Sarah with one of Ira's guns, she made her promise to pop her head in when she returned. "Just let me know you're alive, okay? Else I'll worry."

"It could be a while, an hour or two before I come back," Sarah warned, checking the pistol to make sure it was loaded.

Thanks to her father's tutelage, she was comfortable handling the gun.

"I don't care. I still want to know."

After going back to her room to don sturdy pants, her walking boots, and a coat, Sarah set out, the gun safely holstered on her belt. She'd tucked a blanket into her old book bag and was looking forward to getting out of the house for a while. As she had mentioned to her mother, the moonlight was so bright there wasn't any need for a flashlight. If it had been much brighter, Sarah would have been able to read a book outside if she'd been so inclined.

In the heart of central Appalachia, Perry County was one of the more densely populated areas of the region. It wasn't in the low foothills of Appalachia, nor did it have the soaring ridges and deep valleys of Virginia, but was somewhere in between. Craggy, folded hollows peppered the landscape, looking like nothing more than a green blanket that had been crumpled up by God himself. Sarah had a good idea of how lucky she was to have grown up in a place filled with such natural beauty as eastern Kentucky.

She headed for the path behind the house at the side of the yard that led around the ridge past a rocky outcropping where she liked to sit. The ledge was her thinking place, where she went when she needed some time to herself. But it wasn't her destination tonight. Tonight, she was headed for the pool of water where she felt most at home.

Several years ago, following a painful incident during her sophomore year in high school where she'd overheard Kathy, Randall, and Paul Turner—the boy she'd had a crush on for years—making fun of her, she'd strayed across the property line that divided Browning land from that of their neighbors, the Campbells.

The Campbell family owned most of the mountain, top to bottom, encompassing at least three hundred acres. Their homestead was clear on top, accessed by a road from the other side. For as long as she could remember, her parents had warned her not to cross that line.

"They're good people, but they keep to themselves, and they expect others to let them be, so you need to respect that line," her father, Ira, had told her more than once.

She was curious, avidly so, but she had resisted the urge to explore. She knew there would be consequences if she broke her parents' rule, and they'd be disappointed in her. If nothing else, Sarah was a good girl. But that day, driven by hurt and anger, she'd blown past the boundary with little more than a moment's hesitation.

What she'd found was pure magic.

Thanks to her fast pace tonight, it wasn't long before she heard water trickling rapidly over rocks. There, as she rounded a curve, was a small stream cutting down the mountainside. The branch of water fell into a shallow hollow on the downhill side, with the uphill side on the left forming a higher ledge of rocks and earth that was full of mountain laurel. She skipped across the stream and hurried up the path worn into the ground.

The rocky, shrub-covered outcropping she'd passed below formed a sort of natural dam where a large pool of water had collected. Fifteen feet across and nearly that wide again going in the opposite direction, the pool was surrounded by gently sloping rocks on all sides except the front, where the overflow dropped over the edge in a cascading fall.

Sarah knew from her daytime visits that the water was blue, ranging in shade from light aqua to deeper cobalt, a real, sparkling jewel set secretly into the land. Across the pool from where she stood, a craggy cliff rose about ten feet out of the water, overhanging slightly to form a shallow cave so that the mountain seemed to curve around the pool. It was the top of that cliff that she climbed the rest of the path toward now.

When she reached the top of the boulder where she typically sat, she hesitated. A faint rustling in the trees and brush on up the mountain had the short hairs on the back of her arms and neck standing straight up. Her hand hovered over the butt of the gun, and for the first time, she wondered if coming out had been a good idea.

She stood still for several minutes, barely breathing, but she didn't hear the rustling again. Slowly, she relaxed and dropped her arm to her side. She drew in a shaky breath, then let it out with a huff.

"You're letting your imagination run away with you." She spread out her blanket and sat down. The moon was almost directly overhead, casting a new light on the pool. Tonight, the landscape was stark in the moonlight, monochromatic and eerie. Regardless, the spot soothed her on a primitive level. Sarah had never ventured out to her spot at night, and she was pleased to find it as breathtaking by moonlight as it was in daylight.

She stayed for over an hour before the chill of the night finally penetrated her thick clothing. As she left, she stopped at the pool to rinse the soiled linens, using one of the wet cloths to wipe her hot face. She was glad she'd had the foresight to bring a couple of handkerchiefs, as she'd sat and cried for most of the hour.

She was still deeply anguished by the loss of her father, but the anvil of grief was lifting somewhat. Tomorrow was going to be a challenge, and she might be right back where she'd started emotionally by the time the day was over. But it was a new chapter, and progress was progress, so she'd take it where she found it.

Owen Campbell shadowed Sarah all the way home. Out for a run as the wolf he could become, he'd heard her approaching long before she'd appeared at the pool. When she'd sat down and started crying, her sobs had broken his heart. Having lost both his parents and his brother in recent years, he knew all too well the anguish she was feeling.

He'd wanted to go to her and offer her comfort, but that wasn't really an option. Not only was he not in his human form, but they'd never met.

Though Owen hadn't gone to the funeral home when he had heard about Ira Browning's death a few months back, he'd written Eliza a note of sympathy. He'd kept an eye out toward the Browning homestead since, just in the event they needed something, though given that he was practically a stranger to most of the family, his help might have seemed out of place.

He had also been privy to the speculation about Sarah earlier that day by the eligible—and some not-so-eligible—men who'd been gossiping in the hardware store his uncle owned in the valley. Her attributes were discussed, and several of the local fellows were considering paying her a call.

What Owen couldn't discover was whether Sarah was going to be staying with her mother or going back to school in Berea.

He'd first encountered Sarah while he was a deer, which was the animal he most preferred to shift into. She'd been curious and friendly, chatty and funny, still shy, and all of fifteen. He'd seen her as nothing more than his neighbor's curious daughter whom he'd watched when she came onto his land, more an annoyance than a dangerous trespasser.

They had run into each other a few times after that, mostly with him as the deer, but once, notably, with him as the wolf. He'd been prepared to go to Ira Browning if she'd become a problem; she never had.

Not until she was eighteen and on the cusp of blossoming into a beautiful, enchanting woman. The day she'd gone skinny dipping in his pool, right before heading to college, was the day Owen had run away to his other sanctuary—his family in Laurel County. He'd stayed away until Sarah was safely away at school, else he might have found himself tempted to walk down and introduce himself as a human, not just a curious deer.

In the three-plus years since she'd left for college, he'd missed her more than he would have thought possible. As much as he wanted to deny it, he felt like he had a connection to Sarah. Therefore, hearing the randy bucks at the store talk about her had set his teeth on edge and put him in a snarling, black mood. He'd walked out of his house as soon as the sun went down and shifted into the wolf he was most comfortable becoming when he was in such a state.

He hadn't expected her to show up at the rock. That the moon was full and calling to him didn't help. Full moons always made him more restless, and coupled with his other frustrations, her appearance felt like something of a last straw.

From the time he was a tiny boy, Owen had known he was different from other people. He didn't seem to interact with the world the same way others did, not even his parents, and especially not his father, Hank Campbell. Even though Owen was the oldest son, he and his father had never been close.

Owen was fine with that, a sentiment that made his father even more distant as Owen grew up.

When he was four, he'd gotten lost in the woods. He'd wandered for nearly a day, following deer trails and rabbit paths. He'd been hungry, but he hadn't been afraid. His parents, on the other hand, had been frantic. All their family and neighbors had assembled, forming a search party that combed the mountains for hours.

They'd found him the morning after he disappeared, curled up in a hollow created by a fallen tree. To Owen, the whole thing had been an adventure.

To his mother, it had been a harbinger of things to come.

In eighth grade, after some prodding from his friends, he approached Mallie Johnson, the girl he'd had a crush on since the beginning of the school year. To his shock and horror, his body had started changing, pain tingling down his spine and along his arms, down his legs. Unlike the embarrassing thing that had been happening to him for a while now when he thought about girls, this was scary. Something was drastically wrong, and he knew it.

He fled, running home before anyone could stop him. It was then that his mother sat down and had a talk with him. She told him about shifting, how it ran in her family, how she'd never told his father about it. And she told him he'd have to go away now until he learned to control it.

Owen was devastated.

As the ability came through the Wells family, his mother's brother Eli—also a shifter, as were several of his children—became Owen's tutor in all things supernatural. As time passed, Owen learned how to become a wolf *and* a deer, how to control the shifting, how to harness the energy so that it didn't burst out of him at unexpected moments.

There, on Eli and Amy's farm in Laurel County, surrounded by family, for the first time in his life, he fit in and found acceptance.

Still, his mother's shame stayed in the back of his mind. Even after he grew up and eventually returned home to Perry County, it lingered, tainting how he viewed himself and the world around him.

She'd made him promise on her deathbed that he wouldn't close himself off to the possibility of love. That was the only time Owen had consciously lied to his mother.

No, he'd never subject a woman to his beastliness, and he certainly wouldn't pass his condition on to innocent children so they could suffer like he had. Owen could barely accept himself for what he was, and he wasn't about to let himself be vulnerable enough to let anyone else know the truth.

Even so, his curiosity was insatiable and had been ever since he'd learned about shifting at thirteen. He'd started reading, listening, learning, collecting the tales and folklore surrounding shapeshifting, gathering volume upon volume of stories—fiction and nonfiction alike. While a few of the works came close to what he knew to be the truth, most did not.

For example, the popular belief that shifters could only change during a full moon simply wasn't accurate. That was one of the first myths with which Owen had approached his uncle.

"The moon is there all the time, Eli. It makes little sense that the full moon could affect us so much and the rest of the time, it wouldn't."

Eli, full of the affection Owen's own father denied him, chuckled. "You still feel the warmth of the sun even when it's mostly hidden behind clouds. You still see its light. It still affects the weather, right?"

"Sure, but—"

"Hang on, son. I'm not finished. So, when the moon isn't full, we know it's there. It calls to us, pulls on us, much like it pulls on the ocean to create the tides. But when it's full? That's like the brightest, sunniest day in summer. We bask in the glow, much like a flower opens under the sun. It's simple nature, Owen, not some mystical power."

Not satisfied by the explanation, he had set out to determine the truth for himself. To his consternation, he eventually concluded that his uncle was right. Owen had conceded the fact to him on a visit to Laurel County when he was nineteen.

Eli laughed. "You're so skeptical. You trust nothing if you can't see it. I can hardly wait until you meet a young lady who makes you feel things you can't see or touch. Then maybe you'll understand a little better."

Owen endured the teasing, but only because he knew Eli felt genuine affection for him. He didn't tell his uncle that he had no intention of ever letting a woman get close enough to enthrall him so much that he lost his head. There had been a brief physical relationship with his uncle's neighbor, a widow, the summer Sarah had gone away to school, but physical was all he'd let it be. Owen trusted nothing beyond that.

Instinctively, he knew Sarah Browning could break through all his shields, which was the main reason he took pains to avoid her.

As he "walked" her home now, her obliviousness to his presence sent something dark shooting through him, an unfamiliar longing. It would have been ridiculously easy for him to jump on her and sink his teeth into the soft flesh of her throat.

Conversely, he could shift back into his human form, where he was almost as strong as in his lupine form and carry her to the top of his mountain with no one being the wiser until it was too late.

It had been a long time since he had felt the soft touch of a woman's skin against his, and the emotional and physical need was part of what had driven him out tonight. He wasn't physically aroused by her in his current form, but the mental need was there, riding him hard.

All those dark thoughts raced through his head as what-ifs, but he would never, ever carry out the threat his sheer existence posed. Part of safeguarding those who needed protection was not taking advantage of his superior strength. Owen was a shapeshifter. He wasn't a god or a king. He had no more rights than any other man. There was simply something a little extra in his makeup, that was all.

That said, the feelings Sarah stirred in him gave him cause for concern. If she stayed in the area, they were bound to meet, and he was already drawn to her. If he started running into her regularly, the idea of seeking her companionship might end up presenting a temptation he couldn't resist.

CHAPTER THREE

Not five minutes into her interview with Superintendent Napier, Sarah knew she would not be getting a job as a teacher anytime soon.

"I'm so sorry, Miss Browning. You'd be a welcome addition to the teaching staff at any of our schools. We just don't have an opening, not this time of year. Next summer, we probably could do something. But not right now."

They'd chatted for a few more minutes before he showed Sarah out of his office with a sympathetic smile. "Don't forget what I told you. Come July, I expect to see you back, application in hand."

Sarah kept a brave face until she reached her car, where she sagged back against the cloth seat. She hadn't let her hopes get too high to begin with, but she was still disappointed. It was nearing lunchtime, and she headed over to the drugstore and lunch counter Gilly's parents owned. If she was lucky, Gilly would be at work and they could chat while Sarah grabbed a bite to eat.

Once she'd taken a seat at the counter and placed an order for a turkey club sandwich, she had a few minutes to consider her next move. Gilly brought the food over and set it down, along with a mug of hot cocoa.

"You looked like you needed the sweet," she explained when Sarah sent her a quizzical look. "Interview didn't go well, I take it?"

"No, not in the least. He couldn't help me."

Gilly touched her hand. "I'm sorry. I know you were counting on something coming through. What are you going to do?"

Sarah shrugged. "I don't know. Mama mentioned something about the library hiring. I guess I'll try there next."

Gilly tapped her lip thoughtfully. "You know what? That might work out better in the long run than a teaching job. I think you should go straight over there as soon as you eat your lunch." A customer down the counter signaled for more coffee, and Gilly moved toward him. "Come back and tell me how things go, okay?"

"Okay." Sarah could only eat about half of her sandwich, but she finished off the cocoa. She had the other waitress bag the uneaten food for her, then paid her check. Stopping in at the drugstore had been a treat, especially since she didn't have a job. She'd have to forego eating out in the future if she didn't find employment, and soon.

With little hope, she left her car parked on Main Street and walked up the hill to the library. The building had been built two years prior, and Sarah had only been in it a handful of times. Seeing the line of people waiting to be checked out, she didn't go straight to the front desk, but headed over to browse through the stacks. Several books jumped out at her, and she figured now was as good a time as any to pick them up.

The line was gone by the time she made her way to the front desk. When she placed her selections on the counter, the woman behind the desk gave her a weary smile. Sarah handed over her library card. "I heard that you all might be hiring. If so, then I'd like to put in an application."

The woman—Shirley, according to her name tag—looked her over with renewed interest. "Do tell. Have you ever worked in a library before, hon?"

"No. I was in school at Berea, three years into a four-year degree for teaching. When my father passed in November, I came home.

"I'm sorry for your loss." Shirley removed the cards from the front flaps of the books. "It's difficult to get a teaching job this time of year, I would think, especially without a full certificate under your belt."

Sarah felt her cheeks flush. "Yes, ma'am."

"What all skills do you have? Can you use a typewriter? Answer the phone? Shelve books? Do you know the Dewey decimal system?"

"Yes, to the typewriter and phone. As far as shelving, I know how to find titles when I'm looking for something in particular. I figure filing them back where they go is a similar process, only in reverse. And I know how the Dewey decimal system works. I had to use it for research in college."

Shirley filled out the book cards and handed Sarah's library card back to her. "We don't pay as well as teaching does, but it's a steady job. It's Monday through Friday, nine to five, with half days every other Saturday. We take turns working those. Would you be interested in signing on to stay or just until Mr. Napier calls you in to work for him?"

"I-I don't know. That's something I'd have to answer when and if the time came."

The older woman's indecision was clear on her face. With a tired-sounding sigh, she turned and went to a filing cabinet, where she pulled out a piece of paper. She returned and handed it to Sarah.

"Fill this out. I'm not making you any promises."

"Thank you. I'll do that right now." With a sunny smile for the woman, she picked up her books and went to one of the small, round tables throughout the open area of the room. She read the application carefully before she filled it out. When she was finished, she double-checked all the information to make sure it looked right, and she sent a quick prayer heavenward. "I need this job. Please let this work out."

Books and purse tucked under one arm, Sarah went back up to the desk and gave Shirley the application.

"If you were hired on, you'd be a library assistant. Basically, anything that needed doing, you'd be responsible for it. Whatever we asked of you within reason. It's not as glamorous as teaching."

"I understand."

"How soon are you looking to start if you were to be offered the job?"

"As soon as possible. I knew when I came home that I'd be staying and that I'd have to get a job. I've been helping my mother with everything that needed doing after we lost Daddy, but it's time for me to go to work."

The older woman gave her a kinder look than before. "It isn't easy to give up something we want for family."

Sarah shrugged. "I don't feel like I'm giving up anything necessarily. It's more that my life has changed, and this is the path I'm traveling on now. It wouldn't do me any good to wish for what my life used to be. I can't focus on the past. I have to move forward."

"Moving forward doesn't mean the past doesn't hurt."

That was the God's honest truth. "No, ma'am."

With a decisive nod, Shirley laid her hands on the counter. "I'll tell you what—I still have to get the library director's approval and put calls in to your references, but if you're serious about wanting this job…"

"Oh, I am. I promise you," Sarah said, afraid to hope.

"Good. Then why don't you plan on being here tomorrow morning at eight thirty? Do you have a car, or will you have to get a ride to town?"

"I have a car."

Shirley smiled. "Good." She told Sarah how much they'd pay starting out, an amount lower than she would have made as a teacher, but really not bad, all things considered.

After a few more minutes of discussion, Sarah bid the woman farewell and left. She deposited the books in her car and went into the drugstore to tell Gilly the good news.

"You're kidding," Gilly said, her eyes wide. "They offered you the job on the spot? Oh, Sarah, that's wonderful! Are you excited?"

Sarah laughed. "I am. I didn't expect to be, but I am. Hopefully, this will make Mama smile."

"How is she?"

"As well as expected. She has good days and bad days. I think she's going back to cleaning houses for people sometime this week." Sarah crossed her arms. "I can't imagine what she's going through."

Gilly's smile was sad. "I can, at least a little. I worry so much about Jack, that we'll never get married, that we'll never be together, that we'll end up going to war, and he'll be sent to the other side of the world. He's such a huge part of my life that I can't imagine who I'd be without him. And if we'd been married twenty-five years like your parents were? Losing him would kill me."

Sarah knew she meant it, and she squeezed Gilly's hand. "Before we both start weeping in the middle of the dining room, how would you like to go to the movies with me this Saturday? Assuming I get the job, that is. We need to catch up with each other. We hardly get to talk anymore."

Gilly agreed. "I'd love to. *Operation Petticoat* is still playing, and I know how you feel about Cary Grant. Get up with me on Friday, will you?"

Promising she would, Sarah said her goodbyes and left. As positive a turn as the day had taken, she was exhausted and not a little discouraged. She wouldn't be teaching. Not now, and perhaps not in the future.

But she would be working in a library and the job would hopefully have the chance to help others, to share her love for knowledge. Considering that, when all was said and done, perhaps not being able to teach wasn't the end of the world after all.

CHAPTER FOUR

S ARAH QUICKLY SETTLED INTO HER job at the library. The two-story building was state-of-the-art, barely two years old, with bathrooms on each level. The adult department was downstairs, and a large, expansive children's section took up most of the second floor, along with two meeting rooms and a genealogy/local history room. It was much larger than the previous library, and the patronage had increased to match the new facility's size.

Much as Shirley had described, she did a little of everything, floating around to help whichever department needed her. To her surprise, Sarah found that she really enjoyed the work. She began to think she could accomplish the same goals at the library as she had wanted to through teaching, only with a broader base of the population. She remarked as much to Shirley one day as they were shelving books.

"I love gaining knowledge and always have, and that was one of the primary motivations behind my becoming a teacher. I never expected to find something else where I might share that love. But I've seen you all do it here. When you help someone find a book they're looking for or show them how to use the card catalog, it opens up a new world for them."

Shirley smiled. "It can be a bit like holding the keys to a new kingdom. Oh, the job isn't perfect—no job is. But it has its rewards. Plus, in a library, the people who walk in the doors typically *want* to learn something more often than not. As a teacher? Some of your students are only going to be there because they have to."

"True," Sarah said. "Do you think Ms. Cornett will let me help with the literacy program?"

The program had gained healthy momentum since its introduction. In an area where a decent percentage of the population was still illiterate or barely literate, it had the potential to do a tremendous amount of good.

"She might. You should also ask her about going around to the schools with me when I go. With your background, that would probably be a good fit for you."

Callie Barger, the other library assistant, came around the corner of the bookshelf. "Excuse me, Ms. Combs. Owen Campbell is here, and I can't find that book that came in for him."

"I'll be right there, Callie." Shirley handed the book she was holding to Sarah. "Owen's one of the most voracious readers we have. I'm surprised he hasn't been in since you were hired. He's usually in here every week." She headed for the front desk.

Owen Campbell—her neighbor? Surely it couldn't be. Could it?

Hurrying, Sarah put the book in its place, then eased to the end of the row of bookshelves. She kept the rolling cart in front of her, but surreptitiously looked toward the front desk. Though she'd technically lived next door to him her entire life, she had never laid eyes on the man, and she was curious.

Instead of the scrawny, wizened recluse she'd been expecting, he was tall. He stood straight, his shoulders looking as broad as a hundred-year-old oak. Dark hair that was a little long brushed his collar.

Sarah knew she was staring, but she couldn't stop. There was something very appealing about the way he stood, and as he moved to give Shirley his library card, Sarah glimpsed his hand. It was a strong hand, with long, masculine fingers and a square palm, and she would have given her eyeteeth at that moment to see if his face matched her impression of the rest of him. She didn't glance away until Shirley sent her a questioning look.

When Owen turned, she quickly shifted her gaze to the cart and the one book that still needed shelving. She moved to put it in its place, and by the time she came out of the stacks, he had gone.

"Do you know Owen Campbell?" Shirley asked as Sarah parked the cart at the end of the front desk.

"From up near Firefly Hollow?" When Shirley nodded, Sarah shook her head. "No, I've never met him. His property borders ours. He isn't what I expected."

"He's a complicated young man. What were you expecting?"

When Sarah described what she had envisioned of the reclusive man, her friend laughed. "Oh, my. No, that's certainly not Owen. He causes a stir whenever he comes to town. Didn't you know that? And it isn't because he's a mystery."

Bemused, Sarah shook her head. "No. What do you mean?"

Callie sidled up to the desk, having been blatantly eavesdropping a few feet away. "You've really never met him?"

"No."

The bottle blonde sighed. "Well, he's a dreamboat. Big brown eyes that make a girl melt. And he's completely unaware of the effect he has. One of these days, I'm going to ask him to go for a root beer float."

Shirley frowned. "Callie, you know the director frowns upon that sort of fraternization with the patrons."

"I know. But one of these days, I'm going to do it. He'd be worth getting fired over."

Sarah blinked, but she'd kept her mouth shut. One of the first rules Shirley had explained to her had been to respect the privacy of the patrons who used the library. That included asking them out socially.

"People don't want us commenting on or judging what they choose to read. If you've read a book and think it's good, it's fine to share that opinion. But if you don't like it, or if you don't think the patron should read it, keep your opinion to yourself. Also, don't bother the patrons about their personal lives."

"How do you mean 'bother'?" Sarah had asked.

"It's simple. We live in a small town, and we work with the public. There are things we're going to hear and see that are private. An important part of our job is respecting that privacy. It's an obligation we have to our patrons. We don't intrude on their lives, and we don't gossip about them, especially not to other patrons."

"That has to be a hard rule to enforce. I'll do my best to respect the people who come in," Sarah had promised.

Now, she could almost see the older woman's aggravation with Callie. Before Shirley could call her out, though, the phone rang and two patrons walked in.

"We'll discuss this later, Ms. Barger," Shirley said.

That night as she drove home, Sarah thought about the glimpse she'd gotten of Owen Campbell. When she arrived at the homestead, she went up to change out of her work clothes, then made a beeline for the kitchen to help her mother with supper.

"I got a look at our neighbor today," she told Eliza as she sliced a head of cabbage.

Eliza frowned. "Which neighbor?"

"Owen Campbell. He came into the library and checked out a big stack of books." She eased the cabbage into a hot cast-iron skillet waiting on the stovetop. The thin slices sizzled as they hit the bacon grease in the pan.

"Owen. I've not seen the boy since his mother died, I don't reckon." Eliza opened the oven door to check on the pone of cornbread. Seeing that it was golden brown, she pulled it out and sat it a hot plate before spreading butter on its surface. "How is he?"

"I don't know. I didn't talk to him. But he… I didn't expect him to be so…" She stammered to a halt, her cheeks heating as she tried to figure out how to explain her reaction to the man.

Eliza smiled. "So it's like that, is it? If he looks anything like his father, he's a handsome man. Best I recall, he strongly resembled Hank."

Sarah got down mugs for coffee. "I don't recall much about Hank or Lucy. What sort of people were they?"

"Good people, kept to themselves a lot. Your daddy went to school with Hank. I think Lucy was from down around London or Corbin, somewhere down that way," Eliza said, waving a hand toward Laurel County to the west. "They only had the two boys, Owen and Harlan. Harlan died over in Germany back in… late '53, I guess it was, remember?"

"Vaguely. So how come Owen's a recluse? Do you have any idea?" Sarah considered trying to hide her interest in the man, but with very few exceptions, she didn't keep secrets from her mother.

Eliza's brow furrowed. "No, not really. Like I said, they mostly kept to themselves. Hank worked at the hardware store with his brother, of course, but Lucy stayed home with the boys. We'd run into them now and then in town, but rarely. Harlan was the youngest, and he was a couple of years older than Kathy."

"Hmm. Well, apparently, Owen comes to the library pretty often."

"Maybe you'll have a chance to talk to him," her mother said, hiding her smile behind her coffee mug.

Trying to act as though the idea didn't cause her heart to flutter, Sarah shrugged. "Maybe. We'll see."

She changed the subject, but long after they'd said goodnight and gone to bed, the idea circled through her mind. She envisioned several scenarios, trying to figure out what she'd say, what he'd say, what his voice would sound like, whether his eyes were as dreamy as Callie had declared them to be or not. As she drifted into sleep, Sarah realized she was more excited than she'd been in several months.

As fate would have it, Sarah was on her hands and knees searching for a card that had fallen under the counter when she heard Shirley say, "Owen. How are you doing today? Has it warmed up any out there?"

Sarah jerked in surprise, hitting her head on the shelf above her. "You dirty, spotted milk cow," she muttered, rubbing her head as she repeated the curse her father had often used in front of her and her siblings.

After a muffled laugh, a man said in a deep, smooth voice, "Callie, be careful, or you might knock your brain loose."

"That'd be a pure miracle," Sarah mumbled, then grimaced, mortified.

Shirley coughed. "That wasn't Callie. It was Sarah, our new girl, and I think, your neighbor. Isn't that right, Sarah?"

Shirley held out her hand, and Sarah reluctantly accepted it. Her face felt as though it were on fire. When she was on her feet, she thanked Shirley and sent an embarrassed smile in Owen's direction. To her surprise, he wore a slight frown.

"You're Ira and Eliza Browning's girl?"

"That's right." Sarah held the library card she'd retrieved as if it were a lifeline. "How do you do?"

He nodded. "I was sorry to hear about Ira. He was a good man."

"Yes, he was. Thank you."

Another patron came up, and Shirley directed Sarah toward them. By the time she had finished helping them, Owen was gone.

"Are you sure you don't know him?" Shirley asked as they were setting the counter to rights before closing. "I've never seen him clam up like that."

"No, I've never met him, not that I can recall."

"Hmmm... maybe he was having a bad day, then."

As Sarah finished her duties that day, her mind kept going back to Owen's face. She'd never considered herself to be vain, Joey and his lousy kissing aside, but she had to admit that she would have been more than happy just to sit and look at Owen. She could see why the women in town adored him.

His features weren't delicate, but they weren't painted with a broad, blunt brush, either. Framed by impossibly long, lush eyelashes as dark as his hair, his eyes were a golden brown that reminded her of dark amber. His firm jaw was shadowed, the hint of a beard showing even though it was only early afternoon, and his skin had a warm tone that was surprising given that it was still winter.

She was looking forward to the next time he came into the library. However, she was disappointed by his reaction to her. She gave a fleeting thought to wonder whether he knew she'd been sneaking onto his land and didn't approve, but she dismissed it. There was no way he could have known.

That night, she tossed and turned, unable to fall asleep. Adding to her restlessness was the fact that she'd not been able to go to the pool recently. The cold and nasty weather had kept her indoors.

"I'll ask him what his problem is next week when he comes in," she promised herself with a yawn. "It makes little sense. He doesn't know me."

But Sarah didn't get to speak to Owen at all the next week or the week after that. He seemed to have an instinct for knowing when she was working or too busy to talk to him, coming in only when she was otherwise occupied. If he happened to come across her, he'd frown and nod, then hurry away.

"I swear it's almost like he's afraid of you," Shirley commented.

Sarah was relieved that the other woman verified her own impression of his behavior. "Well, if he is, I don't know why. I'm not the least bit threatening. I wish there was some way to pin him down. Have you asked him about it?"

"I tried," Shirley confessed. "But he turned tail and ran. Shut down just like he did that first day he saw you." She turned and studied Sarah. "All the time I've known him, Owen's been completely oblivious to all the girls I've seen him around. I think he might be sweet on you. Nothing else makes sense."

Sarah blushed. "No, I don't think so. Surely that isn't it."

With an affectionate pat on the shoulder, Shirley headed past her to lock the door. "Oh, I don't know. That could be exactly it. In fact, the more I think about it, the more sense that makes. Anyhow, let's finish up here and try to go enjoy this weather."

A warm front had come through, the first real warm spell of spring. Snow still covered on the ground in patches on the shadowy sides of the mountains, but it was nearly nice enough to be out of doors without a coat. Sarah planned on taking full advantage of the weather and already had her book bag packed for the pool. She hoped to have at least a couple of hours of daylight before the sun started going down.

At home, she hurried to change clothes. With a quick kiss for her mother, she left the house, humming off-key as she walked. She was so intent on reaching the pool, she didn't realize until she was almost upon it that someone else was there, and she came to a stumbling halt. Her eyes felt as if they'd grown to the size of saucers, but she couldn't help staring.

There, across the pool, his hair damp as he shrugged into a T-shirt after obviously having just gotten out of the water, stood too-handsome-for-words, irritated-looking Owen Campbell.

CHAPTER FIVE

O WEN HEARD SARAH COMING LONG before she reached the pool. He'd considered running, but decided instead to stand his ground. Luckily, he'd gotten out of the water minutes earlier, or she would have caught him in the altogether.

She came walking up on the bench of land that connected to the ledge on the other side of the pool just as he was tugging on his T-shirt. Her eyes widened, then a fiery blush raced up her face into her cheeks. "I'm so sorry!" She turned her back on him so quickly she nearly fell. "I didn't realize... I'm sorry."

She kept glancing over her shoulder at him, biting her lip.

As he hadn't yet put on his socks and boots, he yanked his pant legs up and walked across the rocky bridge that formed the front lip of the pool. He stepped out of the pool and moved to stand an arm's length away behind her and waited for her to turn back around.

When she did, she apologized again. "I didn't mean to disturb you. Aren't you freezing?"

He had to struggle to keep his face stern, especially with her seeming so embarrassed and curious at the same time. Her gaze flitted around the clearing, dancing from his shoulders and chest to the trees and back. She was obviously uncomfortable, and with only a twinge of conscience, he did nothing to dispel her uneasiness.

Instead, he crossed his arms over his chest and narrowed his gaze slightly, which he knew made him look more than a little menacing. "You do realize that this is Campbell land, Miss Browning?"

He kept his voice low and tried to ignore the smell of her perfume.

She swallowed nervously but didn't run. "I know." Her chest moved under the light sweater she wore as she drew in a deep breath, and she finally met his eyes.

Owen felt as though he'd been punched. Her eyes were a deep, stunning cornflower blue, framed by thick, dark lashes. Though he'd been close to her before, something about the way the sun highlighted her face left him stunned. As she bravely stood almost toe-to-toe with him, staring him down, waiting for his response, he felt like she could see into his soul.

The notion annoyed him and alarmed him in equal measure.

"I'm aware you've been coming here for some time. It's never been an inconvenience. But now I think it would be best if you stayed on your side of the property line."

The flush in her cheeks faded somewhat, and he ignored the guilt that pricked him. She blinked several times, looking beyond him to the pool as though the words didn't make sense. Then, as he watched, all the fire went out of her.

"I understand. I'm so sorry—I won't come here again." With a quick glance at his face, she turned and went back the way she'd come. There was no longer a spring in her step, no humming of a jaunty tune, and she never looked back.

Long after she'd disappeared, he stood staring after her, much as he had the first time she'd been to the pool. He had to struggle not to run after her and apologize. With a long, frustrated growl, he sat down to finish getting dressed.

When he had gone into the library a few weeks earlier and discovered her working there, it had been like a slap in the face. She seemed to be everywhere he turned, and her appeal grew every time he saw her. He'd tried to ignore her in town and would have avoided the library altogether if he could have.

But he *needed* to go there at least once a week, to smell the books, to feel their bindings, to absorb the atmosphere of knowledge. For someone like Owen, who'd dropped out of school in the eighth grade and finished high school by correspondence course, the library was a sacred space.

Plus, he was working on a genealogy project, and he couldn't afford to let his feelings for Sarah get in the way of completing it.

As he trudged up the mountain to his house, he felt a bone-weary tiredness steal over him. He loathed himself for what he'd done, but he couldn't risk Sarah finding out his secrets. He couldn't risk letting her close.

"Maybe it's time for a visit to Eli and his family down in London," he mused as he reached the small, modern, two-story house where he lived, which he'd built behind the farmhouse, stubbornly unwilling to live in the house his father had thrown him out of now that his mother was gone. "Give us both some distance, let her get used to not coming to the pool. And let me reconcile myself to seeing her at the library."

The more he thought about it, the better the idea sounded, and he headed into the house to pack.

CHAPTER SIX

S ARAH WAS SO MISERABLE AND embarrassed that she didn't even remember the walk back home. All she could think about was how cold and forbidding Owen had looked. If Callie could have seen his eyes just then, the girl wouldn't have considered them remotely close to dreamy. He hadn't scared Sarah, but he'd certainly made her feel unwelcome.

When she reached the outcropping of rocks that had been her thinking spot before her discovery of the pool, she barely hesitated. She felt too exposed to stop there now that she knew Owen had been aware of her trespassing.

Worse yet, she realized she had to tell her mother what she'd done. The last thing she wanted was for word to get back to Eliza from someone else—say from Owen himself.

Though people on the outside liked to make fun of "hillbillies," as the people of Appalachia were derisively called, Sarah had always treasured her culture, which included a deep and abiding respect for the privacy and property of other people, something that was nearly bred into the local genes.

Sure, Hazard was a small town, and like any small town across the nation, it thrived on gossip. But idly gossiping about your neighbors and trespassing on their land were two vastly different things. Crossing onto a man's land without his permission was almost a killing offense in many communities.

Eliza was puttering in the yard when Sarah emerged from the woods. She looked up in surprise, then straightened from the flower bed she'd been clearing out. A concerned frown spread across her face, and she met Sarah halfway across the yard. "What's wrong?"

Sarah shook her head. Arms crossed, she stood there, miserable. "I did something, and you're going to be mad." Adult or not, she knew she was in for a well-deserved lecture.

"Well, that's certainly ominous enough. Want to tell me what it was you did?"

She briefly met her mother's eyes. "Not really. I got caught trespassing on Owen Campbell's land."

Eliza was stunned. "You... you did *what*?"

"I have this spot that I like to go to, and I was going there today, and he was there already. He told me not to come back."

"A spot? How long have you been going to this spot exactly? And where is it?"

Sarah dropped her gaze back to her feet.

"Young lady, you'll look at me when I ask you a question even if you are twenty-one years old."

Her face hot, Sarah raised her head. "Yes, ma'am. It's over the line, about halfway again around the mountain. It's this little pool of water and a big rock. I go there to read and think. I don't do anything while I'm there." Thinking of the time she'd skinny-dipped, she grimaced. When her mother raised an eyebrow, she confessed. "I kind of went skinny-dipping. Once."

Eliza drew in a slow breath and pushed two fingers into the crease between her eyebrows. "How long, Sarah?"

"How long have I been going? Since I was fifteen."

Her mother put her hands on her hips. "You... since you were fifteen? Do you have any idea...? *Fifteen?* Who else knows about this?"

"No one. I... it's a special place, Mama. It wasn't something to share with other people. I'm sorry." She bit her lip harder in an attempt to stave off her tears. "It won't happen again."

"No, it won't. Damn it, Sarah. Anything could have happened to you. Do you know that? Anyone could have come along."

Sarah stood there, a few tears escaping despite her efforts to hold them in.

"What am I going to do with you?" Eliza brushed Sarah's hair out of her face where it had come loose in the wind. "I guess, all in all, you trespassing on the neighbor's land isn't a horrible crime. At least you didn't get pregnant on purpose so you could quit school early like someone whose name we won't mention."

Her sister Kathy had done just that, disregarding their father's views on the importance of education, a decision that had caused a schism between Ira and Kathy for a long time.

Sarah gave a soggy laugh and let her mother enfold her in a hug. As she returned the embrace, she sniffled. "I suppose now I know why he doesn't want anything to do with me at the library. He's known about my visiting the pool for a while, from what he said."

"Oh, honey. And you had a little bit of a crush on him, didn't you?"

"Yes."

Eliza pulled back and studied her. "Well, there's nothing for it. I think you need to apologize to him."

"I did, Mama. And I told him I wouldn't be back."

"Still, I think a nice letter of apology might go a long way in smoothing things over." Eliza linked her arm with Sarah's. "And who knows? Maybe it will make him look on you more favorably."

Sarah did feel she owed him a more adequate apology. She had been trespassing on private property, after all. He was the injured party, such as it was. She had no hope, though, that a letter would make Owen change his mind about her.

"I'll work on it tonight or tomorrow. Right now, I need to lick my wounds."

Later that night after Eliza had gone to bed, Sarah sat at the small desk in her room. The lamp cast a warm glow around the desk and chair, and she stared at the flowers on its china base, lost in thought. She'd started the apology letter to Owen a dozen times, and a dozen times, she'd rejected what she had written. No matter how she tried, she kept coming across as angry and resentful.

"Maybe that's what's wrong. I *am* angry. I love that little pool." Tired, she ran a hand over her forehead.

The house creaked and groaned, its bones settling in to withstand the hell-wind that was blowing. The warm front was giving way to cold air from the north, and the forecasters on the radio were predicting snow to start by the next afternoon. At the moment, the two weather fronts were clashing, and a relentless, howling wind was soaring above the treetops. A hell wind, as her grandmother had called it.

Bending over the paper again, she tried one more time to pen a proper apology note. It might take her the rest of the weekend to figure out the wording, but it was the right thing to do, and she was determined to do it if it killed her.

CHAPTER SEVEN

OWEN DIDN'T FINISH HIS PROJECT until Wednesday. By then, the snow that had come over the weekend had melted. He was itching to get off the mountain and down to Eli's, but he'd had obligations that had to be met first. With those out of the way, he felt free to pack for a somewhat lengthy stay. He figured a couple of weeks would be long enough to forget the look on Sarah's face, even though his conscience whispered that he was a fool.

He had to make a couple of stops on the way, the first being the hardware store to let his uncle know he was going out of town. They weren't close, but Owen didn't like to leave without letting someone know where he was going to be. After that was done, he swung by the post office and picked up his mail. Back in his truck, he thumbed through the stack of envelopes.

Among the usual letters from cousins, a few friends who were in the Army, and the professionals he corresponded with around the globe, one envelope stood out. The handwriting was delicate—elegant, and feminine—and reading the return address caused his heart to skip a beat.

It was from Sarah.

Owen set the other mail aside, next to the stack of books he was planning on dropping off at the library as his last stop on the way out of town. He fingered the envelope, turning it over, then back again, then glanced around the parking lot to see if anyone was watching. Fairly certain he wasn't being observed, he casually lifted the letter to his nose.

With the aid of his enhanced senses, Owen picked up the faint, lingering scent of Sarah's perfume. His eyes closed for a moment, and he held in the breath, keeping it close as long as he could. When he exhaled, he reached into the pocket of his coat and pulled out his penknife. Carefully, he slit the end of the envelope and extracted the letter. The single sheet was folded neatly, and he hesitated before opening it. He wasn't sure he wanted to know what she had to say.

After sliding the letter halfway back into the envelope, he groaned and cursed. There was no way he could make the hours-long trip to Laurel County with the letter on the seat beside him, taunting him. Pulling it back out, he unfolded it.

Dear Mr. Campbell,

After our less-than-illustrious meeting Saturday afternoon, I felt I owed you the courtesy of a more formal apology.

Yes, I have been trespassing on your land for some time now. That was wrong of me; I shouldn't have done it.

I have spent many an hour on the banks of that pool in quiet contemplation, and while I will miss those visits, I will abide by your wishes.

I hope you will harbor no ill will toward me or my family, as they were unaware of my abuse of your trust.

While I cannot be sorry for the time spent beside that lovely pool, I truly regret taking advantage of you and violating your privacy. Please accept my heartfelt apology and my assurances that I will not trespass again.

Warmest regards,

Sarah Browning

Owen was surprised and not a little guilt-stricken. For the millionth time, he wondered if he had done the right thing in evicting her. Re-reading the message, he was tempted to rush down to the library, ask for her forgiveness, and give her permission to use the pool any time she felt like it.

Then he remembered how vulnerable that would leave him.

"Damn it." Despite his inner turmoil, he folded the letter and slipped it back into the envelope, then tucked it inside his jacket pocket, next to his heart. He was tired of arguing with himself. He started the truck, backed out of the parking spot, and went to finish his errands.

After he filled the truck's gas tank and had the oil checked, he glanced at the stack of books sitting so innocently on the seat beside him.

"You'll have to wait until I get home," he told them. He couldn't take the chance of stopping by the library, not even to put the books in the book deposit. Sarah would be too close, and the temptation was too strong at the moment to try to make amends.

The peace Owen sought didn't materialize. In the past, whenever he'd needed to escape the confines of his life, a visit with Eli's family had always set him to rights mentally and emotionally. Not this time. Instead, it was making his irritation worse.

Being an astute man, Eli easily picked up on Owen's unhappiness. He let Owen have three days, during which he worked himself into exhaustion every night helping around the farm. On the afternoon of the fourth day, Eli cornered him in the barn.

"Out with it, son. What's troubling you?"

Owen looked up from the horse he was currying. "What do you mean?"

Eli leaned against a stall door, arms crossed over his broad chest. He gave Owen an indulgent look and waited.

When Owen saw Eli wouldn't let him get away without answering, he let out a low hiss. "Can't I have a bad mood without every move I make being examined?"

"Of course you can. But it's obvious you're hurting, and you're like a son to me. I'd like to help if I can."

Owen leaned his head against the horse's neck, ashamed for having snapped at Eli. "I don't even know where to begin."

Eli moved a crate from the empty stall behind him and turned it up on end. He sat down with a soft grunt. "Try starting at the beginning. Tell me who she is."

He knew his face reflected his surprise. "How did you know it was a girl? Woman, I guess. She's not a girl."

His uncle's answering smile was rueful. "When a man gets to a certain age, it's almost always a woman. Tell me about her."

"Remember the neighbor's daughter who's been coming over to the little swimming hole on my land? The one who went away to school a few years ago?"

Eli nodded. "Sure. I remember how relieved you were when she left."

"Well, she's back." Owen explained about Sarah's father's death, her job at the library, and their encounter at the pool. "I didn't handle it well, but damn it, I didn't know what else to do."

His uncle rubbed a hand over his chin, a look of almost disappointment on his face. "How did she react?"

"It upset her. I felt like a heel. And then, the day I left to come down here? I got this." Laying the comb aside, he pulled the letter from his coat pocket. The paper was becoming worn, he'd read it so much. With some reluctance, he handed it to his uncle, then turned to finish working with the horse.

Eli opened it and read without speaking. When he was finished, he carefully slid it back into the envelope and tapped the edge of the paper on his knee. His expression was pensive, and he didn't speak as he watched Owen finish grooming the horse.

Once the animal was back in its stall, fed and watered, Owen sat down on a bale of hay across from his uncle.

"Why are you so afraid?" Eli asked. "Is it because you don't want to be hurt, or is it because of what you are, what we are?" He handed the letter back to Owen, and Owen tucked it into his pocket.

"A little of both, I guess. I've never fit in with the rest of the world, not really, even without taking shifting into consideration. And I've never told anyone what I am. Harlan didn't even know the full extent of it, and he was my brother. He never accepted me for everything else that I am, so I couldn't see him accepting that I'm a shifter."

"No offense to your late brother, but Harlan was never the most thoughtful person. If he'd been much more close-minded, he would have been a potato."

Owen conceded the point with a nod. "True. But, Eli, there are way more people like Harlan than there are like you. What if I reached out to her, let her in, and she turned out to be like him?"

Eli crossed his ankle over his knee. "Your instincts are better than that."

"Not where she's concerned. She mixes me up inside. I either clam up when I'm around her, or I say the wrong thing. She's home to stay, from what I gather, and I'm not about to move off the mountain. I can't avoid her. I don't know what to do."

"What do you want to do?"

Owen felt his cheeks flush.

Eli gave a soft laugh. "Okay. Well, there's that. What does your gut say? Ignore your head and tell me what your instincts are saying."

Running his hands through his hair, Owen sighed. "I want to be near her. Period. The end."

"Then don't you think you should find out if she feels the same way? What if she isn't like Harlan? What if she's more like my Amy?"

Amy, Eli's wife, was as much a mother to Owen as his own mother had ever been. She and Eli were hopelessly in love, and they had been for decades. Amy accepted Eli—and his abilities—with open arms.

"What if she isn't?"

Eli stood. "Then find out, one way or another. Don't keep torturing yourself and her by going on like this. It serves no purpose." He walked toward the door, then threw a question back that gave Owen pause. "Do you think the kind of person who comes to that pool, who respects it the way your Sarah seems to, could really be like Harlan?"

Owen shook his head. "Not in the least."

His eyes full of sympathy, Eli gestured toward the house. "Me either. Come on. Amy will have supper ready by now. There's no need for you to rush off. I believe you need to think about this for a little while. Stay here like you planned. But you're going to have to give serious consideration to making things right with this girl. I don't think you'll rest until you do."

CHAPTER EIGHT

For the first few days after her encounter with Owen, every time the bell jingled, signaling someone opening the door at the library, Sarah jumped. By the time a week had passed, with no appearance by Owen, her nerves were frazzled.

That Saturday, she met Gilly for lunch after her shift at the library. They took a booth at the back of the drugstore's café, which closed at one o'clock on Saturdays. Once they had their plates, Gilly's mother, Rosemarie, locked the door and turned the sign around to show "Closed."

"There are some advantages to being the owners," Rosemarie said. "You girls take your time and clean up when you're done. Sarah, you ought to come by the house tonight for a sleepover. You haven't done that since you've been home."

"Mother, we're too old to have sleepovers. We're adults now," Gilly said with an impish smile. "But you really should consider it, Sarah. We could stay up all night and giggle just like we used to."

Sarah smiled uncertainly. "I don't know. I hate to leave Mama by herself."

Rosemarie patted her on the shoulder. "I think Eliza would understand. You think about it. Holler if you need anything." She excused herself and headed for the back.

Gilly turned to Sarah. "Okay, are you going to tell me what has you so jumpy? You look like you've not slept in a week."

Sarah pushed her mashed potatoes around on her plate. "I haven't. Not really." She sighed. "You've heard us mention our neighbor, Owen Campbell, right?"

"Owen? Sure. He comes in here from time to time. What about him?"

"He comes in here? That's great. Now I have to worry about running into him here, too." Sarah groaned and let her head fall back against the red Naugahyde booth as she closed her eyes. "I'm so stupid."

"Now, I know *that* isn't true. What makes you say that you are?"

Sarah raised her head and looked across the table at her friend. "Because I got caught trespassing on his land." She explained the whole situation, including the fact that she had feelings for the man.

"Shirley thought he might be shy, that he had a crush on me or something. But no. It turns out he thinks of me as a pest and an interloper. And the worst part? He comes into the library every week, Gilly. I don't know why he hasn't been in this week, but I've almost bolted every time the door opened. Shirley thinks I've lost my mind, and I'm too embarrassed to explain it to her."

Gilly propped her chin on her hand. "Well, that's certainly enough to be embarrassed about, but I can't see Owen holding it against you forever. He's too nice. He always leaves whoever waits on him a good tip, and he doesn't have to." She tilted her head to the side. "So how much of his chest did you see?"

"Gilly!" Sarah ducked her head. "You would pick up on that."

"Of course I would. So? Does his body match his face? Or is he covered in boils and pustules?"

The ridiculous image made Sarah laugh. "No. He was not covered in boils and pustules. He... he was very attractive. Which makes this whole thing that much harder. He's a very appealing man, more so than any man I've ever met."

"That makes you want to chew bullets, I imagine. Tell you what, why don't we go pack a bag for you, and you come spend the night with me? We can drive around, take in a movie, and find you some handsome young men to flirt with. Who knows? Maybe you'll meet the love of your life tonight. What do you say?"

"I guess so. As long as Mama's okay by herself. If she isn't, do you want to spend the night at my house?"

Gilly stuck out her tongue. "Of course. I don't care whose house we stay at, but I want to have some fun. Maybe it would be better to stay at your house anyways. That way, we can get your mother in on our shenanigans." She stood. "I'll go tell my folks, and we can swing by the house and let me get a bag together. Okay?"

"Okay," Sarah agreed. "I'll clean up." As she cleared the table and disposed of her half-eaten food, she sighed. She knew Gilly was right—she had to stop crying over spilled milk. She just wished the spill hadn't hurt so much.

By a week and a half after her lunch with Gilly, Sarah had convinced herself that she was past the blow Owen had dealt her. It didn't hurt that a handsome young insurance agent, Tony DeWitt, had started trying to woo her, coming in the library for a chat nearly every afternoon or 'accidentally' running into her at the drugstore. Though he wasn't Owen Campbell, his interest was a soothing balm to a bruised ego—at least in the beginning.

Now, however, his persistence was wearing on her, and if he kept pushing her to go out with him, she was going to have a very blunt talk with him.

She was working alone in the children's department after lunch, cleaning up after the departure of a group of students from the local grade school, when Tony came in.

"Hey, pretty girl. Why aren't you downstairs, lighting up the place?"

Waving away the compliment, which she knew was nothing more than empty flattery, Sarah moved on to the next section of chairs she was stacking against the wall. "Because I'm working up here, obviously. Why aren't you at work?"

"You know I'm not chained to a desk. I'm getting ready to head over to Buckhorn to visit a customer. Want to go with me?"

With the chairs in their place, Sarah shook her head, annoyed by his persistence. "Thank you, no." Hoping he'd get the message, she moved to the checkout desk, where she glanced through all the new library card applications the students had filled out.

Tony followed, and she hid a sigh of frustration. So it was going to be the hard way, after all.

"Look, Tony, you're a nice man. But if I've told you once, I've told you a hundred times. We're not allowed to fraternize with the patrons." Thinking that if she turned her focus to the paperwork, he might go away, she gathered the papers and headed downstairs.

Undeterred, he followed her. "And I've told you, you don't need this job. You need to find a man who'll pamper you, take care of you. Come on, Sarah. Come with me."

Given that the stairs wound down to open into the atrium at the front door, and sound echoed loudly on the hard surfaces, Sarah hoped no one was in the lobby where they could overhear. To her dismay, not only was *someone* there, the *someone* in question was Owen.

His face was as hard as if it were carved from stone, and he had his hand on the glass interior door to the downstairs. Given the disgusted look he shot her and Tony, he'd heard every word. He moved jerkily, holding the door open for her to pass through.

Tony stopped her with a hand on her arm. "Thanks, buddy, but the lady and I have something to discuss," he said, his tone dismissive even as she jerked her arm out of his grip.

Owen's jaw clenched so tightly Sarah could see a muscle ticking, but after studying her for a long minute, he nodded and went on inside, the glass door closing behind him with a quiet swish.

Sarah tried to count to ten, but that didn't help her temper. She drew in a deep breath and said a silent prayer for patience. "Tony, I need this job. I'm not looking for a man to take care of me. I can take care of myself. You don't need to come here to see me anymore. I will not go out with you. You've been told that a dozen times. You're wasting your time."

She didn't think she had ever seen anyone actually look pole-axed, but at that moment, Tony could have been the poster boy for stunned confusion.

"But I thought…" Clearing his throat, he tried again. "Usually women only get jobs outside the house when they don't have a man to provide for them, so they can find someone to support them. With your daddy gone, I figured that's what you were doing."

Her fingers tightened around the papers. "I know *some* women do that. But this is nineteen-sixty, not eighteen-sixty. Times are changing. I'm not one of those women. I've never been one, and God forbid I ever am. Good day." She hurried to the front desk.

Shirley was frowning. "Everything okay? It looked like he hit a nerve."

"He did. I had to get blunt with him. I hated doing that, but he didn't leave me much choice. Will you be okay if I take five minutes?"

"Of course."

"Thanks." Sarah grabbed the key to the employee restroom and headed toward the back of the building. She used the time to compose herself, and when she came out, she felt much calmer, though still embarrassed.

As she hurried back to the front desk, her steps faltered briefly when she saw Owen standing there talking to Shirley. Squaring her shoulders, she went around the opposite end and helped the next patron in line.

Shirley caught her attention when the patron had been taken care of. "Sarah, do you have any idea when these two books went out? Owen has been waiting for them, and they should have come in while he was out of town."

Sarah took the paper Shirley handed her that had two book titles written on it in a bold, masculine hand. "*The Folklore of Central Appalachia,* and *Haints, Hollers, and Howls,*" she read aloud, then grimaced. "As a matter of fact, I checked them out. I'm sorry. There wasn't a hold notice on them. I've almost finished with them. If you like, I can bring them back in tomorrow."

"No, take your time. I can get them when you're done," he said.

"I thought the two of you were neighbors," Shirley remarked. "When you're finished with the books, why don't you simply take them to Owen's house? It would save him a trip into town."

Sarah would have been hard pressed to say which of them was more horrified by the suggestion, her or Owen. Their excuses ran over each other as they scrambled to come up with reasons that wasn't a good idea.

Shirley looked from one to the other, holding up her hands, and their voices trailed off. "Okay, I see that wasn't a welcome suggestion. We'll plan on holding the books here when Sarah's finished with them."

"I'm fine with that," Owen rushed to say. "Thank you." He picked up the books on the counter and headed out the door.

Once he was outside, Shirley turned to Sarah, hands on hips. "Start talking. What in the world is going on between the two of you?"

Looking around to make sure no one was close enough to overhear, Sarah said, "He caught me trespassing on his land. I wasn't doing anything illicit, I promise. I had a spot that I liked to go to, to read or to think, but even so, I was trespassing. He'd known about it for some time."

"Oh, for heaven's sake. *That's* why he acts like he does around you?"

Sarah nodded. "Apparently so. And then when he came in just now, he overheard Tony say something to me." She bit her lip. "Shirley, I promise you I'm not seeing Tony. I don't want to see him, and I've not encouraged him. I can't lose this job."

Shirley sighed, and Sarah could tell she was a little aggravated. "I know that. I've been watching you. You're one of the best assistants we've had here. I know you follow the rules. Callie, maybe not so much. Tony needs to learn to stay away. It hardly matters if you're encouraging him or not if he's interfering with your job duties."

"I know. And I hope he won't be back." She told Shirley what he'd said. "I know that's a popular opinion even this day and age, but it still aggravates me. My mother raised me to be independent, a true helpmate, not some fragile flower that needs to be 'pampered.' It's fine if some women choose that. I do not happen to be one of them." She snorted.

"Well, if he comes back, I'll have a word with him," Shirley reassured her. "I know you've only been here a few months, but we don't want to lose you."

Sarah smiled and tucked a strand of hair behind her ear. "Thanks. I'm not eager to leave either."

"Now, as to this problem with Owen, do you think you can put on a brave face when he comes in, or do we need to make other arrangements?"

Sarah considered the question. "I think I can handle it. I guess we'll find out when he comes in to pick up those books. If I can't, I'll let you know." She rubbed her neck where the muscles had knotted from the tension of the afternoon. "I'm glad the day's almost over. My head and neck are pounding."

Shirley laid the back of her hand against Sarah's forehead. "You feel a little warm. I hope you aren't coming down with that bug Callie had last week."

"So do I. I can't afford to get sick right now. Besides, on top of everything else, catching that bug would feel like adding insult to injury."

After a miserable night spent tossing and turning, Sarah finally drifted into a restless sleep. She didn't wake until her mother came in and shook her.

"Sarah? Honey, wake up. You're burning up with fever."

Opening her heavy eyelids, Sarah peered up into her mother's concerned face. When she tried to swallow, the pain was excruciating. "I have to go to work."

She tried to sit up, but Eliza gently pushed her back. "Oh, no, sweetheart. I don't think you'll be going anywhere today except to the doctor. You stay right there, and I'll get you some water."

Falling back against the pillows, Sarah asked, "Can you call the library?"

"Of course. And the doctor's office. I'll be right back."

Sarah closed her eyes, too tired to hold them open. She gave a brief thought to the books she'd planned to return that day, but even that didn't keep her awake. Before her mother was downstairs, she'd fallen back asleep.

To her dismay, she was diagnosed with strep throat and wasn't able to return to work until the following Tuesday. When she clocked in that morning, she apologized profusely to Shirley and the library director. Both assured her she wasn't in trouble and that they understood.

"I wasn't kidding when I told you that you're one of the best assistants we've ever had," Shirley said as she was getting ready to go to lunch later that day. "Are you okay with handling things by yourself down here until I get back?"

"Sure. I'll be fine."

Shirley hadn't been gone for five minutes when the door opened and Owen came in. He stopped short, seeing Sarah by herself, but then continued, placing a stack of books on the counter.

"Hello."

"Hi." Sarah's hands, hidden in her lap behind the tall desk, clenched. She made them relax and forced a polite smile as she stood and went to get his reserved books from the back counter. "I have those books you wanted. I'm sorry I didn't get them back in here sooner."

"That's fine. Shirley mentioned you've been ill. I hope it was nothing serious."

"Just strep throat." She took his card and checked the books out to him.

To her surprise, he lingered. "So, what did you think of the books?"

Sarah shrugged. "They were interesting, especially *Folklore*. It was written as more of a nonfiction book than an entertainment piece, though it was still entertaining in its own way."

"How so?"

Seeing nothing but genuine interest in his gaze, she placed the books side by side. She tapped the cover of *Haints, Hollers, and Howls.* "This one is done more like the dime novels that were written about Western life several decades ago or the sensationalized pulp fiction we have today. But *Folklore* takes a more scientific approach, at least in the way it's presented. The other book is a more fun read, but for information, *Folklore* has it beat." She stacked the books and slid them across to him, along with his card. "Is there anything else I can help you with?"

"Not right now, thanks. I'm going to browse." He picked up the books and, with a nod, headed back into the stacks.

When Sarah sat back down, her legs shook. "Probably from being sick," she muttered, refusing to acknowledge any other reason for her weakness.

Shirley returned from lunch before long, and Sarah clocked out. She still had little appetite, but it was nice to take a few minutes to rest. When she came back to the counter, Shirley handed her a folded piece of paper.

"Owen asked me to give you this. It's a list of some books he thought you might find informative. I take it the two of you settled your differences?"

Perplexed, Sarah met the older woman's gaze. "Not in so many words, no. He asked what I thought about the books, and I told him. Did he say anything when he gave you this?"

"No. Just asked me to give it to you."

"Huh. Okay." There were three titles on the list. Sarah folded the paper and put it in the pocket of her skirt. "I'll look at them before I leave. Thanks."

The rest of the day, Sarah ran her fingers across the paper at odd moments, her mind going back to Owen's visit. His behavior utterly confounded her. Tired of worrying, she shrugged his kindness off as an anomaly. Just because he had been civil one day, she wasn't expecting the same treatment the next time she saw him.

She'd had a strong sense of self-preservation ever since she'd overheard Paul Turner laughing with her sister that day in the drama room. If Owen Campbell was trying to get her to drop her guard by being nice to her, he was going to have to do a lot more than recommend some books.

CHAPTER NINE

A FTER OWEN FINISHED SUPPER THAT evening, he settled down at his desk to catch up on the correspondence that had accumulated while he was away. One of the first letters he wrote was to inform Eli of the day's events. With the standard greeting out of the way, he went straight to the heart of what was bothering him.

I don't mind admitting that I'm confused. When I ran into Sarah the other day, a smarmy insurance agent was sniffing at her heels. Then, when I found out she was reading the very books I've been waiting for, I was startled. I handled that badly, something that I seem constantly to do around her. She got sick right after that, from what Shirley said. Strep throat, so nothing I caused, but knowing that just made the guilt worse.

I went to pick up the books today, and the happiness that went through me at seeing her... I don't like it. But then she talked to me about the books.

She's so damned smart, Eli. I wanted to stay there at the counter all day. I don't know what spurred her interest in the subject of the paranormal and Appalachian folklore. It was all I could do not to ask. She volunteered nothing beyond what I asked her, and I could tell I made her uncomfortable.

I've really not handled things well, and I don't know how to rectify that. I left her the names of some books I thought she might find interesting and included one of my own on the list. Maybe next time I go into the library, I'll find the courage to ask her if she's read them.

Given the way I've acted around her, she probably threw the list away as soon as Shirley gave it to her. I certainly couldn't blame her for that.

I will continue to endeavor, as I promised I would, to repair the damage I've caused. Much as you feared, I don't think it's a task that will be easily or quickly accomplished.

Owen sat back, the confines of his chair a familiar embrace of sorts. It was a luxury, crafted from upholstered leather, with wheels on the base, a reward he'd purchased after he sold his first three books. It also made the countless hours he spent hunched over a notebook or the drawing board pass that much faster.

He'd started writing when he was eighteen, a series of illustrated children's books about a shape-shifting boy named Tobias Hedge and his adventures in the Appalachian woods, and through a lucky set of breaks, his books had taken off like wildfire. The boon allowed him to live comfortably.

Instead of a signature, he picked up his favorite drawing nib and sketched out a quick scene of a deer looking up, surprise reflected in its gaze. For whimsy, he added a half-eaten bunch of daisies, one of his favorite treats, hanging out of the deer's mouth. He always added a sketch to his private letters, something to make Eli and Amy smile.

Setting the unfolded letter aside so the ink could dry, he stretched and stood. He looked around the open, airy space that comprised his studio and sleeping quarters. After royalty checks had started coming in with regularity, Owen had built the studio.

He could have lived in the farmhouse, but he wasn't comfortable there anymore. The memories were too strong and too negative. And frankly, he refused to live in a house his father had thrown him out of as a young boy for committing the offense of having had the luck to be born a shifter.

When he'd mentioned to his uncle what he wanted to do a couple of few earlier, Eli and two of his sons had come up from Laurel County to help Owen build the new house. They and their families were the only ones who had ever seen the inside.

Unassuming from the outside, the structure was small but had two stories, along with a porch hidden in the middle of the roof. The downstairs contained his library, where he devoured book after book, his thirst for knowledge never quenched. To the side of the open library was a small kitchen, and attached to the back was a laundry room with a half bath hidden under the stairs.

The upstairs was one large room, the only wall being the divider between the open space and the full bath. At one end, his desk and drawing board sat in front of a large bank of windows. His bed, a king to fit his tall frame, was in the middle of the room, against the wall between the bedroom door and the windows. The foot of the bed faced another window, which was set into the wall beside a wide glass door that opened onto a small deck. Owen had designed a place to watch the sky on the roof above the deck, with stairs leading up into the space.

The house was heated by a woodstove on each floor and met Owen's needs nicely. It was set back almost into the trees, and most people weren't even aware of its existence, those few who cared enough to give him a second thought, believing he still lived in his parents' old house.

Looking out the windows across from his bed, he watched storm clouds gathering off in the distance. Frequent bolts of lightning shot down from the sky, illuminating the purple violence of the roiling clouds. He opened the door, letting the spring air flood into the room.

Lifting his head, he sniffed the wind, his eyes half closing with pleasure. A chill shook him, and he let the wolf emerge enough to enhance the experience of the wind rolling over him. The myriad scents it carried tickled his lupine senses in a way his human side couldn't experience.

He considered going outside for a run. He was wired from his encounter with Sarah earlier in the day, and he could use the exercise to destress. Glancing longingly at the mountain that rolled away from the house, he sighed.

"Too much paperwork, old man. There'll be other runs."

Tamping down his frustration, he closed the door and went back to the desk. As he addressed the envelope and placed the letter to Eli inside it, he wondered again what Sarah had done with the list of books.

"I'll simply have to ask," he finally decided. "There's no way around it."

Down in the valley, Sarah was curled up on the window seat in her bedroom with the window cracked enough to let in fresh air. She heard thunder in the distance and shivered with anticipation. Nothing was as invigorating as a wild thunderstorm, she thought, her attention momentarily diverted from the book she was reading.

One book Owen had recommended, *Tobias Hedge Versus the Opossum,* was a storybook aimed at older children. Given the genre, she'd been surprised to find it on the list, and if he hadn't included two other fairly studious volumes, she would have thought he was sending her a message that he saw her as a child.

Once she picked up the book and glanced through it, though, the recommendation made sense. Inside, she found much more than the typical children's novel. Instead, it was closer in style to the original *Grimm's Fairy Tales*, complete with stunning watercolor illustrations. Unlike Grimm's, however, which were set in Europe, *Tobias Hedge* took place in Appalachia.

As she devoured the book, she recalled what she knew about the series. The author was one she'd heard of at Berea, even though she hadn't had time to read his works before tonight. The series was written for older children, those not quite teenagers, and from what Sarah remembered, it was all the latest rage. A native of eastern Kentucky, the series' author, H.O. McLemore, was reputed to be a brilliant recluse.

Gracie, one of the girls in Sarah's class, had a theory. "I think he's horribly disfigured from fighting in the war, and when he came home scarred and wounded, the girl he was promised to ran away in horror. So he took to his cabin and writes to drown his sorrows."

"Children's stories?" Sarah questioned. "I don't know. I think he'd be more apt to write like Steinbeck or Hemingway if that were the case."

"No, Sarah," another female student had protested. "It's for all the children he'll never have. You *have* to read these books. Then you'll understand."

Sarah had laughed, brushing off their devotion to McLemore as a passing fad. But once she began reading the book Owen had recommended, she couldn't put it down. The words flowed on the page, wrapping around her. The stories were deftly woven, a blend of the folklore that permeated mountain culture with new twists on the traditional tales. Though the writing was original, there were enough glimmers of the familiar present to make it feel comfortably homey.

After pausing only long enough to lay the book down and visit the bathroom, Sarah rushed back in and continued from the spot she'd marked. She might not have understood Owen's puzzling behavior toward her, but the man knew what he was about in recommending books. As soon as she got to work tomorrow, she was going to check out every book they had by H.O. McLemore and devour them all.

CHAPTER TEN

OWEN WAS NERVOUS. NINE DAYS had passed since he'd last been to the library, and he was almost afraid to go back and see Sarah again. What if she hadn't read the books? Perhaps more threatening to his peace of mind, Owen wondered what it would mean if she *had*. He castigated himself for including one of his own titles on the list.

"What are you going to do if she read it and didn't like it?" he asked himself on the drive to town. He'd posed the query a hundred times in the last few days and was still no closer to an answer than he'd been the first time he'd wondered.

He was in between projects and had taken a little time off to do some genealogical research. Writing and illustrating his books was a passion, but researching lineages was something almost as important, satisfying another need. Ever since he'd learned the truth about himself, he'd been determined to find out where the shifting originated. He'd discovered that his family wasn't alone in the special gifts they had, and that the gifts hidden from sight by ordinary people were as varied as the people who bore them.

Shirley had let him know on his previous visit that the library was expecting several boxes of new material from a recent estate settlement. He'd called that morning to see if they had arrived, and when she confirmed they had, Owen was as gleeful as a kid in a candy store.

"I guess this means we'll be seeing you today," she remarked. He could hear the smile in her voice.

"You guess correctly," he assured her.

Torn between his excitement over having new records to peruse and his trepidation at seeing Sarah, he parked in the pay lot near the library. He checked his leather satchel before he got out, making sure the paper and sharpened pencils inside were secure. To get to the library, he had to walk past the insurance agency where Sarah's would-be beau worked. Owen stayed on alert as he went past the building, but saw no sign of the other man.

His heart pounding with anticipation by the time he reached the library, he took a minute to compose himself before going inside. When he reached the front desk and saw only Shirley and Callie working, the moment was rather anticlimactic.

Shirley greeted him with a slightly amused, knowing smile. "You were expecting someone else, I presume?"

Owen felt his face heat, and he gave an abashed shrug. "Maybe. I'm still happy to see you. How are you?" He gave her the books he was returning and leaned against the desk.

"I'm fine, sweetie. And you?"

"Well enough, I guess. So tell me about this new collection. Is it as good as you thought it would be?"

They chatted for several minutes about the new assets in the genealogy collection. Owen was getting ready to go upstairs and start his research when he heard an exasperated sigh coming from the bookcases behind him. Shirley's expression tightened, and Owen turned in time to see Sarah emerge, the smarmy insurance agent right behind her.

"Sarah, sweetheart—" the man started.

"I am not your sweetheart," Sarah grated. "For the last time, Tony, leave me alone."

Owen felt himself go hot and then cold all over, and he straightened away from the desk, fully intending to lend assistance. He never made the first step.

As he watched, Tony reached out to touch Sarah's shoulder. In a flash, her elbow shot back, making solid contact with the other man's midsection, if the grunt he emitted was any sign. The hardback book in her hand flew up to connect with his chin as he bent over from the first impact. The momentum of the blow sent him to the floor, where he lay groaning in pain, his hands over his mouth and nose.

"Oh, no! Tony, are you okay? I am *so* clumsy. This sort of thing happens to me *all* the time," Sarah said, standing over him. To Owen's utter astonishment and not-slight satisfaction, as she bent over the insurance agent, she dropped three of the books she'd been carrying… right on Tony's groin. The man's face, already red from the encounter, turned positively purple. "Oops. Did that hurt?"

A hastily disguised curse sounded from behind him, and Shirley rushed around the counter to where Sarah stood. She quickly took possession of the remaining book, which Owen thought was hovering ominously over the now-whimpering Tony, and drew Sarah back a few steps.

"Oh, this is an unfortunate accident. Sarah, I think you're overset. Why don't you take a break? I'll see to Tony."

"Yes, ma'am." Without glancing at the front desk, Sarah fled toward the back of the library.

Shirley helped Tony sit up and inspected the damage to his chin. "Oh, I think you'll survive. But I don't want to see you back in here pestering that girl again. Because if I do, I'll call Gibson up at the insurance agency. He'll not be pleased when

I'm finished enlightening him. Do you understand my meaning, Mr. DeWitt?"

With a sullen "Yes, ma'am," Tony got to his feet. He didn't look back as he hobbled out the door, wincing with every step. Shirley, Callie, and Owen watched him go, not speaking until the door closed behind him.

Shirley came back to the desk, holding one of the books Sarah had used so effectively in her hand. "Not one word of comment," she told a highly amused Callie. Blood stained the corner of the cover with some soaked into the pages. "Well, that's ruined. Get the information off this and then dispose of it for me. We'll have to order a new copy."

"I'll cover the cost if I may. That was worth watching," Owen said.

Shirley sent him an exasperated look. "I understand why Sarah did it, but I'll still have to have a word with the girl. Mind you, it might be a word of commendation. Don't you have some research to be doing?" She shooed him away from the desk.

Owen smiled and saluted her, nodded to Callie, and headed upstairs, certain of three things: One, Sarah wasn't interested in the least in the insurance agent. Two, she could handle herself well in a difficult situation. And three, he never wanted to get on the wrong side of her and a book.

When Sarah returned to the library floor a short while later, she felt calmer, though she was still humiliated by the whole debacle. It made her want to hit Tony all over again.

Shirley pulled her aside when she reached the front desk. "Tell me what happened. I didn't even know Tony was in here."

Embarrassed, Sarah crossed her arms over her chest. "I didn't either. He was just *there* when I turned around. I figured he'd given up because he hadn't been back in since I told him I wasn't interested. Anyhow, he kept getting closer and closer to me even though I told him to back off. When he touched me, I lost my temper. I'm sorry."

Shirley held up her hand. "Do not apologize. He had no business touching you, especially with you telling him to leave you alone. And you aren't in trouble. But I have to caution you against attacking the patrons, otherwise we'll both hear about it later. With that said, you had every right to defend yourself from unwanted advances. I'm proud of you for the way you handled him, Sarah. Now, why don't you go upstairs and work in the children's department the rest of the day? Tell Nellie I sent you up there."

"Thank you, Shirley."

Taking the rolling cart full of returns for the children's department with her on the elevator, Sarah let her eyes fall shut as the elevator doors closed. Why, she asked herself, did it always seem like Owen was there to witness every humiliating thing that happened to her? When the elevator dinged, she opened her eyes with a tired sigh. He had probably run as fast and far as he could after seeing her attack on Tony. At least he'd been the only patron in the library.

"Hey, Nellie. Shirley sent me up," she told the older lady who ran the children's department. "Where do you need me?"

The gray-haired grandmother looked at Sarah over her half glasses. "Looks like you have plenty of books to check back in. Why don't you start there, and I'll let you know?"

"Yes, ma'am."

It took over an hour to sort through the hundred or so books on the cart. Each one had to be looked up in the file of checkouts and its card replaced in the paper slot at the front of the book. Sarah noticed that several of the books had hold tags.

"Nellie, I thought all books with holds on them got these tags. Isn't that how it's supposed to work?"

"It is. Why?"

"Because I checked a couple of books out a few weeks ago that were supposed to be on hold for a patron. Their cards didn't have tags on them. If they had, I wouldn't have checked out the books. The patron came in looking for the books, and they weren't here."

Nellie pursed her lips and pulled off her glasses, letting them dangle on the delicate chain she wore around her neck. "The patron who had the books reserved wouldn't happen to be a handsome, single man, would he?"

"As a matter of fact… how did you know that?"

The other woman shook her head. "Because that's what Callie does. She takes off the tags, and then whatever man has been waiting for the books calls or comes back in to see what the holdup is. She's determined she's going to catch her a husband, that girl is. Shameful."

That Callie had set her cap for Owen didn't sit well with Sarah. Callie had never made a secret of her admiration of his looks, but removing the tags on his holds seemed like a somewhat underhanded way of getting his attention.

Nellie stood and straightened her skirt. "It's time for me to take lunch. You've been here long enough that you can handle things."

Sarah smiled. "If I have questions, I'll call downstairs. I promise."

The older woman handed Sarah a key ring. "This is for the genealogy room. There's a patron back there now. If he leaves before I get back, which I doubt he'll do given how long he usually stays, make sure he signs out in the register. Lock the room after he leaves."

"Okay. Have a pleasant lunch."

After Nellie disappeared, Sarah started shelving the returned books, enjoying the quiet. With the end of the school year approaching, she knew the peaceful atmosphere was something that wouldn't last much longer. Shirley had warned her that the library became much more active in the summer months. Children, especially those living in town, came to the facility in droves.

As she turned the corner with the cart, Sarah looked toward the genealogy room and groaned. Owen was exiting, walking along with a distracted frown, as though he were trying to puzzle something out. When he saw her, he slowed.

"Hello."

"Mr. Campbell," Sarah said, cringing inside. She'd thought he had left.

He walked to stand beside her. "Owen."

"Excuse me?"

"Owen. It's my name. Mr. Campbell was my father."

She shelved a book and sent him a noncommittal smile. "Okay. Is there anything I can help you with?"

The distracted look came back across his face. "No. I was just taking a break. If you'll excuse me?"

"Of course."

He went toward the restrooms, and Sarah realized she was grasping the handle of the cart so tightly her knuckles were white. She forced a laugh and made herself loosen her grip. Blowing out a sigh, she moved down the aisle of bookshelves and continued putting up the books.

In a couple of minutes, she heard booted footsteps coming back toward the stacks, and she tensed in anticipation. Sure enough, Owen appeared at the end of the row of bookshelves. With his hands tucked into the front pockets of his jeans, he ambled toward her. His dark-blue plaid dress shirt with the sleeves rolled halfway up his forearms made his shoulders look a mile wide. She tried to act nonchalant, but her heart was pounding.

"Where'd you learn that trick you used on the insurance agent?"

"Um." Sarah blinked at him, unsure of how to answer. Should she deny it was a deliberate attack or answer honestly?

Casually, he picked a book up off the cart and thumbed through it. After a minute, he looked up, an eyebrow raised. "Well?"

She frowned. "That's a rather forward question, don't you think?"

He shrugged, looking back down at the book in his hands. "No."

"You're assuming I'm not just clumsy. That it wasn't an accident."

A small smile lifted the corners of his mouth, but he didn't look up. "It isn't an assumption; it's a fact. I've watched you. You're not clumsy."

Completely disconcerted and tired of being toyed with, she said the first thing that came to her mind. "What kind of game are you playing?"

His head jerked up, astonishment on his face. "I'm not playing any game. I genuinely want to know."

"Why? Worried I might use that sort of maneuver on you?" Sarah eyed him from head to toes and back up again. "It's a distinct possibility." Moving past him with the cart, she went to the other side of the bookshelf and tried to pretend he hadn't followed her.

"I think we got off on the wrong foot," he said. "I came on a little strong that day at the pool. I'm sorry."

With a muted growl, she shelved the book she was holding and turned to him. "So you've waited this long to apologize? It's been over a month. Obviously, you weren't too guilt-stricken." Smarting as she remembered how cold he'd been that day, she made a dismissive motion with her hand. "Apology accepted.

Now, if you don't need anything, I have to get back to work. You can get back to whatever it is you were doing."

She walked across the room to the next section of books, hoping he would take the hint. Much to her frustration, he didn't. Instead, he shelved the book he held—in its proper place, she noted—and followed.

"It's genealogy," he said as he came to a stop a few feet away. Hands back in his pockets, he leaned against the wall and watched her finish putting the books away. "What I've been doing. I really am sorry about the way I acted that day. You startled me, and I didn't respond very well."

"Mr. Campbell—"

"Owen."

Sarah counted to ten, then to ten again. "*Mr. Campbell,* I was the one in the wrong that day. I was trespassing. You had every right to throw me off your land."

He scowled. "I didn't throw you off my land."

"Not literally, but you most definitely did figuratively. Regardless, it doesn't matter. I shouldn't have been there. I won't be there again. End of discussion."

Sarah could tell her response didn't sit well with him. He didn't move when she rolled the cart back to the elevator and returned to the desk.

After a minute, he pushed away from the wall and came to stand beside her. "As long as you don't bring anyone else with you, I don't have any objection to you coming to the pool from time to time. Just... just be careful if you decide to come back, okay? And don't go swimming by yourself. It isn't safe." With that, he headed into the genealogy room.

Stunned, Sarah stared after him. She had to make a concerted effort to pick her jaw up from where it had fallen on the floor. When Nellie returned from lunch five minutes later, she was still trying to figure out if she'd imagined the exchange or if it had really happened.

In the genealogy room, Owen mentally cursed himself for being ten kinds of fool. Though Sarah had hid it well, there was still a lingering hurt from that early encounter. From everything he'd seen of her, she didn't seem to be the type of person to hold a grudge for long. Therefore, the only logical reason for her to still be harboring hurt feelings about being forbidden from using Owen's land was that she had a deep, emotional attachment to the pool.

That train of thought almost didn't bear following because if that was the case, if she truly was connected to the land emotionally, it was entirely plausible that she was the sort of woman Owen had dreamed of finding his entire life but never dared believe existed. A woman who might accept him for who he was, all of him. A woman who, if she felt that deeply about something, wouldn't easily forgive the person who came between her and what she loved. And he'd been the one to hurt her.

CHAPTER ELEVEN

WHEN SARAH CAME DOWN FOR breakfast Saturday morning, she found her mother sitting at the table, staring into space.

"Everything okay?" Sarah asked.

"Hmm? Oh, yes. Everything's fine. Did you sleep well?"

"Well enough," Sarah told her with a smile. She made a bowl of oatmeal and added a side of some leftover canned peaches they'd had with supper the night before, then poured a large cup of coffee. Sitting down across from her mother, she ate quietly for a few minutes. When Eliza resumed staring out the open kitchen door, Sarah felt a frisson of concern dance up her spine.

"You sure you're okay?" she asked again.

Eliza blew out a slow breath. "I have a lot on my mind, sweetie. Have you heard anything else from Owen?"

"No. He hasn't been back in since that day I dropped the books on Tony."

Her mother propped her chin on her hand. "Well, hopefully he'll make his mind up whether he's going to be a nice man or an ogre. Personally, I'm hoping for the nice guy. You could do much worse."

"Mama!" Sarah laughed, a little embarrassed, especially since she'd been thinking that very thing.

"It's true. And I'd like to see you married and settled, Sarah. You deserve to be happy."

Sarah frowned. "You make it sound like you're not planning on being around much longer. What's going on, Mama?"

Eliza ran her finger across a groove Jack had cut into the table when he was ten. "I got a letter from Nancy yesterday. She wants me to come to Georgia for a while to stay with them."

Carefully, Sarah laid her spoon down and sat back. "Okay. For how long?"

"I don't know. Until thinking of your father doesn't make it hurt to breathe anymore, I guess."

The ticking of the grandfather clock in the living room was loud. Outside, Sarah could hear birds chirping, dogs barking, children yelling, but inside, it was as though a blanket of silence had fallen over the kitchen.

"How soon would you be going?" she finally asked.

Eliza stood and went to the sink, dumping her coffee down the drain. "I'll wait until after the baby is born and Kathy's all right from that. Do you think you'd be comfortable living here by yourself?"

She realized then that Eliza's mind was made up and that if she hadn't had a new grandchild to greet any day or Sarah living at home still, she would already be packing.

She didn't want to lie to her mother, but her instincts screamed that how she answered the question was monumentally important. "I think I'd be okay. It would be lonely, but maybe Gilly could stay with me sometimes."

"And you wouldn't resent me for leaving?"

"Oh, Mama, no!" Sarah went to her mother and embraced her. "I don't want you to go, but if you need to, then you should. Don't let me be the reason you don't go. I'll be fine."

She felt some of the tension leave Eliza's body. Her mother's hands came up to squeeze Sarah's arms.

"I can't stand being here without him, Sarah Jane." Eliza's voice was choked with tears. "I don't know what else to do."

For several minutes, Sarah held her mother while Eliza cried.

After a while, she released a shuddering breath. "I was so worried about telling you. I was afraid you wouldn't understand and would feel like I was leaving you. You could always go with me. Nancy said they'd love to have you, too." She pulled away to reach for a handkerchief.

Sarah crossed her arms and leaned against the counter. "No. I don't think I'd like that. I'm building something here—I feel it. A life, a career. And I'm not talking about Owen Campbell," she interjected before her mother could say it. "So as much as I'll miss you, I think I'd rather stay here. Will you write?"

"Of course!" Eliza came over and gently wiped Sarah's wet cheeks. "And I expect you to write me back."

Sarah nodded, not looking at her mother. Her tears were still too close to the surface. When the phone rang, she was relieved.

Eliza hurried to answer it, her face breaking into a smile as she listened to the caller. "But she's doing okay? Good. I'll be there as soon as I can. Is Moira with your mother? Okay. Yes, I'll see you soon."

She hung up, and Sarah knew without asking. "Kathy's having the baby."

"Yes. I need to get dressed and go to the hospital. You know how Randall is."

Sarah snorted, then smiled. "I know. If you don't mind, I'll stay here. I'd rather not have to wait with him in the waiting room. I'll see Kathy and the baby tomorrow."

Eliza gave her a sharp look but didn't protest. "Then I'd better get around. I'm glad she's at the hospital and not having the baby at home. You girls definitely have the advantage over us old ladies there."

"Mama, you're not old," Sarah chided. She agreed with Eliza's assessment, though. While a lot of women still relied on midwives to deliver their babies, she was glad the hospital was nearby. New and modern, it provided a much safer alternative than her mother had had when she was pregnant.

Ten minutes later, Eliza was ready to go. "I'll call you as soon as I can."

"Okay. I may go for a walk. If you call and I don't answer, that's where I'll be."

"You sure you don't want to go to the hospital with me?"

Sarah nodded. "I'm sure. I'll be fine." As she watched Eliza drive down the road, she repeated, "I'll be fine. The sooner I get used to being alone, the better off I'll be."

CHAPTER TWELVE

OWEN DIDN'T GET OUT OF bed until noon on Saturday. He'd been up until nearly four o'clock that morning working on a story idea that had come to him yesterday early. By the time he stumbled to his bed, he was exhausted. As a result, his head was pounding from hunger.

He pulled on a pair of plaid shorts and a white T-shirt and headed downstairs to raid the refrigerator. Once his hunger was satisfied, he walked to the front door and stared out across the kitchen garden toward his parents' house. He'd have to get the tiller out soon, but after writing into the wee hours, the last thing he wanted to do was work more. Thoughts turning to the swimming hole, he wondered if Sarah would take him up on his offer and venture back over the property line.

"No, she's too upset," he told himself. "It's way too soon to expect her to be there." Still, the pool sounded like just the place to visit.

He packed a bag with some fresh fruit and a couple of books and started down the mountain. Since he didn't expect to see another human, he didn't bother showering or shaving. He felt decidedly scruffy with a full day's growth of beard shadowing his jaw, and as he scratched his chin, he thought he might try growing out the beard.

When he reached the pool, he almost lost his footing. Sarah was sitting on the rock. Clad in white shorts and a red shirt with its tails tied underneath her breasts, she presented a stunning picture.

Owen wanted to howl. She didn't act as if she knew he was there, so he took an extra moment to gather his composure, being noisy when he started walking again.

She turned, a look of alarm and dismay crossing her face, and started to stand.

"No, no. You're fine. I'm not going to yell or bite your head off," he said as he reached the large, flat-topped boulder. "Do you mind if I sit?"

Wary, she shook her head. "It's your land. You can do whatever you want."

Owen set the bag he was carrying down, then sat on the lip of rock she was resting her back against. He struggled to find something to say, but he was at a complete loss. A few strands of her hair danced across her cheeks, teased by the breeze. Surreptitiously, he inhaled, taking in the smell of her perfume and shampoo. She turned to study him, and he saw that she'd been crying.

"What's wrong?" he asked.

"Nothing. I'd better go, let you have your privacy." Once again, she started to stand.

Reaching out a hand, he stopped her. They both stared at their joined hands, and he slowly pulled back, making the move a caress. He did his best to ignore the awareness the move had caused. "You aren't bothering me. Please stay."

She didn't look at him, but after a minute, she eased back down onto the blanket. "Okay."

Relieved, he pulled out his own blanket along with the fruit and books. He held an apple and orange out to Sarah, but she declined. Placing them on the empty bag, he kicked off his boots and stretched out his legs, then picked up a book and began reading—or tried to.

A good ten minutes later, Sarah said, "It helps if you turn the pages. Makes the story much more interesting."

His face heated, and he gave a rueful shake of his head. "I've heard that."

When she gave a quick laugh, he felt like he'd won a prize. She drew her legs up to sit cross-legged and pulled a book out of her bag. He felt his heart skip a beat when he saw it was one of his—and not the one he'd recommended, either.

"You like that author, then?"

She raised an eyebrow. "Very much. Thanks for the recommendation. I've now read almost everything he's published and am proudly a member of the man's devoted fan club."

"He has a fan club?" That was news to Owen, and he frowned.

Sarah chuckled. "Oh, perhaps not formally. But several of my fellow students at Berea were half in love with him. I can see why now. Yes, they're children's books, but he has a way of writing that pulls you in, makes you almost believe you're there."

She closed the book, marking the page with her finger, and leaned toward him, her tone conspiratorial. "They had all kinds of romantic theories about him. I swear they were convinced he was some fantastical hero who was locked away from the world, writing to quell his misery after losing the love of his life."

Flustered, it was all he could do to speak normally. "Is that what you think?"

She wrinkled her nose, staring at the trees across the clearing. "I don't know. He's probably really a woman writing as a man, so she gets paid better. I'm not sure a man could carry off the romanticism in these stories."

"You don't... but what about male poets? John Donne, Robert Frost, Keats, Byron? They were all romantic," Owen sputtered.

"True, but look at the lives they led. With very few exceptions, some of the most romantic writers we know led lives full of dissipation, debauchery, and vice. None of them hid who they were, either. That's another reason I think this H.O. McLemore is a woman. A man couldn't keep quiet if he was as successful as she is."

Owen didn't know what to say. Without revealing to Sarah that he was, in fact, H.O. McLemore, there wasn't much of a defense he could lodge. Still, he felt he had to try. "William Shakespeare." Laughter bubbled out of her, and Owen felt his smile widen into a grin. "You're laughing at the Bard. I'm crushed." He grabbed at his chest.

"No," she said between chuckles. "I'm laughing at you; I adore the Bard. You know, you aren't someone I'd pictured as being a romantic."

"What if I told you I know H.O. McLemore personally, and I can assure you with one-hundred percent certainty that he is, in fact, a man?" Owen stretched his arm out along the rock behind her, his hand not quite touching her shoulder.

She rolled her eyes. "That's awfully convenient for your argument. And unless I miss my guess, next to impossible to prove."

She had him there. He considered offering her a signed illustration, but she'd seen his handwriting. Until and unless he knew her better, he couldn't take the chance that she might recognize it. He could ask his publisher to write her a letter verifying that he was a man, but Owen figured that would be a waste of time, as she wouldn't believe it was real.

"I guess you'll have to trust me on this," he finally said.

"Uh-huh. Sure I will." She glanced at the sky, then at her watch. "I really have to go. I've been here two hours already."

Owen stood when she did, watching as she folded her blanket she'd been sitting on. "I meant what I said. I don't mind you coming here."

Sarah hugged the blanket to her chest and shuffled her feet, her gaze on the pool. "I appreciate that. I really needed to come here today. Thank you."

"You don't owe me any thanks, Sarah." He held her bag open, and she put the blanket inside.

She met his gaze as she took the bag from him. "Yes, I do. I'll see you at the library?"

He swallowed. "Sure. Are you okay to walk home by yourself?"

Her smile was sad. "I'm used to it. I'll be fine. Bye for now."

Owen watched her go, his curiosity running wild. Something was definitely wrong, but he couldn't press her into telling him what. With a frustrated sigh, he turned back to the book he had no interest in reading.

A shadow passed over the ground, and he looked up to see that a cloud had moved to cover the sun. He gave up on his plans for relaxing next to the water and started packing his belongings. With Sarah gone, he felt a little lost. He figured he might as well be lost at home.

CHAPTER THIRTEEN

THERE WAS NOTHING LIKE THE smell and feel of a baby, Sarah thought as she held her nephew on Monday evening. She'd stopped by the hospital after work to visit Kathy and little Randall, and as she sat in the rocking chair in Kathy's room, she was surprised to feel a twinge of envy.

"You look natural holding him," Kathy remarked from the bed. "You should find a man and have some of your own."

Sarah smiled down at the baby. "Finding a man isn't the problem. Finding *the* man is."

Her sister huffed. "Find one you can stand to look at in the mornings, one who doesn't beat you. Beyond that, they're all the same."

"That's not a terribly nice thing to say," Sarah chided. The baby started fussing, and she stood to hand him to her sister before he could commence a full-blown squall. She turned her back as Kathy lowered her hospital gown to give the baby her breast.

"It may not be nice, but it's the truth. Lord, that hurts."

Sarah chanced a glance over her shoulder. "I thought breast-feeding was supposed to be natural."

"It is. It just hurts at first. After a couple of weeks, the nipples toughen up and you don't mind it so much."

Sarah straightened the flower arrangement someone had brought. "Randall must be proud. To have a son, I mean."

"Oh, he's over the moon. To hear him tell it, he did it all." Her voice softened, and she looked under the blanket to check on the baby. "Did Mama tell you about this crazy idea Aunt Nancy put in her head?"

"About going to Georgia in a few weeks? Yes, she told me." Sarah moved to stand next to the windows and looked out over the parking lot. "But I don't think it's a crazy idea. I think it might be what she needs."

"Pfft. She needs to stop feeling sorry for herself. Nancy coddles her, and so do you. Mama has obligations here to attend to. She doesn't need to go haring off to Georgia. Who's going to help me with my babies? Not Randall, not you."

Astonished by her sister's callousness, Sarah stared at Kathy. "When did you become so cold? It's barely been five months since she lost Daddy. He was the love of her life, her soul mate. You don't just get over that."

Kathy laughed and switched the baby to the other breast. She looked at Sarah with a mixture of pity and condescension. "You're still young. You have your ideals and all that romantic nonsense they put in your head at that fancy school. The rest of us have reality. The sooner you learn that, the easier it's going to be for you in the long run. Mama, too."

Shaking her head in disbelief, Sarah gathered up her sweater and purse. "With all due respect, I think being pregnant and having that baby have addled your mind. I might not have all the *worldly experience* you do, but I know what Mama and Daddy had. It was a damned sight better than what you're describing. And I think Mama's had as much reality as she can take right now." She swallowed, trying to curb her temper before she said something she'd regret. "Now, if you'll excuse me, it's getting late. I need to head home, and you need your rest. Maybe your head will be clearer after you've gotten some sleep."

She stalked out of the room. Any other time, the stunned look on Kathy's face would have made Sarah laugh. It was, perhaps, the first time Sarah had stood up to her. But right now, she just wanted to get home and make sure that Kathy hadn't said anything similar to their mother. Sarah understood how fragile Eliza was, even if Kathy didn't, and such negativity was the last thing Eliza needed at the moment.

By the time she arrived home twenty minutes later, her temper was boiling. That Kathy had said what she had to Sarah wasn't what made her mad. That she'd potentially spouted her negativity and poison to their mother? Sarah didn't know when she'd been so angry.

She sat in the car for a few minutes after she parked, trying to level out her breathing. She counted to a hundred, but that didn't work, so she tried counting backward. When she had calmed down enough not to scream with frustration, she got out and went inside.

Eliza was in the kitchen, filling a pot up with water. "Hey, sweetie. I'm getting a late start on dinner. Did you see the baby?"

"I did. I'm going to change clothes." In her bedroom, Sarah groaned with relief as she kicked off her shoes and pantyhose. She grabbed an old shirt out of the closet and a pair of denim shorts that she'd have been ashamed to wear outside the house because they were so short. After stripping out of her work clothes, she donned a soft, cotton camisole to wear with the shorts. It was too hot to wear her bra for another moment. She pulled on the shorts and the shirt over the camisole, leaving it unbuttoned, then released her hair from the twist she wore for work. The dark, heavy mass fell around her shoulders and down her back, stopping halfway. Even though the trend for women having short hair was becoming popular, Sarah had decided not to cut hers. When the weather grew warmer, however, the temptation was going to be strong to pick up a pair of shears and hack away.

She twisted a rubber band around the locks, drawing them up to a point high on her head. The jaunty ponytail made her smile, although she was still seething over Kathy's remarks. Physical comfort achieved, she headed back down to help her mother with supper.

"I thought we'd have spaghetti if that's okay with you," Eliza said as Sarah hugged her. "And I used some of that strawberry-rhubarb jam we put up last summer to make a tart. I hope you're hungry. You can get started on the salad, if you don't mind."

"I'm angry," Sarah said, getting the ingredients down for the vinaigrette for the greens. "Kathy said some things that rubbed me the wrong way."

Eliza chuckled. "I can't envision *that* happening. The two of you get along so well." She laid a hand on Sarah's shoulder as she passed behind her on the way to the sink. "What did she say?"

Sarah gave the vinaigrette an extra whip with the whisk. "She made some very unflattering comments about men, advised me to find one whom I could stand to look at and who didn't beat me, and said… it hardly matters. I don't think she's fond of the idea of you going to Georgia." She said the last part in a rush, not wanting to say it at all but needing to know if her mother was okay.

"Well, then. All that advice is so valuable I hardly know where to start. What exactly did she say about Georgia? Knowing your sister, it wasn't flattering."

"It wasn't. I don't want to tell you."

"I'm a big girl. I can take it."

Sarah set the whisk down with more force than she'd intended, and the metal tines vibrated, spraying vinaigrette on her arms and face. "Shit."

"Sarah!"

"Sorry. She said that you were selfish for going. The way she talked, I figured she'd said something to you already, and that made me angrier than anything." Taking the towel her mother handed her, she wiped off the mess and braced her hands on the edge of the counter.

Eliza sighed, but she didn't seem overly distraught. "She hasn't, but I'm not all that surprised to learn that's how she feels," she confessed as she drained the pasta. "Do you think she's right, that I'm being selfish?"

"No." Sarah didn't even have to consider her answer. "Absolutely not. Look, I was hurt when you first told me. I won't lie. But the more I thought about it, the more it made sense. I want you to be happy, and I know Jack does, too. If you can't be happy here, then you need to go where you can. It's pretty simple, really."

Her mother visibly relaxed. "Thank you. As for your sister, I learned a long time ago to not let her bitterness get to me. And make no mistake, Sarah—she is bitter."

"I don't understand why. She has what she always wanted—Randall, two beautiful children. I wouldn't want the man, but she set her cap for him in high school. She even got pregnant so they'd have to get married. And as much as I can't stand him, he seemed happy enough to marry her. What in the world does she have to be bitter over?"

Eliza stirred the sauce for the pasta. "I'm going to tell you something about Randall. Don't talk to your sister about this. Understand me? She'd never forgive me if she knew I'd told you." She tapped the spoon on the rim of the pan and set it aside.

"Okay. You have my word." Sarah stopped putting the salad together and gave her mother all her attention.

"When you were in Berea, Kathy left Randall for a few months. He'd stopped working and started drinking more. She came home one day from visiting his mother and found him in bed with another woman."

Sarah was stunned. As much as she didn't understand her sister, she hated that Kathy had gone through that. "How did she keep from killing him? For that natter, how did you keep Daddy from killing him?"

"Ira didn't think he was worth killing, to be blunt. As for your sister, Moira was with her. Kathy got Moira out of there before she saw anything. She came here, and they stayed for four months.

"We almost had her convinced to divorce him, but he started coming around, sweet-talking her. He got a job and stopped drinking so much. Kathy started going to town with him on dates and ended up pregnant again. I think he got her pregnant on purpose, just to keep her. He sees her as a possession, not as a helpmate. She lost the baby, but by then, she was back with Randall, and she wouldn't hear anyone speak of her leaving him."

"Who was the woman?"

"A hooker from down in Combs." Sarah's mouth fell open, and Eliza shot her an innocent look. "What? She was. In any event, your father came down pretty hard on Kathy. You know how he was. He always felt that we should take responsibility for our actions, no matter if the result was good or bad."

"And he didn't think Randall and Kathy had?"

"No. He was willing to do whatever it took to help her, but when she went back to Randall? He washed his hands of the whole thing. I've always thought that's one reason she tried so hard when he was sick. She wanted to prove to him that she wasn't weak." Eliza's mouth compressed in a tight line, and Sarah figured she was remembering Ira's illness.

"So that's why she's bitter. I guess I can understand it." Sarah studied her feet, not really wanting to ask what was circling through her mind but needing to know. "Mama, did Daddy ever... is what Kathy said, right? All men are the same?"

"That's a loaded question, Sarah Jane," Eliza said as she dished out a plate of spaghetti. "The first part is simple—no. Your father never so much as looked at another woman with anything more than friendly admiration, as far as I'm aware. As to the rest of the men in the world..." She sighed. "I'm afraid your sister's assessment might be closer to the truth than not. Please don't misunderstand—there are good men out there. But there are a lot more who are only as good as they need to be to get by."

Her mother's admission unsettled Sarah. "So, how do you know the good men from the bad?"

Eliza laughed. "Oh, sweetie. You have to get to know someone, take time to watch them with other people, with animals. Trust your instincts. And you have to get very, very lucky sometimes. I wish I could tell you there was some obvious yardstick, but there isn't."

Once the food was on the table, they sat down and said a quick prayer of thanks. Sarah was quiet as she thought about what her mother had said. Halfway through the meal, a quiet knock sounded at the front door.

"Are you expecting someone?" Eliza asked. Sarah shook her head, and her mother frowned. "Well, let's see who it is." She went to the door while Sarah buttoned her shirt.

"Can I help you?" her mother asked a minute later.

To Sarah's surprise, a low, male voice answered. "I hope so, ma'am. I was hoping to speak to Sarah for a minute if she's handy."

Hardly able to believe her ears, she came out of the kitchen and stood staring at the man who stood on the other side of the door. "Owen?"

Eliza's eyebrows shot up. "Owen Campbell? Hank and Lucy's boy?"

He smiled. "Yes, ma'am. It's been a while since we've seen each other."

"Well, come on in." Eliza unlatched the screen door. "And it has been a while. Probably at your mother's services. I never would have known you."

Looking nervous, he stepped inside, a small book in his hand. "I don't want to disturb you. I wanted to drop this off." He handed the book to Sarah. "It's pertinent to that discussion we had the other day."

Flustered by his presence, Sarah looked down at the book. When she saw the title and author, she laughed. "Tennessee Williams? *Cat on a Hot Tin Roof*? Really?"

He scowled in mock outrage. "You can't tell me Tennessee Williams isn't romantic."

"Oh, I think I can. What's romantic about a group of people drifting around one another, using the misfortunes and personal crises of others to twist the truth, afraid to reach out for what they really want? It's sad is what it is."

He shook his head, using a hand to emphasize the words. "The *emotion*, Sarah. The pent-up turmoil and longing. Yes, the story is sad, but it's romantic."

"I think you're the one with romantic delusions," Sarah teased.

Eliza was watching their interaction with unabashed curiosity. She turned to Owen. "Have you had supper, young man?"

He looked at her. "What? Oh, no. No."

"Do you like spaghetti?"

Owen's confusion was endearing, and Sarah did her best not to break into nervous giggles as she waited for his answer.

"Yes, ma'am."

When he still didn't seem to understand that Eliza was asking him to sit down with them, Sarah had to turn away to hide her grin.

"Lord help us," Eliza muttered. "Owen, we're having supper. Would you like to join us?"

"Oh! No, I don't want to impose. I only wanted to drop off the book. Thank you, though."

Before her mother could assure him he wasn't imposing, his stomach growled loudly, and his face turned as red as the strawberry-rhubarb jam on the tart they were having for dessert.

"For goodness' sake. Go wash up. You're not imposing. The bathroom's down the hall," Eliza said, pointing him in that general direction. "Sarah, fetch down another plate and feed this young man before he falls over."

When he nodded and went down the hall, Sarah's excitement ratcheted up several notches. She turned and went to do as her mother bade, setting the book on the buffet as she passed, not wanting to get food on it.

Eliza followed her into the kitchen, and when the door to the bathroom closed, she grabbed Sarah's arm. "What in the world? I thought you two were fighting. When did this happen?"

"I'll tell you all about it later. I promise. Mama…" She got a plate out of the cabinet, then grabbed Eliza's shoulders and did a quick, happy dance. When she heard the bathroom door open, she straightened and finished preparing a plate for Owen. She placed it on the table between her chair and Eliza's. "What would you like to drink? We have lemonade, milk, and sweet tea," she told him as he came into the kitchen.

"Tea's fine, thanks." Awkwardly, he sat down, and Sarah brought another glass to the table. Her mother kept the conversation going as they finished the spaghetti.

"We have a tart for dessert," Eliza told him as she and Sarah cleared the table. "Strawberry rhubarb."

Owen's face lit up. "I adore rhubarb."

"This is made from what we put up last summer. Sarah's jam, as a matter of fact. I'm afraid we took shameless advantage of her when she was here for summer break. She has a deft touch with canning."

"Mama, you did not take advantage of me," Sarah protested as her cheeks flushed. Owen was watching her closely as she cut the tart. "She makes it sound like she isn't as handy in the kitchen as I am when she is," she said as she gave him an extra-large portion.

"Well, I do okay," Eliza said with a pleased smile. "Are you planning on keeping the garden this year, Sarah? I hadn't even thought about that. You'll be here by yourself all summer."

At the reminder that Eliza was leaving soon, some of Sarah's joy dissipated. "I haven't really thought about it. I assumed we'd have a garden. It isn't anything I can't handle on my own."

Owen looked at her mother, a slight frown creasing his brow. "You're leaving?"

"Yes. I'll be going to Georgia here in a few weeks to spend some time with my sister. I asked Sarah to come along with me, but she's determined to stay here."

He laid down his fork, and his frown grew. The look he sent her was almost enough to send Sarah's temper soaring again.

"You don't think I can stay here by myself?" she asked him.

Owen hesitated, searching for words. "I don't question your capability. I saw how well you handled that situation in the library the other day. I just don't enjoy thinking of you down here by yourself. No offense, Mrs. Browning."

Eliza waved a hand and took a sip of her tea. "None taken. It eases my mind to know someone will be close by who's concerned about Sarah's well-being."

"I'll be fine," Sarah said, shooting a scowl back at Owen. "I have Daddy's guns, and I know how to use them. I'll keep all the doors and windows locked. Besides, there's a good chance Gilly will come stay with me at least part of the time. Really, there's no reason to worry, Mama."

Her mother smiled. "Sweetheart, I'll still be worrying about you when you have grandchildren." She stood. "Now, if the two of you are finished, I'm going to run you out of here while I clean up. It's supposed to rain tomorrow. Why don't you go on out on the porch and enjoy the evening?"

The suggestion was about as subtle as a brickbat, but Sarah didn't protest. She led Owen to the porch, but she was too restless to sit. "Do you mind walking instead? I've been sitting most of the day, and I'd like to stretch my legs."

"Not at all. I walked down here, and we could head back toward my side of the mountain."

"Let me get my boots on and let Mama know." Hurrying inside, she told Eliza where they were going.

"You might put something else on," Eliza said with a pointed look at her bare legs. "Those shorts are fine for inside the house when we don't have company, but there's no reason for you to tempt the boy into a frenzy. At least not until you know him better."

"Mama!"

The impish grin Eliza sent her made Sarah laugh, and she rushed upstairs to change. Soon, she was back on the porch with Owen, and they set off. He stopped at the edge of the porch to grab a sturdy walking stick he'd propped up there. Neither of them spoke until they reached the edge of the woods.

"I take it your mother leaving is still something of a raw topic. I'm sorry."

Sarah crossed her arms, sending him a quick smile. "It's okay. And it's still a little new, yes. Plus, my sister... never mind. That's not worth getting into."

"She's married to Randall Begley, right?"

"She is. They had their second child over the weekend. I'm the proud aunt of a bouncing baby boy—Randall, Junior."

Owen half smiled. "Poor kid." A stunned look crossed his face, and he quickly apologized. "I don't know why I said that."

Sarah was laughing. "Probably because you know Randall. He's... um..."

Owen nodded. "He was friends with my brother. Drinking buddies, if you want the truth. I never had much in common with either of them. Still, I shouldn't pass judgment. Sorry."

They reached the rock that used to be Sarah's thinking place, and she stopped to lean against the wall the face of the boulder formed. The ground sloped away sharply from the other side of the path, and with the leaves on the trees only half budded, she and Owen had a clear view all the way to the foot of the mountain.

"This is where I used to come before I found that pool on your land," she confessed.

Owen studied the rock and the surrounding landscape. "Where would you sit? Up top?"

"Yes. Want to see?"

"Sure."

She led him up to the top of the rock and gestured to the ledge. "It's a little smaller than your boulder," she said with a laugh. "But it sufficed."

Going to the ledge, she carefully checked around it to make sure no snakes were lurking. Satisfied the rock was safe, she sat. Owen followed suit, and she drew in a breath as he settled beside her. The ledge was so small, they were practically touching all along her right side.

"This isn't bad," he commented. "It has some advantages over my rock." Though he'd said the words casually, the look he sent her was full of warmth.

Sarah ducked her head. "Perhaps. I suppose there are worse places." She let her posture relax so that their shoulders were touching, if only lightly. When Owen didn't move away, she smiled. "So... Tennessee Williams?"

"Yes. I find it difficult to believe that you don't see the romanticism in that play."

"I see the romanticism," Sarah explained. "I saw the movie a couple of years ago when I was in Berea. The tension rolling off that screen was almost palpable, a living thing in the theater. But I don't think unrequited love is romantic. It may be simple of me, but I prefer the story to have a happy, satisfying ending."

"Then I guess you aren't a fan of *Romeo and Juliet*?"

She laughed. "No. First off, they weren't old enough to be as seriously involved as they were. I know it happens all the time. I have cousins galore who had their first child before they were old enough to drive. Shoot, look at Kathy. But I feel more thought should go into marriage than how good a provider the man is or how good a breeder the woman might be." As the last words left her mouth, she flushed.

Owen grinned down at her. "And here you are, the same woman who accused *me* of being a romantic. You've got me beat all to pieces."

"Hush."

He bumped his shoulder into hers, and Sarah rolled her eyes at him, but she was smiling.

"So, the other day at the pool. You'd been crying?"

"I had. Mama had just told me she was going to Aunt Nancy's. I wasn't expecting that." Drawing her legs up to her chest, she wrapped her arms around them and rested her chin on her knees. "And then today, when I went to see Kathy and the baby, she… she made me furious with some things she said about Mama, about her decision. My sister can be extremely selfish, Owen. I love her, but I don't understand her any more than she understands me. And I shouldn't say that, especially to you. It's my dirty laundry. I'm sorry."

He said nothing for a little while. When he spoke, his voice was low. "Don't apologize. I understand what you're saying. I don't know your sister. But I knew my brother, and from what I've seen of Randall, he and Harlan had a lot in common. I can't imagine Kathy can be married to a man like that and not be a little like him."

Sarah nodded. "She is. And she's always resented me. God knows I'm not perfect. I tend to be more stubborn than I ought, and I enjoy getting my way, but I've never tried to compete with Kathy. That hasn't made a bit of difference. Do you know how many times I've been told I'm getting above my raising by going away to school? It bothered me, but I let it go because I knew it didn't matter. But when she said what she did about Mama? That I'm not willing to let go."

"I barely know your mother, but I don't think she'd do something that wasn't in the best interests of all concerned. I know my mother thought a lot of yours. They worked together at gatherings and funerals and things a few times before Mother stopped going to church. And I think you're pretty levelheaded, too. I'm sure your anger is justified."

Tipping her head to the side to study him, Sarah smiled. "You barely know me as far as that goes. How do you know if I'm levelheaded or not?"

Owen returned her gaze steadily. "I know what I've seen. You have a temper, but you're logical. And I'd very much like to get to know you better. If you're interested, that is."

CHAPTER FOURTEEN

O WEN'S HEART POUNDED SO LOUDLY in his ears that he wasn't sure he would be able to hear Sarah when she answered. The declaration had surprised her. He knew that, but he couldn't tell if the surprise was positive or not.

She stared at him for a full minute, then looked away. "Um. I'm not sure I... are you asking me out? Like on a date?"

"That's exactly what I'm asking."

She tucked a loose strand of hair back behind her ear and licked her lips. The movement sent an uncomfortable wave of heat through him. They were sitting so close that he could have easily leaned over and stolen a kiss if he were so inclined. He'd have been lying if he said the thought hadn't occurred to him more than once.

A soft blush rose on her cheeks, and she turned her head in his direction, but kept her gaze on the path below them. "I'd like that."

"You would?" he blurted.

She smiled. "Yes, I would. Were you expecting me to say no?"

He grinned. "I wasn't sure what you'd say."

She shook her head and laughed softly. "Silly Owen."

They didn't speak for a while after that. When a twinkle of light flashed nearby, Sarah drew in a breath.

"What is it?" he asked.

She answered him without taking her gaze from the spot where the flash had come from. "I think it was a lightning bug. It's a little early for them, but I swear, I think it was one." When she was rewarded by a second flash, she clapped her hands. "Did you see that?"

Owen laughed. "I did. And you remember where you live, right? Firefly Hollow?"

Sarah stuck her tongue out at him. "Of course I remember. But it's something I never tire of seeing."

"You should see them up at the homeplace when the grass gets tall in the pasture. They like the alfalfa, I guess, because they float in clouds across the ground."

"That has to be a sight to behold," she whispered.

"It is."

Before long, it was nearly dark, and he knew it was time to escort her home. With reluctance, he stood and held out his hand. "Come on. Your mom will be ready to send out a search party if we don't get back soon."

"She wouldn't do that," she assured him as they made their way back down to the path. "Not unless we were gone until after dark anyhow."

There was a bit of a jump to get back on the path, and he made it easily. Turning, he held out his hands to assist her down. She jumped, but when she landed, her feet went out from under her a little, and she stumbled. Moving quickly, he caught her, pulling her close to his chest.

"You okay?"

She nodded. To his pleasure, she didn't pull away but let her hands rest on his upper arms. They were pressed together from chest to hips, and he sucked in a breath at the feel of her against him.

It was a perfect moment, Owen thought. Sarah was tall, the top of her head nearly reaching his chin. She didn't look at him, but slowly, she let herself relax against him, her head eventually coming to rest on his shoulder. He felt her release a long breath against his shirt, and his eyes drifted shut as he brought his arms more fully around her to deepen the embrace.

He didn't know how long they would have stood there if an owl hadn't hooted nearby, causing them both to jump. Reluctantly, he took a step back, letting one of his hands trail down her arm to capture her hand. Without speaking, he started walking back down the path toward her house, with Sarah a step behind him.

Because of his shifter nature, he could see the ground in front of him clearly, and he stopped as they came to a snake crawling across the path.

"Black snake," he told her over his shoulder. Her hand tightened around his, and she drew in a sharp breath, but she didn't overreact. Given that they were nearly at the same spot where the rattlesnake had cornered her, he was impressed.

"How can you see it? I can barely see the path."

"I have really strong night vision."

"That must come in handy."

He squeezed her hand. "It does. Okay, the snake's gone." They resumed walking, but he slowed as they reached the edge of the trees and drew her abreast of him. "Do you ever go walking at night?"

He knew the answer, but he couldn't tell her that. Not yet.

"Sometimes. But unless it's a full moon, I have to use a flashlight."

"Well, promise me you won't go out without one. I'd hate to see you encounter a copperhead or rattlesnake in the dark and not know it until it was too late."

Sarah looked up at him with an indulgent smile. "I won't, and thank you for your concern. But what do I do if I happen across a poisonous snake and it's between me and the house? Wait for a gallant knight to ride along on his trusty steed and rescue me? I had that happen once before, and I don't look to repeat the experience."

"A gallant knight came riding along? I didn't know we had any of those in these parts."

"No, silly. The snake. I narrowly escaped from a rattlesnake a few years ago. And if I told you what saved me, you wouldn't believe me. I learned to carry a stick and wear sturdy boots after that."

He let go of her hand long enough to tug on the end of her ponytail. "You should put a sharp nail in the end of your walking stick, just in case."

She was horrified. "For what, to spear it? Ewww, no!"

Owen laughed at her expression. It was the first time he had seen her act even slightly squeamish. He wrapped his arms around her and spun her around and around. Laughter spilled out of her, interspersed with delighted shrieks.

When they were both dizzy, he stopped, stepping back from her enough to satisfy propriety and any eyes that might be watching. However, he kept his hands resting lightly on her waist. "There is another option. If you ran across a poor, hapless snake, you could always turn around and come to my house. The path from the top of the boulder continues straight on up the mountain."

Before he could get Sarah's response to his suggestion, her mother came out onto the back porch, and Owen slowly dropped his hands.

Eliza raised an eyebrow, but she didn't chastise him. A smile very much like Sarah's spread across her face, and she came down the steps into the yard. "Did the two of you have a pleasant walk? I was starting to think I might have to gather a search posse to come find you. You didn't take a flashlight."

Sarah laughed and moved to Eliza's side. "Oh, now, Mama, I told Owen he'd have at least until after dark before you sent men with torches out after us."

Owen shoved his hands in his pockets and grinned at her impertinence. From the indulgent look her mother gave her, Eliza didn't mind the teasing one bit.

"It's time I head back up the mountain," he said.

"Not without a flashlight, surely. Sarah, go up to my room and get that big flashlight out of the dresser."

"Yes, ma'am."

Eliza waited until Sarah was safely in the house before she moved to stand a couple of feet away from him. She studied him intently in the light shining out from the kitchen. "Mind if I ask what your intentions are toward my daughter, Owen Campbell? She told me that the two of you had some words over her trespassing. Which she never should have been doing, by the way."

"No, that argument was my fault. I shouldn't have come down on her for being over there." He tried to figure out what to say to reassure Eliza, but he didn't have the words. Finally, he settled on what was as close to the truth as could manage. "I like Sarah. I like her a lot. She's... not like anyone I've ever met. And I want to see what that means, if it means anything, if she feels the same way. And I won't take advantage of her. That's all I can promise you right now."

"Sarah is a very attractive young woman. I'm sure you've noticed that."

As much as he tried, he couldn't meet her gaze. He kept remembering the minutes on the path when he'd held Sarah close. He cleared his throat. "It hasn't escaped my attention."

Eliza laid a hand on his arm, and Owen glanced down at her. She was grinning, looking so much like Sarah that it almost hurt.

"Your mother was a gracious lady. From the way she talked about you, I gather you were her favorite, God rest your brother's soul. I can't imagine that Lucy could raise you to be anything other than a gentleman. And I know you've protected Sarah in the past, though she isn't aware." She gave his arm a squeeze, then crossed her arms over her chest. "I give you my blessing to court my daughter. I know you're young, and I know how powerful attraction can be, especially if it's more than physical. But if you hurt Sarah, I will take it out of your hide. Do we understand each other?"

"Yes, ma'am. We do." Owen wasn't sure whether he wanted to ask her more about what she knew about him or not. He didn't get the chance to decide as Sarah returned with the flashlight.

"I'm going to head back inside now. Sarah Jane, don't stay out here too long. Owen, stop by any time."

He waited until Eliza was inside before saying, "So as to this date…" He let his voice trail off as Sarah handed him the flashlight.

"Yes, as to this date," she responded. "When would you like to… what did you have in mind?"

"Uh, I hadn't really thought much beyond whether you'd say yes or no to tell the truth. I'll probably be at the library tomorrow doing research again. We might grab lunch together if you aren't busy. But that's not really a date."

"I wouldn't mind having lunch with you," Sarah said.

"In addition to the date?"

She moved one shoulder. "Maybe. Depending on how the lunch goes."

Surprised by her coy response, his jaw dropped.

Sarah laughed. "You're the one who asked."

Owen narrowed his gaze and stepped closer to her. Slowly, he reached up and tapped her on the nose with his index finger. "You, Miss Browning, are an imp."

She grabbed his hand and held it. "How long did it take you to figure that out, Mr. Campbell?"

"Oh, about five minutes. So why don't we plan on lunch tomorrow, and we'll figure out what to do about our date, then?"

"Okay. I usually take lunch at noon if we don't get too busy."

"Then I'll see you tomorrow." Raising their hands, which were still joined, Owen kissed the back of hers. Her eyes softened and heated, and it was all he could do not to pull her into his arms.

"Be careful going home," she said.

"Always."

Before the temptation grew too strong, he turned and headed toward the woods. He heard Sarah give a soft sigh behind him, and he groaned inwardly. Somehow, he doubted he'd get much sleep that night.

"A nice, cold dip in the pool on the way home might be in order, old man," he told himself. Adjusting the fit of his pants, he sighed. "Definitely, a cold dunk is in order. A long one."

Sarah stood on the porch and watched Owen go into the woods. She didn't go inside the house until she could no longer see the light from the flashlight. When she did, her mother was at the refrigerator getting some milk. She waited until Eliza had set the milk down, then squealed like a little girl on Christmas morning and jumped up and down.

"He asked me out, he asked me out, he asked me out!" She threw her arms around Eliza, who stumbled against her weight.

"Well, gosh, I wonder what you said," her mother teased. "I'll bet you turned him down."

Sarah laughed. "Oh, Mama. He asked me out. We're having lunch together tomorrow. Can you believe it? He asked me out!" She did a boogie around the kitchen.

"Oh, I can believe it. Given the way he was looking at you, I feel like we need to start planning your wedding."

"Mama!"

"I do. I'm guessing the two of you settled whatever differences you had, if tonight was any indication."

Sarah forced herself to calm down. "We did. But I wasn't expecting this. Oh, my Lord, what am I going to wear?"

To her surprise, her mother started laughing so hard she had to hold on to the counter. "Oh, Sarah. You don't know how long I've waited to see you this excited over a boy. Well, a man, really. It's about time." She met Sarah's eyes, and they both started giggling.

"He's so handsome. There, I said it. I couldn't hold it in any longer."

Eliza agreed. "He is that. He looks very much like his father did at that age. The two of you would make lovely babies."

"Mother! I've not even gone on a date with the man. It's a little soon to be thinking about what your grandchildren would look like, don't you think?"

"It's never too soon for a woman my age to be thinking about grandbabies. Now, let's go find what you're going to wear tomorrow. I'm thinking something blue to match your eyes."

Later that night, Sarah lay awake, staring at the ceiling. The way Owen's muscles had bunched and tightened when he caught her, the solidity of his body when he held her, the warmth of the man, all made for an enticing memory. Heat settled in her breasts and between her legs as she thought about how he'd touched her, innocent though it had been.

Sarah knew about sex, both the crude descriptions her peers had come up with and the more clinical data. Her mother had been frank and forthcoming when Sarah had reached a certain age. Eliza hadn't wanted Sarah to have to learn about intimacy the way she had on her wedding night.

Her mother had explained things while they were canning green beans the summer Sarah turned fifteen. Kathy had just gotten married, and Eliza felt the conversation was necessary, given that Kathy was already pregnant.

"I was very lucky that your father is the man he is," Eliza had told her. "If I'd had to rely on your grandmother's advice, I probably never would have had Kathy, much less all three of you. I'd have run screaming into the night when I saw my first aroused, naked man."

Sarah had been very uncomfortable with the discussion, but she appreciated her mother's forthright attitude, especially after some descriptions her female classmates at college had given of the act. Her roommate during her last semester had picked up a book that would have shocked her mother had Eliza known about it. They'd devoured the book, *The Kama Sutra*, and her roommate had given it to Sarah when she'd left school in November.

Closing her eyes, she let her hands drift down her body, imagining Owen's hands doing the touching. images from the erotic book dancing through her mind. Sarah's imagination was vivid, and she could all too easily picture Owen doing the things depicted in the book.

She didn't know that was where they were heading, but for the first time in her life, she could feel herself losing her head over someone, and it was glorious.

CHAPTER FIFTEEN

WHEN SARAH GOT TO THE library the next day, the first thing she did was find Shirley and pull her aside. She had woken up in a panic at five that morning, unable to get back to sleep as she realized what implications dating Owen might have for her job.

"I need to ask you about the non-fraternization policy. Does it apply if you knew the person prior to starting work here? Even if you barely knew them? Like because they were your neighbor?"

Shirley frowned. "Who are we talking about?"

"Owen Campbell. He asked me on a date." Sarah bit her lip nervously as she waited for Shirley's response.

The older woman winced. "Oh, Sarah. When did this happen?"

"Last night. He came down to the house, and we went for a walk, and... I don't want to lose my job, but he's, well..."

"He's Owen. I understand. I honestly don't know. Let me talk to the director. When is this date?"

"He'll be here today doing research, and we were going to have lunch together."

"The boy doesn't waste time when he moves, I'll give him that," Shirley remarked dryly. "Let me see what I can do. You might have a tough decision to make here."

Sarah nodded her acknowledgement. "I know."

For the rest of the morning, Sarah waited on tenterhooks for Shirley to let her know what the decision was. She'd again been assigned to the children's department. Owen had arrived an hour earlier and gone straight to the genealogy room. His smile had been a little more personal when he signed in, but he didn't mention their lunch date.

Sarah was grateful. She hadn't wanted to explain the situation to Nellie. When the phone rang at ten thirty, she jumped.

"Children's desk, this is Nellie." She shot Sarah a questioning glance. "Oh, okay. I'll send her down. The director needs you downstairs," she said as she placed the receiver back in its cradle.

Drawing in a shaky breath, Sarah stood and thanked her. She hurried down the steps but stopped at the bottom, taking a minute to send a quick prayer heavenward. Shirley was busy at the front desk, and Sarah couldn't read her friend's expression. She reached the back of the library and went to the director's office. The door was open, so she knocked softly.

When the woman looked up, Sarah asked, "You wanted to see me?"

"Yes, come in. Close the door and have a seat."

After Sarah was perched on the chair in front of her desk, the director took off her glasses and rubbed the bridge of her nose. "Ms. Browning, I understand that you've been asked out socially by one of the library's patrons."

"Yes, ma'am. I have been."

"Shirley tells me you and the young man in question are neighbors? That you had a previous association because of that?"

Sarah hesitated. "I knew *of* him, and he'd seen me out and about. But we met for the first time here. I won't lie about that."

A little smile appeared at the corner of the woman's mouth. "Shirley told me you'd be honest. I'm happy to know her faith in you wasn't misplaced. Still, that leaves us with a bit of a predicament. The library has a policy against fraternization, which I am told you are aware of."

"I am."

"Mr. Campbell is a frequent visitor to our facility, and he's been a very generous benefactor. I don't want to endanger that relationship, either by forbidding you from dating him or from having your romance go sour. You see the problem this presents, I hope."

Sarah swallowed, a sinking feeling in the pit of her stomach. "I do."

The director heaved a sigh. "That said, I spoke with Mr. Campbell when he came in a little while ago. I expressed my concerns to him. He made it clear that he would not be deterred unless you also agreed that was the best course of action. He also emphasized how unhappy he would be if you were to lose your job because the two of you are seeing each other. I don't enjoy being put in this position, Sarah. I don't like it at all."

Stunned, Sarah couldn't speak for a minute. "I'm sorry. I didn't ask him to do that. I'll talk to him."

"That's up to you. In the meantime, here's where we are—you need this job, I understand. Shirley and Nellie both sing your praises. Even Callie hasn't been her usual critical self. As far as I'm concerned, you and Mr. Campbell knew each other from being neighbors, and the romance, if that's what it turns out to be, was well underway prior to your starting this job." She stopped to take a sip of coffee.

"Whatever happens with this relationship, you do not let it interfere with your job or this library. If you do, Owen Campbell's preferences be hanged, I'll fire you. Otherwise, keep your head down, do your job, and we'll go on as we are. Do we have an agreement?"

"Yes. Thank you. I wasn't expecting this to happen. I'll do my best not to let you down."

"You're excused, Ms. Browning. Leave the door open when you go."

"Yes, ma'am." Sarah left the office and went back down the hall toward the main room. She ducked into the women's restroom and stepped into a stall. For a couple of minutes, she stood there, heart pounding, and let the relief wash over her. If the director had forbidden her from dating Owen, she didn't think she'd have been able to keep that promise.

CHAPTER SIXTEEN

OWEN WAS A NERVOUS WRECK as he waited for someone to show up in the genealogy room and let him know what was going on. Shirley had waylaid him as soon as he walked in the door and taken him to the director's office. The woman explained the library's policy, a barrier Owen hadn't been expecting. Though he felt he'd made an excellent case for why he and Sarah should be allowed to see each other, he wasn't certain the director agreed.

After he'd been there an hour and had heard nothing, he left the room and went to the desk. Sarah was gone, and for a moment, his heart stuttered.

Before he could ask anything, Nellie said, "She's downstairs talking to the boss. Should be back soon, I'd imagine."

Owen's brow furrowed. "How did you know…?"

She smiled. "I've worked at the library too many years to not be able to read people pretty well by now."

He leaned against the desk. "I don't want to get her in trouble or get her fired."

"Hopefully, it won't come to that, son."

When the elevator dinged, Owen straightened and took a step to the right so he could see who was getting off.

The rolling cart emerged first, and Callie stepped through the doors. The buxom blonde smiled wryly when she saw him. "Gosh, I don't know when someone's looked at me with such disappointment. I feel like I kicked your puppy."

"Sorry. I guess I'll head back into the genealogy room." Once there, he tried to concentrate on his research, but he couldn't focus. After a few minutes, he stood up again and started pacing the small room.

"Why hasn't she come back here? She should know something by now."

Just when he had himself worked up and ready to go track Sarah down and demand answers, a tap sounded behind him.

"Hey," she said. "Are you ready for lunch?"

He caught his breath. "You're not in trouble?"

"No. The director isn't happy, but we are officially sanctioned to see each other if that's what we want."

Though he stepped closer to her, he kept a proper distance between them. "And is that what we want?"

Sarah smiled. "I do, yes."

Blowing out a long breath of pure relief, Owen returned the smile. "Thank God."

"Are you coming back here to work more after we eat?" she asked as he packed his bag.

"I thought I would. Unless you dump me over lunch, in which case, I'll slink back home and cry."

"Well, I can't rule that out, but if you'd like to put your satchel in my locker, you can. Where were you thinking of having lunch?"

"The drugstore has a good hot plate special. If that's okay with you."

"Sure." She led him to the employee lockers, where she got out her purse and let him stash his bag. They left the library and walked down the hill to Main Street.

"I didn't realize you might get in trouble for seeing me," he said. "I'm sorry."

"Yes. The director isn't thrilled, but from what I understand, you didn't leave her much choice in the matter. I'm not sure how I feel about that, to be honest."

He stopped her on the sidewalk outside the drugstore. "I probably came down a little harder than I should have. But I wanted you to make the decision to see me or not without having to worry about losing your job in the bargain."

She studied him closely, her dark-blue eyes serious. "I appreciate that. And after I've had some time to really think about it, I imagine it won't bother me quite so much. But I don't want you strong-arming people to make my life easier."

Properly chastised, he gave her a brief salute. "I promise I'll do my best to respect your wishes. Or at least talk to you first before the strong-arming."

She touched his hand. "Okay. Now, let's get some food. I'm starving."

Lunch went quickly—too quickly, from Owen's perspective. He was pleased that, not only did they have a lot of common favorite authors, their tastes in movies and music were also similar. They both hated musicals and loved Buddy Holly. They weren't in agreement, though, on the rock 'n' roller from Memphis, Elvis Presley.

"I much prefer Sinatra," he said. "Elvis is a little too flashy for my tastes."

Sarah rolled her eyes. "Half the girls at Berea were head over heels in love with him. More than half."

"Were you?"

She dipped her chin and looked at her nails. "Not really. I like his music, but he doesn't hold much appeal for me beyond that."

"So I don't have to worry about you wanting to see his movies, I take it?"

"No," she said, laughing. "Not only do I not like his acting, his movies are mostly musicals, which we both agreed we hate."

"What about country music or bluegrass?"

"Jack's more into country and western," Sarah said, wrinkling her nose. "He and Daddy loved listening to the Grand Ole Opry on Saturday nights. I don't much care for the music, but I miss that family time."

"Mom was a fan as well," Owen said. "And she loved the radio serials, *The Guiding Light* especially. My father bought her a big stereo a couple of years before he died, and she listened to that thing so much she almost wore the dials out."

"Did you all have a television?"

He shook his head. "No. But I've been thinking about getting one lately. You all?"

"Nope. Daddy said if we got one, we'd spend less time being a family. Though I have to admit I wouldn't mind having one from time to time. We had one in the girl's dormitory at Berea, and it was fun to watch now and then."

Owen paid the check and placed his hand on the small of her back as they left the drugstore. "So, have I scared you off yet? Or do you still want to go out?"

"I'm not scared."

Relieved, he took her hand in his and squeezed. "Then what would you like to do?"

"They're re-running *North by Northwest* at the theater this weekend. Have you seen it?" Sarah asked.

Owen confessed he hadn't. "I don't get out to the movies too often. What about you?"

She shook her head. "No. I wanted to see it last year when it came out, but there was school, and then Daddy got sick, so I didn't get to."

"Then we should definitely plan on seeing it. What about dinner? Any preferences there?"

"No, not really. Why don't you pick since I chose the movie?"

"I think I can handle that. So, what day? Friday? And what time should I pick you up?"

"Why don't we say six? And you should come down the mountain. We can take my car, and that way you won't have to drive all the way around. As close as we live, it's ironic that the road takes so long to travel."

"If you're sure, I have no objections."

"I'll even let you drive if you like," she teased.

He waited while she switched out her purse and his bag and then walked her back to the desk in the children's section. "I'll see you before I go today?"

"Sure. Holler if you need anything."

Looking around first to make sure no one was watching, he picked up her hand and planted a quick kiss on the back.

"You shouldn't do that," she scolded, her smile belying her words.

"But it's so much fun." With a wink, he straightened and went back to the genealogy room. Once he was alone in the small room, he let out the grin that had been struggling to break free. It might have been ridiculous for a grown man to feel the way he did, but he couldn't help it. He was giddy, both with excitement and relief.

Later that night, he'd have to write Eli and update him. And maybe ask for some advice on how to proceed with what would be the first courtship Owen had ever conducted.

CHAPTER SEVENTEEN

THE WEATHER WAS WARM FRIDAY night, and Sarah and Owen had the windows rolled halfway down as they drove up in the holler. They'd had dinner and then seen the movie, and as much as she'd enjoyed the film, holding Owen's hand the whole time had been more thrilling than the on-screen action.

"So was it as good as you expected it to be?" he asked.

"It was. Cary Grant never disappoints, nor does Hitchcock. Thank you for taking me. I hope you enjoyed it as well."

His smile flashed in the car's dark interior. "I did."

She felt completely at ease with him at the wheel. He handled the car with a quiet competence that only enhanced his attractiveness. Somehow, that he was a skilful driver wasn't much of a surprise.

"So not to bring up a sore subject, but has your mother decided when she's leaving exactly?" he asked quietly.

"It isn't a sore subject anymore, not like it was. And my aunt Nancy's coming up three weeks from now. They'll drive back down to Georgia together after Nancy's visited a few people."

"Has your sister backed off any?"

She looked out the window, watching as the trees on the roadside appeared and vanished in the headlights. "No. Well, she's shut her mouth, but the disapproval rolls off of her in waves. It's all I can do not to slap the silliness out of her. I don't understand how Mama can stand to go to Kathy's house and stay overnight, much less for several days in a row. And that's an uncharitable attitude for me to take."

"Maybe. Or maybe it's just honest. You're not glossing things over. You shouldn't have to, not with me. I hope you know that."

Sarah gently poked him in the arm. "I don't know you well enough to be completely forthcoming with you yet. I don't want to scare you away."

They'd reached her house, and Owen parked the car. "Not a chance."

She had left the front porch light on, and bugs were swarming it, trying to figure out how to get into the heat of the bulb itself.

"We'll go in the back," she said as they got out of the car. "I don't feel like fighting that horde of skeeters and moths."

They were quiet as they went into the kitchen, and Sarah didn't turn the overhead light on, opting instead for a small lamp on the end of the counter. The glow it cast was intimate, and for an instant, she wondered if it was too intimate. She discounted the thought almost as soon as she had it.

She set her purse on the table. "Would you like some coffee?"

"Sure." Owen had stopped just a step inside the door, and he loosened his tie. "Do you mind if I take this off?"

"Not at all. You've been tugging at it all night."

He gave a short bark of embarrassed laughter. "I was hoping you hadn't noticed that."

As she got the coffee pot ready to perk, Sarah sent him a look over her shoulder. "It was hard to miss. I take it you aren't used to wearing a tie?"

"No. I typically avoid them like the plague."

"Well, next time we go out, you're excused from having to wear one." She got the cream out of the refrigerator.

Owen grinned. "So you want to go out again?"

Sarah flushed, realizing how presumptuous her words had been. "I suppose I wouldn't mind."

He crossed his arms over his chest and smiled. It was an intimate, pleased smile, and Sarah felt something inside her relax.

Once the coffee was ready, they went back out onto the screened porch. The light from the kitchen wasn't terribly bright, but it served well enough so they could see to get to the glider.

"I've been wondering something," Sarah said. "What is it you do exactly?"

Owen stretched his arm along the back of the glider. "A little of this, a little of that. I do a lot of correspondence with people from around the world who are interested in the history of this region. I do some genealogy for people. Sometimes I'll look up deeds, property histories, that sort of thing. When my parents and brother died, I inherited everything, including my father's portion of the hardware store, which my uncle bought from me. I made some investments with part of that money, and they've paid off nicely. I spend some time managing those, as well."

"Did you ever go to college?"

To Sarah's surprise, Owen stiffened. He leaned over and set down his coffee cup, then settled back, but the tension didn't leave his body.

"No. I never graduated high school, never mind college."

Stunned, Sarah gaped at him. "But you're so well-read, so intelligent. You're pulling my leg."

His laugh was self-deprecating. "I am telling you the God's honest truth. I got a high school certificate by correspondence course, but I dropped out of school in the eighth grade."

Feeling that the story behind that was complicated, Sarah put down her own mug and turned to half face him, tucking her legs underneath her.

"What happened?" she asked quietly. "If you don't mind me asking."

Owen's hand rested next to her shoulder, and he turned it so that he was touching her arm. Sarah was wearing a short-sleeved dress, and the way he played with the top of her sleeve sent a shiver down her spine.

"I got embarrassed when I was in eighth grade. There was a girl I liked, and when I went to ask her to go to the spring dance with me, it didn't go well. I had a… I don't know what to call it… a nervous attack of some sort. I left school and ran all the way home. My mother sent me to her brother in Laurel County, and I didn't come back until that fall." He moved his shoulders in an uncomfortable shrug.

"By then, everybody knew about 'crazy' Owen Campbell, and they wouldn't let it go. I finally stopped fighting them and quit school, then went back to my uncle's and didn't come back here until after Harlan died."

"I'm sorry," Sarah said. "I'd heard that you went to Laurel County for a while, but I didn't know you'd quit school. That had to be hard for you in more ways than one."

He shrugged. "I never cared much for school. Learning, yes, but school itself? I would have quit sooner if my father let me. It broke his heart when I dropped out."

The pain that still echoed in his voice told Sarah more than words that his father's heart hadn't been the only one to break. She took hold of his hand, pulling it down into her lap, where she cradled it with both of hers.

The conversation moved on to lighter topics from there. At some point, the night turned chilly, and Owen took off his jacket to slide it around her shoulders. Even so, they kept talking. When she went inside to go to the bathroom and saw that it was nearly one o'clock in the morning, she was shocked. The time had passed so quickly.

Owen was on his feet, looking out into the yard, when she went back outside. He turned to her with a rueful smile. "I checked my watch. I didn't know it was so late. I'm sorry."

Sarah waved away the apology. "No, no. I didn't realize the time either. I was enjoying our talk."

"Well, regardless, I probably should head up the mountain."

Even though she knew he was right, Sarah was disappointed. "I'll get your flashlight." He'd returned Eliza's and brought his own when he'd come down earlier. She grabbed it from where it lay on the kitchen counter and, with heavy reluctance, took it back out to him. "Are you okay to walk home this late?"

Owen's smile was visible even through the darkness. "I'll be fine. Are *you* okay to stay here by yourself? I know your mom is leaving soon, but I worry."

Crossing her arms, Sarah moved to stand beside him. "I guess we'll find out. I'd rather know now when she's only a short car trip away than after she's halfway across the country. But I think I'll be fine. I'll lock up once you leave."

He reached out and touched her cheek. "I don't want to go. I want to stay here and talk more. But I need to go, I guess."

Sarah swallowed, her heart pounding. He brought his other hand up, found the pins holding up her hair, and started removing them. In moments, her hair was cascading down her back. Owen put the pins in his pocket and then threaded his fingers into her hair. The touch was soft but sure, and Sarah closed her eyes against the pleasure of it. She sighed and swayed, and he pulled her closer, his hands cradling her head.

"Look at me," he said, his voice low.

Her eyelids felt as if they weighed a ton each, but Sarah got them open. When she looked up at Owen, the heat in his gaze seared her.

"I'd like to kiss you, Sarah Browning. May I?"

As much as she could with his hands still in her hair, Sarah nodded her consent. She watched as he lowered his face to hers, but when his lips brushed hers, her eyelids fluttered shut again. She grasped his arms, and Owen deepened the kiss.

Though not the first time Sarah had been kissed, it was by far the most pleasurable. Owen's lips were firm but gentle against hers, and when he drew back, she gave a small whimper of protest. The sound halted him as though he had run into a wall, and he dipped his head again.

The next kiss wasn't as sweet, but carried a touch of something hotter. Sarah slid her hands up to wrap her arms around his neck. The movement triggered a response, and he deepened the kiss. Heat flared between them, a little overwhelming, and she turned her head. She gasped for breath as his mouth trailed across her jaw and found a sensitive spot beneath her ear. He lingered there, then let out a long, shaky breath.

One of his hands drifted out of her hair and down her back, pulling her closer to him. His lips trailed up to her temple, and he exhaled on a quiet groan.

"I should apologize for being so forward, perhaps," he said in her ear, "but I won't. I'm not sorry."

Sarah shook her head, struggling to pull her scrambled thoughts together enough to form words. Reluctantly, she pulled her arms from around his neck and stepped back. "I'm not sorry, either." She raised her fingers to her lips as though to verify what had happened was real.

Owen ran his hands through his hair. He shook his head, and Sarah was secretly pleased to see that he looked as stunned as she felt.

"Um, would you like to go for a drive with me Sunday afternoon?" he asked. "I have to go to Whitesburg to pick up some seed for Uncle Eli. If you wanted, we could make a date of it."

"What time on Sunday? If Kathy's up to it, they're supposed to come up here for dinner after church. I wouldn't be able to get away until about two or so."

"That would work for me. I would have to drive, however. I'll need my truck."

"Okay. Then I'd love to go with you. I'd invite you to dinner, but I don't want to torture you by asking you to sit through that." Sarah was surprised when he laughed, as she'd been serious. She told him as much.

Owen ran his hand over his face, no doubt to hide his grin. "I appreciate you looking out for me. I guess we're even now." He reached up to touch her face. "I'll pick you up Sunday. Go on in and lock up. I'll wait until you're safe."

She was sorely tempted to throw herself in his arms and beg for another kiss, but she resisted—just. "I had fun tonight. Thank you again."

"You're welcome. And thank you for consenting to go with me." The heated look came back in his eyes, and he groaned. "Go inside, please. Before I forget I'm a gentleman and cart you off to the top of the mountain."

Shooting him a delighted smile, she hustled into the kitchen. She paused with her hand on the inside door. "Goodnight, Owen Campbell."

He tipped an imaginary hat. "Goodnight, Sarah Browning. I'll see you soon."

Knowing that if she didn't lock the door, he would stand there all night, she forced herself to close the door. The door was solid wood all the way up with no window, so she couldn't see him. But as she turned the key in the lock and slipped the bolt above it, she laid her hand flat against the surface.

Sarah had never felt such an attraction, and she didn't quite know what to do with it. She reveled in the feelings that coursed through her, half afraid of them at the same time. She wondered if her mother had gone through the same thing with her father and determined that as soon as she had time to talk to Eliza alone, she'd ask.

CHAPTER EIGHTEEN

O WEN AND SARAH QUICKLY FELL into a routine. Nearly every evening, they would meet, either at the pool or at her house. Many nights, he'd have supper with her and Eliza. He went into town more regularly than he'd ever gone before, and more often than not, he and Sarah would have lunch together.

They spent hours talking about everything and nothing, getting to know one another. Lurking in the back of Owen's mind were his two secrets—that he was H.O. McLemore and that he was a shifter. He was almost certain that he could trust Sarah with the truth about himself, but he wanted to wait a little while longer just to be sure.

Additionally, he knew she was upset over her mother's upcoming journey, and he didn't want to add to the burden. He knew he had to tell her soon, but he wasn't ready yet.

Friday morning, two weeks after their first kiss and two days before her aunt was due to arrive from Georgia, Owen went into town to finish some genealogy research. After spending a few minutes downstairs chatting with Shirley, he went up to the children's department.

Sarah greeted him from where she was shelving books. "Hi there. I didn't expect you today. I thought you had work to do at home." Sarah reached out and grasped his hand, clasping it for a moment in a private greeting.

"I did, but then I discovered I had forgotten to research one particular family's line. So, as much as I dreaded it, I figured I'd better come in. You know how I hate coming here," he said, tongue-in-cheek.

"I know. It's so admirable that you dragged yourself in."

Owen winked. "I'd better get to work and let you do the same. You busy for lunch?"

"I am," she said, shooting a flirtatious glance in his direction. "I have a date with my boyfriend."

"Lucky guy."

Sarah smiled. "Go do your research."

An hour after he started, Owen was startled to hear a shriek of laughter from out front, followed by a loud clatter.

"What the hell?" He pushed his chair back so fast it tipped over, and he dashed out of the room in time to see Sarah run laughing into another man's arms.

Sarah had been hunched down, trying to straighten the phone cord from where it had gotten tangled under the desk, when she heard someone approach the desk.

"Can I help you?" Nellie asked.

A man answered, "Yeah, I was wondering if I could get a library card."

As soon as she heard him speak, Sarah gasped in disbelief. She straightened, barely avoiding the edge of the desk, to verify that her ears weren't playing tricks on her. Sure enough, Jack was grinning down at her.

Letting out a cry that startled Nellie and the patron browsing the new books with her child, Sarah scrambled to her feet. She tripped over her chair but kept going, and her brother met her halfway around the desk, wrapping her in a big bear hug.

Her eyes flooded with tears, and Sarah held on so tight she knew she had to be suffocating him, but she couldn't let go. "What are you doing here? Oh, dear God, Jack, are you really here?" She pulled back to look at him, touching his face. He was thinner than she remembered, but dressed in civilian clothes. With his Army haircut, he was a sight. "Have you seen Gilly yet?"

He pulled a handkerchief out of his pocket and wiped her cheeks. "Not yet. I was hoping to stash my gear in your car first. I didn't expect you to turn into such a watering pot."

"Why not? We've been so worried about you. How are you here?"

He pulled her in for another hug, bussing the top of her head with a kiss. "I'm out, sis. They gave me a hardship discharge. I'm the only son, and now that Dad's gone..."

Sarah noticed him glancing over her shoulder, and she turned. Owen stood there, a faint frown on his face.

"Owen! Look who's home. I can hardly believe it. Come meet Jack. Jack, this is our neighbor, Owen Campbell." Owen stepped forward, and he and Jack shook hands.

"I've heard rumors he's more than just a neighbor," Jack teased. "From what Gilly says, the two of you have been painting the town red."

"You hush! We have not." Sarah poked him in the ribs. A laugh bubbled out of her, and she threw her arms around Jack's waist, squeezing him tight. "I can't believe you're here. Oh, Jack. Did Mama know you were coming home?"

He let out a put-upon sound, but he was smiling as widely as Sarah was. "No, she'll be as surprised as you were. I didn't want to tell anyone until I knew I was out for good, and by then,

I was practically on the bus home. I figured I'd let my arrival be a surprise. So far, so good."

Sarah headed to her seat, but before she could sit down, Callie came upstairs. "Shirley sent me up here to tell you to take a little extra time off. She expects you back after lunch, but thought you'd be too excited to do much work this morning."

"That's awfully nice," Jack said. "We'll have to thank her on the way out."

"I guess you're pretty eager to visit the drugstore," Sarah said. "And get a root beer float."

He ruffled her hair. "I am eager to visit the drugstore, but not for the float."

"Then I'll grab my purse, and we can put your bag in the car. Owen, will you go with us?"

Owen hesitated, looking truly unsure of himself for perhaps the first time since Sarah had met him. "I don't want to impose."

"Oh, don't be silly. You can put your bag in my car and pick it up when we come back."

"You won't be imposing," Jack said. "Not if what I hear is true, about how much time you've been spending with my sister lately." He grunted when Sarah stepped on his foot, but he hushed.

Owen shrugged. "Sure. Let me get my stuff together, and I'll meet you downstairs."

A few minutes later, while they waited for traffic to clear so they could cross the street, Sarah grabbed Jack's hand. "Let us go in first. I want to see Gilly's face when you walk in."

"You think she'll be excited?" he asked, and the uncertainty in his eyes tore at her heart.

"I think she'll scream and cry and whoop and holler, and there won't be a dry eye in the house."

"Okay, then." He stood to the side of the glass storefront while she and Owen went inside. Gilly was working the counter, and Sarah had to bite the inside of her cheek to keep from squealing. Owen assisted her onto a stool and sat beside her. The drugstore wasn't crowded as it was still early for the lunch crowd, but there were a few people inside, regulars who met for gossip and coffee.

"What in the world are you two doing in here this early? Did they run you out of the library?" Gilly asked as she came down behind the counter.

Sarah tossed a straw wrapper at her friend. "No. We came down to take a break. If you want us to go somewhere else..."

Gilly tossed the wrapper back at her. "You know better. Owen, can't you keep her in line?"

He looked from Sarah to Gilly and back. "There's no right answer here, is there?"

Sarah grinned. "No, there isn't. And aren't you smart for knowing that?"

"So, what can I get for you two lovebirds?" Gilly asked. "Or did you come in here to torture me?"

Sarah tried to keep her answer natural and calm, but she was practically vibrating. "How about a root beer float? I've not had one of those in a while." To her surprise, a shadow crossed Gilly's face. "Sweetie, what's wrong?"

Gilly gave a one-shoulder shrug. "Nothing. It's just that I've not heard from Jack in a while, and you know how he loves root beer floats. I usually get a letter from him every three or four days, but I've gotten nothing since early last week. Have you heard from him?"

Before Sarah could answer, the bell over the door jingled, and Gilly looked up. Her eyes filled with tears, her hand came up to cover her mouth, and then she was running to Jack. He met her with open arms and lifted her off her feet. His eyes closed as well, and for several seconds, Gilly's sobs echoed through the building.

Sarah had to look away, and she hid her face in Owen's shoulder.

"You okay?" he asked, his mouth next to her ear.

She couldn't talk around the lump in her throat, so she nodded. Her joy for them threatened to overcome her. It was too easy for her to imagine herself in Gilly's place, and Owen in Jack's. She realized then how strong her friend had to be to deal with being separated from the man she loved.

With a start, it dawned on Sarah what that awareness meant. Before she could think about it too much, Owen's arm came to rest around her shoulders, and he pressed his lips to her temple. When the rest of the drugstore's customers started clapping and whistling, she turned to see that her brother had Gilly bent over one of his arms and was kissing her soundly.

"Jack Browning, you'd better marry that girl," an older man called out.

Jack straightened, keeping Gilly in his arms, and sent the man a wink. "Just as soon as I can, sir."

"What in the world is going on out here?" Gilly's father asked as he came out from behind the pharmacy counter. He ground to a halt when he saw Jack and covered his mouth, much as his daughter had. "Rosemarie, you'd better get out here," he hollered over his shoulder, grinning. Jack walked over and held out his hand, but George used it to pull the younger man into a hug. Gilly's mother emerged from the back and let out a cry.

It took several minutes for the revelry to die down. By the time he and Gilly joined Sarah and Owen in a booth, Jack was looking a bit harried.

Rosemarie came over to get their order, and she placed a hand on Gilly's shoulder. "You are off for the rest of the day, young lady. Go have fun once you all are done here. But not too much fun," she cautioned, shaking a finger at Jack.

Sarah snickered when he blushed, and he shot her a look that promised retribution. She didn't care. He was home, safe and whole and happy.

"I can't believe you're here," Gilly said once her mother had taken their order. "I'm beside myself. I don't know what to do." She looked across the booth at Sarah. "Did you know he was coming home?"

"No. He surprised me, too. But I guess now we know why he hasn't written to you in a few days."

"I guess so."

The look Gilly sent Jack was so full of love and happiness, it was almost painful to observe. Sarah leaned against Owen, and he put his arm around her.

Jack noticed and raised an eyebrow. "So you're dating my sister. How'd that come about, exactly?"

Sarah glowered at Jack, but he ignored her. From the look he was giving Owen, Sarah had to think Jack was none-too-pleased by the courtship.

"We met at the library, and one thing led to another. Boy meets girl. Boy and girl go to the movies, have dinner, and by some miracle, she didn't decide to give me the boot right away," Owen said. He looked down at Sarah with a half smile, apparently unconcerned with the grilling.

"I heard it was a little more contentious than that, that you'd argued about *someone* trespassing on your land." He turned his gaze to Sarah. "And that's something we're going to discuss, young lady."

Sarah didn't think sticking her tongue out at him in public was the best course of action, so she settled for saying, "No, *baby brother*, I don't think we are."

"We'll see about that."

Gilly goosed him in the ribs. "Leave them alone. There will be plenty of time for this later. Right now, let's just celebrate your being home."

Jack's face softened as he looked down at her. "You're right."

The mood at the table lightened, and Jack even relaxed enough to joke with Owen a little. Before Sarah was ready, it was time to go back to the library.

"What time do you get off work, sis?" Jack asked as they went out to the sidewalk.

"Five o'clock. If you want to meet me at the car, I'll probably be there around ten after."

"I'll see you then. Owen." Jack held his hand out, and the two men shook again. "I expect I'll see you around in the next few days."

"Probably." Owen placed a hand on the small of Sarah's back, and they headed across the street and back toward the library, opposite the direction her brother and Gilly were walking.

Sarah let out a breath. "Mama's going to cry her eyes out when she sees him. She's worried so much," she said as they reached the car to get his bag. "I guess this solves the problem of me staying at home by myself, too, come to think of it."

"I'll admit that I'm relieved he's home for that very reason," Owen said. "Maybe I'll sleep nights now, knowing that you're protected."

Sarah rolled her eyes, thinking he was joking, but his face was serious. "Owen, this is nineteen-sixty, not the pioneer days when panthers and bears and Indians were lurking outside the cabin doors."

"I know what year it is," he said as he held the door to the library open for her to pass. "But I also know that there are a lot of sick and twisted people in the world. A woman, particularly one who looks like you, living alone? You'd provide a lot of temptation for that sort of predator. It's enough to give me gray hair worrying. And before you say it, Miss Independent, it has nothing to do with you being able to protect yourself and everything to do with my protective instincts."

He walked back to the employee break room with her and waited while she locked up her purse and clocked back in.

"Dare I interpret that to mean you aren't simply biding your time with me?" she asked jauntily, her heart pounding as she waited for the answer.

He stopped her with a hand on her arm, his eyes unreadable. "If you knew how much you mean to me, how I feel about you, I'm afraid you'd run the other way so fast I'd be left in a cloud of dust."

Sarah swallowed, her hand coming up to cover his. "I—"

Shirley came in, interrupting them. "I'm sorry to cut your time short, kids. Sarah, Nellie needs you upstairs as soon as you can manage it."

"Okay. I'll head right up." She waited until Shirley had passed, then said, "We need to continue this discussion later, I think."

"Later's probably a good idea. I guess you're going to be busy tonight with your brother. Do you want to cancel our date?"

"Cancel, no. But we'll need to postpone it, I'm afraid. Can we try to meet tomorrow afternoon at the pool? I have to work, but I should be home by two o'clock."

"Then I'll hope to see you there." He walked to the stairs with her, but didn't go up. "I have everything I need, and I should probably get home and finish out this project."

"I hate that I won't be seeing you tonight."

The gentle, open smile she loved so much spread across Owen's face. "We'll see each other tomorrow. That's barely twenty-four hours."

"Might as well be a year, the way I feel. Be careful driving home."

"I will," he assured her. "You do the same later."

With every bit of willpower she possessed, Sarah turned and went up the stairs. Her longing for Owen—for his company, his smile, his hugs and kisses—was growing exponentially. It was ridiculous to feel that way about someone she'd only known for a few weeks. She'd discussed it several times with her mother, who had ruefully admitted she had fallen as quickly for Sarah's father.

"I was sixteen years old when I came in from school one day, and he was there, visiting your uncle Joe. I took one look at him and told my mother, 'That's the man I'm going to marry.' The day after I graduated from high school, we had our wedding. And I never regretted a single day."

Given how hard Kathy had fallen for Randall and how strongly Jack seemed to feel about Gilly, Sarah figured she shouldn't be surprised that she'd tumbled so quickly. She hesitated to put a label on her feelings yet, but she very much suspected she was falling in love with her neighbor.

CHAPTER NINETEEN

THE RAIN STARTED LATE SATURDAY morning, a relentless drizzle that caused a thick, heavy fog to move into the valleys and coves of the holler. Sarah usually loved to sit on the porch and watch the fog roll up the creek, but not when it threatened her meeting with Owen. The fog had caused her to take nearly thirty minutes longer than usual to get home. It was well after two by the time she pulled into the driveway.

She rushed into the house and yelled out a hello but didn't get a response. In record time, she changed into her walking clothes and dug her rain poncho out of the back of her closet. She hurried back downstairs and into the kitchen to pull a bag of food together, most of which she'd prepared that morning before leaving for work. As she laid the poncho across the back of a chair at the table, she saw a folded note with her name on it.

Sarah,

I hope you had a wonderful day at work, sweet baby girl.

The house should be empty by the time you get home. I'm going over to First Creek to visit Olena Brashear. As you know, Jack's out with Gilly and won't be back until this evening. I expect you'll be late getting in as well. Tell Owen hello for me.

Also, please ask him to come to dinner tomorrow. I think it's time he had a sit-down with the whole family, don't you?

Stay out of trouble, have fun, and stay safe.

Love,

Mom

Sarah's eyes stung, and she closed them against the tears that always seemed to hover right below the surface these days. She knew her mother was doing the best thing she could to heal by going to Georgia, and she wanted to see Eliza find her feet again. But Sarah was going to miss her mother, who was truly her best friend in the world. She swallowed, raising the paper to her face to kiss it. "Love you, too, Mama."

With the food packed, Sarah shrugged into the poncho and made sure the doors were locked. As she headed across the yard, she checked her watch and winced. It was nearing three o'clock, and she wondered if Owen would even still be waiting for her. As the thought went through her head, she heard a noise and looked up to see him coming down the path toward her.

"Hey!" she called. "I'm sorry I'm late. It seemed like everything in the world was trying to keep me from getting here on time. And then it's raining to boot."

Owen, clad in a waterproof coat of his own, just smiled. "I don't mind a little rain. I'm glad to see you. I was worrying something had happened." He took the bag of food with one hand and held out his other. Sarah took it and let him pull her close for a kiss.

"I missed you last night," she said. "It was good to see Jack, but I kept wishing you were there."

"They say absence makes the heart grow fonder," he teased. "I missed you, too. So, since it's raining, what do you want to do?"

"I don't know. I brought food, as you can see. We could go back to the house. No one's there."

Owen narrowed his eyes. "We could. Or we could go to the top of the mountain. There's no one there either."

Sarah was surprised. "Really? I thought you said if you ever took me to your house, you wouldn't let me back off the mountain."

His slow, wicked smile turned her heart upside down. "I said that. But we could go to my parents' house."

They'd been slowly walking up the trail toward the pool, but at that puzzling statement, Sarah pulled him to a stop. "Your parents' house? I thought that's where you lived."

"No. Not for some time now." A considering frown furrowed the space between his brows. "It's… complicated. If you'd rather go back to your house, that's fine. I thought I'd offer."

"You throw that sort of mystery out to me and expect me not to hot-foot it up to the top of the mountain? Think again, buddy." She waggled a finger at him playfully.

"Come on, then. As good as this coat is at keeping out the wet, I'm feeling a little like a dog that's been left outside in the cold."

They went up the mountain, which felt like a private haven, shrouded as it was in fog. The branch of water that fed the pool was swollen, running slightly muddy because of the rain, and Owen helped her cross at a narrow spot. Having never been past that point, Sarah gazed around her with avid curiosity. The climb grew steeper after they passed the pool, and aside from Owen pointing out a landmark here or a stunning cluster of wildflowers there, they conversed little.

"How much farther is it?" Sarah asked ten minutes after they'd crossed the branch.

"Not much. We're almost there."

Not a minute later, they reached a flat bench of land that ran parallel to the ridge line, and he led her to some wide steps that had been set into the mountain. When they reached the top of the steps, Sarah gasped.

Spread out in front of them, an open expanse of land spanned the ridge. It was a meadow, on the very peak, with the mountain falling away on all sides. The white, two-story farmhouse in the middle of the field had a wraparound porch. To the far left was a barn, and to the right, behind the farmhouse and its kitchen garden, was a newer-looking building. The additional structure was also two stories and blended into the landscape of the mountain as though it had been carved there.

"Owen, this is beautiful. I'll bet you can see forever from up here when it isn't foggy."

He looked around the clearing, and Sarah could see a sort of peace steal over him. "You can. If you don't have plans for Independence Day, come up here. You can see every fireworks display in every town around here for thirty miles."

"It's a date, then. How many acres do you have here?" Perhaps the most surprising aspect of the view was how flat and open the grassy pasture was. In a region where most of the flat land was spread across river bottoms and where homesteads were carved out of craggy rocks and forests, to find a meadow of any size was a treat. The grass created a soft-looking carpet, one Sarah would be happy to get lost in someday if the occasion arose.

"About eight in the clearing and about five hundred in total."

"Five hundred? I thought you all only had about three hundred."

"My father did. After he died, I started adding to the property."

"So where do you live, exactly?"

Owen pointed at the newer structure. "Over there. I built it a couple of years ago. I'd show it to you, but you know the rules."

Sarah shook her head. "Silly man. One of these days, I may show up on your doorstep and hold you to that rule. What will you do then?"

"Why don't you try it, and we'll find out?"

She leaned against him, nudging him a step to the side. "Let's get you out of the rain before you melt."

He led her up to the front door of the farmhouse and opened it. "After you."

Stepping inside, Sarah was full of curiosity. The house was older but well maintained. Hardwood floors stretched throughout the rooms she could see from where she stood in the open door. The living room was on her left, the dining room on the right. Straight ahead, stairs led up to the second floor, and a hall on the left vanished into the back of the house.

He took her poncho and hung it up, then did the same with his coat.

"It's lovely. Give me the nickel tour?" she asked.

"Of course. Let's start upstairs, shall we?"

Walking up the staircase, Sarah let her hand trail along the polished oak bannister. "I'll bet you never slid down this growing up."

Owen sent her a grin over his shoulder. "Oh, never. I was a perfect little angel."

Sarah snorted and tried to ignore the image of a little Owen that ran through her head. She sternly pushed aside the voice in her head that wondered what a child of theirs might look like.

When Owen showed her which of the four bedrooms had been his, she frowned. "How long ago did you move out exactly? This room doesn't look like you stayed in here since you were much younger."

A fine tension visibly settled across his features. "I wondered if you'd pick up on that. Remember the part about my not living in this house being complicated?"

"Of course."

"Well, that's part of the story. If you don't mind, I'll wait until we're finished with the tour to tell you about it."

Sarah clasped his hand. "Whatever you want."

Back downstairs, he showed her through the rest of the house. When they reached the hall leading to the back, Sarah noticed the pictures on the wall. Owen tried to keep her moving, but she dug in her heels.

"Is this your family?" she asked, pointing to a formal portrait of two adults and two little boys. "It has to be. You *do* look just like your father."

He sent her a quizzical look. "It is. How did you know I look like him?"

Sarah tucked her arm into his, her eyes only leaving the picture long enough to glance up at him. "Mama told me. How old were you here?" She touched the picture with a gentle finger, tracing the curve of younger Owen's cheek.

"Four or so."

"You were adorable. I could just squeeze those little cheeks. Oh, Owen."

Embarrassed by her gushing, he rubbed the back of his neck. "Moving on, let's see the kitchen next." He started walking down the hall, but Sarah didn't move.

"I'm going to finish looking at these pictures, if you don't mind," she teased. "I've seen kitchens before; I've not seen your baby pictures."

"Oh, geez. What is it with women and baby pictures? My aunt Amy's the same way. You look to your heart's content. I'm going to grab the Cokes I stashed over here earlier."

Sarah put her hands on her hips. "Well, wasn't that confident of you? How'd you know I'd agree to come back here with you?" she asked teasingly. When he shrugged without answering, she realized how uncomfortable he was. "Owen?"

He waved away the question in her voice. "I'm fine. It's this house. Makes me... edgy. I'll get the Cokes."

Feeling as though she was on the verge of learning some of his secrets, Sarah wrapped her arms around herself as she finished perusing the pictures on the walls. Seeing Owen's life progress as he went from toddler to young man, she could clearly see a divide. He went from being a happy, smiling young boy to a solemn, guarded teenager. Something had clearly happened to him, and it dawned on Sarah that whatever had occurred probably accounted for his solitary life as an adult.

The last frame didn't hold a picture, but a family tree. It was old and faded, with the names written in a neat, feminine hand. She traced Owen's name and date of birth, reading the information out loud. "Henry Owen Campbell, born October fourteenth, nineteen thirty-three. Son of Henry Duncan Campbell and Lucretia McLemore Wells. Lucretia McLemore..."

Sarah's voice trailed off, and she stood there, staring dumbly at the framed parchment. "No. No, it can't be. He wouldn't... Henry Owen. H.O. McLemore. It has to be a coincidence." Even as she denied the evidence in front of her, she remembered Owen's vigorous defense of the reclusive writer, how he'd often show up with ink stains on his hands, his mysterious research into genealogy and regional folklore.

"The Coke's cold," Owen said, coming down the hall with two bottles in hand. "Why don't we go—"

Even from several feet away, Sarah heard him swallow. If she hadn't been so surprised by the unexpected discovery, she would have laughed at his expression. "Owen?"

He glanced from her to the family tree and back. She watched the guarded expression he'd worn when they first met come over his face, and she felt a pang in her heart.

"I guess we need to talk," he finally said.

CHAPTER TWENTY

WHEN HE'D INVITED SARAH TO the house, Owen had acknowledged in the back of his mind that he might have to discuss sensitive topics. When she'd picked up on the state of his old room, he hadn't been that surprised. After all, her intelligence and empathy were part of what had drawn him to her in the first place. But he'd forgotten about the family tree.

So when he came out of the kitchen to find Sarah with her mouth open in shock, he was flummoxed. He knew he was staring at her like an idiot, but he couldn't help it. He wasn't ready to tell her about his life as H.O. McLemore. His readiness, however, went out the window.

"I guess we need to talk." Edging closer, he gestured with the icy-cold bottles. "Why don't we go to the side porch? It's screened in."

"That's probably a good idea." She preceded him through the living room and out the door. Knowing he'd eventually be bringing her to the house, Owen had cleaned the porch in preparation. He'd even purchased new cushions for the swing, and as they sat down, he wondered if that effort had been for nothing.

He handed her a Coke and set his own bottle aside. Leaning forward, he clasped his hands together between his knees. "I guess you have questions."

"You could say that, yes. I don't know where to start. I have so many questions, so I'll start with the obvious. You're H.O. McLemore, aren't you?"

He'd guarded the secret for so long Owen had to struggle to make himself answer. "Yes. I am."

Sarah didn't respond, and he glanced at her. She was staring down into her drink, a deep, pensive frown on her face. Owen couldn't tell what she was thinking, whether she was angry, hurt, sad, or some combination of the three.

"Were you ever going to tell me?" she asked quietly.

He sighed. "Yes."

She tilted her head and looked at him, and Owen could see that she was both angry and hurt. He couldn't blame her.

"When?"

"Soon, I promise." He struggled for words. "There aren't that many people who know, Sarah. My uncle and his wife, my agent, and my publisher. My mother knew as well. I swore everyone to secrecy, since I didn't want the rest of the world to know about my writing. I wanted to tell you, was going to tell you, but it's not something I find easy to talk about."

She turned away, looking out over the foggy landscape. Her hands were tight around the bottle, and Owen felt a pang of guilt.

"Please talk to me," he begged.

"I don't know what to say. Why wouldn't you want people to know that you're H.O. McLemore? Do you have any idea how wonderful your books are? That's something you should be proud of, not ashamed."

"I'm not ashamed. I've never been ashamed. But I don't want public acclaim. I don't want people traipsing all over my land, trying to get a look at the mysterious writer. I don't want the community speculating about whether I write stories about them or how much money I make from my writing. That's not why I do what I do."

"When I asked you what you did for a living and you told me all those things—the genealogy, the folklore research—was that just your cover story?"

He got up and stood at the screen door that led into the yard. Bracing his hands on the doorframe, he leaned in and let his arms carry his weight. "Not exactly. It's something I tell people to keep them from wondering too much, yes. But it's also the truth. I do all those things. I've never lied to you, Sarah."

"But you haven't exactly told me the truth either, have you?"

The sadness in her voice tore him apart inside, and Owen closed his eyes. "No, I haven't."

She didn't speak, and after a minute, Owen took a chance and looked at her. She studied him as though she'd never seen him before. Drawing in a deep breath, he walked to the swing. He hunkered down and placed a hand on either side of her, leaning close.

"I promise you, swear to you on my life, Sarah, I was going to tell you. Please believe me."

A lock of hair fell into his eyes, and he impatiently pushed it back, only to have it fall right back down. Before he could move it again, Sarah brushed it away, her hand lingering on his face for a bare second before falling into her lap.

"You said your mother knew. What about your father, your brother? Didn't they know?"

"No." He scooted back and sat against the house, legs stretched out in front of him, right knee bent. Picking up his Coke, he took a long swig, holding the cold, sweet liquid in his mouth for a few seconds before swallowing. "No, I never told them. My brother... well, Harlan wasn't much of a reader, and

I knew he'd never leave me alone about being a writer if I told him."

"And your father?"

Owen felt the bitterness rise in his throat and knew it was reflected in the smile he sent her. "Yeah, we weren't close. I wasn't his favorite son." He gave a small shrug, attempting to disregard how much the memory hurt, but from the look Sarah sent him, he didn't think he'd fooled her in the least. When she moved down from the swing to sit beside him on the floor, he hid his relief by taking another drink.

"Tell me why you don't live in this house."

He let the nearly empty bottle dangle from his fingers. "I told you I dropped out of school when I was in the eighth grade. Well, that disappointed the old man pretty badly. That year at Christmas, Harlan and I got into an awful fight. Harlan was only twelve, not quite two years younger than me, but he was big for his age. It didn't matter. We didn't stop until Hank stepped in and separated us. We both had black eyes and bloody noses. Hank was livid. He said some things that I think he regretted as soon as they came out, but he never apologized, never took them back." Owen finished the Coke and set the bottle aside. "Hank Campbell wasn't capable of admitting he was wrong."

"You call your father Hank?"

"Yeah. I haven't called him Dad since that Christmas."

Sarah handed him her soda and wrapped both of her arms around his left one. "What happened?"

"After the fight—we'd torn the living room apart, including Mom's Christmas tree—I decided I'd be better off in the barn. We'd added on a room that Mom was going to use as a chicken coop, but we hadn't moved the chickens out there yet. I commandeered it. I never slept in this house again, not until after my father died."

He couldn't look at her, couldn't bear to see the pity on her face. Her gasp had been bad enough, as were the tears he could feel dampening his arm where her face rested against him.

"The chicken coop? Oh, dear God, Owen. How was it that your mother let that happen?"

"She couldn't stop me. My mind was set. And I didn't stay in the chicken coop. Hank built me a room in the barn loft, complete with a small bathroom. It was actually pretty cozy. I was happier after I moved out there."

"I very much doubt that. What was it he said that made you go that far?"

Owen really didn't want to tell her. It was too close to the truth that he was a shifter. That secret was not something he was close to being ready to share. Still, he had to explain as best he could. "He called me a monster, an animal. Said I was no son of his. That blood didn't matter."

He hadn't spoken to anyone about what his father had said since it had happened. Stopping to clear his throat, he told Sarah what he'd never told another person. "I never forgave Hank for that. Never forgave him for letting me go so easily. For not fighting for me. I refused to live in his house until after he was long dead and buried and my mother needed me here. As soon as she was gone, I built the new house. I'd rather have been tortured than let him know about my writing. He didn't deserve that sort of consideration in my eyes. That old barn burned down while I was living with Eli and Amy. The one out there now, it's new."

She moved her arms so that they were wrapped around his body and not just his arm. He returned the embrace, pulling her closer. Looking down, he saw she was crying silently, and he wiped the wetness away with his thumb.

"Shh, Sarah. I'm okay. It was a long time ago. I've moved past it."

"Have you? Because I don't see how. Your mother must have hated him for what he did."

His mouth tightened. "It changed their relationship, yes. That's something else I've carried with me, the guilt about that."

"Oh, Owen. You can't blame yourself."

"I don't necessarily. But I still feel guilty."

Owen closed his eyes. He buried his nose in her hair and inhaled deeply. The strands were loose and silky soft against his cheek. His heart twisted as he wondered if this would be the last time he'd hold her. Though he hadn't set out to deceive her on purpose, the intention didn't seem to matter as much as the result. Adding to his guilt was the knowledge that he still wasn't being honest about what he truly was.

Sarah finally stirred against him. "Owen?"

"Yes?"

"Is there anything else you'd care to share with me? Any other secrets you've been keeping?"

He didn't know how to answer. She pulled back to look at him, perhaps sensing there was more.

He looked down at her and shrugged. "There are some things I'm not ready to tell you yet. I'm not... it isn't you. I'm not ready to talk about them yet."

"Are they bad things?" A horrified look crossed her face. "You're not married, are you?"

"What? No! No, I'm not married. Never have been. To be honest, I never considered that marriage might be in my future. Not until recently."

Sarah looked dubious. "Then what sort of things are we talking about? Are you a criminal? Have you killed someone? Do you turn into a werewolf by the light of the full moon?"

Though he was fairly certain she was jesting with the last question, it took every bit of control Owen had not to react. He stuttered, trying to figure out how to respond.

Sarah put her fingers over his mouth. "Stop. I shouldn't have asked. You don't owe me any explanations. You already said you're not ready to talk about it, whatever it is. But answer me this." A flash of uncertainty and pain crossed her face, and she wet her lips. "Is there someone else?"

Owen cupped her face in his hands. "No." He kept his eyes on hers. "No. There's no one else, Sarah. Only you." She closed her eyes, and Owen didn't think he'd imagined the relief he'd seen in them.

"Then I'll be patient and wait until you're ready." She turned her head and kissed his palms, first one, then the other. "That said, I think we both need a little space to think about things. I'm going to head back to the house."

She stood, and Owen followed suit. "Sarah, I—"

"I won't tell anyone. You have my word."

He frowned. "I know. I trust you."

"Do you?" she asked, raising an eyebrow.

"Yes. Yes, I really do. You're sure you have to go?"

Sarah wrapped her arms around her waist. "I think so. I need some time to process what you've told me. It's a lot to take in all at once. And I'll be honest, I'm a little upset you didn't tell me earlier. I understand why you didn't, but that's the logical side of my brain. The emotional part is still struggling with why you didn't."

Feeling lower than low, Owen nodded. "Okay. I'll walk you home."

"No. I'd rather you didn't, not today."

He felt the words like a blow, and his jaw tightened. "Are you breaking up with me?"

"Oh, no. I'm not letting you off the hook that easily." Stepping closer, Sarah put her arms around him, her head resting on his chest. She gave him a tight hug, but moved back before Owen could pull her to him. "You may wish I had, however.

Mama wants me to invite you to dinner tomorrow. The whole family's going to be there, Randall and Kathy included."

Owen led her inside to where he'd hung their coats and helped her into the poncho. "You said Eliza wants me there. Do you?"

Sarah sent him a winsome smile. "I want you there, yes. But only if you want to be there. Don't answer me now. Just show up if you decide to come. We eat around one, and Mama doesn't like for people to be late."

Not sure what to say or do, Owen held open the door and followed her out onto the porch. She went down the steps.

He had to grasp the support post in order to keep from going after her. "Will you call me when you get home to let me know you're there and safe? You don't have to say anything else, but let me know you're okay. Please?"

"Of course I will." With a small wave and a sad smile, she set off.

It only took seconds for her to disappear, and as she went, Owen felt his heart shatter. The need to shift, to change into a wild creature and run howling through the woods, was strong. In his animal form, he could express pure emotions easier than he could when in human form. The only time he came remotely close to being that emotionally free as a human was when he was writing. He knew he had to resist the urge to change, at least for a little while.

Once Sarah was safely home, though, he would shed his clothes and transform into the monster his father had feared so much. It had been a long time since Owen had felt such self-loathing, and he growled.

"You took so much from me, old man. I'll be damned if I let you take anything else," he told the house behind him. He'd never been able to tell his father how he felt when Hank was alive, and the house represented most everything Owen resented about his past. He'd hoped that by bringing Sarah there, he'd finally be able to let go of the hurt and the hate, but it hadn't happened. "One of these nights, I'm liable to burn you to the ground."

He grabbed his coat and headed for the house that was his sanctuary to wait for Sarah's call. He didn't want to change while it was still daylight out. With the wolf riding him hard, night couldn't come soon enough.

CHAPTER TWENTY-ONE

THE ENTIRE WALK HOME, SARAH struggled with her emotions. She was hurt that Owen hadn't trusted her sooner with the truth about his being a writer, but she understood why he hadn't, given what he'd told her about his father. That said, she wondered if he really would have told her or not. That doubt, that question, raced through her mind. Even though he'd said all the right things, she would need some time to get back to completely trusting him again.

Another thing that weighed heavily on her mind was Owen's reluctance to tell her what else he was hiding. She would have pushed harder to get him to talk if she hadn't almost been able to feel his pain. As it was, her instincts were telling her she'd end up pushing him further away if she persisted.

When she got home, she was immensely relieved to find her mother there. She greeted Eliza, then went to the phone to call Owen. He answered on the first ring.

"It's Sarah. I'm home."

"Thanks for calling and letting me know. Sarah, I... I'm sorry about everything." He sounded so tense and tired and so very alone that it was all Sarah could do to not cry out.

"We'll talk soon. Bye, Owen." Moving slowly and carefully, as if she would break if she made any sudden moves, she replaced the receiver in its cradle.

"Everything okay?" Eliza asked.

Sarah shook her head. "I don't think it is, Mama. I really don't think so."

Some time later, Sarah and Eliza sat on the back porch, sipping hot cocoa. Eliza had already let Sarah cry on her shoulder. Now that Sarah had calmed enough to talk, she told Eliza a little of what had happened.

"I found out something he'd been keeping from me. It's not bad," she rushed to assure her mother. "He's not married, doesn't have kids. It isn't anything like that. But I'm hurt that he didn't tell me. I kind of stumbled on it, to tell the truth. And it makes me wonder what else he's keeping from me. How much he trusts me, if he trusts me."

Eliza brushed a hand over Sarah's hair. "I'm sorry, sweetheart. I wish I knew what to tell you, but that's something the two of you are have to work out."

"I know. I just… I want so much to be with him. It feels right to be with him, Mama. Like nothing I've ever felt before. And it isn't only that he's attractive," she said, blushing. "Though he is. But he makes me laugh, and he makes me feel safe, and I want to make him smile. He doesn't smile enough. Now, though, I'm worried he won't let me close enough to be a part of his life. Not the way I want."

"Sarah Jane, you're in love with him, aren't you?"

Utterly miserable, Sarah lifted her gaze to her mother's. "I think I am."

Eliza closed her eyes and tightened her arm around Sarah's shoulders. "Oh, sweetheart."

"There's nothing to do but wait. I know that. But, God almighty, it's hard."

"You know, back when I worked with Owen's mother, Lucy, at church, my impression from what she said was that he was a very troubled young man. Oh, not the kind of troubled that would make me worry about you dating him," she hurried to say when Sarah shot her an incredulous look. "It was more that she couldn't reach him. He was maybe thirteen, fourteen, and she'd sent him to stay with someone. He was having trouble in school, I think. Lucy was absolutely heartbroken. Owen was her favorite child."

"Do you know what made him like that?" Sarah kept her eyes on her mug as she waited for the answer.

Eliza considered the question for a minute. "I think she said something about his father and that they'd had a falling out. It hurt Owen, and he would never let her in after that." She looked at her own mug, running a thumb along the rim. "From what I know of Owen, what I've seen when he's here, I'd guess he shut himself away from everyone. I don't think he's used to letting anyone in. He's probably opened up more to you than to anyone in recent years, sweetheart. That has to be hard for someone like him. I don't think I'd give up on him yet."

Sarah felt a small smile coming on. "You think he's worth fighting for, then?"

"I do. I think he's a good fit for you and vice versa. I'd hate to see either of you give up now."

The forest was damp, the scents of decaying vegetation strong in the air. Fog rolled through the trees like a living thing, and the cold, ethereal atmosphere suited Owen's mood to a tee. As soon as it was dark, he'd stepped outside and shifted.

For a long time, he just ran—up and down trails, through the brush—welcoming the sting of the branches as they slapped against his face. It was the wolf's version of a hair shirt, Owen thought, which he very much felt he deserved. Eventually, he found himself at the pool. After getting a long, cold drink, he shook himself and trotted up the path to the top of the boulder. Sitting down, he finally let his pent-up emotions rise to the surface. Anger, grief, guilt—they all warred for dominance within him. They swelled, fighting to get out, to be expressed.

He hadn't run in so long, the emotions threatened to tear him apart. They started clawing their way out of his throat, first emerging simply as yips and whimpers.

When he couldn't hold the pain inside any longer, he howled.

CHAPTER TWENTY-TWO

SARAH AWOKE AT THE CRACK of dawn on Sunday morning. She was so worried about her relationship with Owen, she had only slept in fits and starts. As if that hadn't been enough, she kept hearing a wolf howling in the distance. When she rolled over for what felt the hundredth time at five o'clock, she simply gave up.

Throwing back the covers in disgust, she got up and put on an old sundress. She pulled her hair back into a severe twist, then headed downstairs to the kitchen. She didn't have to worry about waking up Jack, who had taken their parents' old room, as he had stayed in town with Gilly and her family. Free to move around the kitchen, she turned on the small radio Jack had gotten them for Christmas, keeping the volume low, and got to work.

By the time her mother came down three hours later, Sarah had made the yeast dough for rolls. The pot roast they were having for dinner was ready to go in the oven, and she had baked two pies and two dozen cookies.

"Sarah, what in the world? How long have you been up?"

With a quick glance at the clock, Sarah shrugged. "Since five or so. Want coffee?" Without waiting for Eliza's response, she poured a mug and added sugar and cream just the way her mother liked it. She handed the mug to Eliza with a tense smile and turned back to the dough.

Her mother, still dressed in her nightgown, blew out a breath. "Okay, then. I'll sit over here at the table and watch you work. What kind of cookies are these?"

"Peanut butter and oatmeal chocolate chip. And the pies are apple and strawberry. Do you think I should make a cake, too?"

Eliza *thunked* her mug down on the table. "How many people are you expecting to feed today? Sweetie, I think you need to take a break. Sit down here with me."

Sarah braced her hands on the counter. "If I sit down, I'll start to think. And if I think, I don't know if I can bear the weight of my thoughts, Mama."

"I understand." Eliza's voice was quiet, and when Sarah looked over her shoulder, she saw that her mother was twisting her gold wedding band. "Just don't wear yourself out too much. The last thing you want to happen is for dinnertime to get here and you be asleep on the couch."

Sarah snorted laughter. "Yeah, I don't think that'd be the best way to kick off his first sit-down with the family. If he even shows up." She shook herself, stopping the thought in its tracks. "I was thinking about making those noodles Daddy's cousin Helga used to make. What do you think?"

Eliza glanced around the kitchen skeptically. "Well, I think you've already made enough food to feed an army. We still need vegetables, but that won't take any time to do. So, sure. Make the noodles. They sound pretty good, I admit. Do you want my help?"

"No. You've cooked these big dinners for us all these years. Sit back and relax this time. I'll let you know if I need anything." Sarah went back to work, humming along with the song on the radio.

After a few minutes, Eliza got up and topped off her coffee. "I think I'm going to get my Bible and go sit on the porch. Holler if you need me, sweetie." She gave Sarah a quick hug and kiss and disappeared into the living room.

By the time Jack and Gilly arrived, most of the food for dinner was ready.

Gilly looked around the kitchen, her eyes wide. "Wow, Sarah. I made a cake last night. Jack kept trying to get a piece. Maybe I should have let him," she said, handing over the glass cake safe to Eliza, who had come into the kitchen with her. "Are you okay?"

"Sure. I... I'm fine." Sarah went over the food, mentally going through the list in her mind. "The corn and beans need to be heated, the rolls are ready to go in the oven whenever the roast comes out, and the broth for the noodles is on the stove. What am I forgetting?"

"What about tea and lemonade?" Gilly asked.

"Oh, crap!"

"We can take care of that. You need to head upstairs," Gilly said.

Sarah glanced at the clock and grimaced. "I guess I should probably go get cleaned up. Everyone else will be here soon, and I look like a hot mess."

"Why don't you do that?" Eliza took her hand and tugged her toward the stairs. "The last thing you want to happen is for Owen to come in and see you looking like we've kept you in here, chained to the stove."

Sarah nodded. "Okay."

When she climbed the stairs, she realized how much her feet and lower back hurt. She'd been standing for almost seven hours, but the hard work had done its job. She was too tired now to worry about whether Owen would make an appearance.

Deciding that she had time to take a bath, she filled the claw-foot tub, adding Epsom salts and bubble bath. As she sank into the hot water, she groaned with relief. She dunked under the surface fully, holding her breath until it hurt. When she resurfaced, she drew in a deep breath and let it out slowly. Head resting against the back of the tub, she closed her eyes.

"Right now, I'll be happy to get through the day. I hope that isn't asking too much."

When Sarah came back downstairs thirty minutes later, dressed in a blue blouse and white capri pants, the house was full of people. She strained to pick Owen's voice out of the clamor, but couldn't hear him. It was twenty till one, and he should have arrived if he was coming. Masking her disappointment, she hurried into the kitchen.

Kathy, seated at the table with the baby, looked up with amusement clear on her face. "We thought we were going to have to get a wheelbarrow to cart all that food you cooked into the dining room. Surely you're not nervous about your beau coming over."

Sarah ignored the remark and stopped to run a gentle finger down the baby's soft cheek. "Is there anything else we need, Mama?"

Eliza chuckled. "Nothing but our last guest. Oh, you forgot to do mashed potatoes, but we covered that. And the gravy. Speaking of our guest," she said, looking out the kitchen window, "here he comes. Sarah, let him in?"

All the nerves she'd thought she'd conquered by working that morning came rushing back into her stomach, and for an instant, Sarah thought she might be sick. Swallowing hard, she hurried out the kitchen door and stood on the porch steps, waiting as Owen crossed the back yard. He looked up when he was a few feet away and stopped dead in his tracks.

Wearing dark pants and a red dress shirt with the sleeves rolled up, he was so handsome it hurt to look at him. He carried a small book in one hand, and as she watched, he shifted it to the other hand nervously. His expression was guarded, solemn. Sarah pushed open the screen door, and he walked slowly until he was only an arm's length away.

"Hey," she said. "I was afraid you weren't coming."

"Hey, yourself. I almost didn't. I wasn't sure you would want me here, not after what happened yesterday."

"I want you here. But I want you to *want* to be here."

Some of the tension left his face, and he reached up to touch her face. "I do." He let his hand drop and cleared his throat. "I brought you something. It isn't much, but I thought you might… anyhow…" He handed her the book.

Sarah gasped. "Owen, how…? This isn't supposed to be out for another month." The book was the latest volume of the *Tobias Hedge* series. "You didn't have to do this."

He shoved his hands in his pockets, a move Sarah had learned meant he was uncertain, and shrugged. "I wanted to do it."

Embarrassed by the tears that pricked her eyes, she smiled and ducked her head. "Thank you. Is this a borrow, or may I keep it?" She started to open the book, but he stopped her, putting his hand over hers.

"Don't open it here. Wait until you're alone. There's a letter inside. And it's yours. Unless you don't want it," he said teasingly as he moved as though to take it back.

Sarah tucked the book against her chest. "Oh, no. You'll have to pry this out of my hands to get it back."

His smile told her how pleased he was by the statement, and Sarah felt a little more certain of his affections. Taking a step forward, she rested her free hand on his chest and leaned in to place a soft kiss on his cheek, near the corner of his mouth.

Owen sighed and closed his eyes, wrapping an arm around her waist to bring her closer to him. He rested his forehead against hers for a minute, then placed a soft kiss there. He pulled back when Eliza cleared her throat from the kitchen door.

"Not that I want to interrupt the two of you, but dinner's ready. Sarah, bring him in before these boys eat up all that food you worked so hard on."

"Yes, Mama." Clasping Owen's hand, she led him into the kitchen. "I'll introduce you to everyone, and then I'll take this upstairs to my room." Though she tried to hide the book against her body, making sure the title was hidden on the inside, Kathy still saw it when they stepped into the kitchen. She reached for it, but Sarah drew back and grasped the book even tighter.

"Well, must be something if you're that protective of it. What is it, a book of love poems from your sweetheart?" Kathy sneered.

"Of a sort, yes. It's called *The Kama Sutra*. You should look it up sometime. You might find it informative." Sarah didn't expect Kathy to understand the reference, but when Owen, who had sneaked a cookie off the tray, let out a choking noise, Sarah felt her face heat to an almost painful level. Without looking at him, she squeaked out the introduction. "Owen, this is my sister, Kathy. I'm going to put this upstairs."

It was all she could do not to burst out laughing as she hurried to her bedroom. Once there, she looked around, trying to figure out where to hide the book. She knew that as soon as Kathy got a chance, she'd be upstairs searching for it.

"Shit. Where can I put you so that you'll be safe?" she asked the book. Not surprisingly, it didn't answer, but Sarah thought she might have the ideal place. Sneaking back out into the hall, she listened to make sure her sister was still downstairs, then hurried along the carpeted runner into her mother's room. She eased the door closed and went to the vacuum cleaner Eliza had stashed there that morning. Carefully, she opened the compartment that held the bag and placed the book inside. Satisfied, she closed it and stood.

"What are you doing?" her mother asked in a loud whisper.

With a squeak, Sarah turned, her hands going to her chest. "Mama! You scared me to death!"

Eliza looked over her shoulder, then back at Sarah. "Sorry. What are you doing?"

Sarah ushered her back out into the hall, then pulled the door closed. "Owen gave me a book, and Kathy saw it. She's curious, and you know what that means. I don't want her to see it."

"Well, I came up here to get a washcloth for the baby and saw you come in here. Couldn't figure out what in the world you were up to." As they headed back downstairs, Eliza stopped Sarah at the turn of the steps with a hand on her arm. "Is it really *The Kama Sutra?*"

"No! I only said that because of Kathy. How do you know what *The Kama Sutra* is?"

Eliza smiled wickedly. "Never you mind. But Sarah, poor Owen. If you could have seen his face. I don't think I've ever seen anyone turn that shade of red. I expect you'll have some explaining to do later how *you* know what it is. I'd like to know the answer to that myself."

"Not the way you think, I promise. Remember Portia from school?" Sarah asked, waving a hand in front of her face to cool her cheeks. "She gave it to me before I left. I never would have said what I did if I knew everyone was familiar with it."

Her mother was clearly struggling to keep a straight face. If Jack hadn't walked over to check on them at that point, Sarah thought they would have dissolved into laughter.

There was a little chaos as everyone settled around the dining room table, but once they were all seated, they joined hands, and Eliza led them in the blessing. Conversation halted while the food was passed.

"Owen, you must be special. Sarah never cooks, but I guess she made pretty much all of this by herself. I hope you didn't mix up the sugar and the salt again, like you did that one time," Kathy said.

Sarah's hopes for a peaceful dinner evaporated. She knew the expression on Kathy's face too well. Her sister would do everything she could during the meal to punish Sarah for not letting her see the book.

"Kathy, I believe that happened when Sarah was ten years old. And she cooks all the time; you just aren't here to see it," Eliza said. Though their mother's tone was neutral, she sent Kathy a pointed look. "And yes, Owen is special."

Sarah sent her a grateful smile.

"You made all of this?" Owen asked when Jack distracted Randall and Kathy with a question about the baby.

"Um, yes, most of it. I cook when I'm upset," she confessed in a low voice. Because there were so many people there, they all were sitting in closer quarters than usual. Sarah could feel the heat of Owen all along her left side, and he didn't have to move much to be able to speak and not be overheard.

"I'm sorry."

She moved her left hand off the table and touched his leg. "Don't be. I'm not upset now. I just needed a little time to get my head around things."

He covered her hand with his. They left their hands clasped together under the table and resumed eating.

"So what is it you do exactly, Owen?" Randall asked out of the blue, sitting back in his chair to put an arm around Kathy's shoulders. "I've asked around, but nobody seems to know."

"Randall! That's rude, don't you think? And it's also none of your business," Sarah said.

"Now, that's not a nice thing to say, girl. I'm looking out for you. If this fella's serious about courting you, he needs to be able to support you."

Randall's hurt expression didn't fool Sarah for an instant, and her hand clenched around Owen's.

He squeezed back. "It's okay. I do research for people who can't travel down here, and I help my uncle out in Laurel County on his farm every year. I'm perfectly able to support Sarah, if that's something she and I decide needs to happen."

Randall scoffed. "Shoot, you can't make much money at that. Research. Tell you what, I could put in a word for you down at the county garage. If you know your way around an engine, that is. Your brother sure did, I'll tell you that."

"I appreciate the offer, but I'm fine doing what I do now." Owen's tone clearly brooked no argument, but Sarah figured the warning was lost on Randall.

"So, are you going to let Sarah keep working? If you get married, I mean? I wouldn't want my wife out there, exposed to all those men that go in that library. Might give her ideas, if you get what I'm saying." His arm, draped around Kathy's shoulders, tightened, and Sarah saw her sister wince as if in pain. "It's a good thing for a wife to know her place."

Sarah didn't dare glance at her mother. She was afraid of what she'd see.

Owen's voice was icy. "Sarah and I haven't discussed marriage yet, thank you, but when and if we get to that point, Sarah's free to make her own place however she sees fit. I don't hold with the tradition that a woman should stay pregnant and barefoot unless that's what she wants."

Randall's face turned red, but before he could speak, Jack jumped in. "Speaking of garages, I went and saw Mr. Campbell at the Ford dealership yesterday." He looked at Owen. "Kin of yours?"

Owen shook his head. "No. Different set of Campbells."

"Ah. Okay. Well, I'll be starting there on Monday in the service department. I'll be working as a mechanic."

There were congratulations and well-wishes all around the table, and Jack took them in stride.

"That was fast," Eliza said. "I know you were concerned about finding a job."

Jack nodded and touched Gilly's hand. "I was. But now that I have found one, we're going to move the wedding up. We're not going to wait until next year. Life's too short." His pronouncement was met with stunned silence, and then everyone was talking at once.

"Oh, my God. You got her pregnant!" Kathy declared, her eyes wide.

"Kathleen! Watch yourself," Eliza warned. "We have a guest."

Sarah saw the color start at Jack's collar and climb its way up from there. She winced, knowing her sister was about to get lambasted.

"Gilly is not pregnant," Jack ground out. "We haven't anticipated our marriage vows, unlike—"

"Jackson Reese Browning!" Eliza shouted. Everyone turned to stare at her. Eliza rarely lost her temper enough to yell. "God help me get through this dinner without strangling someone, and I swear to you, I'll clean the church every day this week as penance." Lowering her gaze from the ceiling to look first at Jack, then at Kathy and Randall, she nodded once. "As you were."

Randall, perhaps trying to smooth things over, asked Jack, "Where are you all going to live once you're married?"

Jack released a slow breath. "We were hoping we could stay here until we got on our feet a little. Mama, is that okay? I mean, you'll be in Georgia, and Sarah'd be here by herself."

As the implications sank in, Sarah groaned. Her fork clanged against her plate, and she closed her eyes. "Not again. I don't think I can survive another pair of newlyweds."

Randall and Kathy had lived with them when they were first married, and no one in the house had gotten a good night's rest for several weeks. It'd gotten so bad, Ira had had a stern talk with Randall, and they'd moved out shortly after that.

At the end of the table, Eliza made a strangled noise. She held her napkin up to hide her mouth, but Sarah could tell she was struggling not to laugh.

Fighting to keep her own mouth straight, Sarah looked at Gilly. "Do you think your parents would let me rent your room?"

Completely serious, Gilly met her gaze. "No, but Owen might rent you a room."

Eliza hurried away from the table with a choked "Excuse me." Though she went outside, they could still hear her laughter.

"What's so funny?" Moira asked from beside Sarah. "Aunt Sarah, your face is turning awfully red."

Flummoxed, Sarah looked down at her niece, trying to figure out how in the world to answer. Kathy came to her rescue inadvertently by asking Gilly about the wedding.

"Are you still getting married in church?"

"Of course. And I'm planning on wearing white, too," Gilly answered.

"Oh, Christ," Sarah muttered. She let go of Owen's hand and reached for her water, wishing it was something stronger, even though she didn't like alcohol. Any chance she'd had of presenting a halfway-normal family was out the window. She risked looking at him and felt a little less panicked to see that he didn't appear offended but rather amused.

Eliza returned to the table, and the discussion moved back to Jack's new job.

"How come you didn't come to the county garage and put in for work?" Randall asked. "You know I'd have gotten you on there."

Jack took a long drink of tea. "Because I didn't want to worry about my job disappearing next election year. My family's security isn't something I'm willing to risk on politics, and the county garage isn't known as being the most stable place to work."

"Oh ho, how very nice for you, Jackson," Kathy drawled. "I'd rather have a man who's committed to standing up for what he believes in. One might almost say your vote is a commodity if that's the way you feel." Before Jack could respond, she turned her gaze to Owen. "How do you vote, Owen? You can tell a lot about a man from the way he casts his ballots. Take my Randall, for example. He's a straight party man, toes the line the whole way every year."

The tension returned full force as everyone waited for Owen's answer. Eliza had apparently given up trying to control Kathy and Randall, and Sarah guessed she was probably counting the seconds until the dinner was over.

"I vote my conscience," Owen stated. "I'm more concerned with the man behind the stump speech than whether he's a Democrat or Republican."

"That's a shame," Randall replied. "A crying shame. Your brother, God rest his soul, he woulda been sick to death with embarrassment. You don't work a real job. You don't hold faithful to the party. I bet you don't even believe in God. Now, Harlan Campbell? He was a man's man. He died fighting to protect this country from the commies over in Europe. You sure ain't cut from the same cloth. No, sir."

Sarah didn't think there could be another ounce of air left in the room. Everyone had sucked in a breath as the words left Randall's mouth, even Kathy, who finally had the good sense to look embarrassed.

Owen, however, shrugged nonchalantly and picked up his lemonade. "You're certainly entitled to your opinion, as I am to mine. And I'm of the opinion that any man who so idolizes my brother, *God rest his soul*, isn't someone I give two craps and a hoot about. Especially considering that Harlan died in a bar fight over the favors of a whore." He inclined his head toward Eliza. "Forgive me for speaking so frankly.

"Now, we've talked about money, politics, and sex—three things my mother always taught me shouldn't be discussed in polite company. Knowing Mrs. Browning as I do, I can't imagine she didn't teach her children the same thing, which makes it all the more puzzling that all three have come up while we were trying to enjoy this wonderful meal that Sarah prepared for us. It must be some bad outside influence is the only thing that I can come up with." The last part was said as he stared straight at Randall. The look in Owen's eyes dared Sarah's brother-in-law to say a single contradictory word.

"I believe I'm finished here," Randall said, his face a mottled, ugly red. "I'm going outside for a smoke." He pushed back his chair with a scrape and left.

"I hear the baby. I'd better check on him. Moira, come help me." Kathy hurried out of the room, and Sarah felt a moment's pang of sympathy for her sister.

After they left, Eliza sighed, slumping tiredly in her chair. "Owen, I am so sorry. I didn't invite you here today to run the gauntlet like that."

"Don't worry about it, Mrs. Browning. I'm not offended. To tell the truth, I expected something like that to happen. I know how men like Randall work. My brother was one. I apologize for being so crude."

Though Sarah knew her mother was tremendously embarrassed, the smile she sent Owen was genuine. "Son, I think after this you'd better call me Eliza. You've earned it."

After the remains of the disastrous dinner had been cleared away, Eliza invited everyone to move to the backyard and play some badminton. Kathy and Randall declined, citing the fussy baby as an excuse to leave early. Sarah didn't think she imagined the tension level receding as they pulled out of the driveway. She said as much to Gilly.

"That wasn't bad at all," Gilly replied. "And yes, I'm being facetious. But your Owen held his own nicely. You should be proud of him."

"I am. I'm also deeply ashamed, Gilly. Talk about a trial by fire."

Her friend poked her in the ribs. "Hey, at least you know he's not going to turn tail and run away at the first sign of trouble. Come on. Let's join our men and whip their butts."

Sarah shook her head, hiding a yawn. "I can't. I've been up since five, and I didn't sleep last night. Get Mama to go out there with you."

Gilly pleaded with her to reconsider, but Sarah wasn't kidding when she said she wasn't up to it.

"If I sit down for more than five minutes, I'll be asleep, I'm so tired. I'd do you more harm than good."

She helped convince Eliza to go out in her stead, happy to see her mother smiling again. Once they started playing, Sarah stretched out on the glider, wincing as her sore feet throbbed. Even though they'd not let her help with the dishes and she had been resting ever since lunch, she still felt as if she'd walked twenty miles.

The next thing she knew, someone was gently shaking her awake.

"Sarah. Wake up, sleepyhead."

"Owen?"

"None other. Come on. If you don't wake up, I'll have to carry you inside."

Sarah smiled. "Then I'm not waking up. You could kiss me awake. I like your kisses."

He gave a little groan. "Sarah, your mom is standing here."

"I think you're going to have to carry her, Owen. She's exhausted. I heard her tossing and turning all night, and she was up before the sun. Poor thing." Eliza's tone was gentle, though amused. "Do you need Jack's help?"

Sarah felt strong arms slide underneath her, and she pried her eyes a bit. When she saw Owen held her, she rested her head against his shoulder.

"No, I have her. Where do you want me to put her?"

The voices faded away, and the next thing she knew, Sarah was on her bed. Someone tugged off her shoes, and she groaned with relief.

"I'll bet her feet are killing her. They'll be sore tomorrow," her mother said from somewhere nearby. A soft quilt was tucked around Sarah's shoulders, and she smelled Eliza's perfume. "Do you want to stay up here for a while?"

"If you don't mind, I'd like to, Mrs. Browning."

"Eliza. You ought to kick off your own shoes and lie down. You look almost as tired as Sarah. I'll bet you didn't get much sleep last night either, did you?"

"No, ma'am."

"I'm going to head back downstairs. Stay as long as you need to, Owen. I think the two of you need some time together right now. I'm going to close the door, as I'm trusting you." Her mother's voice grew distant, and Sarah figured Eliza was leaving the room.

"I won't abuse that trust, I swear to you."

"I know you won't. There's a frying pan, a shotgun, and a butcher knife downstairs," Eliza teased. "And your mother raised you better than to take advantage of a young woman under her own mother's nose."

The door clicked softly closed. Sarah heard Owen let out a pent-up breath.

"Come lie beside me?" she asked, her voice raspy from fatigue.

"I thought you were asleep."

Sarah opened her eyes enough to see him. "I am. Please?"

He didn't respond for a minute, then nodded. Sarah watched as took off his shoes and unbuttoned his dress shirt, revealing the white T-shirt beneath it. He untucked both shirts from his pants and moved around to the other side of the bed.

Heart pounding, she waited as he eased into bed beside her, drawing the quilt over both of them. Sarah turned over, going into his arms, and Owen kissed her temple. Snuggling her head onto his firm shoulder, she relaxed for the first time in two days and promptly fell asleep.

CHAPTER TWENTY-THREE

THE ROOM WAS DARK WHEN Owen awoke. Crickets chirped, their chorus loud in the silence of the night outside the open window. From somewhere downstairs came the sound of a radio playing quietly. He stretched carefully, not wanting to disturb Sarah, whose back was pressed up to his front. They were snuggled close together in a warm cocoon, and he buried his face in the spot where her neck met her shoulder. His hand was curved around one of her breasts, and as he realized that, his hand contracted.

"Mmmm, that's nice," Sarah whispered, startling him.

"I'm sorry." Owen moved his hand, but she brought one of hers up and kept it where it was. He closed his eyes. "Sarah, that's torture. Your family's downstairs. I promised your mother I wouldn't take advantage of you."

"You're not taking advantage of me. I'm taking advantage of you." She rolled over, her hip brushing his erection. The movement dislodged his hand from her breast, but he barely noticed. Facing him, Sarah threw her leg over his hip, bringing their bodies into contact from chest to pelvis. She kissed him.

"Stop," he managed after a moment, pulling back to draw in a deep breath. "Sarah, anyone could walk in."

"We'd hear them on the stairs. I'm not trying to seduce you, Owen. I just need to touch you a little, have you touch me."

Even as he tried to caution her, his hands moved down her back and pulled her closer. "A little touch turns into something more, and the next thing you know, we're standing in front of a preacher with your brother shoving a shotgun in my back."

Sarah stilled. "Would that be the worst thing in the world?"

"Being married to you? No. Being forced to the altar like that? Yes, it would. I won't compromise you."

He could feel her disappointment, and he gave her waist a little squeeze. "There's nothing I'd like more than to touch you, kiss you, make love to you," he said, his voice going husky as he thought about what all that would entail. "But we can't. Especially not with your mother downstairs."

Sarah buried her face in his throat, and he heard her swallow. "I know."

Owen rolled onto his back, pulling her so that she was once again resting against his side. He ran a shaking hand down her hair, smoothing it back off her face, until he calmed. "This probably isn't the best time to ask this, give our current physical circumstances, but... how do you know about *The Kama Sutra?*"

Sarah snorted, then groaned. "No, it's not the best time. My roommate at Berea had it, and she gave it to me when I left."

"I didn't think Berea was that kind of school," he teased.

Sarah pinched his side. "It isn't. And we probably would have gotten in trouble if our house mother had found it." She rubbed his chest, and then, in a hesitant voice, asked, "How do you know about it?"

"Harlan sent me a copy from Germany. I guess he found it in a brothel and thought it would be hilarious to send his freak of a brother that sort of book. It certainly wasn't something he sent because of any affection or respect."

Sarah propped herself up on her elbow. "He really was a nasty piece of work, wasn't he?"

"Yeah. He was."

"So…"

Owen waited for her to finish, but her voice trailed off. "So, what?" Thanks to his night vision, he could see her pretty well in the dim room, and he watched her tuck her chin and look down at his chest.

"So, did you read it?"

"Did you?"

She raised her head. "I asked you first."

Owen sat up a little, pushing her back onto her back so that he could lean over her. "I read it, yes. Read it, studied it, wondered about it. Your turn."

Sarah's eyes closed. "Yes."

Owen's heart raced, imagining Sarah using the book, and every muscle in his body went rigid. "Damn." He straightened and got out of bed, adjusting his erection so that it wasn't trying to tear through his zipper. "We need to… I shouldn't have… crap."

"Owen? Are you angry?"

He heard Sarah move on the bed behind him, and then her soft hand touched his back. He jerked and moved across the room to stand in front of a chest of drawers.

"I'm not mad," he assured her over his shoulder. "I'm having a hard time not laying you down on that bed and damning the consequences. You should probably head downstairs."

"Oh." She didn't move, and Owen didn't know how much longer he could hold out.

"Sarah? Now would be good."

"It's that bad, then?" she asked, but she started moving toward the door.

"Oh, yeah. I'll be down as soon as I can."

"Okay. I'll leave the door open." She left the room, and Owen heard her pad down the hall to the bathroom. After a couple of minutes, she came out and went downstairs.

Owen finally felt the desire wind down, and he buried his face in his hands. "Too close, Owen, that was too close." Hearing steps coming up the stairs that were too heavy to be Sarah's, the last of his arousal faded. "Thank you, God." He turned to leave the room just as Jack appeared in the doorway.

"I was wondering if she'd tied you to the bed or something," Sarah's brother drawled. He leaned against the doorjamb, blocking Owen's exit. "I'm not sure I trust you with her."

Owen felt his hackles rise, but he tamped down the annoyance. "She's your sister. You aren't supposed to trust me with her."

Jack grunted. "True. So what happened between the two of you that had her so upset? She doesn't cook like that unless she's having a really hard time with something."

"That's between Sarah and myself, with all due respect."

"See, that's where we're not going to agree." Jack took a step inside the room, coming toe-to-toe with Owen. "I think you hurt my sister yesterday, Campbell. And I already have one brother-in-law that's worth far less than a piece of shit on the bottom of my shoe. I don't need another."

Owen met the other man's eyes. All he saw was genuine concern for Sarah, and he gave an internal sigh. "We didn't have a fight; I didn't harm her. We discussed some things from my past, and it was a hard thing for both of us to go through." Jack started to speak, but Owen held up a hand. "No, it wasn't about another woman. It was about my parents. And that's all I'm saying. The rest is between her and me."

"You're sure? That's all it was? Sarah was pretty damned upset."

"It was a pretty damned difficult discussion. We were both torn up afterwards."

Jack was clearly having a hard time believing Owen's explanation, but he stood down. "You know, if you weren't dating my sister, I'd probably like you." He stepped back into the hall.

Owen picked up his boots and followed. "But I am dating your sister. So where does that leave us?"

"It leaves us in a holding pattern until I have more information."

"Then I guess that'll have to do for now."

Owen left not long after he came downstairs, and Sarah, eager to see what was in the book he'd given her, rushed upstairs to retrieve it. She closed the door to her room, and after changing into a short nightgown, curled up on the bed under the blanket she'd shared with Owen.

The book's cover was plain, the title and author's name embossed in gold foil. When she opened it, a thick envelope fell out with her name written across the front. She recognized Owen's bold handwriting.

Laying the letter in her lap, she read the inscription he'd written inside the cover. *"To Sarah, with much devotion. H.O. McLemore."* At the end of his signature, he'd sketched a single red rose. Closing her eyes, Sarah brought the book to her chest and held it close.

After a minute, she laid the book aside and picked up the envelope. The paper was heavy, a thick, creamy stationery that reminded her of the paper her high school teacher had given them to use in art class. She broke the seal and pulled out a folded letter.

Dearest Sarah,

For someone who makes his living with his words, this letter is incredibly difficult to write. There are so many emotions coursing through me right now I hardly know where to begin. I've started this letter a dozen times. Even as I write, I don't know that I'll find the courage to give it to you. And I don't know if you'll accept it even if I do.

This isn't the first letter I've written to you. Far, far from it. There have been others, and maybe someday I'll share them with you. Once it won't shock you too much to read them.

I wouldn't blame you if you hated me right now. I didn't tell you a very important truth about myself. That hurt you, which I never intended. Please believe me if you believe nothing else.

Well, believe one more thing—I care about you deeply. More than I've ever cared about anyone. And I am terrified by how much you mean to me. But I keep coming back to you, knowing that you could crush me if you wished. I can't stay away. I don't want to stay away.

That day by the pool, when you found me there, and I told you to leave, all I wanted was to pull you closer. I wanted to take your hand, touch your face, smell your hair. (Did I ever tell you how much I love the smell of your hair?)

I wanted to find out how you saw the world, know what made you happy or sad. I wanted to make you smile and make you mine. So I sent you away. I couldn't do anything else then; I was too afraid.

When I received your letter apologizing, even though I'd been an ass to you, it took everything in me to not rush to the library and beg your forgiveness. I spent some time with my uncle after that, and he knocked some sense into me. Hard work will do that sometimes.

I thank God every day that he did.

Someday, I'd like to take you to meet him and my aunt and all their brood. They're a noisy bunch, but they are good people. You would like them.

Sarah, I have other secrets. I worry every day and every night that when I finally unearth the courage to tell you about them, you'll hate me. You'll turn your back and walk away, perhaps rightly so, and you'll take my heart with you. I don't know if I'll survive that. But I won't stop seeing you in order to protect myself. It's too late for that. I think it has been since the first moment I laid eyes on you.

I'll close now and leave you with this—even if we part tomorrow, I'll never regret the time we've had. You've brought a light into my world that I didn't know existed, not for me anyhow. I love you, Sarah Jane Browning. I'm not saying that to make you feel obligated to return the sentiment. It's a pure statement of fact. I love you.

Yours in body, mind, and spirit,

Owen

By the time she finished reading, Sarah was crying so hard she could barely see the words. Alongside his signature, Owen had sketched a small deer. It had ears that were a little too big for its body, and the way it stood, it reminded her of the deer she'd seen at the pool. She wondered if Owen had seen the same deer and committed it to memory.

She kept swiping at the tears with one hand and held on to the letter with the other. Laying it down on her nightstand so she wouldn't get it wet and smear the ink, she fought to regain control of her emotions. He loved her. He actually loved her. She'd seen hints of the powerful emotion in him, but the depth of his feelings surprised her.

Shaking, she started laughing with joy, quietly at first, but then louder. Not wanting her mother or Jack to hear, she buried her face in one of her pillows. Owen's cologne was on the pillowcase, and she nearly suffocated herself trying to inhale his scent.

Even through her wonder, Sarah realized that whatever secrets he still held, they caused him tremendous pain. Owen seemed so certain that when he revealed them to her, she'd abandon him. Sarah wondered if that was what had happened with his father, but it made little sense based on what she knew. She couldn't imagine what kind of secret Owen could have had at that young age that would have caused the separation.

She got up, ready to go downstairs and call him to let him know how she felt, but changed her mind. Given that they were on a party line and anyone in the holler could listen in, a phone call was definitely not the way to deliver her message. Sitting on the edge of her bed, she picked up the letter and read it again.

As she stared at the drawing of the deer, she knew what she needed to do. She went down the hall to her mother's room and knocked.

"Come in," Eliza said.

Sarah opened the door. "Mama, I need a favor."

***

When the call came the next morning at eight o'clock, Owen had just sat down to work on an idea for a new book. "Hello?"

"Owen? It's Eliza. Are you busy this morning?"

Puzzled, Owen frowned. "Not too busy. Why? Is everything okay? Sarah?"

"She's fine. But she gave me a letter for you and asked me to call you and tell you I had it. You know, I've not passed love notes since high school."

Taken aback, Owen cleared his throat. "Um, okay. I'll head right down. Thank you."

He hung up, and for several seconds, he stared at the phone. Shaking off the reverie, he went downstairs and pulled his boots on, then headed down the mountain.

When he came out of the woods at Sarah's house, Eliza was in the side yard, talking to a man in overalls. Owen recognized him as Silas Combs, a farmer who lived down at the mouth of the holler. Silas raised a hand in greeting, and Owen nodded.

"Been a while since I've seen you around here," the older man said as they shook hands. "Where've you been keeping yourself?"

"Up on the mountain, as usual. How've you been?"

"Oh, fair to middlin'. Can't complain, and it wouldn't do me any good if I could." He turned to Eliza. "I'll head up after the sun comes out and dries up the ground a little more. We'll get that ground ready to go for you in no time."

"Thanks, Silas. I appreciate it." After he left, she turned to Owen. "I guess you ran all the way down here."

Owen grinned. "Not all the way."

Eliza laughed, then pulled a sealed envelope out of her pocket. "Well, here it is. Sarah bounced out of here with springs in her shoes this morning. Can you come in for coffee?"

"No. I should probably get back up the hill. Are you getting ready to put the garden in?"

"Yes, this evening if all goes well."

"I could come by and lend a hand if that'd be okay."

The smile that was so much like Sarah's spread across her face. "Why don't you do that?"

He bent and pressed a kiss to her cheek. "I'll see you later. Thanks for this," he said, holding up the letter.

"Oh, you're welcome. Have a good day, sweetie."

Owen walked as normally as he could into the woods, even though adrenaline was pumping through his veins. As soon as he was out of sight of the house, he stopped and opened the letter.

Dearest Owen,

I love you, too.

Yours,

Sarah

Owen read the words five times before they truly sank in. When they did, he jumped into the air, letting out a whoop that startled the birds from the trees. Elation like nothing he'd ever felt washed over him. He didn't know what the future held, but the present was pretty damned good, and that was enough.

CHAPTER TWENTY-FOUR

SARAH WAS AMAZED AT HOW quickly Gilly moved to get the wedding plans pulled together. She and Jack had originally planned to get married in June of next year, but without missing a beat, she'd cobbled together stunning results. The flowers, the wedding gown and dresses for the bridesmaids, the suits for the groomsmen—it was almost as though she'd known the wedding date would be pushed up and had planned accordingly.

"If I ever get married, I know who to come to," she told Gilly. They were in one of the private rooms in the back of the church, and Sarah was helping Gilly with her veil.

"I'll be glad to help, and you know it. You might ought to start thinking about your own wedding, you know. I'm expecting Owen to propose any day now."

Sarah bit her lip and met Gilly's eyes in the mirror. "You think so?"

"Oh, yes. Would you accept him?"

"I believe I would." Taking care not to muss the braided twist she'd just finished, Sarah gave Gilly a hug. "I'm so glad my brother is marrying you."

Gilly reached up and squeezed her hand. "So am I."

The wedding went beautifully, and by two o'clock, Gilly and Jack were on their way to a honeymoon at Cumberland Falls. Gilly's parents had given them a week in the honeymoon suite at the nicest hotel in the area as a wedding gift.

Sarah rode home with her mother, her aunt Nancy, and Owen, who drove them in Sarah's car. Nancy and Eliza kept up a steady stream of chatter in the back seat, but Sarah was lost in thought.

Owen reached a hand across the seat to touch her arm. "You okay?"

"Yes. Just thinking about things." Sarah turned her hand over and captured his fingers.

Once they reached the house, Eliza insisted Owen come in and eat with them. They lingered over the late lunch, and by the time he left, it was nearing five o'clock.

"I'll walk you out," Sarah said. When her mother and aunt both giggled, she sent them repressive looks.

"Hold on," Eliza said. She hurried around the table and gave Owen a long, solid hug. "You take care of my baby girl while I'm away, all right?"

"I will," he promised.

"And take care of yourself, too. I think a lot of you, young man."

Owen gave her another hug and murmured something in her ear too low for Sarah to hear.

Eliza pulled back and studied him, a soft smile on her face. "Oh, I think I can do that."

As they walked out to the edge of the woods, Sarah sent him a curious look. "What was that all about?"

Owen grinned at her. "I'll tell you later. What time are they leaving tomorrow?"

Because the wedding date had been pushed up, Eliza had convinced Nancy to extend her visit by a week. Sarah had noticed her mother getting more and more antsy. Eliza was nearing the end of her ability to remain in the house she'd shared with Ira. Sarah had talked about it briefly with Owen, but was trying to ignore Eliza's departure as long as she could. She figured she could fall apart once her mother was gone.

"Early. Probably as soon as it's daylight, if I had to guess. They've got a long drive ahead of them."

They didn't stop walking until they were in the woods, out of view of the house. Owen pulled her close, and Sarah rested her head on his shoulder. They stood there for a while, simply holding each other.

"What time do you want me here tomorrow?" he finally asked.

Sarah pulled back and shrugged. "I don't know. I can't think today." Rubbing her eyes with the heels of her hands, she sighed. "Anytime is fine, I guess. Whenever you can and want to."

"Okay. Listen, you call me if you need me. Promise me that, Sarah." He cupped her face and tipped her chin so that she met his gaze. "I'm only a phone call away."

Lifting her hands to touch his face, Sarah rose up on her toes and kissed him. The kiss contained some heat but was a more gentle, affectionate exchange than anything. Breaking away, she wrapped her arms around his neck tightly. "I love you."

Owen's arms tightened around her waist, and he straightened, holding her off the ground effortlessly. "I never tire of hearing that, you know. I love you, too."

With reluctance, Sarah let her arms down from around his neck, and Owen set her back on her feet. "I guess I'd better go in. I'll see you tomorrow."

"Call me. I can be down here in ten minutes."

Blowing him a kiss, Sarah started the walk back to the house. She knew she only had to make it one more day, and then she could fall apart. She was very glad because she didn't know if she could hold herself together much longer.

Later that night, after everyone had gone to bed, a knock came at Sarah's door. She opened it to see her mother standing in the hall, a small package in her hands.

"Mind if I come in?" Eliza asked.

"Of course not."

Eliza walked over to the window, stared out into the darkened yard, and sighed. "I'm going to miss you, but I'm so very ready to be gone from here. I hope you understand that, sweetie."

"I do. I'll miss you, too, but I want to see you happy again."

"I'd settle for content, to tell the truth." Eliza turned and held out the brown paper-wrapped package.

As Sarah took it, she was surprised that it didn't weigh more. "What's this?"

Eliza's cheeks turned red. "Something I think you're going to need. Go ahead. Open it."

Curious, Sarah sat down on the edge of the bed and un-wrapped the paper. When she saw the contents, she blinked and looked back up at Eliza, not understanding. "Condoms?"

Her mother twisted her hands in front of her and moved to sit next to Sarah. "Let me start by saying that I'm not ushering you to go out and have sex. I want to make that clear. I'm not giving you permission. Of course, you're twenty-one, so you're responsible for your own self, but still. I'm your mother."

"Um, yes. You are."

"I've seen the way you and Owen look at each other, Sarah, and I know it's only a matter of time. I'd like to see you wait until you're married, but I won't shun you if you don't."

Sarah didn't know what to say. She'd expected her mother to give her a parting gift, much as Eliza had when Sarah had left for college, but she certainly hadn't expected *condoms*. Considering that birth control for women was illegal in most states, the gift was significant.

The situation struck her funny bone, and she laughed. It was a simple snicker at first, but before long, it had turned into a full, rolling belly laugh. Within seconds, she and Eliza were holding on to each other for support, the hilarity taking them over.

"Oh, Mama. What am I going to do without you?" That quickly, Sarah's laughter turned to tears.

"I suspect you're going to do just fine, Sarah Jane." Eliza held her, and when the storm was over, she handed Sarah a tissue. "Now, back to these condoms. Do you remember how to use them?"

"Yes. That was a hard lesson to forget." She shared a grin with her mother as they remembered the incident in question. Shortly after Kathy had announced her pregnancy with Moira when she was seventeen, Eliza had sat both girls down with a box of condoms and a bunch of bananas. What had started as a serious lecture on sex education had quickly devolved, and all three of them had laughed until they cried.

"That was one of the first times I think I really felt like an adult. And probably the last time Kathy and I did anything remotely close to a sisterly activity."

"I wish that was different. But she's changed so much since she married Randall. We can only do what we can do, Sarah."

"I know."

Eliza looked down at her painted toenails. "There are other ways to prevent pregnancy, like the vinegar sponge approach. That and condoms are what your father and I used." When Sarah winced, Eliza sent her a look. "I'd rather have you a little uncomfortable with the discussion than expecting a child before you're ready. It's ridiculous that women don't have more control over when they bear children. In this day and age especially. Maybe by the time you have grown daughters, that will have changed."

"I know. And I appreciate the advice."

"The kit contains condoms, sponges, and vinegar. Promise me you'll use these things if you and Owen decide to become intimate."

Though embarrassed, Sarah was deeply grateful Eliza had taken the time to obtain the devices for her. She nodded. "Okay. And I'm not planning on it. I promise you. But if we do… and if I run out of these," she said, lifting the box, "what do I do?"

Eliza raised an eyebrow. "Well, if you run out of these things, you'd better be married. Or else I'll come back up here and borrow Jack's shotgun." She bumped Sarah's shoulder with hers. "But if something happens and you need more, go to Rosemarie. I talked to her about it last week."

Mortified, Sarah stared at her mother. "Mama! You talked to Gilly's mother about this? About me and Owen? I'll never be able to face her!"

"Of course you will. And if it makes you feel better, she had the same talk with Gilly as soon as she found out Jack was home. Back when we were growing up, Sarah, women had little choice in the matter. Shoot, we still don't. But Rosemarie and I both feel like our daughters should have that choice."

"What if Owen won't use condoms?"

"Well, that's simple. In order for him to get what he wants, you have to get what you want. And that's him wearing a condom. But I doubt he'd have much objection. He strikes me as a reasonable man."

"And if we both want it?"

Eliza looked at her askew. "Maybe I should have this conversation with Owen, too."

Just the thought of *that* scenario sent them both off into another round of giggles. Once the humor died down, Sarah sighed. "If things don't work out between us, I may come to Georgia."

"If you need to come, don't hesitate. But I'm betting you won't need to. I think Owen's a good man, and I think you'll have a ring on your finger by the end of summer, if not sooner."

Sarah smiled, wistful. "You think so? Gilly said something similar to me. If he proposes, will you come back for the wedding?"

Her mother gave her a one-armed hug. "Of course." She smoothed Sarah's hair and kissed her cheek. "I'll let you get to sleep. We're going to have a hard day tomorrow, and we need to face it as rested as we can."

"Goodnight, Mama."

Eliza closed the door behind her, and Sarah stared down at the box. Curious, she sifted through the contents. She found and unfolded an instruction sheet, and her eyes widened as she read how to use the vinegar and sponges.

"Oh, my. That's not what I expected." She thought the sponge went inside the condom, but apparently not. She put the paper back and closed the box, then tucked it into her nightstand. Sarah wondered if she'd have the courage to bring up the subject of contraception to Owen. As she thought about Kathy and how miserable her sister seemed to have become with her life, talking to Owen about condoms didn't seem like a hard thing to do after all.

CHAPTER TWENTY-FIVE

S ARAH'S MOTHER AND NANCY WERE on the road
before seven o'clock the next morning. Their parting had
been difficult, but Sarah held back most of her tears until
they pulled out of the driveway. That said, they probably hadn't
even reached the mouth of the holler before she was upstairs,
stretched out across her bed, sobbing into her pillow. After the
tears stopped, exhausted by her grief, she fell asleep.

A persistent knocking woke her sometime later. Groggy and
disoriented, she stumbled to one of her windows, which overlooked the backyard, and raised the glass. "Hello?"

Owen's face appeared over the edge of the roof. "Hey. Are
you okay?"

"I'm sorry. I fell asleep after they left. I'll let you in."

"Hang on. I'll come up." He disappeared, and a few seconds
later, his shoes came up over the edge of the porch roof to land
on the metal surface. He went to a nearby oak and climbed up its
trunk. Easing out onto a branch that hung out over the roof, he
dropped onto the sloping surface with an agility that surprised
her. In no time, he'd grabbed his shoes and was standing outside
her window, a silly grin on his face.

"Knock, knock."

Sarah felt her own smile start, and she slid up the screen so he could come in. "Well, I can't say this has ever happened before."

"I hope not." He set down his shoes and replaced the screen. "Hi."

"Hi yourself." Remembering she was clad in her nightgown, Sarah grabbed her robe and put it on. "Come on downstairs. Have you eaten?"

"Not yet. You?"

"No. I was too upset to eat earlier."

Once they reached the downstairs, he stopped her. "Don't I get a hug?" With a choked sigh, Sarah wrapped her arms around him and clung tightly. She didn't cry again, but the pain was still there.

"Did they get on the road okay?" Owen asked.

"Yes. You should have seen Mama's face; she was so excited. I shouldn't feel so bad that she's going, not when she's so happy."

"Sure, you should. I imagine she felt something very similar when you left to go to college."

Sarah let out a deep breath against his chest. "I would bet she probably did. I snuck a present into her suitcase last night, just like she did for me every time I left for Berea. It's the little things sometimes, you know?"

"I do."

Feeling some of the sadness loosen, she moved back. "How do you feel about pancakes?" Owen's stomach growled, and Sarah laughed. "I guess that answers that question. Come on. I'll feed you."

After they'd eaten, cleanup went fast, a task Sarah was pleased to note that Owen stepped in to help with without being asked.

"So what do you want to do today?" he asked as he dried his hands on a dishtowel. He slung it around her neck and used it to pull her closer, dropping a kiss onto her nose.

Sarah rested her hands on his chest. "I don't know. All the chores are done, and the laundry's caught up. What do you think?"

"We could drive over to Buckhorn to the lake, rent a boat, go swimming. Have a picnic."

"That sounds nice. But the more I think about it, I'd rather not be around other people. Would you mind if we stayed here? We could still have a picnic and swim up at the pool."

"We could do that. I'll have to run back to the house and get my swim trunks."

Sarah pulled away and sent him an impish grin. "Or you could go skinny-dipping." Owen's eyes widened, and she laughed. "You can borrow Jack's swim trunks. He left them in the washer and forgot to pack them. They should fit you."

He shook his head. "You are impertinent. I don't know. I'm liking the idea of skinny-dipping."

Sarah felt her face heat, and she swiped the dishtowel from him. "Behave."

"Me? You started it."

"No, not me." She swatted him with the towel. "Let's get a picnic packed, and I'll go change."

Once the basket was packed, Sarah gave Owen Jack's swim trunks, pushed him toward her brother's bedroom, and excused herself. Upstairs, she dug through her dresser, pulling out the new bathing suit she'd gotten when she and Gilly had gone to Lexington two weeks earlier to shop for a wedding dress. The cornflower-blue suit was more daring than anything Sarah had ever worn. Though not terribly revealing, the two-piece left her midriff bare. After putting it on, she considered the box her mother had given her and thought about throwing it into her bag, but she was too embarrassed. She pulled a flowered sundress on over the bathing suit and, after stopping by the bathroom closet to get two large towels, hurried down to Owen.

"I'm ready." She made sure she had her house keys, and they set out. "Did the trunks fit?"

"They did."

The day was partly sunny. Clouds were moving in, and Sarah figured it would probably rain later. As they got closer to the pool, Sarah felt her tension ease, and she breathed freely for the first time in days.

"I needed this. Thank you," she told Owen as he helped her up over the large step up onto the top of the boulder. They spread the blankets out on the rock and sat down. "It's probably still too cool to swim, don't you think, being only May?"

"Probably. We might have to stay here for quite a while today before it gets warm enough to get in."

Chin resting on her upraised knees, Sarah turned to look at him. "Yet you were swimming in there a couple of months ago. Weren't you freezing to death?"

Owen shrugged. He unbuttoned his shirt and removed it, leaving him clad in his T-shirt, then stretched out on his back beside her. "Not really." He squinted against the sun to look up at her and grinned.

"Uh-huh. I'll bet you jumped out about as quick as you jumped in."

"It wasn't a long swim," he conceded. "So…"

"Mmmm. So."

"We haven't really talked about my letter," Owen said softly.

"I know. And I've wanted to talk to you about it, believe me. I don't suppose you've written me another letter, have you?"

"Maybe."

She poked him in the belly, and he jumped. "Where is it? Can I have it?"

"I don't know. I think I need a letter back from you first."

"I sent you a letter!"

"You did. And I keep it with me all the time. But I'd like something a little longer."

"You... you stinker." With a growl, she started tickling him.

Owen's eyes flared with surprise, and he grabbed her hands. Pulling her close, he tucked a hand behind her head and rolled so that she was underneath him. "Oh, you've done it now." Without warning, he ducked his head into the curve of her neck and blew against the bare skin of her shoulder, making a rude noise. At the same time, he started tickling her ribs. Within seconds, Sarah was shrieking with laughter, begging him to stop. He did, hovering over her with a grin. Her hands captured in his, he drew her arms up over her head. The movement brought their bodies more firmly into contact. "I have you now."

"So you do. What are you going to do with me?"

He lowered his head, rubbing her cheek with his. "I figured I'd love you."

Sarah's heart melted. He lifted his head enough to kiss her, and his grip around her hands loosened. The kiss, which started out slow and gentle, quickly picked up in heat and intensity. Before long, they were both breathing hard.

When Owen again buried his face in the curve of her neck, he let out a deep groan. "Sarah, you destroy me."

She turned her head so she could kiss his ear. "You do the same thing to me." She ran her hand through his hair. Owen shuddered, and she did it again.

"Okay, this is not a good idea," he said. Before Sarah could stop him, he levered himself up and stood. "I'm going to take a cold swim. You stay here."

Blinking with surprise, Sarah sat up. "Owen?"

"Unless you want to find yourself in front of a preacher today, stay up here." He took the path down to the pool, and after several seconds, there was a splash. Sarah moved to the edge of the rock to look down into the pool. Owen surfaced as she settled down to watch. His clothes were in a pile on the rock alongside the water.

"Cold?" Sarah called down to him, her heart racing at the picture he made. The water was clear enough that she could see the tops of his shoulders and part of his chest, and her hands itched with wanting.

He shook his hair out of his eyes. "Not cold enough," he replied and ducked back down under the water.

Sarah tried, she really did, but the temptation was too strong. Before she could let herself think, she stood and stripped off the sundress, then ran down the path. Owen resurfaced just as she jumped into the pool.

"What the hell? Sarah!" When she came back up, he was glaring at her. "Get out! I'm not strong enough to turn you away right now."

Instead, Sarah swam over to him, her teeth chattering. Her toes barely brushed the bottom of the pool, but Owen was standing, and she used his shoulders to hold herself up. "If you want me out, you'll have to put me out."

She closed the distance and kissed him.

CHAPTER TWENTY-SIX

O WEN WAS AGHAST. HE'D THOUGHT she understood the danger, but apparently not. Still, he had to try again. Pulling back, he gasped for breath. His heart raced, and his lungs struggled as though he'd run a mile. "Sarah, I mean it. I want you too much right now." He grasped her arms, intending to pull them from around his neck, but he couldn't find the willpower to do it. She was too close at hand and too close to naked.

"Please don't make me go," she whispered.

As though they had a mind of their own, his hands slid from her arms and down her back, pulling her hips closer to his. Sarah wrapped her legs around his waist. The movement brought her into full contact with his arousal, and they both gasped.

"Oh, God. Sarah, we can't do this."

"I know, but I want... Owen, please. Do something. I need you to do something. Make the ache go away."

She moved her hips against his, and Owen almost exploded on the spot. The rush of pleasure, the need to be inside her, nearly drove him to his knees. With the last ounce of willpower he possessed, he disentangled her limbs from around him and gently pushed her away. He was so aroused he was surprised the pool wasn't boiling. From the Sarah's panting, he figured she was in the same state he was.

"Look, we have to think about this." He spoke more to himself than to her, and when she started back toward him, he held out his hands. "Just stop. Give me a minute." His thoughts racing, Owen tried to figure out what to do. He wanted Sarah, of that there was no doubt, but he knew she was vulnerable at the moment.

They had options, he knew. They didn't have to have actual sex in order for both of them to achieve satisfaction. If they didn't take the edge off the desire, though, they were liable to tear each other apart trying to stop it.

Sarah went to the edge of the pool and boosted herself out, then hurried up to the top of the rock. With a curse, Owen followed.

"Wait. Sarah, hang on a second here."

"No. I can't... I shouldn't have been so forward. I'm sorry." Her voice was choked with tears, and after a brief struggle, she got back into her dress.

Frustration and fear caused his temper to flare. Owen started to yell but stopped himself just in time. Instead, he lowered his voice and carefully modulated his words. "I'm not saying no. Please, please listen to me."

She gathered up the blankets and shoved them into the bag. Owen stepped closer to her and gently placed his hands on her shoulders. They went rigid, but she didn't move away.

"We can't make love, Sarah. Not like this, all in a rush. And as much as I would kill to be inside you right now, we have to wait for that. But there are things we can do. Things that will make the ache better. It's not full lovemaking, but I think it will be enough. For now."

Her shoulders drooped under his hands, and she let him turn her around to face him. The misery on her face sent a guilty lance through him. Cupping her face, he whispered kisses over her eyebrows, nose, and cheeks, finally settling on her mouth. It took a moment, but Sarah finally responded and kissed him back. Owen kept the kiss light. When he lifted his head, she didn't look as upset as she had before.

"What exactly do you have in mind?"

"Let's go back to the house," he said. "We'll need privacy."

He thought she was going to refuse, but then she closed her eyes and nodded. "Okay."

Sarah was so nervous as they went back to the house, wondering what was going to happen, that Owen had to guide her like a child. Her behavior, her eagerness despite his best attempts to ward her off, mortified her. She'd jumped on him like a shameless hussy, not the proper young woman her parents had raised her to be.

Once they reached the back door, she turned to face him, unable to meet his eyes. "I shouldn't have come on to you like I did. I'm so sorry. I can't tell you how much. I forced myself on you, and that was wrong. I don't expect you to come in."

He took the key from her hand and unlocked the door. "Go inside."

Eyes downcast, Sarah turned and went into the kitchen, keeping her back to the door. She didn't want to see him leave, and she waited for him to shut the door behind her and go, but he followed her. He locked the door and laid the key on the kitchen table. When his arms came up and pulled her back into him, she shut her eyes, a hot tear escaping down her cheek. It landed on his arm.

"Tears? Oh, Sarah, no." Turning her, Owen wiped the wetness away with his thumbs. "Look at me."

He forced her to meet his gaze, and he took her hands, sliding them up and around his neck. "Hold on."

Before Sarah could react, he stooped and lifted her into his arms, then started toward the stairs. "Owen?"

He stopped at the foot of the stairs, and the heat in his eyes kindled an answering flame in her. "If you want me to stop, tell me. Tell me in plain words. Because otherwise, I'm taking you upstairs, and I'm laying you down on that bed. Then I'm going to show you exactly how much I want you."

Sarah could hardly believe her ears. In answer, she leaned up and kissed him. Owen's arms tightened around her, and he started climbing.

Once they were in her bedroom, he stood her on her feet and closed the door. "I know no one else is here right now, but leaving the door open doesn't feel right."

The room was stuffy, and Sarah opened a window halfway while Owen did the same to the other one. He kicked off his shoes, came back around the foot of the bed, and held out his hand. Trembling, Sarah walked to him. He drew her in, holding her tighter than he'd ever held her. Even as innocent as she was, his arousal was obvious.

"I need to ask you some things," he murmured, his lips moving against her temple. "How much you know about this? I don't want to do anything that's going to frighten you."

"I don't understand," Sarah answered, dazed by the heat of him, the solidness of the muscles pressed so firmly against her.

He gave a faint groan, and flags of color appeared across his cheeks. "Have you ever... how far have you... how much experience do you have?"

"Um, I don't have any. I've only ever been kissed. I've read books, and Mama was very frank." She blushed, remembering the contents of her nightstand. "She gave me a box of condoms before she left."

Owen's eyebrows shot up, and he swallowed. "She did?"

Sarah nodded. Moving a step away from him, she got the box out and handed it to him, then hid her face against his chest.

"I'll be damned." He rubbed his chin on her hair and ran his hand up and down her back in a soothing motion. "Remember those secrets I told you I have?"

"Of course."

"I think it's time for me to let you know one of them."

Drawing back, she frowned. "Just one?"

Owen placed the box on the nightstand and sank down on the edge of the bed. "For now. One's about all I can handle."

Her desire muted somewhat by concern, Sarah sat beside him. "Okay. I'm listening."

He cleared his throat and coughed. He picked up an empty glass from the nightstand. "Could I have some water?"

"Sure. I'll be right back." Hurrying down the hall, Sarah filled the glass. When she returned to her bedroom, Owen was hunched over with his elbows resting on his knees, his hands laced behind his head. He thanked her when she handed him the water and downed most of it in one swallow. Sarah sat back down and waited.

"There's no easy way to say this—I'm not a virgin."

"I'm sorry?"

He sent her an unreadable look. "I'm not a virgin. Considering that enlightening conversation at the dinner table between Kathy and Jack a few weeks ago, I thought it was something you needed to know before we... we…" He gestured to her, then the bed.

A sharp sense of disappointment went through her. She knew men were held to a looser moral standard than women, but she had never considered that Owen might have been intimate with someone. He was so reticent, so reserved, the revelation was a tremendous shock.

"Do you mind explaining?" she stammered.

He fidgeted. "After my mother died, I gave some serious thought to moving to Laurel County. There wasn't much here for me, just the land, and I have family there. So I went down for a few months, stayed with Eli and Amy. It was summer, hotter than Hell itself, and I was hurting." He rubbed his face. "There was a woman, a widow, who Eli knew from the community. She had a farm near his, and he sent me to help her out. We ended up being intimate."

Sarah was dumbstruck. "Oh. I see."

"Do you?" His smile was sad. "It lasted a couple months, and it was two people helping one another through a bad time. She was lonely, and I was trying to find my footing. You have to understand, Sarah," he said, looking down at his hands. "From the time I was thirteen years old, I was convinced I'd never know that sort of affection. I never thought I'd marry, have children. So when we came together that summer, sex was all it was."

Sarah had wrapped her arms around her middle. "But did you love her?"

Owen shook his head. "No. I truly cared for her, wished her nothing but happiness, but we were using each other, and we both knew that. After that summer, I've not seen her except in passing. I came back here, back to the mountain, and I've been celibate since." He blew out a deep breath. "I had to tell you before we went any further. You have the right to know."

Unsure of what she felt, Sarah turned her head and studied him. He didn't look proud of what he'd confessed, but he didn't seem ashamed either. She wasn't sure if she was more comforted by the fact that he hadn't loved the woman or not. "And she was the only one?"

Owen met her gaze squarely. "She was the only one."

Satisfied he was telling the truth, Sarah dropped her gaze to her feet. "I don't know what to say."

"Are you angry?"

"No. I'm disappointed, I guess. And jealous. Though that's ridiculous. I should be grateful you had someone when you needed her."

"I don't think it's ridiculous."

"No?"

He shook his head. "No. If our situations were reversed, I'd have a very hard time dealing with that, I think. Just thinking about it upsets me, so I can imagine you're not thrilled."

Sarah gave a little snort. "No, I'm not thrilled." She picked at the hem of the sundress. "Did you ever tell her you loved her?" She felt as much as saw the start go through him, and then he was on his knees in front of her.

"No. Sarah, look at me." When she met his eyes, he told her again, "I never told her I loved her. You are the only woman I have ever said those words to, and you're the only woman I've ever loved. And I never told her about my writing, either. It wasn't that kind of relationship. Please believe me."

Though certain her sister would have called her all kinds of a fool, Sarah believed him. One of his hands was resting above her knee, and she put her hand on his. "I do."

Owen closed his eyes and laid his head in her lap. Only then did Sarah notice he was trembling. With her free hand, she brushed his hair back off his face.

"I love you so much," he rasped. "And I'd give anything to go back and not have been with her. But I can't. All I can do is promise you I'll never look at another woman as long as I live, Sarah."

"How experienced was she?" Sarah hated herself for asking, but she needed to know. If the woman turned out to be a modern sophisticate, she didn't know how she'd handle the revelation. Sarah was forward thinking, but she wasn't sophisticated and certainly wasn't experienced. The only reason she'd let Owen so close was because she was in love with him.

If it turned out he didn't feel the same, the pain that would cause didn't bear thinking about. Needing to be closer to him, Sarah slid off the bed and onto the floor. Her skirt pooled around her, draping over Owen's thighs.

"She was a widow. Her husband had been gone for several years, and she was young when he died. So I wasn't the first man to be with her after his death. But there weren't a lot of men either." His cheeks turned bright red. "It was a long, rainy summer. And we... let's just say that I learned a lot. Hopefully, I can make things good for you."

Sarah's stomach fluttered. "Why would you think you'd never marry or have a family?"

He played with her fingers and shrugged. "You know about my father, how things were between us. After I moved out to the barn, I let go of the idea that I'd ever have a normal life. It was easier than deluding myself."

Tightening her grip on his hands, Sarah kissed one, then the other. "And now?"

Owen swallowed. "Now, I'm finding that maybe I've been ridiculous about the whole thing."

"No, not ridiculous. Maybe misguided. Reasonably so, given what you went through." Cautiously, she laid her palms flat against his chest. "So, how does this work? How do we...?"

He slid a hand into her loosened hair and pulled her close for a lingering kiss. Sarah's hands curled against his shirt, and she moaned in protest when he broke the contact.

"There aren't any rules," he said in a husky voice. "You tell me what you like, what feels good, what doesn't. If you want to stop, all you have to do is say so."

"But I don't know what I like." Sarah's eyes fluttered closed as Owen kissed his way along her jaw to her ear. When he lightly nipped her earlobe and tugged with his teeth, she arched toward him with a gasp.

"Do you like that?"

She nodded. "Mmmm, yes."

He brought his mouth back to hers. "Open your mouth. Let me in." When she complied, he tightened the grip his hand had on her hair and tilted her head back. What followed was an erotic dance with Owen leading with his lips and tongue. The intensity was almost too much, and Sarah pulled back, gasping for breath. Undeterred, he trailed his open mouth down her throat to lick at the pulse beating frantically in her neck.

"Owen, please…" Her hands were curled tightly around his shoulders, and she forced herself to relax.

He raised his head to look at her. "Please what? Stop?"

"No. Please *don't* stop."

The hand that had been in her hair slipped down, curving around her neck. His thumb brushed against the place he'd just kissed. With his eyes on hers, he brought up his other hand and unbuttoned the bodice of her sundress. He moved her hands off his shoulders and pushed the straps of the dress down over her shoulders, leaving the top of her swimsuit exposed.

He tugged on the dress. "Take this off."

Sarah looked down at where his hand rested against her stomach, under her breasts. "The whole thing?"

He smiled. "Whatever you're comfortable with."

Tamping down her nerves, Sarah put her hand over his. "What about you? You'll still have your shirt on."

"That's easy enough to fix." He pulled the T-shirt off over his head. Sarah hummed with admiration as his muscled chest came into view. Even so early in the year, his skin was darker than hers, and a light dusting of dark hair covered his chest. The patch narrowed to a point as it disappeared into the waistband of his pants. "Your turn."

Cheeks warm, Sarah rose to her knees and drew the sundress over her head. Clad only in the bathing suit, she fought the need to cross her arms over her chest. Instead, she reached tentatively out and placed her hand just over his heart.

"You can touch me," he whispered. "I'd really, really like it if you did."

Growing bolder, she let her hands roam across his chest. As her confidence increased, she explored his muscles with a less tentative touch. When she skimmed the skin above his belly button, Owen sucked in a breath. Sarah stopped, her eyes flying to his.

"You're getting into slightly dangerous territory there," he explained.

"Oh. Do you want me to stop?"

The shake of his head was slow and definitive. "No."

A very long while later, they were lying together, legs entwined. Owen was playing with her hair, and she was tracing the muscles in his arms. "Do you regret what we did?" he asked softly.

They'd stopped short of total intimacy, but a lot of Sarah's innocence had been stripped away that afternoon. She didn't have a single twinge of guilt about that, either.

"No. Not in the least. Do you?"

"No." He brushed her hair back off her face. "You're going to have to marry me, you know."

Sarah was stunned. It took her a long minute to recover enough to speak. "Is that a proposal?"

"No. But it's coming. I wanted you to know that." He kissed her. The kiss had a different feel to it, a deeper intimacy, than the kisses they'd shared previously. Sarah rolled onto her side so that she was facing him. She slid her leg between his and closed her eyes at the feeling of his muscled, hairy legs against hers.

"What we did—is that what sex feels like?" she whispered.

Owen hesitated. "Not exactly. It's more intrusive, more personal. Not in a bad way, but it's different."

Sarah ran her hand down his chest. "Did you do this sort of thing with her?"

"I don't want to talk about her. That was years ago, in the past. Let it stay there?" He traced his finger down her arm.

Sarah frowned. "It's not that I'm asking for details. I'm asking... oh, hell. This is embarrassing." She covered her face with her hands, but Owen tugged them down.

"Don't hide. We can talk about anything here, no fear of judgment or reprisal, as long as we don't deliberately set out to hurt each other. Okay?"

"Okay."

"What is it you want to know?"

She moved her shoulder. "I don't know. I guess what I'm asking is… you said you've read *The Kama Sutra*. Did you try any of that with her?" From the red flush that spread across his face and the way he winced, Sarah knew he had. She felt a flare not only of jealousy, but of curiosity as well. "Can you show me?"

Owen stared at her. "Show you…?"

"What I mean is, if you tried the things in the book, then you know how they work. Or how they don't work. So, can you show me those things?" She would never know where she'd found the courage to ask him.

"All of them?" Owen rose up on his elbow to look down at her.

"Um, maybe not quite all."

Looking as though he couldn't quite believe he was having the conversation, Owen shook his head. "We are definitely going to have to get married."

Sarah sat up and planted a kiss on his bare shoulder. "And then you'll show me?"

When Owen turned and pounced on her, bearing her backward on the bed, Sarah shrieked. He tickled her, his touch quickly turning into a caress.

"Yes, minx. And then I'll show you."

They spent the rest of the day in bed, something Sarah felt she should probably have been embarrassed by, but she couldn't muster the emotion. Mostly they talked, but they also touched each other, loved each other. For the rest of her life, Sarah knew she would look back on that day as one filled with magic and love.

When dusk finally settled in and Owen reluctantly said goodbye at the back door, Sarah almost wept.

"Soon, Sarah. Very soon I'll have you installed on the top of the mountain with me, and we'll never have to say goodbye again." He pressed her against the doorjamb with an intense kiss. "I love you. Love you so much."

"I love you," she said. "I'll see you tomorrow evening after work?"

"Of course. Be careful on the road tomorrow. And call me if you need me tonight." He came back for another kiss. "I don't want to go."

"You could stay."

"No, I couldn't. I've compromised you enough as things stand. I won't give the neighbors anything more to talk about."

With one last, intense kiss, he was gone. Sarah locked the house for the night and went upstairs. As she laid her clothes out for work and drew a hot bath, she couldn't stop thinking about everything that had happened. Owen had as good as proposed to her. If things continued as they were, she'd not be surprised to find herself married by the end of the month.

CHAPTER TWENTY-SEVEN

OWEN COULDN'T STOP SMILING As he walked home. Last week, he'd reached out to a contact in Laurel County who designed jewelry to start the man on creating a ring for Sarah. When he'd hugged Eliza goodbye the night before, he'd asked her to call him with Sarah's ring size, a task Eliza had been all too happy to perform.

All he had to do was plan how and when he wanted to propose. The ring would be ready in a couple of weeks, but Owen wasn't sure he could wait that long.

The only shadow on his happiness was the knowledge that he'd have to confess to Sarah that he was a shifter and that any children they had could be like him. Though he was fairly confident that Sarah would accept him for who he was, there was still a niggling self-doubt in the back of his mind.

When the phone rang at six the next morning, though, everything changed.

Sarah had just gotten up and stumbled downstairs to the kitchen to start the coffee when someone knocked on the back door. Startled, she cautiously approached the door and flipped on the porch light.

"Sarah, it's me."

Sarah recognized Owen's voice and quickly undid the lock. As soon as she opened the door, she knew from the look on his face something was drastically wrong. Her heart stuttered, then took off. "What's wrong?"

"I just got a call. My uncle's house burned down last night. I have to go to Laurel County."

Sarah stood back and let him in, then wrapped her arms around his waist. "Oh, no. I'm so sorry. Is everyone okay?"

"No." Holding on to her as though she were the only anchor in a turbulent sea, he said, "Eli's in terrible shape, from what his son Trent said. They're taking him to Lexington. Everyone else got out okay, but Eli went back to get something, and a timber fell on him. They barely got him out."

Sarah closed her eyes. If his uncle didn't survive, it would devastate Owen. She said a quick prayer for the man and his family. "Is there anything I can do?"

With one last squeeze, Owen pulled back. "No. Just pray. I don't know how long I'll be gone. Five of their kids, teenagers, are still at home, and I'm probably going to be helping watch them." He pulled a piece of paper out of his pocket. "This is Trent's in-laws' number and their address. They don't live far from my uncle's farm. If you need to get up with me, they'll know how."

"Okay. I wish there was something I could do. Do you need me to go with you?"

Owen kissed her hard. "I would love to have you go with me, but I don't know what I'm going to find when I get there. We might all end up sleeping in the barn until we can figure something out. Besides, you have obligations here. I won't ask you to give them up."

"Well, if you get down there and need me, promise me you'll call. Obligations be hanged, Owen."

He kissed her again and wrapped her in a hug that lifted her off the floor. "I love you so much. I'll contact you as soon as I can, okay?"

Sarah nodded and touched his face. "Okay. Promise me you'll be careful. Don't rush too much on the road. You won't do anyone any good if you wreck getting there."

"I'll be careful. You do the same." After one last kiss, he was gone.

Sarah sat at the kitchen table. Even if his uncle recovered, the loss of their home would be devastating. Her mother's parents had gone through a house fire when Sarah was a little girl, and the loss had almost been like a death in the family. With a heavy heart, she got ready for work. If there was anything worse than feeling helpless and having to stand by while someone you loved hurt, Sarah didn't know what it was.

Late Thursday evening, nearly eleven o'clock, Sarah was reading and thinking about going up to bed when the phone rang. Scrambling up from the couch, she hurried into the kitchen. "Hello?"

"Sarah? It's me."

"Owen! How's your uncle?"

"Holding his own, the doctors say. They're still not sure how things are going to turn out. He's in Lexington. How are you?"

"I'm okay. I miss you, but I'm okay. How are you?"

He gave a short laugh. "Exhausted. They lost everything. Their oldest daughter's up in Lexington with Amy, and the rest of us are trying to figure out what to do. I don't know when I'll get another chance to call you. I'm sorry."

Sarah had to clear her throat. "It's okay. I understand. Do you need anything?"

There was a long pause on the other end of the line, and she thought the connection had been lost, but then Owen said, "There is something. If it isn't too much trouble, can you write to me? Let me know how you are, what your days are like? I'll try to write back, but I can't make any promises right now."

"Of course I can. Do I send it to that address you gave me?"

"Yes. I have to go. As soon as I can, I'll be in touch. I love you."

"I love you, too. Stay safe for me?"

"You, too, Sarah Jane."

The buzzing of the dial tone sounded in her ear before she could respond, and Sarah reluctantly hung up the phone. She stood with her forehead braced against the wall while tears streamed down her cheeks. Her heart screamed for her to go to him, but she knew that having her down there was the last thing he needed to worry about right now.

Her book forgotten, Sarah shut off the lights downstairs and headed to her bedroom. She didn't know how much help it would be, but she was determined to send a long, detailed letter to Owen first thing in the morning. Hopefully, it would reach him by Monday, perhaps even as early as Saturday, depending on how the mail was running. As anxious as she was to see him again, she knew she'd have to be patient. She had the sinking feeling that it could be weeks before he returned home.

"So it will have to be an excellent letter. And hopefully, he'll be able to write me back."

CHAPTER TWENTY-EIGHT

OVER THE NEXT TWO WEEKS, Sarah wrote to Owen nearly every day. She only received two letters in response, both much shorter than she would have liked, but she understood. Several times, she considered driving down there to be with him, but rejected the idea. The last thing she wanted was to show up, get in the way, and cause more trouble for him.

Jack and Gilly had returned from their honeymoon. Much to Sarah's relief, living with them wasn't a problem. They were much more circumspect than Randall and Kathy.

Owen's absence didn't go unnoticed at the library, with both Shirley and Callie remarking on it. Sarah explained the circumstances, but by the time Owen had been gone for three weeks, Callie was looking at her with pity.

The attitude angered Sarah, and she talked to Shirley one day when they took lunch together. "She acts like he's deliberately staying down there to avoid me. I can't say anything to her because that will make it worse, I expect."

"I'd say you're right. Ignore her. Do *you* think he's avoiding you?"

Sarah dropped her gaze to the table. "I don't want to think that, but the longer things go and I don't hear from him, I'm wondering a little."

"Well, have you tried calling him?"

"Yes. The number he gave me just rings and rings. No answer. And I've tried calling at different times during the day, on the weekends, in the evenings. I don't know what to think."

When Shirley's mouth tightened in to a grim line, Sarah realized Shirley was also having doubts about Owen's reasons for not being in closer communication.

"What should I do?" Since Eliza had left, Sarah had grown closer to Shirley, and she valued her opinions.

"Honey, I don't know what to tell you. Have you written him and flat-out asked him what's going on?"

"No. I've been waiting to see if I hear from him. I thought about driving down there, but I don't want to appear forward. Besides, if he is… done with me, I don't want to find out in front of his whole family."

Shirley patted Sarah's hand. "I think you need to write and ask him what's about it. I understand he's under a lot of pressure right now and you don't want to add to that, but you deserve to know. And as much as I hate to admit it, I have to think something else is causing him to not write or call. You need to find out what."

So that evening, after she'd finished the garden chores and helped with supper, Sarah went to her room and started writing. Like the first letter she'd ever written Owen, it took her several tries to get right, but when she finished, she was satisfied. She hoped she was wrong, that her suspicions were just her own insecurities rising to torment her.

CHAPTER TWENTY-NINE

O WEN WAS IN A FOUL mood from the time he woke up on Wednesday morning. Though his uncle was doing better and was expected to be released from the hospital later that week, not much else had gone right in several days. They'd started clearing the ruins of Eli and Amy's farmhouse over the previous weekend, and it rained the entire time, making the stinking heap of burned wood a dangerous, soggy mess. Owen could finally coordinate with a local contractor to bring in a bulldozer, and on Tuesday, they'd made decent headway. Work had ground to a halt, though, when Eli's fifteen-year-old son, Tad, fell and broke his arm.

Leaving Trent in charge, Owen had rushed Tad to the hospital to get the arm set. That took several hours, and by the time they made it back to the neighbor's farm where everyone was staying, it was dark. The rest of the children were in an uproar, stress and the disruption of their lives wearing on them, and it took everything in Owen's power to settle them down that evening. Five of them were still teenagers, and three of the four were shifters, which added another level of stress to the situation.

Once he had gotten them quiet, Owen walked outside to see Trent off. "It's a good thing the Hayses went on vacation last week. Otherwise, we'd all be sleeping in the barn until we get the new house built."

Trent, who had to have been as tired as Owen was, nodded. "I'm glad you're here to help. I don't know how we'd handle this without you. And I know you're making a sacrifice by being here."

Owen clapped a hand on the younger man's shoulder. "You would all do the same for me. That's what family's for. Get yourself home and get some rest. I'm hoping to get a little sleep tonight myself."

"Will do. Cora should be here in the morning by eight or so to look after Tad. At least you won't have to worry about having him underfoot tomorrow."

They said goodnight, and Owen went inside the farmhouse. As he passed the table in the hall where the phone sat, he paused. He missed Sarah with a longing that was nearly a physical pain, and the desire to call her was strong. He knew he should have called sooner, but every time he'd started to, something happened. Just as he moved to pick up the receiver, he heard soft footsteps.

"Owen? My arm hurts," Tad said from the foot of the stairs.

After glancing at the phone with regret, Owen went to Tad. "Come on. I'll get you something for it." Maybe if he got up early enough the next morning, he could call Sarah for a few minutes. If he went much longer without hearing her voice, he'd end up going crazy.

Tad was up and down the rest of the night, and Owen with him. He finally got to sleep after four, but was up again by six. There had been too many nights like that in the past few weeks, and Owen was feeling the effects.

So when, on Wednesday morning, Tad's sister Julie casually mentioned that Owen had received a letter from Sarah the previous day, Owen only felt a bit guilty for losing his temper.

Luckily, Trent's wife, Cora, showed up before he could fly completely off the handle. Taking in the situation with one glance, she herded the children out the door. "Go take a few minutes for yourself, Owen. Lord knows you deserve it."

Thanking her, he hurried up to his bedroom and sat on the bed. As he opened the envelope, he held it to his nose, hoping for a whiff of Sarah's perfume. Her letters had been his salvation over the past few weeks.

Dear Owen,

I hope this letter finds you well and your family. Hopefully, your uncle is recovering quickly.

I debated long and hard on whether I should write this letter. I don't want to add to your burden. But I've not heard from you in a while now, and I'm concerned. I've tried calling, but I can't get through. The phone just rings.

Please tell me you're okay.

Owen, I don't want to think you're avoiding me. I certainly don't want to think that you're trying to tell me you don't want to be with me anymore. But I am concerned. Your last letter came over two weeks ago. Knowing how fond you are of writing letters, I'm worried.

I won't write you a lengthy diatribe. I'm not blaming you for not writing or calling me. But I would ask that you please let me know if you're okay and if you want to hear from me again. I'll honor your wishes, but I need to know.

Regardless of your response, I want only the best for you. I only want you to be happy, whether that is with me or not.

I hope to hear from you soon.

Love,

Sarah

Owen read the letter three times before the words made sense. Once they did, he stared at the paper in disbelief.

"Where the hell did *this* come from?" he muttered. His not writing to Sarah had nothing to do with diminished feelings; he simply hadn't had time. He figured that would have been obvious given what he was going through, but apparently not. He felt a burst of anger and picked up a pen and a piece of paper. He knew the message back to Sarah was terse, but he hoped it would be enough to reassure her.

A loud thump sounded from outside, and Julie screeched with outrage or pain. He wasn't sure which. Hurrying to the window, he saw that she and Tad were arguing.

"Shit! What now?" He quickly signed the letter and addressed the envelope. Sealing it as he hurried downstairs, he prayed to God for patience. He needed as much help as he could get.

Sarah came in from work Saturday afternoon feeling tired and out of sorts. Summer had arrived with a vengeance, and the humidity had ratcheted up into nearly unbearable levels.

"Hey, girl. You look like a wrung-out dishrag," Gilly said from the front porch.

Despite her fatigue, Sarah laughed. "Gee, thanks. I appreciate the comparison."

"That's what I'm here for. A letter came today. That might perk you up a bit. It's on the table in the kitchen."

"Why didn't you say so?" Fatigue forgotten, Sarah rushed into the house. When she saw the envelope addressed to her in Owen's familiar handwriting, she almost wept.

"I guess you'll be going upstairs to read it?" Gilly asked, having followed Sarah inside.

Sarah didn't answer, but grabbed a knife from a drawer and slit the envelope. She drew out the letter, and when she saw it was only one page, her heart climbed into her throat. One page couldn't be good news. Tossing down the knife, she unfolded the paper.

Sarah,

I'm sorry I've not written sooner. I have a thousand and one things to do here, and all of them are urgent. That doesn't leave much leisure time.

Eli should be home this weekend. It was close, but the doctors think he'll make a full recovery.

I'll call you as soon as I can, but I don't know when that will be.

O.

For long minutes, she just read and reread the words. Without speaking, she handed it to Gilly, then turned to get a glass for some water. Hands trembling, she filled it as Gilly read.

"Leisure time? What does he mean by that? Writing to let you know he's still alive shouldn't be leisure time."

"I don't know what he means. And he didn't answer any of my questions except about his uncle. How would you interpret that?" Her hands clamped onto the edge of the sink.

"I don't know what to think." Gilly folded the page and put it back in the envelope. She laid the letter on the counter and tapped it with her fingers. "Maybe we need to take a trip."

"No." Of that, Sarah was certain. "Like I told you, I don't want to just show up. I don't want him to be forced into a confrontation in front of his family. And if he really is that busy, he doesn't need my interference."

"You have doubts, don't you?"

Sarah hesitated. "I don't want to."

"But you do."

She nodded. "I do. If he weren't such a prolific letter writer, Gilly, I wouldn't think so much of it. But that's what Owen *does*—he corresponds. His lack of correspondence is speaking to me louder than any words."

Gilly moved to stand beside her at the sink. "Sarah, that week Jack and I were on our honeymoon, did something happen between the two of you?"

"What do you mean? We didn't argue."

"No, that's not what I mean. Were you intimate?"

Sarah crossed her arms. "We, um, sort of?"

Gilly looked at her, eyes wide.

"I'm still a virgin. But we... I guess I'm not as innocent as I was."

"Well. I see."

Sarah turned anguished eyes to Gilly. "What are you thinking? That he got what he wanted and decided it wasn't worth buying the cow?"

"Sarah! That's not quite how I would have put it, no."

"But that's what you're thinking, isn't it? It's what I'm thinking. Gilly, he wasn't a virgin," she confessed in a near whisper. "There was someone else, a widow who was his uncle's neighbor. And he's down there, and I haven't heard from him except for that." She gestured to the letter. "He didn't even sign it with love, just 'O.' What else can I think?"

Gilly put her arm around Sarah's shoulders and squeezed. "I don't know. I really don't know."

CHAPTER THIRTY

S ATURDAY MORNING, OWEN WENT TO London to pick
up supplies for Eli and Amy. Eli had come home from
the hospital the day before, and the Hayses had installed
his uncle and Amy in their downstairs parlor. It wasn't an ideal
situation, but Owen hoped that, in a couple of weeks, they'd be
able to have Eli's new house finished enough that the family
could move in. Several men from the community had come by
the day before, and an old-fashioned house raising was planned
for Tuesday.

He stopped in the pharmacy to pick up some things Amy
needed. As he waited for the prescription to be filled, he pe-
rused the aisles of goods. When he came to the card section, he
stopped. He still hadn't had a chance to call or write to Sarah.
His conscience was giving him a good pounding over that, but
he was so tired he knew if he talked to her, he might say something he shouldn't.

Oh, he didn't think he'd say anything that would hurt her
feelings, but he might let more slip about his family and the
shifter thing. Until he could sit down with her face-to-face, he
was better off remaining silent.

The pharmacist called his uncle's name, and Owen made his
way back toward the counter. At the end of the aisle, he bumped

into a woman carrying a baby. Reaching to steady her, he apologized. "I didn't see you come around the corner. I—" Owen broke off as he recognized her.

The woman's eyes widened. "Well, I'll be damned. Fancy meeting you here." Kathy looked him over with a raised eyebrow. "You've gone all country on us."

Owen looked down at himself. Clad in jeans and a checked shirt open over his T-shirt, with a full beard covering his jaw, he knew he looked different. "I've been a little busy lately. How's Sarah?"

"Fine, as far as I know. I haven't seen her in a few days. She said something about your family having a house fire?"

"Yes. My uncle's house. I'm helping rebuild it. What brings you down this way?"

She shifted the baby to a more comfortable position. "Randall had something he needed to do for the county, so I came along."

"There you are," a woman said from behind Owen, and he felt a soft hand touch his elbow. "I've been looking all over for you. Are you ready to head back?"

When Kathy's eyes widened, Owen frowned. Looking down at the petite blonde, he softened his expression. "Sure. I just need to get Eli's medicine first."

"Is this your cousin?" Kathy asked, drawing his attention back to her.

"No. This is Nora Caudill. She's a neighbor. Nora, this is Kathy Begley. I know her from back home."

The two women nodded at each other politely, but Kathy's expression turned to stone.

Nora touched Owen's arm again. "I'll be out front in the truck when you're ready to go. It was nice meeting you." With a smile for Kathy, she excused herself. They both watched her go, and when Owen turned back to Kathy, he was surprised by the loathing he saw on her face.

"You know, I really thought you were different. I'll be sure to give Sarah your regards, shall I?" Lifting her chin, she stalked away, leaving Owen staring after her, trying to figure out what he'd said.

Surely, Kathy hadn't thought he and Nora… no. Dismissing the thought as absurd, Owen got in line to pick up his uncle's medicine, but he couldn't shake the feeling that he was missing something important. He paid for the prescription, then hurried out to the truck where Nora was waiting.

"Sorry it took so long," Owen said. "I hope I didn't keep you waiting."

"Not at all," Nora assured him as he climbed inside. "Who was your friend?"

"Kathy? She's Sarah's sister. The girl I'm dating," he explained as they headed back to the farm. "I really appreciate you giving me a lift into town. Hopefully, those new spark plugs will fix Eli's truck, and I won't have to bother you again."

"It wasn't any bother. I was coming in anyhow. Call me anytime you need to." The smile she sent him was friendly. Perhaps, Owen thought, a little too friendly. He thought about the ring he'd picked up at the jeweler's a short time earlier and grimaced. Resolving to call Sarah that evening, he said little the rest of the trip back to Eli's.

As many of Owen's intended plans had gone lately, the phone call never happened. When Nora pulled into the driveway to drop him off, Julie came running out to meet them.

"Daddy fell! He says he's okay, but Mama wants to take him to the hospital. They're arguing, Owen."

Owen hurried inside and, much to Eli's chagrin, agreed with Amy's assessment. Though Eli wasn't hurt too badly, he'd torn several stitches. Amy, exhausted from keeping her bedside vigil in Lexington, stayed at the farm with the children while Owen drove Eli.

Because of the seriousness of the injuries his uncle had sustained in the fire, he was checked into the local hospital overnight as a precaution. Owen stayed with him, sleeping in fits and starts. By the time they were back at the Hayses, half a dozen other crises had developed, which needed to be dealt with. Vowing that he'd call Sarah before the weekend was over, Owen's encounter with Kathy completely slipped his mind.

CHAPTER THIRTY-ONE

Late Monday morning, Sarah was up to her elbows in strawberries, prepping them to make jam, when she heard a vehicle in the driveway. Glancing out the window, she was shocked to see Kathy. She wiped her hands on a towel and opened the door for her sister.

"Thanks," Kathy said, setting the baby's bag down in one of the kitchen chairs. She looked around and raised her eyebrows. "You're busy today."

"Yes. Mr. Combs's strawberries came in this weekend. Ours didn't do anything, so I got six flats from him to make jam since the library was closed today. If you want to take some home with you, feel free. Where's Moira?"

"She's with Randall's mother. Thanks for the offer, but I'll pass."

Not sure what to say, Sarah pushed her hair back off her face. Feeling how loose her ponytail had gotten, she reached up and redid it. "So, what brings you out here today?"

To her surprise, Kathy's cheeks flushed. "We need to talk."

Sarah studied her sister. For once, the derision and smugness were gone, and Sarah was hard-pressed to name what had taken its place.

"Think we could go on the porch and sit? I can lay a blanket out for the baby. He could use some sun," Kathy said.

"Sure. I'll get a quilt from the couch. Go on out, and I'll be right there. Do you want something to drink?"

"No, I'm fine."

Worried, Sarah got the blanket and went out to the front porch. She made a soft nest partially shaded from the sun and took little Randall from Kathy. After pressing a soft kiss to his forehead, she laid him down, then joined Kathy on the swing.

"First, I'm sorry," Kathy said. "I know we haven't gotten along the last few years, and I know I'm to blame for a lot of that. But I am sorry, for whatever it matters."

"Sorry for what?" Sarah asked, frowning. "What's going on, Kathy?"

"Randall and I went to London on Saturday. I ran into Owen."

Sarah's heart started pounding, and she knew instinctively that she wouldn't like what came next.

"He wasn't alone. He was with a woman."

"His aunt or a cousin?" Sarah asked.

"No. He said she was a neighbor. And when he introduced us, he didn't say I was your sister, only that he knew me from back home." Kathy didn't look at Sarah.

Her throat was as dry as parchment, and Sarah had to try three times before the words would come. "What did she look like?"

"Short little thing, blonde. Maybe ten, fifteen years older than us." She must have seen something in Sarah's expression because she stilled. "That mean something to you?"

Sarah gave a faint laugh, looking out over the front yard as her heart broke. "Oh, yes. That means a lot. It explains a lot." Her hand came up to cover her mouth, and she laughed. The sound emerged with a harsh edge, nothing of humor in it. When Kathy's arm came around her shoulders, Sarah stiffened.

"I'm so sorry, Sarah. So damned sorry."

Giving in to the tears, Sarah let herself cry.

Some time later, all her tears spent, Sarah straightened from where she'd been leaning on Kathy. The initial shock still reverberated through her, but she was starting to think past it. "Do you think there's any chance they weren't together?"

"I don't think so."

"Why not?" Sarah could tell Kathy didn't want to answer her, but she persisted. "Why not? I need to know, Kathy."

Kathy looked down at her hands laced together in her lap. "When a man and a woman have been together, they look at each other a certain way. Touch each other a certain way. You just know, Sarah. Especially if you've been cheated on. Or if you're the other woman."

"He touched her?"

"No, she touched him. But it was there. And I told him what I thought of him, too. I expected better of him, and I'm sorry he wasn't."

The baby whimpered, and Kathy bent to pick him up. "I need to feed him. Will you be okay if I go in for a few minutes?"

Distracted, Sarah waved a hand toward the house. She searched her memory for what Owen had told her about the woman he'd been with, but he'd been vague. He hadn't said the widow's name or described her at all. As much as she wanted to believe that Kathy was mistaken, she very much doubted she was.

Sarah didn't move off the swing for a while. Kathy came back out and sat beside her, the baby in her arms. Sarah held out her hands, and Kathy passed little Randall to her.

"Maybe I heard you wrong earlier," Sarah said, keeping her tone deliberately light, "but I could have sworn you implied you knew what it was like to be the other woman."

When Kathy smiled sadly, Sarah's heart sank further. That was something she hadn't believed was possible, but there it was.

"The baby isn't Randall's."

Her words were another shock and a blow, even though Sarah didn't like Randall. "Oh, Kathy."

"I'm leaving him, Sarah. I've tried and tried, but I can't stand living with him anymore. That's the other thing I came out here to tell you."

Sarah looked down at the baby, who was blissfully ignorant, and groaned. "Does Mama know?"

"No. You're the only one I've told."

"Who's the father?"

Kathy reached over with a tissue and wiped drool off the baby's chin. "Randall's boss from the garage. Clay Morton." Sarah was incredulous, and Kathy shrugged. "It just happened. And I'm glad it did. I'd never have found the courage to leave Randall if I hadn't met Clay. We're leaving together tomorrow."

"What about Moira? Have you told Randall yet?"

"No. He'll find out when he gets home from work tomorrow. I wanted to warn you, as he'll probably show up here first, looking for us. And Moira'll be with us."

Sarah swallowed, finding everything hard to take in. "Where are you going?"

"It's probably best that I don't tell you. Clay's arranged a good job for himself, and as soon as we get where we're going,

I'm filing for divorce. When that comes through, we're getting married."

"So you won't be staying around here?"

"We figured it might be better to go someplace where we could get a fresh start." Kathy stood with a groan and stretched. She picked up the quilt the baby had been using and shook it. "I want you to know something—I didn't tell you what I did to hurt you. I hope you believe that."

"The thought had crossed my mind," Sarah admitted. "Why did you tell me? You didn't have to."

Kathy looked across the valley, the quilt draped over one arm. Sarah was surprised to see her struggling with tears.

"Randall has been cheating on me since we were in high school. Sometimes I knew about it; sometimes I didn't. I don't want that for you. You deserve better."

"So your advice to find a man who doesn't beat me and all that? Should I disregard it?"

Her sister laughed, and in that instant, she looked freer than Sarah could ever remember seeing her. "You find a man who treats you like a queen, who puts you above all others. You find him, and you hold on to him. And don't you dare settle for anything less. Do you hear me?"

Standing, Sarah handed Kathy the baby and wrapped her arms around them both. "I hear you. Will you at least promise to write now and then?"

"Of course. You'll do the same?"

"I wouldn't have it any other way."

Long after Kathy had gone, Sarah stayed out on the porch. She stared at the landscape, not feeling comforted, but feeling as though she were in an alien world. It was as if everything she'd held dear had been turned on its end.

When the phone rang, she jumped, startled. Thinking it might be Owen calling with an explanation, an apology, something, she nearly killed herself getting inside. Ignoring the blood that ran down her shin from where she'd hit it when she tripped, she grabbed the phone with a breathless "Hello."

"Yeah, is Dellie there?" a woman asked. "This is Maude. She's 'specting my call."

"Oh. No. Sorry. Try again." Sarah hung up and slumped down, landing on the floor with a *thunk*. Her back pressed against the wall, she looked down at her skinned leg. One spot was bleeding more profusely than the others, and as the blood dripped off her calf and splattered on the linoleum, she started laughing.

"Sorry, try again," she whispered. "I don't think so."

Sarah didn't think things could get any worse, but that evening after supper, someone knocked on the door and proved her terribly wrong. She and Gilly, who were finishing up the jam making in the kitchen, exchanged a look and went to answer the door together. When Sarah saw who was on the other side, a chill went down her spine.

The deputy sheriff's face was solemn in the falling dusk. "Ladies, I'm looking for the family of Kathy Begley."

"Kathy's my sister," Sarah managed to say. "What's wrong?"

She never remembered falling or that the deputy had to help Gilly get her to the couch while Jack rushed in from where he'd been working outside. Instead, what stood out was the horrible knowledge, the tears, the pain, and the disbelief. Sarah remembered the sound of Jack's voice trembling as he called their mother and the seemingly interminable drive to the hospital, to Kathy, after Eliza had been told the devastating news. She remembered the long, long wait in the hospital waiting room and the kindly young doctor's grim face as he came out to apprise them of Kathy's condition. Most of all, she remembered the realization that none of their worlds were ever going to be the same again.

CHAPTER THIRTY-TWO

F ATE CONSPIRED AGAINST OWEN AT every turn. He finally got the time to sit down late Sunday evening and call Sarah, but when he picked up the receiver, the line was dead. After a quick trip down to Nora's, taking Tad and Julie along as chaperones, he discovered that a car wreck had taken down the line.

"It won't be back up until midweek, at least. I'm sorry," Nora said. "And it's out all the way into London, from what I hear."

Ready to pull his hair out with frustration, Owen thanked her. "Not your fault."

Returning to the Hays farm, he cloistered himself in a bedroom and wrote Sarah a long letter, pouring his heart and soul into it. He'd been away from her so long he didn't much care if he gave away his secret. He simply wanted to be with Sarah.

Monday morning, he gave the letter to Amy to mail for him. "Promise me you'll send this? It's important that it goes out today."

She gave him an impatient look. "Owen Campbell, you know I will. Get on with you."

He gave her a smacking kiss on the cheek and headed out for his meeting with the contractor who was organizing the rebuild.

Until Eli could recover a little more, Owen was in charge of that task.

Things moved fast on the house. Tuesday, over twenty men showed up to help, and they came back each day that week. By Thursday, Eli was well enough to sit in a chair under an oak tree and supervise with Amy hovering to ensure he didn't overdo.

Owen joined them at lunchtime, stripped down to his pants and a sleeveless T-shirt. "It's coming along so quickly you all might move back in here this weekend. I can hardly believe it. If you ever wondered how your neighbors felt about you, now you know."

"It's overwhelming," Amy said. "I don't know how we'll ever repay all these folks. They won't take money. And you, Owen... sweetie, I don't have words enough to tell you how grateful we are that you've been here." He clasped the hand she held out to him and squeezed.

"Well, I think we need to cut the boy loose," Eli said, clapping him on the shoulder. "I've never seen anyone champing at the bit so much to get home but not say a word about it. We've held you up long enough."

"I figured I'd head back Sunday or Monday if you all are comfortable with that. I'll stay longer if I'm needed, but I am anxious to get home."

"You need to let me give you a haircut before you go home. Your Sarah won't recognize you." Amy touched his hair, which Owen had taken to tying a bandanna around to keep it out of his face. "Are you going to shave?"

He rubbed a hand over his beard, which was almost as unruly as his hair. "I don't know. I've kinda gotten used to it. I might trim it up a little."

"We'll sit down tonight and take care of that. It's the least I can do," Amy said. "We don't want to send you back to your girl looking like a wild man."

"I'm hoping to get a letter from Sarah today or tomorrow. She should have received the one we sent out Monday by now. I've not been as diligent about writing her as I should have been," Owen said.

"I'm a little surprised by that," Eli replied. "We were wondering if something had happened between the two of you."

Astonished, Owen looked from his uncle to Amy. "You know how busy I've been. I wasn't avoiding her or anything like that. I love Sarah."

"That's what made your not writing that much more puzzling, son. I'm glad you sent that letter out to her this week. If we were wondering, she might also be." Eli carefully got to his feet. "I see that Stidham fella over there. I've been wanting to talk to him."

Owen and Amy watched him go. Owen was troubled by what Eli had said. He asked Amy if she felt the same way, that he'd been neglecting Sarah.

"Honey, that's something you'll have to ask her. Hopefully, you'll get to do that soon."

"Hopefully. That's why I was so eager to get that letter out to her, so she'd understand." Without that letter, he was terrified Sarah would write him off as a lost cause. The letter was a good start at an apology, but he'd feel better once he saw her in person.

He couldn't get home soon enough.

When Owen came down to breakfast the next morning, he found Amy and Eli seated at the kitchen table with their daughter, Julie. The girl's eyes and nose were red, and she wouldn't look at Owen as he came to a halt at the end of the table.

"What's wrong?"

Amy heaved out a rough sigh. She and Eli exchanged a look, and Eli gestured toward her with his uninjured arm. "You tell him."

Amy pushed a familiar-looking envelope across the table to Owen, who stared at it in confusion.

He picked up the envelope, the skin all over his body prickling with warning. It was the letter he'd written to Sarah that explained everything. "I thought this got mailed. Amy?"

"Julie has a confession to make. I'm so sorry, Owen. I thought it went out."

Still not believing what he held in front of him, Owen looked at Julie. "Explain. Now."

Her face turned bright red, and she started crying. "I just wanted to read it. I didn't mean to hurt anyone. I've never read a love letter before, and I wanted to see what it said. I'm sorry." The teenager buried her face in her arms and sobbed.

Fear and anger raced through Owen. He wasn't even aware that he'd stood until Eli followed suit. He looked at his uncle, not seeing him. Instead, he imagined Sarah's face growing colder and more hurt every day that went by that she didn't hear from him. His heart sank even as his temper soared, and he started cursing.

"Henry Owen Campbell! Watch your mouth!" Amy scowled at him, clearly appalled, and Owen attempted to calm himself down. Looking down at Julie, he shook the letter at her.

"Do you have any idea what you've done? Do you? This was a private letter, Julie. The things I wrote in here were for one person's eyes and her eyes only. I poured everything I felt into this letter so that Sarah wouldn't worry, so she'd know I was coming home to her. And you took it and kept it? What's she going to think now, huh? That I've abandoned her, that I'm done with her—that's what. Damn it!"

Owen stormed out of the house. His anger carried him across the driveway to the pasture fence, where he slammed his hand into one of the slats. Head bowed, he had to swallow against the sick fear that clawed his belly. He heard someone come up beside him and saw Eli's boots stop next to his.

"I'm sorry, son."

"Sorry's not going to fix this. Do you know what Sarah's probably thinking right now? And I can't even call her." The phone lines were still out, and Owen started thinking about where he could get access to a phone.

"Look, I know you were going to leave in a few days, but I think you should go now. We've gotten enough done that Amy, Trent, and I should be able to handle it from here."

"I don't want to walk out on you and leave you in the lurch," Owen protested half-heartedly.

Eli sighed. "In what possible universe could you possibly think you'd be doing that? I've made it forty-five years on this earth, the last twenty-five or so on my own. I think I can manage."

"You're sure?"

"Of course I'm sure. Go get packed up. You can get on the road in fifteen minutes, if you hurry, and be in Hazard this afternoon. You can deliver that letter in person."

The idea was too appealing to resist. "Okay. But you call me if you need anything. I can be back down here tomorrow if I need to be."

Eli wrapped his arm around Owen's shoulders and started steering him back toward the farmhouse. "Son, I think it's going to take more than a day to straighten this out. You don't worry about us; worry about yourself for once. You need to make that commitment to Sarah. She needs to come first now. We'll be fine."

When they went back inside, Owen saw Julie was gone.

Amy was washing the breakfast dishes, and she wiped her hands on her apron, turning to him with guilt written all over her face. "Sweetie, I can't tell you how sorry I am. I didn't know she hadn't mailed it until I saw it in her room this morning. Are you going home?"

"Yes. Hopefully, I can straighten this mess out." He wrapped Amy in a tight hug. "Don't worry too much about it."

"Well, now, you know I will until we hear from you. I'll pack you some biscuits and sausage for the trip."

Owen dashed upstairs and gathered his things, throwing them haphazardly into his bags. In five minutes, he was packed. When he left the bedroom, a forlorn Julie was waiting for him in the hall.

"Do you hate me?" Her voice trembled, and Owen felt a little of his anger melt.

"I'm not thrilled with you right now. But no, I don't hate you." He tipped her chin up with one finger. "You've hurt me with what you did, Julie, and you've hurt the woman I intend to marry. I'm not quite ready to forgive you yet."

Though she sniffled loudly and Owen could see that she wanted to cry, she held back the tears and gave him a stiff nod. "I understand."

He ruffled her hair. "Try to stay out of trouble?"

"I will."

Amy and Eli saw him off with hugs and kisses. Just as Eli had said, Owen was on the road in fifteen minutes. He checked his watch and the truck's gas gauge. He'd stop to fill up before he left London, and hopefully, he'd be in Hazard by lunchtime. He'd go straight to the library, and if necessary, he'd get down on his knees in front of God and everyone else and beg Sarah's forgiveness.

As he drove, he realized how stupid he'd been for not making more of an effort to contact her. If he had, then Julie's stealing the letter wouldn't have been as grievous an offense. So, as much as he wanted to blame his young cousin, Owen knew that if Sarah told him to go jump in a lake, it was more his fault than anyone else's.

Owen made good time on the road, arriving around the time he'd thought he would. After he parked the truck in the pay lot down the street from the library, he sat there for several minutes, collecting his thoughts. He didn't want to rush inside willy-nilly and fumble his way through the explanation.

He didn't see Sarah's car, which gave him a moment of concern, but then he remembered she was sharing it with Jack and Gilly. "Well, no time like the present. Suck it up, Owen." He made sure he had the letter tucked inside his shirt pocket and, with a fervent prayer that he'd find the right words, headed into the library.

Callie was manning the front desk. Instead of the friendly smile she typically greeted him with, her eyes widened with alarmed surprise.

A frisson of warning raced across Owen's back. "Hey, Callie. Is Sarah handy?"

"She's not here. You need to talk to Shirley." Callie dropped her gaze to the desk, her posture stiff.

Owen scowled. "What do you mean, she isn't here? Where is she?" Callie didn't answer, and Owen reached out to touch her shoulder. "Callie, where's Sarah? What's going on?"

Callie picked up the phone and dialed. "Owen Campbell's down here. He's asking about Sarah." She hung up and stood. "Shirley will be right down. I need to shelve these books. Excuse me." Before he could stop her, she hurried away.

His heart racing, Owen paced in front of the desk. Shirley finally appeared with a grim look on her face, and Owen knew then that something was terribly wrong.

"Where is she? Is she okay?"

"Come with me." She started toward the back of the building, but Owen didn't budge.

"Not until you tell me where Sarah is. What's going on?"

Shirley grasped his arm and tugged. "Come on. We have to discuss this in private."

Scared half to death, Owen followed her.

She led him into the employee break room and shut the door. "Sit down, Owen. Did you just get back in town?"

He sent her a frustrated look but sat. "Yes. Now, please, tell me what's going on. Is Sarah okay?"

Shirley clasped her hands on the table in front of her. "In a manner of speaking, she is. But her sister isn't. Sarah's probably at the hospital with her right now, if I had to guess. They've all been taking shifts."

"Kathy? What happened? Did she have an accident?"

To his surprise, Shirley pressed her lips together and looked away. She picked up a napkin and blotted her eyes. "No. It's awful, Owen. I'm surprised you haven't heard the news even down in London."

"Our phone's been out for over a week. Shirley, you're worrying me. What happened to Kathy?" He made to stand, but Shirley stopped him.

"You need to know before you go over there. From what Sarah has told me, and from what people are saying, Kathy was planning on leaving her husband for another man. He found out, and he... he didn't take it very well."

"Oh, dear God. Did Randall go after her?"

Shirley's lips trembled. "It's so much worse than that. Owen, he called the other man to their house. He attacked Kathy and then killed her lover. Then he killed their children, and then he killed himself. All of it in front of Kathy."

Owen's vision narrowed to Shirley's white face and her trembling hands. The room faded around them. He thought about the baby Kathy'd been holding just a week ago, about little Moira, and nausea roiled in his stomach. "No," he whispered, shaking his head. "Why? Why would he do that?"

"From what Sarah said, he did it all to punish Kathy. That's why he didn't kill her, so she'd have to live with what he did."

He didn't realize he was crying until Shirley handed him a napkin. Unashamed, he wiped his face. "When did this happen?"

"Monday evening. I know they tried to call you, but they couldn't get through."

Owen felt her words like a stab to the heart, and in that moment, he hated himself. "How's Sarah? You've seen her, I take it?"

"She's holding up for now. Her mother's on her way from Georgia, should be here today sometime. Sarah and Gilly have been taking turns sitting with Kathy, and Jack has, too. They've all been staying here in town with Gilly's parents." Shirley went to the refrigerator and got out a pitcher of cold water. She offered Owen a glass, and he accepted it.

Shirley poured herself one and sat down again. "I want to ask you something. This is coming from Sarah's friend, not from your librarian. Understand me?"

"Of course. Ask away."

"Where the *hell* have you been, and why haven't you contacted Sarah? Do you know what she's thought? What we've all thought? She's called you, and you don't answer. She's written, and you don't answer. I'm ashamed of you, Owen Campbell."

Owen flinched. "I don't have any excuses. None. I didn't consider how my not writing or calling looked until this week, and by then, it was too late." He looked at where his hands wrapped around the glass. "Do you think Sarah would see me if I went to her?"

"You know, I'm not sure. If this hadn't happened with Kathy? I think you would have walked in the door today and gotten knocked flat on your behind, and you would have deserved it. But now? The girl has had about as much tragedy as she can cope with. She can't take much more. So I don't know if she'd see you or not, but I think you'd better try. If you care about Sarah at all, you'd better try."

CHAPTER THIRTY-THREE

SARAH WAS STANDING AT THE window, staring out across the hospital parking lot, when Kathy stirred on the bed behind her.

Turning, she moved to her sister's side. "You're awake." Sarah thought her bruises looked a little better, and her eyes didn't seem to be as swollen. If there was an inch of skin on her sister that hadn't been cut, bruised, or battered, Sarah would have been surprised.

Kathy grimaced as she tried to sit up, and Sarah helped her get into a more comfortable position. She poured her sister a fresh cup of water.

Kathy drank about a third of it before she handed it back. "Thanks."

"The doctor was in a little while ago. He thinks you might get to come home tomorrow," Sarah said. She sat down in the chair beside the bed.

"I won't go back to that house."

"No. You won't have to. The rest of us can go get your belongings, and you can stay with us at the farm."

Kathy plucked at the blanket. "Heard from Mama yet?"

"She called early this morning. She and Nancy are in Tennessee and should be here later today."

Kathy slumped against her pillows with a tired-sounding sigh. "Did you bring anything to read today?"

Sarah smiled. "Of course." She pulled two books out of her bag and held them up so Kathy could see them. "Which would you like me to read?"

"The McLemore, please."

Sarah was at Kathy's bedside the first day after the shooting, keeping vigil. The silence in the hospital room had been deafening, and out of self-defense, she'd pulled out a book and started reading aloud. By sheer accident, the book was one of Owen's that Sarah hadn't yet returned to the library.

When she'd stopped reading, Kathy, who had been silent ever since she'd been brought in, had spoken, her voice a bare whisper. "Don't stop. I like that."

So Sarah had continued reading to her sister. The action soothed them both, even though Kathy's choices so far had been mostly Owen's books. Calling herself ten kinds of fool, Sarah felt closer to him by reading the words he'd written. She thought maybe the reading helped her pretend he hadn't left her and helped Kathy pretend everything she loved hadn't been destroyed.

"This is new," Sarah said as she put the other book aside for later. "Well, new to me. It's been checked out ever since I started reading the series. It finally came in to the library last night, and Shirley grabbed it for me. This one's called *The Summer Folly of Tobias Hedge*."

Kathy's battered mouth moved in what Sarah thought was a smile. "I like Toby. He's funny."

"He is at that," Sarah said as she opened the book. "But I like Hootie Grey Feather, too."

Toby and Hootie were a deer and an owl, respectively. Toby was a young teenager who could shapeshift, and Hootie was an old man whose spirit roamed the land as an owl when he slept.

Together with Minerva, a shape-shifter who turned into a surly bobcat, they had adventures. The stories were always centered on traditional Appalachian myths and folklore. Hootie and Minerva usually ended up getting Toby out of trouble, as they were older and wiser. Owen had done an excellent job of blending fiction with folklore.

"So what's Toby into this time?"

"Let's find out." Slipping off her shoes, Sarah curled her legs up under her and started reading.

"The morning was cool as Toby gamboled through the woods, fog nipping at his heels. It was late spring, and the young buck was in a playful mood. He hadn't been able to change into his deer form in recent days, and the energy soared through him as he ran. He stopped here and there, nibbling on soft green leaves and tender shoots, but he didn't linger anyplace very long. He wanted to get to the pond, where he was meeting his friends.

Toby's excitement turned to uncertainty when he reached the cool, serene pond, for there, sitting on a rock in the bright sun, sat a girl.

'Oh, no,' Toby thought. 'What do I do?' His parents had warned him against interacting with humans while in animal form, but they'd always been more worried about hunters with guns. They'd said nothing about what to do if he encountered someone close to his own age.

Moving slowly, Toby approached the girl. She didn't see him at first, as she was enraptured by the book she held. Feeling bold, he edged closer, stepping on a small twig as he did. The sound startled the girl, and she looked up, straight into his eyes.

Toby's heart sighed and fluttered. She was the most

beautiful girl he'd ever seen. Her eyes sparkled a deep blue that fairly shone with intelligence. Creamy white skin and dark, shining hair completed the picture. He'd never seen her before and wondered where she'd come from, who her people were.

She smiled. 'Are you really standing here?' she asked. 'I've never seen a deer before except in pictures.'

Toby thought that was strange indeed, but he couldn't ask her about it while he was in deer form. A sweet, tart scent reached his nostrils, teasing them. Looking around, he realized the smell was coming from a sliced apple in the girl's lap. Apples were one of his favorite foods, in deer or human form, and his mouth watered. Even though he knew he shouldn't, he moved closer and cast a longing glance at the fruit.

The girl took the hint and offered him a slice. He moved carefully so that he didn't scare her and took the apple from her fingers. It was so good and crisp he huffed out a sound of deep satisfaction as he ate. He'd never had an apple so sweet, and he figured the girl must have worked some sort of magic over the apple to make it taste so good. He went back for more, and she freely gave him the rest of it."

Sarah stopped reading as a memory tugged at her. The encounter Toby was having with the girl was exactly like the encounter she'd had with the deer at the pool the summer she graduated from high school. The description of the girl in the book fit Sarah herself.

"No," she marveled, "I'm losing my mind."

Kathy glanced at her but didn't speak.

Shaking herself, Sarah continued reading.

"Intrigued by his new friend, Toby lingered at the pond for

a while. He eyed the girl's brown bag with curiosity, hoping there might be more apples.

'Oh, you probably won't like what's in there,' she told him. 'My granny packed my lunch for me this morning. It's probably egg salad or tuna. I doubt that'd be to your taste.'

Toby agreed. He wasn't much of a fan of egg salad."

"Sarah, are you okay?"

Sarah wasn't aware that she had stopped reading until Kathy spoke. Feeling as though she were in a fog, she looked at Kathy, then down at the book in her hands. There was no way Owen could know what she'd said to the deer that day at the pool. None. Unless he'd been eavesdropping, and since the deer hadn't sensed him nearby, Sarah didn't think that was how he'd known.

"It's not possible..." she whispered. "I mean, I know the book's about a boy who can... but it isn't possible."

Kathy rose up a little in the bed. "You have the strangest look on your face right now. Are you okay?"

The irony of Kathy asking *her* that question made Sarah laugh. "Yeah, I'm fine. I just... I'm okay." With an effort, she turned her attention back to the book long enough to finish reading the story. She didn't remember any of it later. Her mind raced as she started putting together puzzle pieces—the deer's odd, human-like behavior, Owen's certainty that Sarah would reject him once he revealed all his secrets. Everything made a strange sort of sense. As she finished the story, another thought occurred to her. She'd gone skinny-dipping that day at the pool.

"That little... I was naked!" she burst out. "And he was there."

"Who was where when you were naked?" Kathy looked completely confused.

Sarah was saved from having to answer by a soft knock on the door. She and Kathy turned, and Kathy inhaled sharply when they saw who the visitor was.

"Mama!" Kathy struggled to get up, reaching for Eliza, sobbing.

Their mother hurried across the room. "I'm here, baby. I'm here." Eliza tucked Kathy into her arms carefully, mindful of her injuries, tears streaming down her cheeks.

Nancy had stopped in the doorway, and she gestured to Sarah. Understanding, Sarah gathered her bag and joined her aunt in the hall. She closed the door behind her, and Nancy held her arms open for Sarah, who accepted the hug gratefully.

"Let's get some air, shall we? They're going to need a while."

"There's a little area downstairs the nurses showed me. We can go there," Sarah said.

The tiny garden was deserted, and Sarah tossed her bag on top of the picnic table that sat to one side of the green space.

"How are you?" Nancy asked. She walked around, stretching her legs and her back.

"Okay. Coping. Did you all just get in?"

"Yes. We drove straight through from Knoxville. What a mess, Sarah. What a damned tragic mess." She sat beside Sarah and pulled a pack of cigarettes out of her purse. She offered one to Sarah, then lit her own when Sarah declined. "Have you all talked to the funeral director yet?"

"Jack spoke to him earlier this week and again yesterday, I think. Kathy isn't able to talk about it, and we wanted to wait until Mama got here. He understood. I expect we'll have to take care of that tomorrow."

"God damn Randall Begley. Have you heard from his family?"

"Oh, yes. His mother blames Kathy for everything. Said he should have killed Kathy instead of himself. They had to sedate her, she was so upset. Randall's father is almost as upset, as you can probably imagine."

"Well, they lost a son and two grandchildren, so they have every right to grieve. But Kathy's not the one who pulled the trigger on that gun. He could have let her walk out. They'll never see it that way." Nancy stubbed the cigarette out in the tray on the table. "So, what about you? Eliza said you'd been having some problems with your beau. Have you straightened them out?"

"No. I've still not heard from him. I guess Mama told you he went to London?" When Nancy nodded, Sarah continued. "Well, Kathy came up to the house on Monday. That's when she told me she was leaving Randall, but she also came to tell me she'd seen Owen with another woman. She and Randall had been down there, and she saw him."

Nancy looked surprised, and Sarah shrugged. "I wasn't expecting it either. I tried again to call him after... well, after. I think he gave me the wrong number because it just rang and rang unanswered. He'll show up one day, or he won't. Not much I can do at this point." She sighed.

"I hate that things have turned out like that between the two of you. I was rather impressed with him when I met him. I never would have expected him to act like that."

"Neither did I, Nancy." Sarah thought about the connection she'd made between Owen and the deer a short while ago. "I must be more tired than I thought."

Her aunt sent her a quizzical look. "What makes you say that?"

Sarah laughed. "It's nothing. I imagine you all are exhausted as well."

"It wasn't a peaceful trip, no. We didn't stop to eat lunch today. Neither of us could really think about it but I'm getting a little hungry now. Have you eaten?"

"No. We could get something from the cafeteria."

Nancy stood and held out her hand. "I was thinking about the drugstore, actually."

Sarah grimaced. "That's probably not a good idea right now, unfortunately. I made that mistake on Wednesday. I was stared at like I was a leper or questioned nearly half to death. Until some of this with Kathy blows over, I'm avoiding public places as much as I can."

"I was afraid of that. Cafeteria it is, then."

After a quick lunch, they returned to the floor where Kathy's room was. As they got off the elevator, Nancy asked Sarah about her job. "Are they accommodating you, or are you in trouble?"

"They've been wonderful. The director promised to hold my job as long as she can. Hopefully, I'll be able to go back in a week or two."

As they passed the waiting room, Sarah glanced inside. The sight of a tall, dark-haired man stopped her dead in her tracks. He had his back to the hallway, but when she gasped, he turned.

"Owen." Sarah couldn't move as he hurried toward her, concern etched on his face. When he reached out for her, however, she slapped his hand away with a smack that echoed in the small room. Not waiting to see how he would react, she ran down the hall and into the ladies' room.

Both stalls were thankfully empty, and Sarah locked herself inside the smallest. She pressed her back against the door, heart hammering in her throat. For a minute, she thought she might throw up. Her hands were clammy, and she couldn't think beyond the knowledge that Owen, finally, was there.

When Sarah calmed down enough to come out of the bathroom, Owen was waiting for her in the hallway. He'd been leaning against the wall, hands shoved in his pockets, but when she came out, he straightened.

He looked tired, and Sarah was shocked to see that he appeared to have lost ten pounds, maybe more. The beard was unexpected, but he wore it well. She laughed bitterly to herself. He seemed to wear everything well.

"Your mom needs to see you," he said. "Sarah, I—"

She cut him off by simply walking away. As much as she'd prayed he would return, she didn't have the least bit of interest in having a discussion with him at the moment. She was too tired and devastated by everything that had happened that week to care what he had to say. She went straight to Kathy's room and tapped on the half-open door.

"Come in," Eliza murmured. "Kathy's asleep. They gave her something to help her rest." She met Sarah near the door and pulled her into a hug so tight Sarah thought she might suffocate. She didn't complain, though.

Eliza pulled back and looked at her. "You look tired."

"I could rest. You don't look like a bundle of energy yourself."

Taking her hand, Eliza glanced over her shoulder. "I'm going to stay here with Kathy. If you could, take Nancy over to Gilly's parents' house and let Gilly get her settled in. Then I'm going to have Owen take you home. The doctor came in while you and Nancy were at lunch, and he's sending Kathy home tomorrow. We'll stay here while you, Gilly, and Jack get some rest."

Her emotions on a rollercoaster, Sarah started to refuse to take anything from Owen, but her mother stopped her.

"Look, I know the two of you have some problems you need to work out. But right now, I don't care. You're both adults, and I expect you to act like it. Whatever's going on between you, put it aside for now. At least until we get Kathy home. Okay?"

"Yes, ma'am."

"Owen?" Eliza prompted.

"Whatever you need," he responded.

Eliza nodded. "Good. I'll tell Nancy. You two wait in the hall."

Sarah and Owen took up positions on either side of the door. Sarah kept her eyes forward and tried to pretend he didn't exist. Nancy joined them after a couple of minutes, and they made their way to Owen's truck.

Even though the ride to Gilly's parents' was short, it felt like a special torture for Sarah. Nancy had ensured Sarah sat in the middle of the bench seat. Owen was pressed all along her left side, and as he shifted gears, she could feel the muscles in his thigh bunch and relax. She held herself as stiffly as possible, but it didn't help.

Gilly came out on the porch as they pulled up, and even from the driveway, Sarah could see her eyes widen.

"When did you get in?" she asked Owen as she walked up to the truck. "We figured you'd been eaten by wolves."

He had the grace to blush. "A little while ago. Nancy, I'll carry your bag in."

"Thanks, Owen." Nancy got out of the truck. When Sarah attempted to follow, she said, "No. You stay here. I know you're not happy to be riding with him. I'm sorry."

"I'll manage. Get some rest," Sarah said as she gave her aunt a quick hug. While Nancy updated Gilly on the plan, Sarah moved over to take Nancy's spot. She let her head rest against the back of the seat, and her eyes drifted shut. She hadn't slept in days, her dreams running red with blood every time she laid her head down on the pillow.

When Gilly spoke to her through the passenger window, she was startled awake.

"I'll pack up your things and bring them home tonight when Jack and I come back. We'll see you in a little while, okay?"

"Okay. Thank you."

Owen got back in and backed out of the driveway. Sarah waved at Gilly and Nancy before turning to face forward. Sarah didn't speak until they neared the turnoff for the road that led to Owen's house nearly twenty minutes later. "If you want to, drive to your place. I'll walk down. I need the exercise."

"You sure?"

"Yes."

He took the turn, and before long, the foot of his driveway came into view. It was nearly hidden and, unless someone knew it was there or was really looking, was easy to miss. Owen steered the truck off the road and started the climb around the side of the hill.

"How's your uncle?" Sarah finally remembered to ask. Her thoughts had been racing around in circles so much she felt lucky to string the words together enough to form the question.

"Better. He finally got to come home last Friday, and he's been steadily improving ever since. We almost have their house rebuilt, too."

"Already?"

"Yeah, it's gone pretty fast." They topped the hill, and Owen's parents' house came into view. He drove past it and stopped the truck in front of the newer house. "I was starting to think I wouldn't ever get to see this place again. Sarah, I'm sorry—"

"Stop. Just stop. I can't do this right now. I only want to go home and sleep."

"We will talk about this though, right?"

"Yes. But not today." She didn't wait for him to come around and open the door, but got out on her own.

"If you don't mind waiting, I'll put my bags inside and walk you home." Owen had his bags in hand and was already halfway to the front door. "You're too tired to go on your own."

"Fine." She knew she was being snappish, but she didn't care. If he got offended, that was his problem. She started toward the steps that led to the path home. She heard him curse behind her, but she kept walking, her only thoughts involving getting home and going to bed.

Owen caught up with her quickly, and Sarah was thankful that he didn't initiate any conversation. At the house, she unlocked the door and led him into the kitchen, where the dishes were still piled up from Monday night. The jars of jam she'd canned were still waiting on the counter for their lids, and a line of sugar ants was marching from the back door toward the sink.

Sarah felt like crying. "Oh, damn it. I forgot what a mess we'd left this place in."

Owen started rolling up his sleeves. "I can take care of this. You go rest. I'll get this cleaned up in no time."

His willingness to step in and take care of her was too much. The irony was the final straw, and, temper flaring, she spun around to face him.

"Oh, I'm sure you'll do a *wonderful* job. Please make yourself at home. When you're finished here, Jack started painting the house Monday evening. You can finish that. And I'm sure we can find something else for you to do when you're done with that chore. Just forgive me if I don't believe you'll finish any of them. Where were you, Owen?" Her voice had grown louder and louder until she was shouting. "Where the hell were you? Damn you! I needed you, and you weren't here. Why are you here now? Go now before I need you again and you aren't there!"

Owen's face had turned to granite, and she could almost see him reining in his own temper. Angry, hurt, and wanting to lash out, Sarah stalked over to him and shoved him with both hands. He didn't budge.

"Why, Owen? Why weren't you here? I needed you, and you weren't here. Why? Why, damn it?" She screamed at the last, and the tears hit. Sobbing, she curled her hands and beat her fists against his chest, pain from the last couple of weeks overwhelming her at last. "Why, why, why?"

His arms came around her. Sarah fought, but Owen wouldn't release her. Instead, he drew her closer. The grief took its sweet time winding down, and by the time her tears slowed, Owen had picked her up. Sarah realized he was taking her upstairs, but she didn't protest. She was just too exhausted.

In her bedroom, Owen set her on her feet. "Where's a nightgown?"

Sarah gestured toward the chest of drawers.

He walked over and pulled out a gown. "Do you need help? Need to use the bathroom?"

"I don't know."

Owen matter-of-factly started undressing her, his touch impersonal as he helped her out of her clothes. Once she was stripped down to her panties, he eased the gown over her head. He let her settle it around her hips as he opened the bedroom windows, letting in some fresh air.

"Let's go wash your face. You'll feel better." Taking her hand, he led her down the hall and into the bathroom. He wet a washcloth and wrung it out, then gently used it to blot her face. "I'll let you take care of more personal business. I'll wait for you in your room."

After he closed the door, Sarah stood at the sink for a minute, trying to get her body to cooperate with her brain. She used the bathroom and washed up, then got back down the hall. Owen was waiting in her room, where she let him tuck her in bed.

"I'll be downstairs if you need anything. Just holler."

Exhausted, Sarah was asleep almost before he'd finished placing the sheet around her shoulders.

CHAPTER THIRTY-FOUR

OWEN PULLED THE LETTER FROM his pocket and laid it carefully on Sarah's dresser, then left her bedroom and went to the top of the steps, where he sat down. Resting his head in his hands, he let the emotions he'd been holding a tight rein on since he'd gotten back to town shudder through him. Unlike Sarah, whose tears had been violent and noisy, Owen's were silent.

If he hadn't known it was Kathy in the hospital bed, he never would have recognized her. Her face was swollen from the beating, and from what he'd seen of her arms, the rest of her body had fared no better. Owen had gotten into a few altercations over the years, brotherly tussles with Eli's son Trent and once with Harlan after they'd reached their late teens. Those battles had been rough, and Owen had come away from them sporting various aches, pains, and bruises, but nothing like what Kathy was suffering. He couldn't imagine the beating she had endured at Randall's hands. If the man hadn't killed himself, Owen would have gladly murdered him without regret.

The thought of Kathy's children devastated him, but Sarah's pain almost destroyed him. She had needed him, and he'd let her down. Owen couldn't lie to himself anymore—he hadn't written, not because he was tired or too busy, but because he had been hesitant to put every part of his heart out there.

As he'd told Shirley, he really had no excuse. He'd wanted to protect himself, so he'd held back. Sarah deserved better than him, and Owen suspected she knew it. She would probably never forgive him, and it would be no less than he deserved. God knew he would never forgive himself.

Once his emotions were under control, he went downstairs and started cleaning the kitchen. Owen knew a lot of men, his father included, considered dishes and cleaning women's work. He'd never understood that. Work was work. If something needed to be done, then whoever was most able to do it should do it. It was a philosophy he'd always believed and Eli had helped reinforce.

Owen spared a few thoughts for Eli and Amy as he worked, but he realized that his responsibility wasn't in Laurel County anymore. If he wanted any chance at working out his relationship with Sarah, he had to put her first, no exceptions.

Once the kitchen was clean, Owen did a little straightening around the house. He stepped out onto the back porch with the garbage and glanced over at the garden. It wasn't in terrible shape, but the weeds were getting a decent hold. Knowing exactly what he needed to do next, he went back inside and grabbed the key to the shed off the wall. Thanks to the day he'd helped put the garden in, he was familiar with where all the tools were, and in hardly any time, he had the garden mostly put to rights. He was putting away the hoe and preparing to get out the lawn mower when he heard Sarah scream.

The blood was everywhere, coating Sarah's hands, arms, legs, and torso. She frantically brushed at it, trying to shake it off, but it clung stubbornly. She couldn't get it off.

The next thing she knew, someone was shaking her.

"Sarah, come on, wake up. You're having a nightmare. Sweetheart, please. Open your eyes."

"Blood, there's so much blood," she mumbled. When she finally came awake, the stench of it still burned in her nostrils, and she coughed. "Get it off me. Please, Owen, make it go away."

He sat down on the bed beside her. "Shhh, it's okay. Look at me. That's a girl. Look at me. You had a bad dream. There's no blood, Sarah. It was only a dream."

Sarah focused on his face, and the horrible visions faded. He was brushing strands of hair off her damp face, and Sarah brought her hands up to his wrists. She felt his pulse race against her fingertips and the warmth of his skin against hers, and she relaxed.

"You okay now?" he asked.

"Yes. I think so."

Owen closed his eyes and rested his forehead against hers. "When I heard you scream… God, Sarah." His breath rushed out across her lips, and Sarah had to fight not to kiss him. They sat like that for a few minutes, and she felt the last vestiges of the nightmare slip away.

"Do you want to talk about it?" he asked.

"I don't know. All I remember about it is that I'm covered in blood, and I'm alone and scared. That's all I remember, but it's horrible. I can taste the blood; it's so strong." She drew her knees up to rest her head on them, forcing him to move back. "I wonder if it's because Kathy was here Monday and I feel guilty. I didn't stop her or talk her out of leaving. I knew she was going to. I should have said something."

"What could you have done? If she'd stayed here, Randall might have come gunning for all of you. You could have been killed, too, Sarah."

"I know. And that's hard to take as well."

"How did he find out? That she was leaving, I mean. Do you know?"

Sarah scooted back so that she was propped against the pillows. Hot, she kicked off the sheet. "From what one guy at the garage told Jack, he overheard Clay telling Randall that he and Kathy were in love and that they were leaving. They got into an argument, and Randall threw a punch or two. Clay let him, and Randall left, headed for the bar." She looked down at the counterpane bedspread, tracing its pattern with a fingertip. "The baby wasn't Randall's. Kathy told me when she was here Monday morning."

Owen's eyebrows shot up. "Oh, God. And Randall found out?"

"I guess so." She tipped her head to the side. "She came to tell me she'd seen you in London. And that you weren't alone. Were you with *her*, Owen? The woman you had the relationship with?"

He grimaced, but he nodded. "I was, but not the way you think. I needed a ride into town, and Amy called Nora before I could stop her. Amy didn't know about us. I couldn't very well explain it to her in the kitchen over breakfast. And after three years, I didn't think it mattered. It didn't matter, not to me. But she's their neighbor, so Amy called her and..."

"Did it matter to her?"

Owen studied his boots, then shrugged. "I don't know. I got the feeling I wouldn't be rebuked if I wanted to renew our acquaintance, which I didn't. I don't. I'm not interested in her or anyone else outside this room."

Her chuckle was dry and rough, Sarah knew. "I'm not sure I believe you."

He didn't seem surprised. "I can understand why you'd think that. I've done badly by you, Sarah. I know that. I want to fix things."

"And if you can't? If things between us are irretrievably broken? What then?"

"I refuse to give up. It's taken me a while to understand the whole picture, to realize what it means to make a full commitment. I wish I'd known a few weeks ago, but I didn't."

As much as she wanted to believe him, it was hard. She knew she wasn't in the best frame of mind to make any sort of decision. While she hadn't intended to discuss their relationship so soon, a question kept plaguing her. "Why? Why didn't you call or write? Why are you here now, after so long?"

Owen stood and went to her chest of drawers. He picked up an envelope and brought it over to her before sitting back down on the bed. "I was afraid I'd get hurt. That's the why. Plain and simple. No excuses. So I told myself I was too busy and that you'd understand why I wasn't in contact. Plus, I didn't think it would take quite so long to get back here. The phone line got taken out late last week by a wreck. Tad broke his arm, Eli ripped his stitches out, and I used all of that as an excuse to protect myself."

Sarah set the letter aside. "Why'd you come back now?"

His mouth twisted in an annoyed grimace. "That letter. It was supposed to go out in the mail on Monday. Instead, it got waylaid by a fourteen-year-old who wanted to read a love letter. When she confessed this morning, I realized what I'd done by not contacting you. Then, when I got to the library and Shirley told me about Kathy…" He shook his head. "I'm sorry."

"So am I." When they heard two car doors slam, Sarah glanced at the clock on her nightstand. "That's probably Jack and Gilly. I should get dressed." She looked at Owen, and it occurred to her that Jack probably wouldn't take his presence in her bedroom very well, but before she could warn him, the front door opened.

"Sarah? We're home." Gilly was coming up the stairs. Sarah tried to nudge Owen off the bed, but he wouldn't move.

Gilly came to a stop in the bedroom doorway and stared at Owen. "You shouldn't be here." She shot a worried glance over her shoulder. "Jack's already talking about going up to your house to have a word or two. You are not his favorite person right now."

"I'm not his favorite person on a good day." Owen stood. "I'll go face the music, see if he wants my help with the grass or what." He touched the back of his hand to Sarah's cheek and left.

Gilly leaned against the doorjamb, watching him go, then turned back to Sarah. "Are you going to let them sort it out themselves?"

Sarah went to the closet and pulled out her most comfortable clothes. "Yes, I think I am. I'm not sure I'm ready or willing to forgive Owen yet, and if Jack doesn't get the anger out of his system now, he might never. If I decide to forgive Owen and we end up married, they probably need to be over any grievances one or the other has first. Don't you think?"

Gilly rubbed her hand over her face. "Yeah, makes sense. I just hope they don't hurt each other too much. We've had enough of that this week."

CHAPTER THIRTY-FIVE

J ACK WAS STANDING ON THE back porch, hands on his hips, studying the yard, when Owen came downstairs. "Somebody's been working in the garden. Is Sarah okay?"

"She had a nightmare," Owen answered. From the way Jack swung around, Owen guessed he was not expecting to see him there. "And I'm the one who was in the garden. I was about to get started on the grass when Sarah woke up screaming."

"You! What the hell are you still doing here?"

"Just trying to help. Some things needed doing, and I was here. That's all."

Jack was practically vibrating with anger. "You've done enough, thanks very much. Leave. Now."

Owen held up his hands. "Okay." He knew better to argue or try to reason with Jack. The look in the younger man's eyes said he was itching for a fight. Owen figured that with the week the family had had, on top of his mistreatment of Sarah, it wouldn't take very much to set a spark to Jack's temper. He edged around Jack and walked down the steps.

"What? Nothing to say to defend yourself, Campbell?"

With a low hiss of frustration, Owen turned to face Jack. "Are we going to do this, then?"

"Oh, I think so." Jack launched himself off the porch at Owen, tackling him to the ground.

The grass cushioned the impact of the fall somewhat, but it still knocked the breath out of Owen. "You're heavier than you look," he panted as he blocked Jack's first punch. He braced his stomach muscles and let the next one make contact. While Owen wasn't immortal, he could take a heavier beating than the average man, and he figured letting Jack get a few blows out of his system would go a long way toward defusing the situation. He didn't want Jack to feel as if he was winning too easily, however, so he heaved upward and flipped Jack off of him. As Owen scrambled to his feet, he saw Gilly and Sarah come out onto the porch from the corner of his eye.

"Jack! Don't you think that's enough?" Gilly asked.

"No." Back on his feet, Jack circled Owen, looking for an angle of attack. "Not even close."

"Well, try to not bruise each other where Kathy or Mama can see it," Sarah said. "That's the last thing we need, the two of you looking like you tried to kill each other."

"But it's okay to hit him where the bruises don't show?" Jack asked. "I want to make sure I understand you right, sis."

"If the two of you want to spend the rest of the evening scrapping around out here, who am I to stop you? Try to stay away from the garden and the flowers."

Owen turned to look at her, and when he did, Jack pounced again. Owen stayed on his feet, but keeping himself upright took his focus away from blocking Jack's punches. After one particularly stinging blow, Owen grunted. He tried to get Jack in a headlock, but Jack danced away from him.

"What's the matter? You afraid to hit me, Campbell?"

"No. I just don't want to hurt you."

Jack laughed. "As if you could. Come on. Take your best shot. Right here. Prove to me you're man enough." He tapped his chin, angling it upward toward Owen.

Owen's temper flared at the taunting words, but he rolled his shoulders and pushed back his anger. "Your sister asked me to avoid your face. I'm not going against her."

Jack sneered. "I figured you'd hide behind the women. Good to know I was right."

Owen let out a low growl. "Watch yourself, Browning."

"Oh ho, the big man doesn't enjoy being called a mama's boy. What's wrong, Owen? Did I hurt your feelings?" Jack stepped in and shoved Owen's shoulder with one hand. Owen looked down at where Jack had pushed him, then slowly raised his eyes to meet Jack's. The words were too close to what Harlan used to say to him when they were boys. A flash of anger went through him, rapid-fire, and Jack's eyes widened.

"You should *not* have said that." With a roar, Owen tackled Jack. They rolled onto the grass, and Owen punched Jack in the stomach, the shoulder, and the face. He didn't hit hard enough to bruise but enough to sting, and he knew Jack would feel it the next day. Jack snapped Owen's head back with a right uppercut. "You aren't the only one who's had an awful week or two, Browning."

"Yeah, well, I can't kill Randall, so I'll have to settle for you." Jack flipped them so that he was straddling Owen, then drew back his fist. Before he could let fly with the punch, though, a cold jet of water hit him in the back of the head. Jack rolled off Owen and tried to get away from the water, but it followed him.

"That's enough!" Sarah aimed the hose at the ground while Jack sputtered and coughed. As she stood over him, fury rolled off of her in waves. "What is wrong with you two? I thought a few little punches here, some sniping there, and you'd be over your mad. Instead, I think you're trying to kill each other."

"Sarah, we're just—" Owen started, but she turned the water his way, soaking him with an icy blast.

"Hush! I don't care what you were 'just.' What I know is that the two of you needed to blow off some steam. I get that. Well, you'd better be unsteamed now is all I can say. Because I am not explaining to Mama why her baby boy and my… my whatever-the-hell-you-are put each other in the hospital." With one last blast for each of them, she threw down the hose and stalked toward the house.

Gilly, standing by the spigot, twisted the knob and followed. She stopped at the kitchen door. "Here are some towels and a couple of beers. Go make friends somewhere. But neither of you is getting back in this house until you shake hands and apologize. And mean it!" She slammed the kitchen door, and Owen heard the lock slide into place.

Jack, still on the ground, stared at the door with astonishment. "She locked me out. My wife locked me out."

Wearily, Owen got to his feet and went to the other man. He held out his hand. "Come on."

Jack took the offered hand and got to his feet with a grunt. "Where are we going?"

"Somewhere we can talk."

Owen took Jack to the pool. It was the nearest, most comfortable place they could speak privately, and Owen hoped Jack would see the invitation as the olive branch he intended.

"So this is where you bring Sarah?" Jack asked, looking around.

"Yeah. She found it on her own a few years back." Owen led him to the top of the rock. "Have a seat."

Jack got out his pocketknife and opened his beer, then held out the knife to Owen.

Owen shrugged. "I rarely drink, but I'll make an exception today."

They sat side by side on the ledge Owen and Sarah liked to use as a backrest. Owen took a swig of beer and grimaced at the taste. "Tastes like piss. Nasty stuff."

Jack shot him a sidelong look. "How do you know what piss tastes like?"

"I don't. But I still think beer tastes like piss. Looks like it, too." He went to the branch and dumped the beer, then rinsed and filled the bottle with fresh water. "There, now we can pretend we're having a beer together."

Laughing, Jack shook his head. "So what are you?"

"What do you mean?"

"I mean, what do you turn into? You're not big enough to be a bear, I don't think."

Owen paused, hanging in midair for several long seconds. With a grunt, he dropped on his butt. "What are you talking about?"

Jack rolled his eyes. "Come on, Owen. I saw the flash in your eyes. So what are you? Maybe a wolf?" When Owen sucked in a breath, Jack winced. "Damn. Does Sarah know?"

Owen considered trying to brazen it out, but he didn't think that would work. Besides, he needed to find out the extent of Jack's knowledge. "Not yet. I figured I'd tell her after everything calms down a little. How'd you know?"

"The flash. You hid it pretty fast, but it was there." He studied Owen with consideration. "Are you kin to the Muncys from over in Harlan County?"

Owen shook his head. "Not that I'm aware of. Why?"

"Guy I was in the Army with, Harold Muncy—big guy, six-and-a-half-feet tall, three hundred pounds—we were in the same unit. He was a shifter, turned into the scruffiest black bear you've ever seen." Beer finished, Jack went to the stream and filled his bottle. He took a long drink and topped it off, then moved to look out over the pool.

"And he just told you what he was?"

"No. We were out on practice maneuvers one night and got lost. Harold was always bragging about how he was a mountain man, could find his way home from anywhere. He was a nice guy—funny, affable—but it rubbed some of the Yanks the wrong way. So they got into our bags and swiped our compasses and maps. And we got lost."

"Ouch. That had to be hard to live down."

Jack smiled. "Nah. Because Harold got us back to base exactly like he'd said he could. They couldn't believe it. Harold told them that next time we had R and R, he'd take us all camping and show us how he did it."

"Oh, boy."

"Yeah. Oh, boy. So we get out there in the woods, and Harold pulls out two quarts of 'shine. I don't know where he got it, never asked."

"Quarts?" Owen interrupted to ask. "Not pints?"

Jack shook his head. "Quarts. There were six of us in total. So, Harold gets the four other guys drunk off their asses. He'd been out drinking with them before, knew how well they held, or didn't hold, their liquor. He worked them like a pro. They never even suspected what he was doing." He came back and sat down. "I didn't touch the stuff. Dad always warned us kids against moonshine. He knew too many people who got destroyed by drinking it. And Harold didn't ask me to. I think he wanted me to know his secret."

"So once they're falling down, about ready to pass out, he asks them if they want to know what the secret is. They begged him to tell them, and he stands up and says, 'Okay, boys. You want to know? Here it is.' And just like that—" Jack snapped his fingers. "—his face and arms changed. He made a pitiful looking bear, let me tell you, but that's what he was. Scared the living daylights out of one guy so bad, he peed his pants. The rest of us were too scared to move, myself included. I thought he'd slipped me something. Then, he changed back and started laughing like a loon. 'I can smell you Yankees from twenty miles away,' he said. 'I followed the smell of your carcasses back to base.'"

Owen laughed, picturing the scenario in his mind. He shook his head, though, at the man's recklessness. "Why in the world would he take a risk like that? Most of us would never be so bold. It only takes the wrong person knowing, and that's all she wrote. It's all torches and pitchforks from there on out."

"He knew that. That's why he made sure they were all stupefied drunk. Even if one of them remembered it, anyone they told wouldn't believe them. After that, he talked to me about it. He seemed to be relieved to have someone to share the burden with."

"He sounds like quite a character, this Harold."

Jack's smile held a terrible sadness. "He was. He got sent over to Asia in January. Hadn't been there two weeks when he stepped on a land mine. I think it's what he wanted, in a way. The girl he'd loved for half his life rejected him to marry a man who wasn't a shifter. He couldn't handle that. So he enlisted, and that was that."

"I'm sorry." There wasn't really much more Owen could say. The loss was tragic, and words wouldn't change that.

"Yeah, me, too. There's been too damned much death lately." Jack picked up a small rock and tossed it into the pool. "Why'd Randall have to kill them anyhow? He could have let her go, been the injured party. Son of a bitch would have had women lined up to soothe him."

"Because if he let her go, everyone would know he was a failure," Owen said. "That's the way my brother would have seen it anyhow. As an assault on his manhood."

"Did Sarah tell you that Randall raped Kathy? Before he shot Clay, he raped her, and he made Clay watch. How the hell does she get over that?"

Owen closed his eyes, sick at the thought. "I don't know."

"I want to go get him out of the ground and kill him all over again. If I believed he'd know I was doing it, I would."

"They've already had his funeral?" Owen asked, surprised.

"Yesterday. His brother stopped by the garage today and let me know his parents won't be at the kids' funerals."

"But those kids are their grandchildren."

"Not to them, not anymore. They're Kathy's children, and they blame her for all of this." Jack rubbed his eyes, and he looked years older than he had the last time Owen had seen him. "Speaking of my sisters, what are you going to do about Sarah?"

Owen peeled the label off his bottle, scowling at the paper as it tore. "Beg her forgiveness. If I can get that, then I'm planning to marry her as soon as I can. I know I've hurt her, and I haven't handled things the way I should."

To his surprise, Jack clapped him on the shoulder. "How much of that is because you're an ass, and how much is because you're a shifter?"

The question startled a laugh out of Owen. "Two halves of the same coin, I'm afraid. I just hope I can get Sarah to understand and to trust me again."

"For what it's worth, I hope you can. But if you ever treat her like you have the last few weeks again, I'll kick your ass. I won't pull my punches next time."

Owen stared at Sarah's brother in shock. "Pull your... you sneaky son of a gun. You were trying to find out how easy I was to make angry."

"Did you really think I'd let Sarah get involved with you again if you had a temper like Randall's? After what happened this week?"

"No. And I'm not upset that you did it. I understand your reasoning."

Jack smiled. "Good. Oh, by the way, I don't think you're a mama's boy. But that sure didn't sit well with you."

"No, my brother used that taunt against me when we were growing up. After the last few weeks, I'm worn a little thin, and you touched a nerve." Owen stood, and Jack followed suit. "Did you all have any idea Randall was like that? That he'd go off the way he did?"

"No, he never so much as raised a hand to her that I ever saw. None of us would have allowed that if he had. But now, looking back, I wonder."

They started down the trail.

"Wonder about what?" Owen asked.

Jack rubbed the back of his neck. "Well, they stayed with us off and on after they got married. I don't know if Sarah's told you this or not, but they were loud. Like, really loud. The first few weeks they were married, nobody else in the house slept well."

"You mean when they were...?" Owen's face heated, and he saw that Jack's had as well.

"Yeah. And now that I'm married, I'm wondering about that. Whether it was all for show, or he was hurting her and we didn't realize it. Or if that was his way of marking his territory, so to speak. Hell, I don't know."

"I'm surprised your parents didn't say something to them, especially with you and Sarah still at home."

Jack stopped as they came out of the woods and crossed his arms, much like Sarah did when she was uncomfortable. "Dad said something. It would die down for a while and then start back up again. After about the third time, Randall and Kathy moved out." He used his chin to point to the back porch where Sarah and Gilly sat talking. "Think they'll let us back in the house now?"

"Only one way to find out."

As Jack pled their case to Gilly, Owen thought back over everything they'd discussed. He had a lot to answer for, and he wasn't sure how to make up for all the hurt he'd caused. The idea of what Kathy had gone through, not just on Monday evening but throughout her married life with Randall, made Owen look at Sarah's sister in a whole new light. And what Jack had told him about his friend, Harold, made Owen look at himself differently as well. He thought he'd been brave and stoic by hiding himself away from people. Instead, he'd been doing the same thing Harold Muncy had done, only slower. He'd been punishing himself for being what he was born as, something he couldn't change.

Owen was tired of hiding. If Sarah hadn't looked so tired, he would have swept her away and confessed everything right then and there. He wanted a life with her. Period. End of story. And right at that moment, he chose to live instead of just existing.

All he could do was hope she still felt the same way.

Later that evening, after Owen had gone back up the mountain and Gilly had gone to take a bath, Sarah and Jack sat out on the front porch. They'd spent many a summer evening playing in the front yard, chasing fireflies and playing card games or checkers with Eliza and Ira. Kathy had been there, too, but less so in recent years, and Sarah and Jack had gotten close.

"What do you think I should do?" she asked him. She pushed the swing with her foot, sending it gently swaying.

"About what?"

"About Owen, of course. The two of you seemed to have come to terms with each other."

Jack stretched his arm across the back of the swing. "I like him. Despite how he's acted lately, I like him. He's not without flaws, but I believe he's essentially a good man."

Sarah turned and tilted her head. "What about him not contacting me for so long? Do I ignore that?"

"No, ma'am. Not even close. But sis, good men sometimes do stupid things. It doesn't mean they aren't good men. It simply means they're human."

"And you really think he's a good man? That I should give him a second chance?"

"Yeah, I do."

"Hmmm. I once asked Mama how to tell the good men from the bad. She told me some things to look out for, and then she said that it still comes down to being very, very lucky." She stopped the swing and stood, then bent down and hugged Jack. "I think Gilly is very, very lucky. Goodnight."

"Night. Don't let the bedbugs bite."

Sarah smiled as she went inside and climbed the stairs. Jack's opinion meant a lot to her, but she had to make up her own mind. She had to trust her instincts and believe in her heart that Owen was the right man for her. She had to trust him again with her heart, her body, and her soul even. Tonight wasn't the time to decide something that important, but Sarah thought she'd know soon what her answer would be.

CHAPTER THIRTY-SIX

WHAT SARAH HELPED HER MOTHER do the next day was one of the hardest things she'd ever done in her life and something she hoped she'd never have to do again—plan her niece and nephew's funeral. Jack drove her into town, where they picked up Eliza. Nancy was with Kathy, waiting to drive her home as soon as the doctor released her.

Sarah, Jack, and Eliza were all three exhausted by the time they finished at the funeral home, and hardly a word was spoken on the drive back to the house. Though it had only taken a couple of hours, it felt like a lifetime had passed.

Owen had offered to help finish painting the house, and they'd gratefully taken him up on it. He and Gilly were sitting on the porch, taking a break. They stood and came to meet the car.

"Nancy isn't here yet with Kathy?" Jack asked as they got out of the vehicle.

"No. She called a little while ago. The doctor had just come in, so they're going to be an hour or two still," Gilly said, greeting him with a kiss. "Several of the neighbors have stopped by, and there's plenty food inside if you all are hungry."

Food held little appeal to Sarah at the moment. She squeezed Gilly's hand as she walked past her on the way to the house. "I'm going to change clothes."

Upstairs, Sarah felt as though she were moving through a fog. She changed out of the dress she'd worn to the funeral home and hung it up, then pulled a loose sundress out of the closet. She stood staring at it as though she'd never seen it before. A knock on the door startled her out of her reverie.

"Just a minute," she called, and slipped the dress over her head. The bodice laced up, and she tightened it as she walked over and opened the door.

"I wanted to check on you," her mother said.

Standing back, Sarah let Eliza in and closed the door behind her. "I'm okay," she said as she moved to one of the open windows.

"Are you?"

Sarah unpinned her hair and started brushing it. "No. I'm not. But things are what they are, and I don't know what to do to change any of it."

"What do you want to do?" Eliza sat down on the bed and slipped off her shoes with a tired sigh.

"I don't know. I feel like someone came in during the middle of the night and swept me away to some alternate reality. This is my life, but it isn't. Everything's changed, and everything that was good a week or two ago is gone."

"Oh, sweetie, believe me, I understand. What about Owen? He's here."

Sarah straightened the bottles on her dresser. "Is he? Do you think he's really here to stay, or is this all for show?" she asked, using the hairbrush to gesture toward the end of the house where Owen was painting.

Eliza patted the bed. "Come sit down. Tell me what in the world happened with you two. We've not had a chance to talk about it."

Desperately needing her mother's feedback, Sarah sat. She told her mother everything, only leaving out the details of the day she and Owen had been intimate and her crazy suspicions that Owen might be more than human.

When she finished, Eliza shook her head. "What did this epic letter say?"

"I haven't read it yet. I didn't have the energy."

"Are you afraid to?"

Sarah glanced at her mother with a huff of laughter. "Scared to death. Because if he's not apologetic, it's over. And if he is apologetic, then I have to figure out if I'm strong enough to trust him again. I don't want it to be over."

Eliza put her arm around Sarah. "He doesn't act like it's over."

"That makes it harder, not easier. Oh, Mama, what should I do?" She covered her face with her hands.

"You know I can't tell you that, Sarah Jane."

"How did I know you were going to say that?" Sarah picked up a rubber band from the nightstand and twisted her hair into a ponytail. "But I'm asking anyhow. I need your advice, Mama. Please."

Eliza ran her hand down the arch of the wrought-iron footboard. "If it were me, I'd start by reading his letter. Whatever else happens, I think that's necessary." She sighed. "The next few days are going to be incredibly difficult, perhaps even more so than when your father died. I wish he were here, Sarah. I wonder how much of this would be different if he were still here."

"Has Kathy talked to you yet about what happened?"

"Some. She wants to go back to Georgia with Nancy and me as soon as she's able to travel. I think that's probably the best thing for her."

"There are many people around here who think she got exactly what she deserved for cheating on Randall. Did she tell you that the baby wasn't his?" Sarah asked.

"Yes. And I think she knows how people feel. I certainly don't condone what she did, but it's ridiculous to blame the victim for the crime."

Sarah stretched her legs out in front of her and studied the almost-healed scrapes from where she'd tripped on Monday. "When she was here Monday, she seemed so happy, so content. We were kids the last time I saw her like that, Mama. We actually talked, spent time together as sisters."

"I've been doing nothing but thinking this past week. I wonder how long Randall had been abusing her," Eliza said. "Because it makes little sense that he'd go from being neglectful and unfaithful, which we know he was, to murderous. And I'm starting to think she's been hiding a lot from us for a very long time. That's something I'm going to have to live with for the rest of my days."

"You can't help someone if you don't know they need help. We all missed it, Mama. Not just you. And from what little Kathy said, I think she wanted to hide how he treated her. She was ashamed of it."

"That doesn't matter. She's my daughter. I should have known."

"Well, she's my sister, and I saw her that day. I should have stopped her, made her stay here."

"That's ridiculous! There's no way you could have known what he was capable of. None of us did."

Leaning in to look directly into her mother's eyes, Sarah said, "Exactly. None of us knew."

Eliza threw her hands in the air. "Fine. You've made your point." She stood and headed for the door. "It's going to be rough when Kathy gets here. I'll have to sit her down, go over the arrangements. Take a walk, get out of here for a while. You probably won't get a chance for the next few days."

"I think I will if you don't need me," Sarah agreed. "Mama, what about after the funeral? Is everyone going to come to the house?"

"No. Gilly said Silas and Ethel Combs stopped by while we were out. They've offered to have the wake at their house. I think that'll be the best for everyone." She stopped at the door. "The next few weeks are probably not going to be easy for any of us, especially in town. I don't blame your sister for what happened—the responsibility for that lies on Randall's shoulders—but I resent that the scandal's going to be hard on the rest of the family. I have to get over that, I know."

"We'll weather it. And as far as blame goes, Clay's the one who had to open his mouth. If he'd just kept his own council, they could have left without Randall being any the wiser until it was too late."

"And then he might have come up here, killed you and Jack and Gilly."

Sarah crossed the room and laid her hand on Eliza's. "Mama, we can second-guess until the end of eternity, and it won't change what happened. All we can do is move forward and try to pick up the pieces."

Sarah only felt a little guilty that she made sure Owen was busy in the front yard before she sneaked out the back door. After a mad dash into the woods, she slowed to a walk. She needed to go to the pool, to gain some perspective on everything, and she didn't want him to know she'd gone.

When she reached the pool, she climbed to the top of the boulder and sat with her legs dangling over the edge. The day was warm and clear. Sarah leaned back and braced her weight on her elbows, turning her face up to the sun. It didn't take long for the sunshine and fresh air to work a little magic, and Sarah was surprised by a yawn. She considered the blanket she'd brought with her.

"What the heck. I should be fine." She spread the quilt and, using her book bag as a pillow, stretched out and promptly went to sleep.

When she woke up a short time later, the mysterious deer was standing over her, sniffling her hair.

CHAPTER THIRTY-SEVEN

AFTER NANCY AND KATHY ARRIVED, Eliza shooed Owen off with a smile and a small basket of food. A little perturbed as he'd gotten a good start on painting the house, he resisted at first.

"But I've just gotten this side prepped. I'll stay out of your way."

Eliza touched his arm. "Sweetie, I think you need a break. Take a walk in the woods. Take in the scenery. But I want you to go." When Owen's shoulders slumped, she sighed. "Oh, for heaven's sake, Owen. You can come back. I'm not banishing you. And don't worry about the painting supplies. Jack can take care of those."

He scowled. "Okay. I guess I'll see you tomorrow, then. Tell Sarah I… never mind. Thanks for the food."

Still feeling out of sorts, Owen headed home. He didn't see Sarah asleep on the rock until he was almost on top of her. Eliza's pushing him out the door suddenly made a lot more sense.

Putting the food basket down carefully, he squatted beside her. A silky strand of dark hair had come loose from her ponytail and fallen across her face, and Owen brushed it back. Sarah mumbled, but didn't awaken.

Indecision filled Owen. He wanted to sit there beside her, watch over her, and protect her while she slept. However, he realized she had snuck out and not let him know she was coming to the pool because she wanted to be alone. He didn't want to infringe on her privacy, but his instincts told him to not leave her by herself.

The sun felt good on his back, and the musical sound of the water flowing down the rocks of the stream made for a soothing lullaby. He could understand why Sarah had fallen asleep; he was tempted to curl up with her. But he didn't even want to think how she'd react to *that*.

It occurred to him that he could do both—stay near and give her the solitude she wanted. All he had to do was shift into the deer. The decision made, he went up the hill to change.

He realized that once he told Sarah the truth about his being a shifter and revealed to her that he was the young deer, she might not take his presence on the rock with her today well. But it was a chance he had to take.

He stripped and folded his clothes into a neat bundle, then hunkered down. Centering himself mentally, he envisioned his inner deer. His scalp started tingling, then the nerves all along his spine and, finally, his entire body. The tingle became painful, almost unbearably so. Owen's muscles stretched, his bones reshaped themselves, and that simply, he was changed.

The shock of it all left him panting. He hadn't been able to shift recently, having been too tied up with the rebuild. Feeling elation at being in animal form again, he shook himself all over. Once he'd recovered from the transformation, he stretched his neck and haunches. Hungry and needing calories, he trotted back down to the rock and munched on some grass around the boulder's perimeter. He'd seeded the grass the previous fall just for that purpose. As he ate, he kept a close eye on Sarah.

Appetite satisfied, he got a drink of water from the branch, then carefully approached her. He could smell her shampoo and, giving in to temptation, he stretched his neck and sniffed her hair. She stirred, and before he could move back, she opened her eyes.

For a couple of seconds, she stared at him. Then, with a small shriek, which she quickly muffled with her hand, she sat up. Owen stepped back warily, waiting to see what she'd do.

"You," she breathed, her eyes wide. After looking around as though trying to figure out if she were still asleep, her gaze came back to rest on him.

Owen couldn't read her expression. He dipped his head, flicking away a curious fly with the twitch of one ear. When Sarah remained silent, he huffed questioningly.

"You know, you don't age much," she said. "It's almost like you only exist sometimes."

Owen froze. Something about her tone made him wonder if she knew... but no, she couldn't. A twig snapped in the woods, and he turned toward the sound, but it was only a squirrel. When he looked back at Sarah, she had sat up and was watching him, her eyes still heavy from sleep. Her legs were bent, and the skirt of the sundress covered them, with only her toes showing. Feeling playful, he stepped closer and lowered his head to sniff at her toes.

Sarah jerked her feet back. "You stinker. Keep your nose to yourself." Her tone was scolding, but a smile played around her lips.

Emboldened, Owen reached out again and gently clamped the edge of the quilt between his teeth. When he tugged, Sarah's laughter echoed around the clearing.

"Stop that! You're feeling your oats today, aren't you?" She slowly raised her hand. Owen held still and let her touch him between his ears. "Wow. This is incredible," she whispered.

He turned his head so that her hand moved along his fur, then repeated the movement in the other direction. Sarah picked up on the message. She ran her hand down his neck and across his shoulder.

When she reached up and gently tugged on one of his ears, he pulled away with a shake of his head. His ears were very sensitive, and her light touch tickled. She did it again, and he snorted. He took a step back so that he could shake his head more fully.

Sarah laughed again. "Are you ticklish? I'm sorry. I won't do it again."

Owen didn't believe that for an instant, but he eased back over and settled down beside her. They weren't touching, but they were close enough that Sarah could easily pet him. After a while, the long, soothing strokes of her hand down his neck slowed, and she let her hand rest on his shoulder.

They sat like that for a long time, with Sarah not speaking at all. It was odd, Owen thought, being so near her and not being the least bit physically aroused. The connection between them went so much deeper than the physical, and he thought that if he only ever had moments like this with her, it might be enough to sustain him for the rest of his life.

One of the first questions he'd asked Eli once they'd started his training was whether Owen would be still be attracted to humans in his animal form or if the attraction would shift to his animal counterparts.

Eli had assured him that cross-species physical attraction wasn't possible. When he shifted into the deer or the wolf, his uncle had explained, he was still human in spirit, so the emotional connection could still be there with a woman.

Regardless of Eli's reassurances, Owen had always worried in the back of his mind. Sitting next to Sarah, he realized that if there was ever going to be a time he'd be aroused, it would be with her. He was immensely relieved to know that Eli had been correct.

"So I've not been very happy lately," Sarah whispered. "There's been a lot going on in my life, and it's mostly been bad. I have some tough decisions to make, and I'm not sure what I'm going to do."

Owen's heart raced. He knew that his listening to her private thoughts was something she wouldn't forgive. Standing up with a clatter of his hooves, he moved away from her.

"Don't you want to hear what I'm thinking?" she asked.

He snorted and went to the branch to get another drink, frantically trying to figure out what to do. As hard as he found the idea to swallow, he knew he had to walk away from her. When he heard someone coming up the path, he whirled around to see who it was. The wind was coming from that direction, and he easily scented Jack. Sure that Sarah would be safe, he took off up the hill.

It wasn't until he got back to the rock where he'd hidden his clothes and had changed back into human form that he remembered the basket Eliza had packed for him—the basket he'd left sitting on the rock beside Sarah—and he cursed.

Sarah had been working her way to addressing the deer as "Owen" when Jack came up the path, startling him away. She swore under her breath as she waited for her brother to join her on the rock.

"What are you doing up here?" she asked.

"Looking for you. Mama needs you back at the house. I wouldn't normally come over here and bother you, but she said it was important." He frowned. "Where's Owen?"

Sarah scowled. "How should I know? I haven't seen him."

Jack pursed his lips. "You haven't? Because I could swear that's the basket of food Mama packed for him." He pointed behind her.

Sarah turned. Sure enough, a basket sat there, a basket that hadn't been there when she'd gone to sleep. She had been so distracted by the deer's presence that she hadn't even noticed.

The food being there was too much of a coincidence, and for a few seconds, Sarah thought she might faint.

"Sarah? You okay?"

She ran a hand over her face. "Yeah. Maybe he passed by here and left it. What does Mama need? Is anything wrong?"

"No, but I think Kathy's asking for you."

Sarah stood to shake out the quilt, then stuffed it in her bag. "Grab that basket, will you? We can't leave it here. The animals might get it." She said the last part with a strong sense of irony. She had an idea one animal in particular might get into the basket, and she snorted. Oh, yes, she and Owen were going to have to talk, and soon. She could hardly wait to see how he explained that basket.

CHAPTER THIRTY-EIGHT

THE DAY OF THE FUNERAL arrived with rain clouds and thunder. While Sarah got dressed, she tried to keep her mind as blank as possible. The task wasn't easy. The reality of the loss of Moira and the baby was hitting home.

It was such a senseless waste. The children had been so innocent, so sweet, so undeserving of the fate they had been handed. Sarah was struggling to keep herself as calm as possible. She was torn between anger at Kathy for placing them in the situation and grief for her sister for the living hell her life had apparently been. On top of that was her own guilt for not having seen what Randall really was.

Kathy was staying two doors down the hall, tucked away in the room she'd had as a girl. Jack and Gilly had offered her the use of their bedroom, but she'd declined.

Though she seemed to be recovering, albeit slowly, from the physical trauma, her mental recovery hadn't even remotely begun yet. She couldn't stand to be touched by anyone other than Eliza, and any loud noise startled her so badly she trembled for an hour afterward. When the day of the visitation came, Kathy had refused to come out of her room.

"I can't. I can't go. I can't face them, what I did to them."

Eliza had spent over an hour closeted away with Kathy. When their mother came out of the bedroom, the decision had been made. "She's not going, and I don't think she should. I don't think she can handle it. Nancy, can you stay with her?"

Nancy had agreed, and the rest of the family had gone without Kathy.

On the day of the funeral, Kathy remained steadfast in her determination to avoid the services. Sarah finished dressing and went down the hall, where she knocked on the open bedroom door. Kathy was sitting in a chair, looking out the window. She had one of Moira's dolls clasped in her hands and was absently playing with its hair.

She answered Sarah's knock without turning. "Come in."

Sarah moved to stand beside Kathy's chair. She didn't understand how Kathy could not need to go to the funeral, not need the closure the services would provide, but she had to respect her sister's decision.

"I know you think poorly of me because I'm not going to the funeral. I can imagine what the townsfolk are going to think." Kathy's voice was rusty from disuse.

Sarah fetched the footstool and pulled it over so she could sit beside her sister. "I'm perplexed, but I don't think poorly of you. I guess I don't understand, but my understanding isn't necessary. As for the rest of the town, hang them."

Kathy snorted. "Well, then I guess I think poorly enough of me for both of us." She shifted her gaze from the window to look down at the doll in her hands, seeming oblivious to the tears that tracked slowly down her cheeks. "Owen came back."

Sarah cleared her throat. Her sister's silent grief was almost more than she could bear. "Yes, he did."

"You've not made up yet. How come?"

Shifting so that her back rested against the bed, Sarah clasped her hands around one knee. "Because I'm afraid he'll hurt me again. And I feel incredibly vain and shallow saying that to you after what you've been through."

Kathy sent her a sidelong look. "Hurt comes in all shapes and sizes. Just because he didn't do to you what Randall did to me doesn't mean your hurt isn't as bad in its own way as mine."

Sarah tilted her head. "How can you compare the two?"

"I can't. I don't. I hope to God you never know what I've been through. But don't diminish your own feelings because of this." She waved a hand. "Are you going to forgive him?"

"I don't know. I think I am. Does that make me gullible?"

"Not necessarily. I've been watching him these last few days. I don't like the way he did you, but he doesn't act like... well, he doesn't act like Randall. And he doesn't act like Randall's friends either. Did you talk to him about the other woman?"

Sarah found it a little odd that Kathy was so eager to discuss her love life, but considering what the rest of the day held, maybe it made sense. Her sister was probably desperate for a distraction.

"I did, briefly. You were right; she is someone he's been with. But he only accepted a ride from her that day. They were together years ago and only for a few months." Seeing Kathy's skeptical look, she held up her hand. "I know, I know. But it would be very easy for me to verify whether he's lying. Besides, he wrote me a letter, and he said the same things in the letter as he told me in person. I finally worked up the courage to read it yesterday."

"I hope you're right. I need to believe there's still something good in this world."

Eliza interrupted to let Sarah know it was time to go. As she stood, she held out her hand to Kathy, letting her sister decide whether to accept her touch or not. After a brief hesitation, Kathy clasped Sarah's hand, squeezing tightly. It wasn't the hug Sarah wanted to give her, but Sarah knew it was all Kathy could handle at the moment.

Four hours later, the funeral was over. The babies had been placed together in one casket and laid to rest next to Ira in the family cemetery. Sarah wondered how the family had gotten through it all. She'd never expected to be back in the cemetery again so soon, staring down into a dark hole in the ground. She'd certainly never imagined the next funeral would be for Moira and the baby. She hated thinking of him as little Randall. She didn't even want the son of a bitch to have that much claim on the child.

Throughout the funeral and graveside service, she'd leaned heavily on Owen. He said little, but he was there from start to finish. He anticipated her needs almost before she knew she had them and was so quietly solicitous of her that Sarah felt like weeping all over again.

They went straight to Silas and Ethel Combs's house after the burial. Sarah had always held the older couple in high esteem, but their generosity in opening their home for the wake left her speechless with gratitude and affection.

An hour into the gathering, Sarah stepped out onto the back porch for a brief respite.

Eliza, apparently having the same idea, came out a few minutes later. "You look like you're considering making a run for it."

"I am considering it," Sarah said. "I know I shouldn't."

"Why not?"

Eyebrows raised, Sarah blinked at her mother. "What?"

"Sweetie, I think you've done enough. You deserve some time to yourself. And I'm fairly certain there's a young man who'd like to spend some alone time with you as well. Why don't you find him and have him take you home? If you want to go somewhere after that, you should."

Sarah let out a tired breath. "What about you?"

"I'm fine. After we're done here, I'm probably going to go home and sleep for a while. But I know you, and I know that you're champing at the bit to get out of here. You still don't like crowds."

"No, I don't," Sarah admitted. "Especially when it's this kind of crowd for this kind of purpose."

"So go find Owen. Make him show you his house." Sarah had confided Owen's living arrangement to her mother during their discussion the other day.

"Maybe that's not a bad idea."

"It's a *good* idea," Eliza stated. "I'll make your excuses to Ethel." She turned to go back inside, then stopped and came back to Sarah. In a voice that was almost a whisper, she said, "Just make sure you take that box I gave you."

"Mama!"

"Don't be afraid to live, Sarah. Especially not now. Love you, baby girl." With a quick hug, Eliza disappeared inside the house.

Sarah was left standing on the porch, her mouth open. As the wind picked up, she studied the sky. The storm front that had been threatening all day was almost there. If she was going to get Owen and leave, she should probably do it before the rain started.

As she reached for the door, Owen opened it from the other side. "Hey. Your mom said you needed me?"

"She would, wouldn't she? I was thinking about leaving. Do you want to go?"

"Sure. Do you want to go home or what?"

"Yes. I need to change clothes. But after that, could we go somewhere to talk?" She didn't look at him as they walked around the house to the field where he'd parked his truck.

"Of course we can. You tell me where." He looked up at the sky as he held the door open for her. "I don't think our usual spot's going to work."

Sarah waited until he'd gone around the truck and slid in behind the wheel. "I was thinking we could go to your house."

Owen paused in the act of starting the truck. "M-my house? Not the farmhouse, but my house?"

"Mm-hmmm, if that's okay."

She heard him swallow from across the cab. "We can do that."

At her house, she hurried inside and greeted Nancy. "I'm going to Owen's house with him. I don't know when I'll be back. How's Kathy?"

"Sleeping. You take as long as you need, honey. We'll be here."

In her room, Sarah changed out of the funeral dress. Once she was clad more casually, she grabbed her book bag and threw some things in it. Heart pounding, she slowly eased open the drawer to her nightstand.

Sitting beside the letter Owen had written her was the birth control kit. Sarah put the letter in her bag, and without letting herself think about it too much, she grabbed the box and put it in as well. After slipping on her tennis shoes, she went back downstairs and out to Owen's truck.

"Ready?" he asked.

"I guess so. We're driving around?"

"Unless you know a shortcut," he told her with a smile.

Sarah shook her head. "I guess we're driving, then."

When they got to the top of the mountain, Owen parked the truck, got out, and walked around to open Sarah's door. Thunder rumbled as they walked to the house.

Unlocking the door, Owen pushed it open and stood back for her to enter. "After you."

Sarah's initial look at the inside of Owen's house was surprising. The first floor was open and airy, with high ceilings and comfortable-looking furniture. A small dining area was to the right, in front of the kitchen, with a bar separating them. To the left was the living space. A stone-faced wall with a woodstove covered most of one wall, and a wide table sat before the tall windows that fronted the house. Bookcases flanked the woodstove, and the table was covered with stacks of papers and books.

"Is this where you write?"

"No. This is where I research. I write upstairs. Want to see?"

"Please." Sarah followed him past the kitchen to a set of stairs set against the back wall.

"Half-bath back there and the washer," he said, pointing past the stairs. "Side door goes out to the patio."

The stairs were lit by tall windows set high into the wall. When they reached the upstairs hallway, Sarah could see out the windows and into the treetops beyond.

Owen directed her down the hall, which was lined with more bookshelves. "Full bath here, complete with tub and shower."

Sarah glanced in the room he indicated. Past the bathroom, the floor opened up into his bedroom. To her right was a door that went out onto a balcony. The bed was straight ahead and seemed to stretch halfway across the room. At its foot, on the opposite wall, was another woodstove. Beyond the bed, the room went on a good fifteen feet or so. A dividing screen separated the sleeping area from the work area.

Sarah approached his studio with reverence. "So this is it, where you make the magic."

Owen gave her a brief smile. "Yes." Low cabinets formed a U-shape around the outer walls. Most were less than three feet tall, but the cabinets to her left were taller. On the right, they were interrupted by a drafting table. The center of the area was occupied by a round table, and several sketches were laid out on its surface.

Walking to the bank of windows that looked out over the front of the house and into the kitchen garden, Sarah turned and caught Owen watching her. She smiled sheepishly. "It's not like I pictured it."

"How'd you picture it?"

"More like a rustic cabin, I guess. But it's very modern, very sleek."

He stepped over to the table and straightened the drawings. "Are you disappointed?"

She shook her head. "No. Where does the door go?"

"I'll show you."

Stopping only to toss her bag on the bed, Sarah followed him. He unlocked the inside door and the screen door and stood back for her to precede him. The door opened onto a large deck, which overlooked a slate-rock patio. The view was breathtaking, unobstructed by trees.

"You really can see for miles from up here," Sarah breathed. "I don't see how you can bear to tear yourself away from it."

Owen's hand trailed down from her shoulder to her waist. "There's more."

Turning, Sarah saw a set of stairs that seemed to vanish into the roof. Eager to see where they led, she crossed the deck. "Oh, this is incredible." Stunned, she looked back at Owen, who was climbing the stairs slower than she had.

Carved out of the roof was an area with low walls. The surface was flat, and even though the roof was all around them, it didn't interfere with the view. Sarah felt as if she were on top of the world. "What is this place?"

He shoved his hands in his pockets. "I like astronomy. This is where I come to stargaze."

Sarah was astonished by how much the house spoke to her. It felt like a sanctuary, and she could see why it brought Owen such peace. "You've built yourself an aerie up here on top of the mountain."

His mouth tightened. "I've been hiding up here, rejecting the world. Don't romanticize it; it's nothing but cowardice."

"Owen. Don't say that." Sarah moved to touch him, but he backed up a step.

"Let's go back downstairs. We need to start this talk we've been putting off."

She followed without protest, but when he started for the hallway and the stairs, she stopped him. "I'd prefer to stay up here."

His shoulders stiffened, and he faced her with a scowl. "Why?"

Gathering her courage, Sarah took his hands. "Do you love me?"

Owen swallowed. "More than anything."

"And you want to be with me?"

"Oh, yes."

"And do you give me your word that you'll never again do what you've done these last few weeks? No matter what, you'll always stay in touch? Even if you're angry with me?"

"Yes," he whispered. "Sarah—"

Pressing two fingers across his lips, Sarah rose onto her tiptoes. "Shh, Owen." Sliding her fingers away, she replaced them with her lips.

A few seconds later, Owen took over the kiss she'd started. He clamped her against him, his arms like a vise, and kissed her as if he were starving for the taste of her. Sarah met him at every turn.

His hands seemed to be everywhere at once, and still he wasn't touching her enough. She moaned against his mouth, wanting more. Her head fell back, and when his hot mouth moved down to the base of her throat, she gasped.

She fought to get her hands under the hem of his shirt, and once she had, she jerked up the fabric. "Off. This needs to come off."

Owen pulled back, his eyes hooded and hot with arousal. "Sarah, we should stop now."

Even as he said the words, she was shaking her head. She looked straight into his eyes. "No. I don't want to stop. I want to keep going. Show me, please. Show me everything."

His eyes widened. "Do you know what you're asking?"

"Yes."

"Why now? There are things we need to discuss, important things I need to tell you."

"I know we need to talk, and I promise you, we will. But right now, I want to be with you. All the way, in every way. I want to be with you. I don't want to spend another minute apart from you. If the last couple of weeks have shown me anything, it's that. If that isn't what you want, then I'll go. I don't want to pressure you. But if it is, please… don't turn me away. Tomorrow isn't guaranteed, and I don't want to lose another minute with you."

He stood, head bowed, hands clenched at his sides. Sarah thought he was going to say no, but then he groaned. He took a step, bringing them so close together she could feel the heat radiating off of him. "If we do this, there's no going back. We'll be married this week. This is permanent. Is that what you want?"

"Yes. Yes. More than anything."

He searched her eyes. Finally, to Sarah's relief, he seemed to see what he wanted. Moving slowly, he drew her to him. "I love you so much, Sarah Jane Browning. I hope you know that," he murmured against her mouth.

"I do. I really do."

The kiss escalated into a white-hot need, and they were both breathing hard by the time Owen lifted his mouth from hers. With a heated groan, he lifted her into his arms and carried her to the bed.

Some time later, they were curled up together. This time, they hadn't stopped. This time, they'd made love completely. Boneless and content, Sarah kept one hand on his back and raised the other to push his hair from his face. The sight of white speckles peppered through it made her smile. "You have paint in your hair."

"I'm not surprised. It's near impossible to get out." He reached up and traced her lips with his index finger. "You are so beautiful. I could lay here and look at you forever. Do you know that?"

"I might let you if you promise to let me look back." Sarah put a hand to his chest. "So that's what sex is all about."

"No."

Startled, Sarah laughed. "No? You mean the books have it wrong?"

Owen shook his head. When he raised his head, she saw his eyes were damp. "No, I mean what we just did wasn't sex. It was love. We made love."

The raw emotion on his face stole her breath. "Oh, Owen. Yes, we certainly did."

CHAPTER THIRTY-NINE

OWEN COULD HARDLY BELIEVE THAT Sarah was in his house, much less in his bed. He'd dreamt of having her there so often he kept surreptitiously pinching himself to make sure she was real.

When she noticed what he was doing, she wrinkled her nose. "What are you doing?"

"Pinching myself," he admitted sheepishly. They were lying side by side in his bed, and Owen couldn't stop touching her. Her face, her arm, her hand. He let his fingers trace the lines of her body. "I keep thinking I'm going to wake up and discover this was all a dream."

Sarah touched his jaw. "It's real. I promise you."

Owen excused himself to deal with the condom, then hurried back to the bedroom.

Sarah was sitting up on the side of the bed, the bedspread pulled around her. She glanced up at him with a shy smile. Cheeks flushed, her lips swollen from his kisses, the picture she made nearly stopped his heart.

"Do you want to take a bath?" he asked. "You're probably sore."

"I don't want to impose."

Owen went to her and hunkered down, his hands resting on either side of her hips. "Sarah, love, you aren't imposing. If I have my way, you'll be living here by the end of the weekend. I don't want you to suffer because of what we did. The bath will help."

"Okay."

He stood and held out his hand. Owen chuckled. "You'll have to let go of the quilt."

Sarah laughed. "I know. I'm not as comfortable being naked as you are."

Owen tugged, and she came to her feet. He ran his free hand down her hair. "We'll fix that soon enough."

"Owen!" She hid her face against his chest, and Owen slid his arms around her. He sent a prayer of thanks heavenward and guided her down the hall into the bathroom.

When she saw the tub, she let out an admiring sound. "Where in the world did you find a bathtub so big? I've never seen one this size."

"I read about it in a magazine while I was planning the layout for this house. I enjoy soaking in the tub in the winter and figured I'd indulge myself. It's big enough for two."

"I noticed," Sarah said dryly. Then the meaning behind his words sank in, and her eyes widened. "Oh. You mean... oh."

"Just because it's big enough for two doesn't mean we have to share," he hurried to assure her. "I thought I'd mention... never mind. I shouldn't have said anything. I'll get the water started and get out of your hair."

"My hair. I need to get the rubber band so I can pull it out of the way." She disappeared back down the hall.

He put the stopper in and turned on the taps, cursing himself for being too eager. While he waited, he pulled out a box of Epsom salts and poured a little into the water, then followed that with a dollop of bubble bath. Checking the water temperature, he adjusted the taps.

"Towels," he muttered. "She'll need towels." He got two fluffy towels down from the storage closet and placed them on the wide ledge of the tub.

When Sarah came back in, she was twisting her hair up as she walked. She stopped inside the door to finish the job.

"I'll let you be," he said and walked past her. "Holler if you need anything."

"Owen? Will you stay?" The question was so tentative he barely heard it over the rush of running water. She was biting her lip as she looked up at him uncertainly.

Seeing that the tub was nearly full, he went back and turned off the water. "Are you sure?"

"Yes."

"Then I'll stay. Check this and make sure it isn't too hot," he said.

Sarah bent to swish a hand through the water, and Owen's mouth went dry at the sight of the curve of her bare hip. He looked away quickly, but not fast enough, as a tingle of arousal started in his groin.

"Feels wonderful," she said as she straightened. "So, um, how do we do this?"

He stepped over the tall side easily and sank into the water. He patted the ledge. "Sit here and swing your legs in. Sit between my legs." When she swung her left leg over the rim, he saw the rust-colored stains on the inside of her thighs and grimaced.

Sarah noticed his gaze and looked down. "Oh. Um, I think that's normal, too."

Owen didn't care if it was normal; he'd hurt her. His face must have conveyed his turmoil, because when Sarah slid into the water, she moved to frame his face with her hands.

"I'm okay, Owen. It had to happen. Please don't be upset." She kissed him tenderly, then turned and settled back against him with a sigh. "This feels so good. Thank you for suggesting it."

He shifted, getting comfortable, and relaxed against the slope of the tub.

Sarah leaned into him, and under the water, her hands skimmed along the muscles in his legs. "So I finally garnered the courage to read your letter yesterday. The doodles were a nice touch."

Thinking of the deer he'd drawn, complete with a landscape including birds, a squirrel, and Hootie the owl, Owen scowled. "Doodles?"

Sarah leaned her head back and looked up at him, her lips pressed together to hold in her laughter. "Mm-hmmm. I particularly liked the hearts and flowers with our initials." When his scowl deepened, her laugh bubbled out.

Owen growled, exasperated. "God save me from teenage girls. Julie must have 'enhanced' the letter. I'm sorry."

"It's okay. I think it's cute, even if her stealing the letter was almost a disaster."

Owen huffed. "I don't think it's cute. If Amy hadn't discovered Julie had it, I wouldn't have come home when I did. I could have lost you forever."

"No." Sarah's voice rang with certainty. "No, I don't think so. Oh, it would have been more painful than it has been, but I think we would have found our way back to each other."

"I hope so." He pressed a kiss to her hair just above her ear. "Promise me something, though?"

"If I can."

"If we are blessed enough to have children, make sure they're all boys."

Sarah slid her arms over his and laced their fingers together. "I don't think we get a choice in the matter."

Owen groaned into her neck. "God help us, then. We'll probably have half a dozen girls."

"How many daughters does your uncle have?"

"Three. Claire is twenty, and the other two are teenagers. Joline is sixteen; Julie's fourteen. Jo's boy crazy like you wouldn't believe, and Julie's about half as bad. They caused me more trouble than all the boys put together, and there were three of them. Tad's fifteen, and Greg and Noah are thirteen. They're twins. Trent's the oldest, at twenty-three, and he's married with his first child on the way."

"I can't imagine having that many kids in one family. Oh, I know most of the people around here do it, but I think it would be a madhouse all the time. It was bad enough with the three of us growing up. Do you want kids?"

Owen hesitated. "The idea of you having my children scares me to death. Do you know how dangerous childbearing is?"

Sarah turned to face him, sliding her legs over his so that she was sitting in his lap. "I do. But we have an excellent hospital with wonderful doctors. It's safer now than it has ever been." Her hands slid around his neck, and she rested her head against his shoulder. "I want babies with you, Owen."

"You might not after we talk."

"Is it time for you to finally reveal this big, dreadful secret you have?" she teased.

"Yes. It isn't a joke, Sarah. I wouldn't blame you if you walked away once you know."

She traced the shell of his ear with a delicate finger. Owen scowled and batted at her hand.

To his surprise, she grinned. "Your ears really are that ticklish, aren't they?"

Between the comment and the expectant look she was sending him, Owen realized she knew. When she used her fingertip to lift his chin, he realized he'd been staring at her, mouth agape. He sat up quickly, causing her to squeal and tighten her arms around his shoulders. Water sloshed out of the tub, but he ignored it.

"You know. How do you... when did you...?" His voice faded as he stared at her. "Sarah? Explain?"

She shrugged. "I don't know as much as you apparently think I do. And I'm not sure I believe what I know. Or think I know." She smoothed her hands over his shoulders and the top of his chest.

Owen realized she was nervous. "If you've soaked long enough, why don't we get out of here and go somewhere that we can talk a little easier?"

"Okay."

He helped her step out of the tub, then pulled the plug. Once they were dried off, he started toward the door.

Sarah cleared her throat. "Um, would you mind closing the door? I need to use the facilities."

"Yes, ma'am. I'll see you in a few minutes."

In the bedroom, Owen opened his dresser and pulled out a pair of pajama bottoms. While he didn't mind being naked, he wanted Sarah as comfortable for the upcoming conversation as was possible. Leaving his chest bare, he grabbed a soft T-shirt for her to wear and moved to straighten the bedclothes. Figuring she might want to cover up, he folded the sheet and bedspread back to the foot of the bed. He stacked the pillows against the tall headboard and stood back, eyeing his handiwork critically. Satisfied, he went back down the hall in time to hear the toilet flush.

"I'm going to get something to drink," he called through the bathroom door. "I laid a shirt out for you on the bed. Do you want anything?"

"Just something cold," Sarah answered.

When Owen came back upstairs, she was in the bedroom and clad in the shirt. She wasn't on the bed as he'd expected.

Instead, she was standing at the round table, looking down at his sketches. Owen set the pitcher of water and two glasses on the nightstand and moved to stand behind her. He undid the rubber band around her hair and tossed it on the table, then slid his arms around her waist.

"I know it's terribly nosy of me," she said, "but I am officially your biggest fan. I couldn't help myself; I had to look."

"I'll forgive your nosiness for a kiss," Owen murmured against her neck, then bit the soft skin lightly. He felt a shiver run through her, and she moved her head so that he had better access.

"I'll be glad to pay up. But we need to finish that discussion first."

"I know. Come on. Let's get comfortable."

Sarah settled in against the pillows and tugged the sheet up over her. He filled a glass with cold water and handed it to her, then filled his own.

Stretching out, he drew in a deep, steadying breath. "Tell me what you suspect."

Crossing her legs, Sarah gave a little shrug. "What I suspect should qualify me for the loony bin. I feel ridiculous even saying it. But as crazy as this seems, I believe you might be a shapeshifter who turns into the most adorable deer I've ever seen. A deer who looks remarkably like Toby from your books. It's the only thing that makes sense. It's why you sign your letters with a drawing of him, isn't it?"

"How'd you figure it out?"

Her eyes widened. "You mean it's really true?"

Owen realized then that she had doubted her own judgment. "It is."

She smiled and gave a small laugh. Shaking her head, the laughter increased to a soft, tinkling roll even as her smile widened into a grin. "I'm sorry. I just... I can't believe it. And

I know it has to be true, or maybe I really have fallen down the rabbit hole, but it's incredible."

"How did you put it together?"

"*The Summer Folly of Tobias Hedge*. I was reading it to Kathy the day you came home." She shrugged. "You like apples, and you hate egg salad. Do you remember that 'conversation' we had at the pool the summer I graduated from high school? Of course, you could only snort and shake your head at me since you were a deer."

Owen closed his eyes. "And Toby ate the girl's apple."

"Yes, he did. And turned his nose up at her egg salad." Sarah moved to stand on her knees over him and put her hands on her hips. "I went skinny-dipping that day. Where were you?"

It didn't take much of a tug to send her tumbling into his arms. Owen rolled onto his back and settled her against his chest. "Up the hill, hiding behind a rock. I could hear you, but I couldn't see you. I wouldn't spy on you like that, Sarah. That's why I left the other day before you revealed any secrets to me. Or rather, to the deer."

She smiled down at him. "*Deer* Owen. I find it amazing. And as soon as I'm convinced I'm not crazy, in about fifty years or so, I'll probably stop reacting like this. But for now, it's just amazing."

He grunted. "You say that now. Wait until we have a teenager or three running around, changing. Then you'll rue the day you met me."

Sarah's expression went blank. She obviously hadn't considered the implications of having children by a shifter, and Owen felt his heart sink. Certain that she would start distancing herself, he braced for rejection.

"That's what happened to you and your father, isn't it? You hit puberty and changed, and he couldn't handle it. Oh, Owen. I'm so sorry."

Owen rubbed his cheek against hers. "You constantly amaze me. Did you know that?" He kissed her with an intensity that threatened to start something they couldn't finish right then. Remembering her question, though, he pulled back with reluctance. "And to answer your question, yes. He wasn't a shifter, and he didn't understand it."

"So, where did it come from? Your mother?"

Owen fell back on the bed. "Yes. It comes through the Wells family."

Sarah leaned across him, her weight on one arm. The position caused her shirt to ride up, revealing the edge of her panties. Owen stroked the smooth skin of her legs, soothing himself almost as much as he was trying to soothe her.

Sarah, however, seemed remarkably calm. "So Eli... he's a shifter?"

"Yes."

"And his kids?"

"Four of them are."

She frowned. "But not all of them? How come?"

Owen shrugged. "Genetics. It's like blue eyes or curly hair, as far as I can tell. I got the gene; Harlan didn't. Sometimes it skips entire generations. There's no rhyme or reason to it, which makes the condition that much more dangerous."

"Did you always know you were a shifter?"

"No. I found out the hard way when I was thirteen. My mother was afraid to tell me; she had hoped I wouldn't turn out to be a shifter. She didn't get her wish." He rubbed his eyes, remembering the weeks and months that had followed his first transformation. "That's why I'm telling you now. I won't go into a marriage unless you're aware of what all that entails exactly. She didn't tell my father until I was four years old. He never had a choice in the matter. I don't want to do that to you."

Sarah rubbed her hand across his chest, curling her fingers in the hair and tugging. "So if we have children who are shifters, what does that mean? Do they have to go into training when they reach a certain age? I'm guessing that's why you were sent to London, to Eli, right?"

"Yes. I had to go through what I did because of the way I was taught about shifting. Eli's kids had a much easier time of it. They were told as soon as they were old enough to understand and keep a secret."

"Do parents know right away if a child has the gene or not?"

"Some do; some don't. Sometimes the signs are dormant until the children reach puberty, and sometimes it's apparent from the time they start to walk. Every child is unique."

She appeared to consider his words, a slight frown between her eyes. "Okay. So do your cousins change into deer also? Or are there other creatures, like bobcats?"

"Like Minerva, you mean? It really depends on the person. Most people can only change into one animal, and a few can change into two."

"Really? What about you? Can you change into something other than a deer?"

Owen sat up, tipping her back so that she was lying across his legs. "You're enjoying this a little too much," he teased. "Are you sure your family doesn't have a shifter somewhere you aren't telling me about?" He slipped his hand under her shirt, moving it up the soft skin of her abdomen to cup her breast.

Though Sarah's eyes softened, she didn't let him distract her. She covered his hand with hers and used her free hand to pinch him under the arm.

"Ow!"

"Answer the question, please. I can tell that you don't want to. That must mean you change into something else. So what is it?"

Resigned, Owen confessed. "A wolf."

Pushing his hand aside, she slowly sat up. "A *wolf*? As in a howl-at-the-moon wolf?"

"Yes."

She stared at him, mouth open in shock. "A black-and-gray wolf, by chance?"

Owen nodded tersely. "Yes." He watched her put two and two together.

"That was you all those years ago. You're the one who saved me from the snake."

When Sarah was seventeen, she'd come face-to-fang with a deadly rattlesnake while out on one of her walks. A large, angry wolf had come along out of nowhere and torn the snake to shreds, saving her life. The event had seemed so surreal that over the intervening years, she'd almost convinced herself that she'd imagined it.

He couldn't read her expression. Given that he'd pretended ignorance on several occasions, he almost expected her to slap him and storm out.

Instead, she sagged back and teared up. "How long have you been looking out for me?"

"Since that day. Does that change things for you?"

"No. It surprises me, that's all. I was expecting the deer, not the wolf. I have to get my head around it." She pursed her lips and studied him with a considering gaze. "Is that something you'd let me see you as?"

He looked down at the place where her hand rested on his belly. He trailed his fingers across hers. "Why would you want to see that again?"

"Owen. You can't seriously not know." When he shrugged, she sighed. "Oh, my dear, sweet Owen. If I could turn into a creature as magnificent as a wolf, wouldn't you want to see *me*?"

CHAPTER FORTY

FROM THE STUNNED LOOK ON Owen's face, Sarah realized he had expected a much different reaction. At first, she was a little insulted, but then remembering what he'd told her about his childhood, his confusion made more sense. She brought his hand to her mouth and placed a kiss on his knuckles.

"I don't know," he finally answered. "That's something I'll have to think about. The wolf... it's the deepest, darkest part of me. I only go there when I'm in the worst place mentally. I don't want to show you that right now. Not today. There's been enough darkness today."

Sarah touched his face, her heartache flaring as she thought about the funeral. Deliberately, she focused her mind away from the babies. "Yes, there has. Okay. So is shifting like you explain it in the *Tobias Hedge* books?"

"Mostly. It's a lot less magical, but the basic mechanics are the same. There's no glow, no mist, just a physical transformation."

"And you can do it at will?"

He shrugged. "Most of the time. If I'm getting sick, which is rare, or if I'm extraordinarily tired, it doesn't work. And I can prevent it from happening, though that's harder when I'm upset. That's how Jack figured it out. I lost my temper."

"Jack knows?" Sarah sat up and pulled away. "For how long?"

Owen sat up as well. "Since the day we had the fight. He guessed, and I had to tell him. And I'm pretty sure your dad knew. Your mom too. Ira came up to see me after the incident with the snake."

Sarah was flabbergasted. Her hurt must have shown on her face because he rushed to explain.

"I hated that I didn't talk to you first, but Jack wouldn't exactly wait for answers. And what with the funerals and all the work related to those, I haven't had an opportunity to discuss it with you. Until now. Please don't be hurt. I didn't deliberately tell him and not you. And your dad guessed, I think. He never flat out told me he knew I was a shifter, but the implication was there. God, I'm such a screwup."

"They never said a word to me." She closed her eyes, feeling a little foolish that she was the last person in her family to know about Owen's gift. When she looked back at him again, his misery was plain to see. Some of the sting faded. "Is there anything else, anything *at all,* that you haven't told me? If so, please just blurt it out now. I can't take any more surprises."

"That's all. You know everything."

She let out a sigh. "I'm crazy for doing it, but I believe you. But if you ever hide something from me again, I'll have your..." She glanced down at his lap. "Well, it won't be pleasant."

Owen cringed. "Cross my heart. You know everything."

After a gentle kiss, Sarah pulled back. "So, did you start to change into the wolf when you and Jack were fighting?"

"No. My eyes flashed."

"Flashed how?"

He sighed. "It's easier to show you than explain. Okay?"

"Okay."

He closed his eyes and drew in a deep breath. When he raised his eyelids, his irises had taken on a golden hue that glowed in the dim light coming through the windows. The pupils had shifted a little also, taking on a more animalistic slant.

"Whoa. That's… wow!"

He blinked, and his eyes were back to the warm amber brown Sarah loved. She touched the skin around his eyes and shook her head, astonished. "Does your vision change when you do that?"

"A little, but not much. I know you have a lot of questions, but can they wait? I'm getting a little hungry."

When her stomach growled, they both laughed. "I guess I'm a little hungry, too."

She followed him downstairs, where Owen insisted she have a seat on one of the stools at the kitchen bar. "You've cooked for me several times. It's only fair I return the favor," he teased. "Is soup and grilled cheese sandwiches okay?"

"Of course." She watched him move around the kitchen with competence. "I guess you have to be fairly self-sufficient, living alone."

He opened a large jar of soup and emptied it into a saucepan. "I do okay. The soup's Amy's. She makes a huge batch every time she knows I'm heading down there and sends it home with me."

"Eli and Amy sound like wonderful people. You're lucky to have them."

"I know. I can't imagine what my life would have been like if they hadn't been there. Speaking of them, I've been thinking about something. I wanted to run it by you first."

Sarah propped her chin on her hand. "Okay. I'm listening."

"They lost everything in the fire. Furniture, clothes, everything. And I have that house sitting over there." He pointed toward his parents' house. "It's full of furniture that's going to waste. It wouldn't fully outfit them, but it'd go a long way. There are a few pieces I'd like to hold on to, but I'd like to give the rest to them. I don't plan on ever living in that house again unless you want to."

With a frown, Sarah tilted her head. "I wouldn't force you to go back there, not as much as the place bothers you. For goodness' sake, give it to them. You don't need my permission to do that. It's your house, Owen."

He buttered the bread for the sandwiches. "It'll be your house soon enough."

Sarah wet her lips. "You say that, but I don't recall any formal proposal. So maybe it will be, maybe it won't." When he looked at her with consternation, she gave him an innocent look. "What?"

He went to the stove and turned off the burner, then came around the end of the counter. "You stay right here." He dashed upstairs but returned in less than a minute, a fierce look on his face. When he held out his hand, Sarah's heart soared. With not a little anxiety, she placed her hand in his.

Owen drew her to her feet and wrapped his arms around her. She let her hands rest lightly on his chest, and as much as she wanted to, she couldn't meet his eyes. She felt incredibly shy and, to her shock, terribly afraid.

He touched her cheek with his hand. "Look at me."

Sarah shook her head and buried her face against his chest. "I can't." She laughed. She bit the knuckle of her thumb.

"Sweetheart, if you don't look at me, I can't show you what I have in my hand. Sarah, come on. Please?"

Drawing on her courage and feeling somewhat ridiculous for being so missish, she raised her head.

Owen smiled and gave her a brief kiss. "That's my girl. Now, there's something I've been wanting to ask you for several weeks now. Thanks to an entire load of bad luck, I've had to wait longer than I expected. I want you to know that I'm not jumping in here blind."

"Okay."

He pushed her hair back off her face with one hand, keeping his other arm firmly around her waist. "You mean the world to me. I knew from the first time I saw you, when you were fifteen... remember?" Sarah nodded, and he continued, "From that first time, I knew you were special. When I saw you again that summer before you left, I told myself it was a good thing you were going. Because I knew you could break my heart without even trying. It wasn't until you came back last fall that I realized how deep I was already in. And then we got to know each other, and I didn't want out anymore. I didn't want to hide anymore. So with that in mind..." He went down on one knee.

Sarah could scarcely breathe, she was shaking so hard. Her hand came up to cover her mouth, and she realized she was crying.

Owen held up a trembling hand. Nestled in his palm was a blue velvet box, and as Sarah blinked tears away, he opened it.

"Sarah Jane Browning, will you do me the honor of becoming my wife?"

So overcome she could barely see the ring, Sarah just nodded. She tried to answer, but she couldn't speak. She settled for throwing her arms around his neck. He stood, wrapping his arms around her to lift her off the floor.

"Is that a yes?" he asked in between kisses.

"Oh, yes." She hugged him so tightly he grunted. "I love you so much, Owen. I would be thrilled to be your wife."

He pulled back enough to kiss her. When they came up for air, he whispered, "I love you more than you can know."

After several minutes of kissing and holding each other, Sarah finally calmed down enough to ask for her ring, and Owen slipped it on her finger. It fit perfectly.

"Your mom gave me your ring size before she left for Georgia," he confessed.

Sarah gazed down at the ring with amazement. It was a beautiful piece, a large star sapphire surrounded by a swirl of diamonds. "It's gorgeous."

"I wanted something that matched your eyes."

"Oh, Owen. I love it. Thank you."

His stomach growled in response. "I guess we'd better eat, huh?" He finished putting the meal together and came around to sit beside her at the bar.

"So what kind of wedding do you want?" he asked.

Sarah thought about it, sadness rising inside her, threatening to overwhelm her as she thought about the funerals and Kathy's devastation. "I don't know. A few weeks ago, I would have said something similar to what Jack and Gilly had. Now, though? After everything the family's been through, I don't think that'd be appropriate. Does that make sense?"

Owen ran his hand down her back. "Sure, it does. I'm sorry. I guess if you want to wait a few months, we can." Sarah sent him a look, and he sighed. "Yeah, I guess not."

She leaned over and kissed his bare shoulder. "It's okay. We can always do a big to-do for our first anniversary if we want. What's important is that we're together. I feel so guilty, being so happy when so much sadness has happened, especially to Kathy."

"I think she'll understand. We'll keep this as low-key as possible."

"That's probably best." She looked down at her soup and blew out a breath. "I'd like to be married before Mama and Kathy leave. And I'd planned on going back to work next week, probably Wednesday."

"Okay. Then why don't we go to the courthouse tomorrow and get our marriage license and then plan on getting married on Monday? That'll take care of the three-day waiting period. Is that enough time for you?"

"I think so. I'll recruit Gilly's help. Are you okay with getting married at the house? I'd like Kathy to be there, and I doubt she'll leave to go anywhere else."

He pressed a kiss to her temple. "Sure, that's fine. Do you think it'd be okay if I invited Eli and Amy to come up? He's an ordained minister. It'd be kind of nice if he were the one who married us." Owen frowned. "Maybe we should clear all this by your mother before we plan everything and just show up in her parlor on Monday."

Sarah smiled. "Do you really think she'd mind as long as you marry me?"

"Probably not, but I'd rather make sure first."

"Then we can do that. But even if she says no, I'd still like to plan on Monday."

He picked up her hand and kissed the back. "It's a date."

Owen walked her home that evening, and they made the announcement to the family.

"We don't want to have a big celebration right now given the circumstances," Sarah explained after the subdued but sincere congratulations were given. "But we'd like everyone to be with us when we say our vows."

Eliza hugged her, then Owen. She stepped back and took one of each of their hands in hers. "Of course we'll be there. Do you want to have the wedding here?"

Sarah smiled at Owen. "We were hoping to, actually."

They obtained the marriage license the next day, and all the women helped with planning the tiny wedding, even Kathy, who said, "I want you to be happy. And this gives me something to focus on. Something to hope for."

Before Sarah knew it, Monday rolled around. The ceremony was set for one o'clock.

As Eliza helped her get dressed, her mother kept sniffling back tears. "I am so happy for you both. You've found a good man, Sarah Jane. I hope you have decades of happy years together."

"So do I," Sarah whispered.

Jack was waiting at the foot of the steps and offered his arm to her. "You sure about this?" he murmured. Sarah sent him a chiding look, and he grinned. "I'm teasing. I like Owen."

"I know. I like him, too."

As they went into the parlor, Sarah only had eyes for Owen. Standing in front of the fireplace next to his uncle, he was so handsome in his gray suit that she could hardly stand it. He'd shaved the beard, and as Jack escorted her across the room, the smile she loved so much spread across Owen's face. Jack placed her hand on Owen's and gave her a quick hug.

Sarah barely remembered to speak her lines, and the ceremony itself was a blur, but the image of Owen's smile, radiant and happy, would be with her forever. The feel of his hand around hers, the moment he slid the ring onto her finger and the moment when she gave him his ring, the quiet reverence in the room as they pledged their lives to one another—those were the memories she wanted to preserve.

That night, as she and Owen made their way to the top of the mountain and their new home together, she asked to stop at the pool. The moon was full, shining down on them from the dusky sky as though in blessing.

"Here's where it started," she said. "It's incredible to think about, almost too hard to believe. We've come so far."

Owen kissed her with deep passion, and Sarah could feel the love in his touch.

He rested his head against her forehead. "And this is only the beginning. Just imagine the stories we'll have that we can tell our grandchildren."

Sarah laughed, happier than she had ever thought possible, even through her grief. Owen picked her up and twirled her around and around. When they were both dizzy, he put her back on her feet with another kiss.

She kissed him again. "You'll have to write everything down so we can pass our story on to our children."

And he did.

Want more? Keep reading for a sneak peek at *Kathy*, the second book in the Firefly Hollow series, available now.

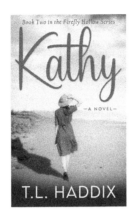

Book Two in the Firefly Hollow Series

Kathy

—A NOVEL—

T.L. HADDIX

Out of the darkness comes the fire...

Life changed forever for Kathy Browning one fateful day in 1960. Fleeing the tragedy that haunts her, she left her hometown, seeking safety and shelter with her mother in coastal Georgia.

Three years later, she's moments away from ending the pain once and for all when she's interrupted by family friend Charles Kelly. Thwarted, Kathy lashes out - but she finally gets the help she needs.

Charles has been intrigued by Kathy ever since a chance meeting at a dinner party. There's more to her than what she shows the world, and he wants to warm himself with the fire she keeps hidden. But until she heals from the past, he has to settle for being friends.

Kathy is terrified when her affection for Charles changes into something more intimate. The last time she trusted a man, he nearly destroyed her. But she uncovers a depth of passion and love in Charles that calls to her, a wild devotion she might lose forever if she can't find the courage to reach beyond the devastation of the past.

CHAPTER ONE

JUNE 1963

C HARLES HUSTON KELLY DARED NOT take his eyes off the dark-auburn-haired woman walking tentatively toward the waves. If he looked away, he feared she might vanish forever. He'd come to the beach to watch the pounding surf after a long, strenuous estate battle finally drew to a close, needing to be near the elemental pull and push of the ocean so as to clear his head. He'd never expected to encounter the woman who'd been haunting his dreams for months, ever since he'd first laid eyes on her at a dinner held by a friend.

But there she was, staring out at sea, the wind whipping her hair wildly, plastering the skirt of her dress to her body in a way that revealed her curves without being lewd.

Since he'd spotted her, she'd edged down toward the sea farther and farther with slow steps. Her shoes lay discarded ten feet behind her, apparently forgotten. That simple clue, as well as her hesitant steps, struck fear in his heart.

Praying he was wrong, he set off down the sand, battling the gusty wind as he walked as calmly as he could as quickly as he could. *Let me get to her in time, God. Please let me stop her before she vanishes into the waves.*

He had no doubt she *would* vanish, as strong as the surf was this afternoon. She'd go under before he could get to her, and that would be the last anyone ever saw of Kathy Browning—at least alive. After having watched her for what felt like hours but was in fact a fraction of that time, he knew that was her intention.

Can you blame her? a voice inside his head whispered. *After what she's been through, losing her husband and children, most people would be hard-pressed to find a reason to go on living.*

"Yes, I can blame her," he ground out as he hurried along. "Damn it, she's too young to give up. There has to be a better way to stop the pain."

He'd been trying to convince himself of that for eleven years, ever since he was nineteen and had been summoned home from school following his father's death. A gun accident, they'd called it, sugarcoating the truth for his mother's sake and the sake of his family's reputation, a treasure more priceless than gold in the society of Savannah.

The reality had been suicide, Charles knew. A last-ditch effort of a man in tremendous pain, both physically and mentally, to make the hurt go away. Charles still wasn't sure his father hadn't been trying to simply blow away the nearly continuous migraines that had crippled him for years, a lingering reminder of a war that had been victorious on paper if not in sheer casualties.

As he approached Kathy, he swallowed hard. He wasn't sure what he'd say, what he'd do to stop her if she was determined to carry through with killing herself, but he had to try to save her if he could.

CHAPTER TWO

"I CAN DO THIS. I HAVE to do this. God, please, why can't I just *do* this already?" Kathy Browning bit her lip so hard she tasted blood as she pushed her hair out of her stinging eyes for what felt like the thousandth time. She'd been standing on the beach, facing her fate, for hours it seemed, and she was so tired she could barely stay upright.

Every time the waves came in, she had to battle her desire to run away, back the way she'd come, back to her room at the house she shared with her mother. Back home... *No, never that*, she thought as pain nearly broke her in half.

That's why you're here, remember? To make all that awfulness go away. Just do it already, Kathy. You'll feel so much better when you get it over with. The whisper in her head had a distinct voice, a sneering tone she knew well, one she still heard in the nightmares that kept her awake most nights.

"Randall, why can't you leave me alone?" she whispered into the wind.

She knew the voice didn't really belong to Randall Begley, the man who'd been her husband. Well, most days she was fairly certain it wasn't really him. Some days... she wondered. The things he whispered made more sense than what the people around her said.

Thinking about the people in her life brought another jolt of pain. Her sister, her brother, her mother….

"Oh, God, I can't think of you. If I do, I'll never be able to do this." She choked back a sob and lifted her foot, preparing to take another step into the abyss that beckoned.

"Kathy? That is you! What in the world are you doing down here today? It's a little blustery for beachcombing."

The words jerked her attention away from the ocean, making her jump. She'd been so intent on her task she'd not realized she wasn't alone. It took her a few seconds to focus on the man's face, to recall his words and process them. To recognize him.

"Charles. Hello. I…" Her voice faded into nothing. She just didn't have the strength within her to speak to another human being. Dismissing him, she turned her eyes back to the sea.

"It's been a while since we've seen each other. How are you? Roy said you've been under the weather."

Roy Morris was her uncle by marriage through her aunt Nancy. He was a senior manager at a large, well-known area department store, and he was an associate of Charles's somehow, though the exact connection escaped her at the moment.

"I'm fine," she managed stonily. Anger crept up inside her with surprising speed, and it took almost more strength than she could muster not to bite his head off at the mention of her recent "illness." She'd not been sick; she'd had surgery. A hysterectomy, to be precise, and the impetus for her latest dive into despair.

"Good, good. That's… good," he said. An awkward silence spread between them. "I saw your mother this past Monday. I stopped in to buy my sister a birthday gift. She helped me pick something out. Your mother, that is. Not Daphne. A lovely lady, your mother. Very nice, very kind."

Kathy closed her eyes as her throat tightened with guilt and grief. Her mother *was* nice and kind.

"She doesn't deserve to lose you like this."

The words were delivered quietly but in a stern voice that had her opening her eyes to stare at him.

"What did you say?" she asked hoarsely. "What did you just say to me?"

Charles met her gaze head-on, though he did lift a hand to the bridge of his glasses to push them back up on his face. "I said your mother doesn't deserve to lose you like this. They might never find your body, and if they do find you, with the way this surf is pounding? What do you think will remain? You don't want to leave that for her."

An image of grotesquely disfigured humanity flashed in her mind, making her flinch. She knew all too well what a battered body could look like. "You heartless... why did you have to show up here today?"

He shrugged, and even though the question had been rhetorical, he answered. "I had court—the conclusion of a long case we fought very hard to win. I needed some fresh air."

He was a lawyer, she remembered then. Angry more with herself than with him, she lashed out. "You lost, boohoo. Isn't that just too bad? You should've gone to a bar, had some pretty little thing stroke your ego. Or does your type run more to debutantes?"

Though his jaw tightened a fraction, he showed no other sign that her words had landed blows. "I didn't lose. I won. I do that quite frequently." He leaned in as though confiding a secret. "I'm very good at my job. Why don't you let me take you home? It's getting late."

Bitterly disappointed and feeling foolish—and to her horror, foolishly relieved—Kathy growled. "You don't give up, do you?"

To her amazement, he smiled, though he was still watching her like a hawk. "It's part of my charm. Come on. Where's your purse?" He held his arm out toward the parking lot on the other side of the sandy dunes.

After a full minute, Kathy gave in and went to pick up her shoes. "I didn't bring it. I left it at home." She'd made a small pocket on the inside of her slip, and she'd tucked her driver's license, along with a personal memento or two she'd wanted to take with her, into it.

"Then it's a very good thing I happened along," he said as he walked behind her. "This is one of my favorite beaches. I live not far from here, just a couple of miles down the road."

Kathy didn't respond. She was even spared having to give him directions, as he'd once driven her and Eliza home from a Sunday dinner with Roy and Nancy. In fact, she crossed her arms and didn't say another word until they were a few blocks away from her house.

"If you don't mind letting me off at the corner, I can walk from there," she told him when he stopped at a red light.

"Oh, I think I'll drop you off at the door if it's all the same to you." There was that implacable tone again.

"I guess I don't have a choice, do I?" She snorted. "Of course I don't. When did I ever? The story of my life."

"We always have choices. The right ones are just hard to see sometimes." He pulled into the small driveway right behind her mother's car as Eliza was getting out. "And just in time."

Kathy's heart started racing as soon as she saw her mother. There were letters on her bed that she needed to get to before Eliza saw them. Grabbing her sand-coated shoes, she fumbled for the doorknob. "If you mention a word of this to anyone... promise me you won't."

Charles's smile wasn't unsympathetic. "I can't make that promise."

"Damn you. Thanks for nothing." Ashamed of her behavior even as she spoke, she couldn't bring herself to apologize. She hurried out of the car and, with a waved hello for her mother, into the house, pleading under her breath the whole time. "Please don't tell her. Please, please, don't break my mother's heart."

No, that job would be hers and hers alone. And given how much Eliza had already lost, it was a job Kathy should never, ever aim to complete. With any luck, today wouldn't be the day she devastated the only person who'd held her together after the worst days of Kathy's life. But Kathy was plain out of luck. She had been for most of her life, it seemed. She'd been born out of luck, and she'd never been able to catch up.

In the house, she made a beeline for her bedroom and shut the door with a sigh of relief when she saw the letters still intact on the pillow. She grabbed them so tightly the paper crinkled in her hands, and then she dashed to the closet to stow them away until she could come up with a proper use for them.

Charles had *known*. He'd known what she had planned from the instant he walked up to her, though Kathy couldn't figure out how exactly. And he didn't strike her as the sort of man who wasn't thorough, which meant at some moment in the very near future, someone would be knocking on her door and asking questions to which she didn't have the answers.

"You blew it, Kathy. This time, you've really done it," she whispered as she sank onto the bed, tired to her bones.

Even if she'd had a means of killing herself at hand, at that moment, she didn't have the energy to do it. It had taken every bit of her courage to go to the beach in the first place, and she'd pondered that decision for days. All she could do was wait and hope she could somehow manage to find the strength to go on one more day. As it was, all she wanted to do was rest.

"I could sleep forever," she said around a yawn as she lay down, pulling her daughter's favorite doll from where it had been sitting on her pillow. She wrapped her arms around the raggedy little cloth toy, unaware of the tears that tracked down her cheeks, and let herself embrace sleep's oblivion.

CHAPTER THREE

A S SOON AS SHE'D SEEN Kathy's face, Eliza knew something was drastically wrong. She hesitated on the driveway, looking after her daughter, then faced the man getting out of the low-slung, expensive car. As much as she wanted to check on Kathy, she needed answers first.

"Charles. What in the world is going on?"

"Mrs. Browning." Charles's face was somber. "I ran into Kathy at the beach, and… she's upset. She's tremendously upset. I think you need to keep a close eye on her. I think she's all right for now as she's pretty mad at me, and that's replaced… but for later, I'm not so sure." He looked at her intently, as though trying to convey a message he didn't want to speak aloud.

Eliza very much feared she understood, but perversely, she needed to hear the words. "What was she doing at the beach?"

He looked away briefly, toward the street. "I can only guess based on what I saw."

"Then make a guess. This is my daughter's life we're talking about, isn't it?" She clenched her purse tightly to her chest, bracing for the blow.

"Yes. She might never speak to me again, but I don't care. You need to know. I realize she's been through a hard time over the last few years, but surely… well. Surely there's another way. She just needs to find it."

There was something in his eyes, his voice, Eliza thought as her heart sank. "Unless I miss my guess, this is not your first encounter with someone who carries a load that's too heavy. Is it?"

He shook his head. "My father, unfortunately."

Eliza closed her eyes briefly. "I'm so sorry. Just how certain are you that she… that Kathy was trying to kill herself?" she asked softly. "I have to be sure."

"I'm one hundred percent certain. She was working up the courage to walk into the waves. I watched her for a while before I stopped her. I needed to be sure myself."

She could tell it pained him to say the words. What surprised her, however, was her own reaction. Hearing the truth was almost a relief. She knew the pain would come later, when she was alone and able to grieve. For now…

"I can't tell you how glad I am that you happened along. Charles, I'll be in your debt forever. I'll see that she gets the help she needs. This has been coming for a long while now. In the back of my mind, I suspected what she was thinking of doing. I should have done something sooner, but I didn't want to believe what was in front of me."

"Don't blame yourself." His voice was low, full of emotion. "That's a road you can't let yourself go down. If there's one thing I've learned through the last eleven years, it's that the what-ifs will destroy you if you let them. If there's anything I can do, please don't hesitate to ask. I think a lot of Roy, you know. I'd like to help if I can."

Eliza reached out to him. "I appreciate that. Like I said, I'll never be able to repay you for what you've already done. I'd best go in and check on her."

"Of course. Good luck."

She hurried inside, her head reeling. Kathy's door was closed, and after a brief hesitation to gird herself, Eliza opened it without knocking. Her breath escaped in a rush when she saw Kathy curled up on the bed, sound asleep. Moira's old doll was held tightly in her arms. Even if she'd not seen how upset Kathy was or talked to Charles, Eliza would have known something was drastically wrong just from seeing the doll. It was usually kept in a box in the back of Kathy's closet.

"Oh, my baby, what in the world are we going to do?" She approached the bed quietly, almost timidly, and brushed a dark curl off Kathy's tearstained cheek. Traces of sand lingered on her arm, her knee, her dirty feet.

For a moment, Eliza wondered if Kathy had taken something, but her breathing was soft and regular. Eliza saw no evidence of pills or a bottle or a glass nearby, and she was fairly confident there were no medications in the house her daughter could have used.

After they'd first come to Georgia three years earlier, Kathy had turned to sleep to help get her through those days. Eliza imagined that was what she was doing now, shutting out the world in an effort not to face the hellish demons that haunted her.

Moving carefully, Eliza covered Kathy and left the bedroom, pulling the door around but not closed. She wasn't sure how much time she had before Kathy woke up, but she'd use what she had to the best of her ability.

"I'm not letting go of you without a fight," she said as she stood in the kitchen, staring out the window over the sink. "I'm not letting that bastard, Randall Begley, steal you from me too. He's taken enough already. He's not taking anyone else." And if she had to go to Hell and fight him for Kathy's soul, she would.

Kathy is available now in eBook and print.

WANT MORE?

www.tlhaddix.com
www.facebook.com/tlhaddix

If you'd like to stay up to date on news and new releases, giveaways and freebies, sign up for the newsletter at:
www.tlhaddix.com/newsletter

Romantic Suspense novels
(written as Alex Collins):
www.authoralexcollins.com.

For a look at quirky romantic comedy in various genres, released under the pen name I. Ronik, visit www.ironikauthor.com.

Ingram Content Group UK Ltd.
Milton Keynes UK
UKHW011943080523
421401UK00004B/406